Praise for Baker & Goodman's

Against the World

Life's journey is *Against the World*. We all have something to learn.
Marcia Crosthwait

The Nurseketeers reunite for their sophomore year, and what an adventure it is! They are starting to mature into young women, although someone is a bit slower than the rest... They band together to help each other through burgeoning love, tragedies, and personal soul searching. This book shows how they truly embody their motto of "One for All, and All for One."
Daryn Herrington

Baker and Goodman pull you in to *Against the World* and put you in Robin's footsteps to share all her life lessons as she endures inequality, loss, love, and hardships to discover her true self!
Chelsie Gabel

Against the World would make a great movie. I thoroughly enjoyed following Robin on her journey to become a woman in the early 1970s. The story captures the essence of the times when women were fighting for equality with men and the personal challenges that everyone faces. The book captures the innocence of youth and the trials associated with becoming a strong woman.
J.D. Buchert

A young woman struggles to balance her college education, reconnecting with her mother, while exploring her sexual identity.
Amy Clark

Against the World

JOY DON BAKER
&
TERRI GOODMAN

Published 2019
Printed in the United States of America
ISBN: 978-1-7322535-5-1
E-ISBN: 978-1-7322535-3-7
Library of Congress Control Number: 2019918680

Written by Joy Don Baker & Terri Goodman
Cover design: *Fresh Design*
Interior design: *JETLAUNCH.net*
About the Authors photo: *Kelly Williams Photography*
Author photo back cover: *Simao Ago*

For information:
Baker & Goodman
Watauga, TX
admin@bakergoodman.com
www.bakergoodman.com

Table of Contents

Chapter 1

WELCOME HOME, ROBIN. The placard stopped Robin in her tracks, forcing the deplaning passengers to flow around her.

"*Gram!*" she called, as a radiant smile peeked from behind the sign.

Robin ran straight into her grandmother's open arms. "I never expected you to meet me here. What a surprise! What a *wonderful* surprise."

"I couldn't wait another hour to see you. The five months since Christmas vacation seems like a century. Let's collect your luggage and you can fill me in on finals and what's going on with your roommates. Then we can decide how to make the most of the precious ten weeks that you'll be home for the summer. Did I mention that I've missed you?"

Robin hugged Gram again and they joined the crowd heading for Baggage Claim. "Finals were fine and all four of us passed. I made the honor roll, and so did Katie. Leslie struggled some, and Frannie's superhuman effort kept her from flunking out, so the Nurseketeers will march together into our Sophomore year. We're moving to Kirkwood Hall and we got a suite on the first floor."

Gram pointed, "That one looks familiar."

Robin grabbed a suitcase from the carousel. "The other one should be close by Gram. Keep an eye out for it."

"What about *your* summer plans, Robin? That is, of course, after you spend every minute of this weekend with me."

"That's my plan exactly!" Robin grinned. "First on my list for Monday is to look for a job. Mr. Davis wrote a nice letter of recommendation, but he doesn't know anyone in Chicago in the restaurant business. He told me when I find a position that I want, no matter what it is, to have them call him."

"How kind," Gram said. "You were fortunate to work at the SteakHauz. Mr. Davis is an exceptional employer."

"A restaurant or drug store here would be an option, but I'd prefer to do something with better pay and maybe more responsibility. I was thinking of Marshall Field & Company. It's got an excellent reputation for community support and the employee discount would probably make up for tips. What do you think?"

Gram smiled but didn't say anything.

"What's so funny?" Robin said.

"I was just picturing some tired woman with three kids in tow getting short with you because you're not ringing her purchases up fast enough."

"She can wait until I'm through. There's no reason to rush and make mistakes. By the way, I think this carousel has gone around a zillion times already, and I still don't see my suitcase."

Gram's grin widened. "You might want to think twice about working where the customer is always right... even when they aren't. It *would* be a great opportunity for you to develop some restraint, but are you sure you're up for that kind of responsibility?"

Robin's defensive expression morphed into a grin. "I love you, Gram. You've always had a knack for telling me just what I need to hear without lecturing me. Why hasn't that wonderful trait rubbed off on me in all the years I've lived with you? I guess *in your face* is a better description of me, huh?"

"Sweetheart, I'm proud of the woman you're becoming. There's no one on this earth who doesn't have some behavior they should work on. Being blunt isn't the worst trait you could have, but the saying *you catch more flies with honey than with vinegar* hasn't been around for centuries for nothing."

"Okay. I'll put, *learn to be nice,* on my to do list for the summer. Seriously, Gram, do you think that Marshall Field is a good idea?"

"I certainly do. I have a friend who retired after years of working there. Perhaps she would write a letter of recommendation to go with Mr. Davis's."

"That would be wonderful… my suitcase!" Robin exclaimed as she grabbed the handle and yanked it from the carousel. "It's about friggin' time."

Gram smiled. "Robin, perhaps you should start practicing verbal restraint *before* you start interviewing."

"Yes, Ma'am. How about this? My, how nice that my suitcase has finally arrived. Shall I retrieve it so that we can be on our way?"

"Good idea," said Gram, grinning back. "Let's go find a cab."

"Whoa!" Robin exclaimed. "Stop! Where did all the houses go?" Robin stared through the cab window. "This was a neighborhood when I left for school and now it's an office complex. How could this happen just since Christmas vacation?"

"It's the first phase of the Old Town Renovation Project," Gram replied. "They razed everything between here and Division practically overnight. A whole neighborhood gone, and office buildings halfway built in five months."

Still shaking her head in disbelief, Robin said, "Thank heaven our house is safe. We're half a mile north of Division." Gram's sad smile gave Robin pause. "What?"

"Only for a while, I'm afraid. Our neighborhood will be next, but they haven't disclosed a time frame for Phase II. I received a letter in January describing the project in general. There were no details, but the letter made it clear that our neighborhood was included in the renovation."

3

"They're going to tear down our house and you didn't tell me?" Robin huffed.

"Hold on! What would you have done if I'd told you?"

"Well, I..." Robin stammered.

"You're upset and ranting. I didn't see the need for that when I didn't have any solid information."

"I'm sorry, Gram. I didn't mean to be critical, but who would have thought that someone could just kick us out of our house? You've lived there for 40 years and I've lived there almost my whole life."

"So we have, but I've had time to put the situation in perspective. Our neighborhood has become shabby and unsafe. This project has made our property valuable again."

"You're amazing. You get kicked out of your house and find a way to make it a good thing."

"Jumping to conclusions usually prevents one from arriving at the best solution to a problem. You'll discover that in time."

Robin grinned. "Is that your way of saying I'm a hothead?"

Gram laughed. "I might have been hinting that you could work on that. You already know that it often gets in your way."

"I know, I know... and I *am* working on it... at least I'm trying."

"I'm told that accepting the developer's offer is wise because folks who hold out until the bitter end can lose their homes to eminent domain. That's the tragedy of being stubborn rather than realistic."

"Gram, it *could* be a good thing. You can move to Dallas! I'll be there for at least three more years, and it would be wonderful having you there instead of a thousand miles away. You *have* to consider it. You'd *love* Dallas, and..."

"Slow down," Gram said, holding up both hands. "It might be years before they're ready for the next phase of the project. If I sell before the developers want it, I won't get enough for the house to move, and there's your mother to consider."

"I thought we agreed that getting her to leave that drunk of a husband is a lost cause. I can't bring myself to refer to him as my father. What difference does it make if you're here or not?"

"Sweetheart, it's not easy for me to turn my back on Aileen. Even though she can't muster the courage to escape an abusive relationship, you never know. Something could happen to change that, and as long as I'm here, she has a safe place to go."

"Gram, she's an ungrateful mouse! How can you even think of staying in Chicago just to give her a safe haven, especially since she's never going to take advantage of it. She's a pathetic excuse for a daughter AND a worse mother. She let you take me away without a whimper. She just sat there and watched us gather my things and walk out forever. That was the best decision she ever made, though it was hardly a decision. I don't think it would have been long before he quit hitting on me and started to get physical. I'm eternally grateful that you rescued me."

"We made the right decision. You've been a treasure for me all these years. Watching you grow up healthy and safe was all I ever wanted."

The cab pulled to a stop in front of Gram's house. "I'll carry your bags up to the porch," the driver said.

"You are kind, young man." Gram paid him the amount on the meter plus a generous tip.

"Thank you, ma'am," he said, smiling broadly. "I hope you and your granddaughter have a lovely summer."

Robin giggled. "Imagine the stories he hears. I'll bet most passengers don't pay any more attention to him than I did all the way home. Do you think that's rude?"

It was Gram's turn to laugh. "No, Sweetheart. I don't think so. I believe the best cab drivers pretend to be part of the vehicle, unless the passenger engages them in conversation. Let's get you settled in and have some dinner. Then you can tell me about the girls and what, besides work, you plan to do this summer. We have ten short weeks and I don't want to waste a minute."

"When I'm not working, I plan to spend my time with you. I'm gonna make up for the two years of high school that I wasted hanging around with Jake and his pathetic band of losers. What a jerk I was! I shoulda been doing stuff with you. I hope you know how sorry I am that I ignored you. Everything you warned me about was true; I just didn't want to listen. Well, Jake is history and you and I are going to have a super summer together."

"That was wonderful," Robin said, leaning back in her chair. "I've been looking forward to your lamb shank baked potato soup since Christmas vacation. Shall we do the dishes, or sit and talk for a bit?"

"I'm stuffed," said Gram. "That's a great excuse for visiting. The dishes won't go anywhere, I promise. It's wonderful that you four suitemates will be together again next year. What are they planning for the summer?"

"We promised to write and keep each other up to date. Katie wants to work at the Indian Clinic in Atoka. She told me that a lot of the older Choctaw people don't trust White medicine and won't go to the clinic, even when Indian medicine isn't helping them. Katie thinks that they would be willing to go if one of their own worked there."

"Katie seems like such a grown-up young lady. I'm pleased that her family has taken you under their wing. It's a comfort to know that you have a home away from home since Chicago is so far from Dallas."

"Gram, you'd love Katie's family. Her mother is a lot like you. She's capable and wise. She takes care of everything without raising her voice or getting excited. She has a good sense of humor, too. Katie's Dad and her two older brothers spend all their time running the farm, and her little sister, Naomi, is starting to talk about going to Crestmont. She'll start college the year after we graduate.

"Just about everything about Katie's life is perfect, except for the prejudice that goes with being a minority. Fortunately, she didn't have any problem at all at Crestmont. If I were full-blood

Choctaw and anyone picked on me, I'd set the bigots straight in a New York minute!"

Gram grinned. "I have a perfect picture of *that* confrontation."

Robin shrugged. "Of the four of us, Leslie's the one who has to work the hardest for her grades. She's the first in her family to go to college and I'm not sure she'd be at Crestmont if it weren't for her athletic scholarship. Remember, it was Leslie's car, *Nellie,* that Katie and I drove to Atoka for Thanksgiving last year since Leslie was flying home for the long weekend. She'll probably spend her summer splitting her time between her folks' grocery store and keeping herself in shape so she can make varsity next year."

"You said Frannie passed. I'm so glad to hear that."

"I swear that little bitch drove me friggin' nuts..." A sheepish smile crept across Robin's face. "I mean, Frannie drove me crazy for most of the year. She's a complete disaster on her own because her mother has always done everything for her. Can you believe that when she got to school, she'd never done her own laundry, ironed, made her bed, or even cleaned up after herself? She's a prima donna when it comes to clothes and makeup. It used to take her forever to get ready no matter where we were going." Robin took a breath and with a satisfied smile said, "I am happy to report that she's come a long way."

"I'm glad to hear that. It's hard to imagine someone so close to adulthood who can't take care of herself."

"The four of us promised we'd stay in touch. We even talked about a chain letter, but we never worked out the details. When I get a job, I might start the chain by writing to Katie."

"I expect that letters will be flying back and forth. I doubt that any of you can afford long-distance phone calls. Shall we take care of the dishes?" Gram suggested. "We should also make a list of meals you're looking forward to so that we can shop for the ingredients."

"That was a breakfast fit for a queen, Gram. Thanks for letting me sleep late. I can't believe it's after 10," Robin said, pushing back from the table and stretching.

"You won't be job-hunting until Tuesday. Take advantage of the Memorial Day weekend and sleep late while you can. Let's plan for an early dinner. I can't imagine that we'll be hungry for lunch."

"I'm stuffed! I may never be hungry again."

"I thought we might take a walk after we get the dishes out of the way. The weather's lovely, and it won't be long before it's too hot for a leisurely mid-day stroll."

"Great idea. I'd like to see what's happening with the construction we passed on the way home. I wonder how long it will be before our neighborhood will be consumed."

"I have no idea, but it could be sooner than I expected," said Gram, filling the dishpan with soap and water. "There was no sign of construction when you were here for Christmas and look how much they've accomplished in just five months. I may have to make some decisions sooner than later."

"That could be a good thing," Robin said. "The neighborhood certainly isn't getting any safer, and this way, the house will be worth more than if you just sold it to get away."

"I'll have to think of it as a blessing in disguise." Gram said. "Except for leaving the house where I've lived for so long, and all the hassle of packing and moving, it could be rather an adventure."

"I love how you see the best in everything. Why couldn't your sunny personality have rubbed off on me? I just can't keep what I'm thinking, from flying out of my mouth. Sometimes what I say even surprises me. Well, maybe I'm not so surprised as I wish I hadn't said it, or maybe I wish I'd said it differently."

"That, My Dear, sounds to me like you're growing up," Gram said with pride. "I just might be rubbing off on you after all." She finished drying the sink. "Well, that does it. No sign of breakfast anywhere. Let's go for that walk."

Robin locked the door and followed Gram down the steps to the street. "Let's go check out the construction," she suggested.

"They might have one of those big pictures that shows what the project's going to look like when it's done."

They ambled down the quiet street, careful not to trip on the uneven concrete sidewalk. "Remember when we used to wave at our neighbors on our Sunday walks?" Gram asked. Nearly everyone we knew is gone now. The neighborhood's nothing like it was even ten years ago. It's slipping away and the changes are all bad. Even the laundry and the grocery store on Sedgwick near Division are boarded up. It's not safe anymore. The neighborhood's poverty-stricken, and the hopelessness makes people defensive and dangerous, like Jake and his cronies.

"I don't think I ever told you what Jake did, the day I left for college," Robin said. He stole a carton of cigarettes while I was standing outside the store with the rest of the gang. At that moment, I knew you'd been right all along."

"I could tell something had happened when you rushed back home, but I thought it best not to prod. I knew you'd tell me in due time. I'm just glad he didn't get caught, at least not that time. Can you imagine what would have happened to you if the police had been called and you'd been right there? I think we'll just put all that behind us. It's ancient history and we needn't give Jake another thought."

"I am the luckiest person in the world. I am planning to spend the rest of my life making you glad that you saved me, and that you put up with me the last two years of high school when I was acting like a jerk."

Gram smiled. "That's a bit melodramatic, but I'll admit that it's good to hear." She stopped and pulled Robin into a hug. "A grandmother wants nothing more than to know that she's done her best."

They walked in silence until Robin said, "Look, I think that sign on the corner is just what we're looking for. Come on," she said hurrying across the street.

"So, here we are," Robin pointed to the *You are here* arrow, "and there's our house." She pointed to an area higher up on the sign than she could reach. "This phase ends at Division and our street is only three blocks further north. We'll certainly be included in the next phase of the project."

"You're probably right. It looks like the streets north of Division are going to be residential. I like imagining nice homes replacing mine. That's better than shops and office buildings. Robin, look! St. Michael's is included in what they're planning for residential. I do hope they plan to leave it alone. That church was here when my family first settled in the city. I don't go often, but occasionally, I attend mass. I find the sanctuary comforting when I'm troubled about something." Gram grinned at Robin. "I spent a fair amount of time there during your last two years of high school."

"I'm so ashamed of that time, Gram."

"I'm teasing, Sweetheart, though I did find myself there looking for strength on more than one occasion."

"There's a lovely church not far from Crestmont. Please think about Dallas. It would be wonderful to have you there. We wouldn't be thousands of miles apart. You'd like my friends. I know there'd be lots for you to do and you'll love the weather."

"Hooooold on!" Gram laughed and held up her hand. "I understand that I won't have years to consider moving, and I'm not opposed to Dallas. It's just not a decision that I can make without giving it serious thought. Rest assured we'll talk about it; the subject is not closed."

"Gram," said Robin insistently.

"What is it, Robin? Is something wrong?"

"Nothing's wrong... just, whenever I'm with Katie and her family, I can't help thinking how nice it would be if I didn't resent mother, *The Mouse*, so much. She never stood up for anything... even me! I never have a pleasant thought about her. I call my father *The Brute* and sometimes worse because that's all he ever was."

"I agree that's sad, Robin, but it's understandable."

"I know. I'm not saying I'm wrong, but I'd like a reason to change the way I feel. What if I spent some time with her? I know we can't just show up over there, but we could take her somewhere where she wouldn't be scared. We could go to a restaurant at lunchtime when the Brute's at work. Or, maybe coffee in case he shows up unexpectedly for lunch. He doesn't need to know that we met. Do you think there's any chance she'd do it?"

"I don't know. I haven't been over there in some time. I stopped dropping by when I realized that Aileen's anxiety level increased with every passing minute, even though it was only the two of us. It seemed she was afraid that Harold might barge in any moment. I can understand that; he would be furious if he found me there."

"I'll bet The Brute doesn't want you around because he thinks you'll talk her into leaving, and SHE doesn't want you around because she wishes you could. That makes her even more afraid of him."

"Could be, Robin, but whatever the reason, I decided it was better for everyone if I left things alone. Aileen knows that she is always welcome in our home. That seemed to be the best I could do; leave her alone and be there if she needs me."

"That's sad. Katie's family makes me want to try and change things. I want to talk to my mother, and I promise I won't be upset if she refuses."

"That's silly. Of course, you'd be upset. I'm glad that you realize it's a possibility, so you won't be surprised if the results are disappointing."

"I thought of something. Do you think that she'd leave The Brute if we could take her where he'd never find her? Like to Dallas? If you could bring her with you that would be a wonderful reason to move there, in addition to being close to me."

"It's something to think about, but don't get your hopes too high. Rational as that solution may sound, this is anything but a logical situation. Aileen's decisions are motivated by fear, not logic. Besides, we're not sure we can get her to visit with us in the first place."

"How can we let her know that we want to visit? If we can't risk dropping in, what *can* we do? Do they have a phone?"

"They had a phone a while back. I have the number. We can try it and see if it still works, but we can't call until we have a strategy. If she does answer the phone, we'll have to be ready with a compelling story. If she has time to consider her options, she'll push us away."

"Then we have to be practically outside her door when we call. If she answers, we can say that I'm home from school and would love to see her, and we've come just to take her for a cup of coffee. I think coffee would be best because it's not likely he'd come home mid-morning. Then we'll hang up and get over there before she can tell us not to come. Once she opens the door, we'll try our best to get her to come with us. We don't even have to go into the house."

"It's a good plan, and we can certainly try it, but I want to be sure that you understand what a small chance there is that we'll be successful. Aileen is terrified of Harold, and I expect that has only gotten worse over time."

"I understand," Robin assured Gram. "If we try and I don't get to see her, then at least we tried."

Chapter 2

Robin smacked her alarm at 6:30, then tiptoed down the stairs to grab a quick breakfast and plan her job-hunting for the day.

"OH, I didn't think you would be up yet," Robin said, joining Gram at the kitchen table.

"I've been up just long enough to enjoy a cup of coffee and glance through the paper." Gram replied.

"Mind if I take a look at the employment section?" Robin asked, pouring herself a cup of coffee."

"Would you like a good breakfast to get your day started?"

"Thanks, but I'm going to stick with a little toast and jam so I can get a quick start."

"Stores don't open until nine, so there's plenty of time," Gram assured her as she stood to fry eggs and bacon to go with Robin's toast.

"I suppose you're right. I've gotten used to getting up at the crack of dawn because that airhead roommate of mine needs an hour to get ready in the morning. The rest of us can be ready and out the door in about 20 minutes."

"Well, some folks just take a little more time to primp than others. Perhaps she will learn where she can shave off time as she matures."

"I doubt it. Frannie has to try on half her closet even after she decided what to wear the night before. She is a bit of a ditz, Gram, you gotta admit."

"Hmmm… so, where are you planning to start your job search? Simpson's Drug Store might be looking for help."

"That wouldn't be my first choice. That's the corner where Jake and his friends hang out and I don't want any part of them. Besides, I don't expect Mr. Simpson can pay what I want to make. My plan is to check out Marshall Field downtown. The station's a five-minute walk from the house and it's a short train ride downtown. By the way, did you get a chance to talk with Mrs. Hornsby about a reference?"

"Yes, she'll be happy to do that. If you would drop over there this morning on your way to Marshall Field, she'll give you the letter. We thought that would be better than mailing it."

"Thanks, that's super!" Robin jumped up and gave her grandmother a big hug, almost knocking the plate of eggs and bacon out of her hand. "Thanks for breakfast and for everything you're doing for me."

Robin ate absent-mindedly while perusing the newspaper. "It might be worth checking out what's available in the neighborhood on my way downtown. Close would be nice. You know that big Pizza restaurant about four blocks from here," she asked? "They're looking for waitresses."

"I know that one," Gram answered. "I don't walk over that way anymore, although I do like their pizza. The characters who hang out in the doorways and on the corner don't look like stable folks. I wouldn't want you to walk the streets after dark."

"I'll pick up Mrs. Hornsby's letter and stop by the shipping place next door to Simpsons to make copies on the way downtown."

"That sounds like a good plan."

"Let me help you with the dishes?" Robin said as she carried her plate to the sink.

"No, sweetie. You go get ready for your interview, then come show me how you look."

Robin bounded up the stairs, showered in record time, and dressed in a white blouse and black skirt. She looked for the lipstick that Frannie had foisted upon her. *"I'm not sure why women have to wear this crap, but maybe it will help me get a good job that pays well."*

Gram's knitting needles were clicking ceaselessly when Robin found her sitting in the living room. "Whatcha making?" she asked.

"I've been knitting scarves and mittens for the homeless for winter," Gram responded. "Someone should benefit from this hobby of mine. Turn around and let me see how you look."

Robin complied. "Ahh. Very professional. I know you'll find the perfect job today."

"Do you think it's too early to drop in on Mrs. Hornsby?"

"No, Eleanor gets up early like me. Dawn comes too quickly to sleep late now that summer is here." Gram put aside her knitting and walked with Robin to the front door. She pulled her in for a hug. "Enjoy the search and be safe out there. I love you so much."

"I love you too, Gram." Robin waved to her grandmother, then walked on to Mrs. Hornsby's house. She rang the bell and Mrs. Hornsby peeked out the glass beside the front door. From her expression, she didn't recognize Robin. Then a smile creased her face and she opened the door.

"Robin?" Mrs. Hornsby questioned.

"Yes, Ma'am. Gram said you might be willing to write a letter of recommendation for me."

"Come in, Child. I've begun a draft on a note pad, but I thought we might improve on it and add personal information to make it solid. Then you can type it up for me."

"Cool."

"I also have a fresh pot of coffee. Would you like some?"

"No, thanks. I had a cup with Gram, and a huge breakfast."

"Then let's get started. Tell me about where you have worked."

"During this last school year, I worked at the Rob Rory Steakhauz in Dallas. I've worked almost every position in the restaurant. Mr. Davis is a great boss. It's a policy that each employee can work any station. My official job was waitressing, but the nice thing is we all share equally in the tips. I hope my summer job turns out to be something new and," she grinned, "pays enough so I can save up some money."

"What do you spend your money on, Robin?"

"Well, I save for tickets to fly home to spend Christmas with Gram and back home for the summer, and for spending money at school. My scholarship covers tuition, books, and housing, but that's it. Gram helps me with the big things, but I'm responsible for the rest."

"That's impressive. Thank you for sharing that with me. Let me finish the letter now. Why don't you set up that portable typewriter there on the kitchen table and we can complete our little project."

"Mrs. Hornsby, thank you for doing this for me."

"Marshall Field is a wonderful place. I worked in the jewelry department for most of the years I was there and loved it. If you do work there this summer, please look up Delores Parker and convey my best wishes to her. I'll have a cup of coffee while you type."

Robin settled in front of the typewriter and carefully rolled in a sheet of paper. She skimmed the draft that Mrs. Hornsby laid beside the machine. "Thank you so much," she said, and began to type.

To Whom It May Concern:

Miss Jennifer Lynn (Robin) Hart is the granddaughter of my special friend. I have known Robin most of her young life. I know that she is a willing and hardworking young woman who has obtained a scholastic scholarship to aid in the pursuit of her nursing career. She has worked part-time during the entire school year while attending Crestmont University in Dallas, Texas.

Robin is a resourceful young woman who will go far and would be an asset to any establishment for which she works. I wish her the best and highly recommend her for employment in your fine business.

Sincerely,
Eleanor Hornsby

Robin typed the letter without a single error. She removed the sheet from the typewriter and handed it to Mrs. Hornsby to reread.

"Perfect," Mrs. Hornsby declared, "and your typing skills are impressive. There's not a single correction. Have you ever considered being a secretary?"

"Thank you for the compliment, but I am going to be a nurse."

"That's a fine career," Mrs. Hornsby said as she signed the letter, tucked it into an envelope, and handed it to Robin. "I wish you the best in your job hunt," she said as she walked Robin to the door.

Robin danced down the steps contemplating her prospects with two letters of recommendation in hand.

Robin stopped at Simpson's Drug Store on her way to the train. It wasn't yet nine, but the store was open. She and Gram had been going to Simpson's all her life. She walked to the back where Dick Simpson, the pharmacist and owner, was rearranging items on the shelves.

"Hello, Mr. Simpson. Gram mentioned that you might have a job opening."

"I'm sorry Robin, I did have a position, but I filled it yesterday afternoon. I needed someone to stock, sweep, haul boxes, and assist my wife with the inventory. I'm sorry I didn't know you were looking for a job. I know you'd make a great employee."

Robin smiled at the compliment. "Well, thanks for your time, Mr. Simpson."

"You bet. Say hello to your grandmother for me. Best of luck with the job hunt."

Robin paused at the spot where she'd been standing when Jake stole the carton of cigarettes just nine months ago. *"I should have reported Jake back then. I chickened out, certain it would all fall back on me and keep me from leaving for Crestmont. I need to grow some balls and not let that jerkwad anywhere near me. Aaaagh makes me mad just thinking about it."*

Robin scanned the neighborhood as she made her way to the train station. *"Gram was right about the neighborhood deteriorating. The blocks beyond Simpson's are all but shambles. There were more homeless than residents."* She watched an old man pee on a pile of rubble as if the world were his own private bathroom. *"I don't want to walk through this area in the daytime, let alone at night."*

One of the ads from the paper turned out to be a high school hamburger joint on the way to the station. That wouldn't do, and tips would be terrible. The next train stop had two ads for her to check out. The first was a small restaurant suggesting home-style meals. A man sweeping the floor stopped and asked if he could help.

"I want to talk to the owner about a waitress job?"

"Mr. Jason don't come in till later. I can git you an application, but I think he done filled the last waitress job."

Robin completed the application and left her reference letters on the owner's desk.

The second place was called Cub Corner and it made her skin crawl. Through the open doorway, she saw the sticky floor strewn with peanut shells and knew it had never felt the brush of a broom. The smell of stale beer wrinkled her nose. At the far end was a raised platform pierced with a single floor-to-ceiling gold pole. One of the barflies beckoned. "Hey, you, Red, c'mon in," he slurred. "I got a perrrrrfect spot for you." He patted his lap and Robin quickened her pace back to the train.

Tuesday was always busy in downtown Chicago and Robin enjoyed the hustle and bustle. She stopped at a stationery store to make copies of her letters, pushed through the glass doors of Marshall Field. A cheerful clerk greeted her immediately. "May I help you?"

"Yes please, I am looking for the employment office."

"Certainly. Take the elevators to the fifth floor" she said, pointing toward the far wall. "Then, turn right and go to the back of the building. Someone in the reception area can assist you. Have a good day, Madam."

"Thank you, and you have a good day too."

The elegant elevator transported Robin silently to the fifth floor. As promised, the receptionist asked, "May I assist you?"

"Yes, I am looking for the employment office?"

She pointed. "It's the third door on your left down that hall."

"Thanks for your help."

"Good luck," she said, then whispered, "You'll love it here. Marshall Field is a super place to work."

Robin nodded and crossed her fingers. "*This is the best option by far.*" Robin opened the door to the employment office and another smiling woman asked if she could be of assistance.

"I understand from the paper that you are hiring summer help. I would like to apply for a position."

"Yes, we're hiring. Have a seat while I get an application packet together for you. When you've completed the forms, Mrs. Hall will review them and meet with you." The girl returned with a pen and a clipboard holding a stack of forms.

It took Robin 15 minutes to complete the paperwork. She clipped a copy of her two letters of recommendation on top of the application and returned the clipboard and pen to the receptionist. She returned to her seat and unfolded her copy of Mr. Davis' letter. She had nearly cried the first time she read it.

To Whom It May Concern:
Re: Ms. Jennifer Lynn (Robin) Hart

My letter is about a special young woman who joined our staff at the end of August last year. She worked her schedule dependably throughout the school year and covered shifts for others who called in sick. When she needed time off, she planned well in advance, negotiating with other employees to avoid upsetting the restaurant's schedule.

We at Rob Rory's SteakHauz expect our employees to learn to cover all stations and be able to fill in wherever they are needed, no matter the job. All employees must be willing to pick up a mop or whatever it takes to make ready for our patrons. Robin has been a model employee who embraces our philosophy and functions competently in every position in our restaurant.

I do hope you value this gold mine of energy and the commitment she brings to whatever is expected of her. She is passionate about her work and about those who work with her.

We value Robin's willingness to learn and highly recommend her for any position she seeks while she is in Chicago. I have included my contact information should you wish to speak with me in person.

Sincerely
Rory Davis
Owner, RobRory's SteakHauz

Lost in the memory of the Davises and her job, Robin almost missed hearing her name.

"Jennifer," called a woman a second time.

Robin stood quickly and reached for the woman's outstretched hand. "I'm Jennifer," she said, "but everyone calls me Robin."

"Well, Robin, I'm Mrs. Hall, the Human Resources Director. I will be interviewing you this morning. Your nickname fits well with your red hair." She gestured toward the chair beside her desk. "Please take a seat. I have reviewed your application and your letters of recommendation. We have three positions left to fill. One is in the jewelry department, one in the men's shoe department, and one in sports equipment. Before we go further, I have a few questions for you."

Robin sat up straighter and nodded.

"Tell me how you handled an unpleasant diner at Rob Rory's Steakhauz. I'm sure every restaurant faces those challenges."

"Well, most of our diners during the day are local business-people and nice families in the evening. However, there was one afternoon that a group of businessmen came in who were different from the Steakhauz' usual clientele. It seemed they were just having a good time. I wasn't their waitress. One of the men got a little too friendly with his hands for my friend working the station, so I switched with her. I was respectful but persistent with him and that seemed to work okay. I stayed out of his reach, and when he got too loud, Mr. Davis stepped in. He told the man he would have to leave if he could not treat the staff with respect. The guy huffed, but I think it embarrassed him, so he settled down. The men finished their meal and left, and I haven't seen them in the restaurant since then. Interestingly, they split the bill three ways and the other men left huge tips and that guy left nothing. Can you believe that? The guy was rude and should have been the one to tip big time! You've gotta be a real jerk to leave it to your friends to cover for you..." Robin sucked in a breath.

"That sounds like a good learning experience. What would you say is your biggest weakness when interacting with other people?"

Robin sat quietly as the seconds ticked, pacing her heartbeats, and took a deep breath. "Sometimes I speak before I think, but I'm getting better at managing that. I try to take another breath and pause before I say anything. Most of the time that works." Robin watched Mrs. Hall's face. *"I've said too much and now I won't get the job. Shit..."*

"That is an insightful disclosure, Robin, and it seems like one that was difficult for you to make."

"Yes, it was, but I want to put my best foot forward and be as open and honest as I can. I want this job and I am looking to learn as much as possible over the summer to help myself and the store be successful. I will do what you ask of me and demonstrate reliability. Mr. Davis taught me the value of a flexible staff and I am willing to work where and when you need me."

"Thank you for that. I want you to meet Mrs. Parker, the manager of the jewelry department. I think that might be the right spot for you. Please wait outside while I see if she has the time to interview you now."

"Thank you, Ma'am. I am yours as long as you need me."

With each passing minute, Robin worried that she had talked herself out of the job.

A tall-regal looking woman walked toward Mrs. Hall's office. Robin thought, *"I want to look like that. She walks like she's somebody."*

The woman entered Mrs. Hall's office and closed the door behind her. Five minutes passed while Robin watched the clock. The door opened and Mrs. Hall motioned for Robin to join them.

"Robin, please meet Mrs. Deloris Parker from the jewelry department. She'd like to ask you some questions. You're welcome to use my office for your conversation."

Robin reached for Mrs. Parker's hand and said "It's nice to meet you, Ma'am. I am Jennifer Lynn Hart, but everyone calls me Robin."

"Yes, so Mrs. Hall has told me," Mrs. Parker smiled as she shook Robin's hand. "Please have a seat. I understand you are interested in a position here at Marshall Field and Mrs. Hall has recommended the jewelry department?"

"Yes ma'am, I am interested in that position. I know I could do the job for you if you will give me the chance."

"First things first. I read your application. You haven't worked in a department store before. How do you believe your previous experience will relate to meeting our needs here at Marshall Field?"

"Well, I suppose a customer is a customer and I've worked with all kinds of personalities, including demanding diners. I suspect that customers in a jewelry department will also expect me to pay attention only to them."

Mrs. Parker chuckled at Robin's accurate description of the privileged clientele of the high-end jewelry department. "Quite right, Robin, quite right. If you were to get this position, what do you think would be the biggest hurdle you will have to overcome?"

"I think I can manage the customers well, but I don't know anything about jewelry. My Gram and I aren't made of money, so jewelry is a luxury that we can't afford. I have a lot to learn about the merchandise, like what is in good taste and what isn't. I hope that you will teach me."

"Thank you, Robin. If you will step back out to the waiting area and have a seat, Mrs. Hall and I will talk for a moment and she will get back to you."

"The longer they talk, the better my chances," Robin thought. The minute hand had made only two revolutions of the clock face when Mrs. Hall's office door opened, *"Damn. I knew I blew it!"*

Mrs. Parker nodded to Robin as she passed, giving no clue whether the job was on or off.

Mrs. Hall stood in her doorway and beckoned Robin to approach. When Robin reached the office, she stuck out her hand. "Congratulations, young lady, I have a job to offer you. Step back into my office and we can discuss the details."

Elated, Robin hesitated. "Did you say I got the job?"

"Yes, you did," she chuckled. "You impressed Mrs. Parker and she is ready for you to start orientation tomorrow. Be here in my office at eight. I'll give you a pass until you have a badge and I'll show you where you come into the building. The main doors don't open until nine."

When Mrs. Hall quoted her salary, Robin almost choked. The figure was nearly twice what she earned at the Steakhauz, including tips. With what she could save over the summer, she'd be able to work fewer hours during the next school year. *"I can't wait to tell Gram!"*

Robin left Mrs. Hall's office with a smile on her face and a large packet of materials under her arm to read in preparation for her orientation. She reached the house without being fully aware of how she'd gotten there. She burst into the living room and spilled the whole day's events from start to finish in one excited monologue.

"I am so proud of you!" Gram said. "You got a wonderful job on your first day out. What are you going to wear tomorrow?"

"Uh, I haven't given that a thought. I've got to read the pile of material Mrs. Hall gave me. I'm sure the dress code is in there somewhere."

The next morning, the sun was shining and so was Robin. The security guard tipped his hat and said, "Welcome to Marshall Field and have a good day, Miss."

"Thank you and the same to you."

On the elevator, Robin bumped into a young man. "Oh excuse, me."

"No problem. By the way, I'm Titus Smithers the Third. My Dad's on the Board here and I'm on my way to orientation. I'm working here this summer."

Robin shook his hand and said, "Well, Titus Smithers the Third, I'm Robin Hart the First and I'm pleased to meet you. This is my first day, too, and I suspect we will be in orientation together."

Mrs. Hall greeted them. "Right on time, you two. You'll spend the morning with me learning about Marshall Field's policies, procedures, and benefits. Then after lunch, you'll orient to your department. You may be interested in our incentive program. After two weeks of employment, you will be eligible to apply for the Lead Trainee position. You will need a letter of recommendation from your department manager."

"Yep, that sounds interesting."

Robin's thought was interrupted when Titus muttered to no one in particular, "I've got that in the bag."

Chapter 3

Robin stood at one end of the counter sorting charge tickets. "Robs! Hey, Robs," came a hushed, but insistent voice. "That you, Robs?"

Robin shivered as if someone had dropped an ice cube down her back. She clenched her fists at her sides and took a calming breath, then raised her head slowly to face Jake. "Son of a bitch!" she hissed through clenched teeth, "What in the hell are you doing here?"

Jake leaned in conspiratorially. "Cool that you're here, Robs. Stroke of luck. I could use your help."

"Help?" Robin retorted. "You're shittin' me. I wouldn't help you cross a busy street! I would, however, be delighted to push you into one."

"C'mon, Robs. Get off your high horse. A girlfriend always helps her man."

"Girlfriend! Are you crazy? The association between your name and that word slipped permanently from my vocabulary last August. Girlfriend in your dreams, you piece of shit."

"Robs," he began.

"You must be high on something," she continued. "Oh, how silly of me… of *course*, you're high on something. Get lost, Jake. This place is way too classy for the likes of you."

Jake wheedled, "Listen, Robs, I need your help. The guys and I have a good business going. We lift high-end stuff, then unload it at a discount. You workin' here will be a big help. There's good money in it and I'll cut you in."

"Don't say another word, Jake. See that tall guy over there? He's got eyes in the back of his head, and you're just who he's looking for. Try something stupid, Asshole, and see what happens."

Jake shook his head. "You just wait, Robs. When you see how little you make here compared to what helping me out would be worth, you'll change your mind. I guarantee it." He winked and walked away.

Robin breathed deeply, clenching and unclenching her fists. *"That asshole! I should tell Security to keep an eye out for him. But… that could be a bad move. Just to keep my eyes open and my mouth shut."*

"I have the tickets sorted and the department's quiet. Would now be a good time for me to take lunch?"

"Certainly, I appreciate your doing those tickets for me. I'll relieve you as soon as I get these bracelets back in the case. You've earned a leisurely lunch," Mrs. Parker said.

"That was quick," Robin said with a smile. "I've restocked everything that we showed customers this morning."

"Thank you. If you go now and come back at 1:00, you can enjoy an extra ten minutes as a reward for your initiative. Robin, I'm pleased that you joined us for the summer. The recommendations from your employer in Dallas and from Eleanor Hornsby were impressive. I knew right away if Eleanor recommended you, I was making a good decision."

Robin absently sipped her lemonade while she replayed the confrontation with Jake. *"You fuckin' asshole! Just who the hell do you think you are, waltzing back into my life and expecting me to do anything but spit in your face."* For an instant, a grin replaced her scowl. *"If we'd been anywhere but here, I WOULD have spit in your face!"*

Robin jumped when a tall young man holding a lunch bag and a can of Coke interrupted her thoughts. "Mind if I sit at your table? Looking out the window at lunch lets me pretend that I'm not spending the glorious days of summer inside." When she hesitated, he continued. "I don't mean to intrude, but this is the last window seat left. That looked like some pretty intense thinking you were doing just now."

"Sure. The table's big enough that I can pretend you're not here... in case I want to think about something intense," she added smiling. "Or I might just look out the window with you."

"Guy Mason," said the young man, holding out his hand.

"Robin Hart, intense thinker," Robin smiled, giving his hand a firm shake.

"Summer help or new prisoner from the glorious outdoors?"

"Actually, I was hired for my ability to think intensely," Robin said, "but just for the summer. I hear that after mid-August, intense thinking is no longer considered an attribute."

"You're quick," he said. "That's impressive. I like you already. I work in men's clothing. I've been working here summers since high school and they take me back whenever I'm home. They pay a premium at Christmas."

"Home from where?" Robin asked.

"Northwestern. I'm in pre-med. I'll be a junior in the fall."

"Cool! I'm in nursing. Just finished my freshman year at Crestmont University in Dallas."

"Dallas! That's a ways from home."

"They offered me a scholarship, so it was a no-brainer. There's no way I could manage college on my own dime. Crestmont's a good school, and you won't believe the weather. Summer's a bitch, but it's glorious from September to May. Texas missed the memo on what winter's supposed to be like."

"Sounds like I'd be grateful for an inside job in summer. Maybe I should broaden my horizons."

"Northwestern *is* a great school, but I'll admit… I get both a great school AND decent weather," she grinned.

"Touché," Guy grinned back. "Hey, it's almost 1:00 and I gotta get back. Thanks for sharing your table with me, Robin. See you around."

"I gotta go, too." Robin gathered her things. "See ya."

Robin watched Guy leave the lunchroom. *How refreshing! A guy who's the polar opposite of Jake! There's hope for humanity after all!*

"Gram, do you think buying a short gold chain would be extravagant? Your ring ends up buried inside my blouse. A shorter chain would show it off, not hide it."

"I'm pleased that my ring is that important to you. I expected that you would tuck it away in your jewelry box."

"I was so happy when you gave it to me after I'd been such a shit…"

Gram peered over her glasses and cleared her throat.

"Oh… sorry…" Robin winced, "…after I'd been so ungrateful my last two years of high school. It meant so much that you still loved me. I never take it off. Good thing it's waterproof."

"I have an idea. I'll buy a chain that's the right size for the ring, and you can use the one you have for your pendant."

"How about we buy it together? I *do* work in the jewelry department after all. And, I get a discount! It will be *our* chain for *our* ring. Can you meet me at the store on Saturday at 5:30 when I get off? Then we can celebrate and have dinner out."

"It's a date! We'll take each other out to dinner."

"Hey, Robin! Wait up."

She turned to see Guy hurrying along the sidewalk to catch up with her. "Hi, Guy," She said. "I like the sound of that. *Hi, Guy!* It's catchy, like *Later, Gator.*"

"This is your first Saturday, isn't it?"

Robin nodded. "I have no clue what to expect. I've always hated shopping, especially in crowds, so I've never been a Saturday shopper."

"It'll be busy, for sure. The challenge is to make everyone think they're important," Guy said. "There'll always be someone waiting for your attention while you're helping someone else. The trick is to make eye contact and smile. Then say things like *I'll be with you in just a moment* or *Thank you for your patience. I'll be right with you.* People don't seem to mind waiting when you acknowledge them. When you ignore them until it's their turn, they're more often rude than pleasant."

"That sounds like great advice. Thanks," Robin said. "Left to my own devices, I'd probably do just the opposite. I'm not famous for gentility and tact. I'm a *Say-it-first, then-think-about-it-after* kinda person. Gram made it clear that working here would be an opportunity for growth and development."

"Your Gram… can I presume that's your grandmother? …is a wise woman. That must be something unique to grandmothers. My Granny is my sage. Seems to me that the most important things, or at least the most practical things I've learned, are those she taught me."

"Gram's amazing. She's wise, for sure, but the thing that gets me most is that she never loses it. She never lets anything push her off track. Like if someone made her angry, that wouldn't keep her from remembering all the good things about that person at the same time. Or when something interferes with plans, she acts like it's an opportunity instead of an inconvenience. "

"Yep. I think I read something like that in the dictionary under *Grandmother.*"

"You'll get a kick out of this. When I was a kid, we'd planned to go to the zoo and I talked about it all week. When Saturday got here it was raining. I was crushed and she was grinning. She said, *Lucky for us, it's raining. Let's go to the planetarium! We can go to the zoo any time, but we'd never have thought of the planetarium if the sun were shining.* Can you believe that?"

"I believe it," Guy said with a smile. "It sounds like something Granny would say." Guy held the door open for Robin. "That was cool, running into you. The ten-minute walk went by in a flash."

Robin smiled, "Time to put your sage advice into practice. *I'll be right with you,*" she said, exaggerating her smile. "How'm I doing?"

"You're on track for *Lead Trainee*!" Guy grinned and waved as he turned toward the men's department.

"Good morning, Robin." Mrs. Parker smiled as Robin approached the jewelry counter. "Welcome to your first Saturday shift. It'll be a busy day. Try not to let impatient customers get the better of you. If you need help, just let me know."

"I'll be right with you. Thank you so much for your patience."

Mrs. Parker grinned. "My star employee has been reading sales etiquette. I'm impressed!" Then she said, "Seriously, Robin, if it gets overwhelming, call me. I don't want you quitting in frustration."

"I'll do my best, Mrs. Parker. I really will."

Customers arrived at 9:00 on the dot and Robin discovered that Guy's sage advice made the morning pass without incident. Eye contact and a pleasant word managed to keep people satisfied to wait their turn. *"I gotta stop by his department on break and thank him."*

At 10, Mrs. Parker shooed her off for a 15-minute break. She walked through the men's department, but Guy was engrossed with a customer. Disappointed, she continued to the break room to drink her lemonade, then trudged back to the jewelry counter and worked non-stop till noon.

"Hungry?" Guy asked. "Mrs. Parker said you can take lunch now if you'd like. I thought you might like a break from practicing gentility."

"What kind of pull do you have with Mrs. Parker? The counter looks way too busy for her to be sending me to lunch."

"I was her fair-haired boy my first summer here. To hear Mrs. Parker talk, you're walking in my footsteps. It will be busy all day, so there's no good time to go to lunch. Let's go make the most of the 28 minutes we have left."

Robin grabbed her lunch bag from the refrigerator and joined Guy at the last window table. "So, how's your day going? I stopped by on break but you were selling a suit to a big handsome black guy and I didn't want to interrupt."

"You shoulda stuck around. That was Gayle Sayers. He plays for the Bears and he's as nice as he is good-looking. I was in high school the first time he came in and I could barely say *May I help you;* I was so tongue-tied. Last Christmas he brought me an autographed copy of *I Am Third,* his book. You can tell I'm a fan!"

"It's cool that you know someone famous and talk like he's just a regular guy."

"He is. The next time he's in, I'll introduce you." Guy continued, "Anything interesting happen for you today?"

"The best thing I have to report is that so far I haven't pissed anyone off. Thank you for the lesson in customer management. Your advice was on target and I'm most grateful. I certainly wouldn't have thought of it myself."

Guy smiled. "I'd love to claim credit for your success, but it was Mrs. Parker who taught me that approach. Small world, isn't it."

"Gram is going to meet me when I get off this evening. We're going to buy a gold chain for my ring," Robin explained, pulling the ring from inside her blouse. "I'm getting a shorter chain so it will sit right here. You get off at 5:30, don't you?" Guy nodded, and Robin continued, "Do you have time to meet me at the jewelry counter? I'd love for you to meet Gram."

"Great idea! I'd like to meet her, and I bet there's a story behind that ring, too. You don't have a boyfriend whose gone off to war, do you?"

"Heavens, no. I don't have time for a boyfriend right now. Classes, studying, and work take up all 36 hours of my day at school, and the only boys I know in Chicago don't qualify for the position. How about you? Are you harboring a damsel in distress somewhere?"

Guy laughed. "Well, not exactly."

When he didn't say anything more, Robin asked with a teasing smile, "You're not hitting on me, are you, Pal? Just so you know, I'm in the market for a really cool friend who's smart and witty and doesn't have a hidden agenda. I'm taking applications."

"Hmmm. I know someone who just might be interested." He waved his napkin.

Robin looked at Guy with a grateful smile. "I'm glad we met, Guy. I spent Thanksgiving with one of my suitemates on her farm. When I met her soulmate, that's what she calls the boy next door, I thought how cool it would be to have a friend like him." She took the napkin from Guy's hand and pretended to read it. "When would you like to set up your interview?"

"Mrs. Parker, I'd like to introduce you to my grandmother, Maureen Kelly. Gram, this is my supervisor, Mrs. Parker."

Gram reached for Mrs. Parker's hand. "Eleanor Hornsby mentioned you on more than one occasion."

"It's nice to meet you. We do miss Eleanor. All of us learned from her over the years," said Mrs. Parker.

"Now I hear that Robin is learning from you. She's a bright girl and I'm sure that she'll make you proud. Every new experience is an opportunity for learning," Gram smiled at Robin.

"Gram and I are going to buy a chain for my ring, Mrs. Parker. Why don't I show her what's available since there are customers waiting for you?" Mrs. Parker nodded and turned to the first person in the substantial line at the counter.

"There are so many styles," Robin said holding a velvet display board for Gram to examine. "I want one that's lightweight and won't kink. These box chains are attractive, but they aren't as flexible or durable as the diamond cut. What do you think of this one?"

"Sweetheart, I must admit that they're all lovely. We need to choose the one that's the right length and the most comfortable."

"The most common length is 16 inches, but I think I'd prefer 14. That narrows the choice significantly because we only have four styles that come that short. Of course, we can have any length shortened, but that's such a waste."

"Show me the ones you like, and I'll tell you, which I like best," Gram suggested.

"Okay. These three. They're not all the same price, Gram. I should tell you how much each one costs before you pick."

"Of course not! We're choosing an heirloom. We want the *right* one, not necessarily the *least expensive* one. After all, you're working now, and you have your discount. Soooo," Gram said, studying the three chains that Robin laid on a separate display board, "I like *this* one."

"Gram, you picked my favorite! If we both like it best, it *must* be the right one."

Mrs. Parker rang up the purchase and handed Robin a box with the chain nestled on a silky cushion.

"You both have good taste," came a voice from behind them.

"Guy! I'm so glad you stopped by. I want you to meet Gram."

"Gram, this is Guy Mason. He works in the men's department. He knows famous football players, and he submitted an application to be my friend."

Guy smiled at Gram, taking one of her hands in both of his. "I am so pleased to meet you. I suppose "Mrs. Gram" isn't what I'll be calling you."

"Kelly. Mrs. Kelly will do nicely. It's nice to meet a new friend of Robin's. Your application must have been quite impressive. My granddaughter has exceptional taste in friends." Gram grinned at Robin. "At least she does lately."

They separated outside the store, Guy heading for Washington Station and Robin and Gram to find a restaurant quiet enough for conversation. "How does *The Village* sound," Robin asked. "It's a bit pricey but I thought we could split some filling pasta dish and maybe get an extra salad. I've heard one entrée is waaaay too much for one person."

"We're celebrating, so *The Village* it is! It's not much of a walk and I'm sure we're early enough to get in without reservations."

"I've been thinking…"

"About what, Sweetheart?"

"About visiting my mother. I'm off on Wednesday and Thursday. I think we should try for Wednesday. If we're successful, we can meet again the next day. The safest time to visit should be from 9 to 11. Harold will be gone to work by 9, and Mom will be back in the house in case he shows up for lunch."

"That's perfect, as long as the weather is good. With construction, bad weather can make for an unpredictable schedule. If the weather is iffy, I don't think we should risk contacting Aileen. Fortunately, none of the forecasts I've heard mention rain."

"We'll call from the payphone outside the grocery store, a block from their place. If she'll meet us, we can go somewhere for coffee and visit for an hour or so. I want so badly to let her know that I care about her. Until I spent time with Katie's family, I hadn't felt anything but resentment for her letting you take me without blinking an eye. Don't misunderstand, Gram, I wouldn't have wanted to grow up with anyone but you, but it pissed me off that she didn't say one word about loving me or missing me or anything. She just watched while you packed my things. She didn't even get up to hug me when we left. I've never forgotten that day."

"That's understandable. You were just eight, and Harold made Aileen's life a living hell, which made it hard for her to act like a mother. Harold makes it hard for her to do anything."

"I understand that now. Watching how the men in Katie's family behave made me realize what a beast Harold is. They're gentle and respectful and supportive. I realized that Aileen had absolutely none of that. I want to let her know that I don't blame her anymore."

"Aileen should hear that from you. I can't promise, after all this time, that she has any emotional energy left to share with you, but I know that your words will lighten her heart, even if she can't show you how much it matters."

"Gram, thanks for being with me in this. I don't think I could approach her alone. Can we do it next Wednesday? If she won't see us... well, I haven't thought about what if she won't see us."

"I think she will. Anyhow, we'll see."

Robin smiled in anticipation.

Chapter 4

"Mom, this is Robin. Don't hang up. Gram and I are waiting for you at the grocery store on the corner. Please come meet us. We have a little time to visit and you can be back in plenty of time in case Harold comes home for lunch. Please come."

"Robin? Is that really you?" Aileen was hesitant, her voice a mere whisper.

"Yes, Mom, it's me. Please hurry so we'll have time to visit before you have to get back home."

"Robin. I'm not sure…"

"Don't say *no*. We're just a block away and you have to come. Say you'll come."

"Well…"

"Mom, say you'll come." Robin's voice was insistent. "We're right here and there's not a lot of time."

"Well… Okay… but I won't be able to stay long. Harold may come home."

"I know, Mom. Come quickly so you can get back in plenty of time. Come now."

"But…"

"Now. Right now. You're wasting time. I want to see you." Robin hung the receiver on the cradle, and her dime clinked as it dropped somewhere inside the black payphone.

"Gram, do you think she'll come?"

Gram could see the uncertainty in Robin's eyes and assured Robin with a nod. "She'll come. I know she wants to see you and I don't think she'll let the opportunity pass."

They stood on the corner facing the direction from which Aileen would come. Ten minutes crawled painfully by before she appeared. Aileen stopped and stared at her mother and Robin, her face and her feet frozen in place. Gram grabbed Robin's hand and approached her daughter. "Aileen," she smiled, and Aileen melted into her embrace.

"Mother, it's so good to see you..." Gram opened her arms and Robin entered the awkward embrace, at a loss for words.

Gram released them and smiled. "Let's sit in the park across the street." Her daughter and granddaughter followed wordlessly.

They sat on a shaded bench facing a profusion of pink azaleas. "How lovely," said Gram. "Just the spot for a long-overdue family reunion."

Robin found her voice. "Mom, I'm so glad you came. I'm not angry anymore, not at you. I understand what Harold does isn't your fault, and that leaving him can be more frightening than staying. I'm grown now, and I want you to know that I'm fine. I want to bury the old memories and remember you from today. Gram's always told me that you care about me, and I want to believe that."

Aileen sat up and opened her mouth to speak. Then she sagged back and lowered her gaze to her hands in her lap. "Robin. I'm sorry. I'm so sorry. I wanted so much to have a child, but I wasn't brave enough to keep you. I didn't deserve you."

"Wait." Robin took both her mother's hands in hers. "Forget that! That was long ago. Gram taught me that yesterdays do not determine tomorrows. Today is ours to take advantage of, so let's forget yesterdays and concentrate on the rest of our lives.

"I want to tell you about my first year in college. I got a scholarship and I'm in the nursing program at a terrific university in Dallas. I have a ditzy roommate who's a terrific kid who needs to grow up, and two suitemates who are cool. I want to share all that with you. You and I can both thank Gram for taking care of us and love each other just because we can. Can you do that? Can you just love me without caring about the past or worrying about the future? You don't need to do anything except spend time with me."

Aileen's tentative smile spread slowly across her face. She held her daughter's gaze, then sat up straighter and opened her arms. Robin entered the embrace while Gram looked on, pleased.

"Aileen, what time did you say you had to be home to prepare lunch for Harold?"

"Let's sit here together and visit for a few more minutes," Aileen replied, "then I'll hurry home. I'd hate to take a chance on spoiling such a special morning."

"Can we meet tomorrow?" Robin asked eagerly. "Let's not waste a day. Is this the best place for us to meet?"

"I think we can. Let's meet right here." Aileen hesitated. "If something goes wrong, I'll try to call you. We still have a phone, though it wouldn't be a good idea for you to call me."

"Okay, then. Tomorrow. Could we come earlier so there'd be more time to visit? What time could you meet us?"

"Nine feels safe. Let's leave it at nine." Aileen stood.

Gram and Robin each hugged Aileen. "Thank you, Aileen," Gram whispered. "That was a brave decision. I'm proud of you. You've made Robin happy. I'm not sure what I'm going to do with her until tomorrow morning."

"Gram's right, Mom. I am a happy camper. Thank you for coming and letting me know that you care. I'm serious about ignoring the past. No sorries. Let's just look forward."

The next morning, Aileen was sitting on the bench when Gram and Robin arrived. She rose and hurried toward them. "Let's walk and talk," she said. "Mornings are lovely. We can enjoy ourselves before the sun has a chance to broil the city. There's a café a few blocks from here where we can stop for coffee. Have you two eaten breakfast?"

"Robin was in the kitchen at 6:30, watching the clock and ready to leave. I had to feed her to keep her in her chair."

Aileen's smile didn't reach her eyes. "Explaining how and why things happened wouldn't change anything, so I'm grateful that you've forgiven me. I feel sure that we can work out ways to spend time together this summer."

"Mom, if Gram and I lived far away from here where he couldn't reach you, would you consider coming to live with us? Would…"

"Oh, Robin," Aileen interrupted, "I couldn't do that. He would find me no matter where I went."

"Don't close the door so quickly, Mom. It's just an idea. Sometime soon, Gram will have to sell the house because they're going to tear it down. We don't know when it will be, but that gives us an opportunity to explore options. You never know what the future will bring. You have to keep your mind open to possibilities."

"But…" Aileen began.

"No, really! Just keep an open mind. There is no harm in dreaming."

"You're right, Robin. I'll try."

"That's all anyone can ask," Gram said. "Now let's settle into this cozy booth and order something sinful to go with our coffee?"

They sipped coffee, nibbled cinnamon rolls, and planned their next clandestine meeting. "Aileen, what arrangements can you make to be out of the house during the day that would appear normal to Harold? Something that would include your not being home at lunchtime. Do you ever go shopping with a friend?"

Aileen's shoulders drooped. "I don't have friends. I can't risk having someone at the house when Harold goes into one of his rages. It's difficult to make friends if you can't reciprocate and it's awkward to visit someone's home and never invite them to mine."

"That's sad."

"Do you ever go shopping, just by yourself?" asked Gram. "If you planned a shopping trip, you could spend time with us at my house. We could do more than have a coffee before you had to run off."

"I suppose I could. Stores don't open until 9 and it wouldn't be practical for me to be home for lunch. Let me think that over. I would have to start talking about it today to give him time to get used to the idea. I'll go shopping next Wednesday. The traffic will have died down by nine, so I'll plan my trip from 9:30 to 2. I'll be home in plenty of time to have dinner ready when Harold comes home. Yes, that sounds reasonable. I'll just have to think of why I need to go shopping. It's not his birthday. I'll think of something."

"Mom, that's terrific! We'll have a late breakfast ready when you come. I'm so excited!"

"If for some reason you must alter our plans, Aileen, will you be able to call and let me know? Robin and I can still come here to visit on Wednesday if the shopping trip doesn't work out."

"I'm sure I can manage a call." Aileen said, "I do so want to go to the house, Mother. It's been a long time. Robin, you have made such a difference in my life this summer. I haven't been this excited about anything since, well… since longer than I can remember. I want to spend every moment that I can with you two. Mother, thank you for encouraging Robin to contact me."

"She did that all on her own, Aileen. I will say that I was pleased, but I didn't have anything to do with it."

"We should be going," Aileen said. "It will be close to 11 when I get back to the house. I'm looking forward to next Wednesday." Aileen walked with them to the bus stop, then gave Robin a hug. "You are lovely. I'm so pleased that you've given me the opportunity to know you. See you on Wednesday." She walked toward her house with a spring in her step.

"Gram, can you believe it! She's going to come to the house. We have to find a way to make her think about the possibility of leaving that dirtbag. I'll admit that I'm selfish. If she won't come, then I'm afraid that you might consider staying in Chicago, even after you sell the house. If she will come, there's nothing keeping you here. We can be a family, Gram. Doesn't that sound great? A family! She just has to see that leaving him is the best thing to do."

Robin lifted her head when she heard Guy's voice. "Thought I'd check to see if you could slip away for your break."

"She can go," said Mrs. Parker from the other end of the counter.

"Thanks. Back in 15," Robin gave Mrs. Parker an appreciative wave. "Guy, I hope I didn't give you the wrong idea when I said you could interview to be my friend. I meant friend, not boyfriend. I think you're great and I love spending time with you, but boyfriend wasn't what I had in mind."

Guy grinned. "No problem at all! I'm cool with that."

Robin smiled. *"That was easy. Pressure's off... but he sounded relieved that I wasn't up for a boyfriend. That was odd."*

"Want a Coke?" Guy asked. "Save the drink you brought for lunch."

"You sure? I'm used to pinching pennies. I don't want to waste any of yours either."

"Definitely sure. I'm a lucky guy whose folks can afford to send him to college. I work because those same folks expect me to be industrious and productive. They pay the bills and I work for spending money and Christmas presents."

"Christmas presents?"

Guy laughed out loud. "Guess that did sound kinda off the wall. My family's big on Christmas and birthday presents... not expensive things but presents that you think a lot about before you give them and mean a lot when you open them. It wouldn't work if my parents had to pay for the presents, I pick out for them."

"Your family sounds cool. Are you an only, or part of a herd?"

"Small herd. My older brother, Gary, is a pathology resident. Elsa's in her second year of law school, and Reid is 15. Not sure what my folks were thinking… but I do have a good idea what they were doing."

Robin said. "I love how you say things… you make me laugh."

"So… other than a wise and wonderful grandmother, who else is lucky enough to be related to you?"

"I'm it! I guess they broke the mold. My parents discovered they weren't parent material and quit before they did any more damage."

"It sounds like you just might be serious."

"Unfortunately, I am. My dad is a drunken bastard and my mother just wasn't strong enough to stand up to him. The best part of the story is that Gram and I lived happily ever after."

"I like the ending, but the beginning and the middle will have to wait or Mrs. Parker will never let us take a break together again."

"Wow. Where did *that* 15 minutes go? Any chance we can have lunch together? I've got stuff I want to tell you."

"There's something I need to tell you, too," Guy added.

"Now I'm intrigued. You've kicked my curiosity meter up to max." She turned to dash back to work. 'Oh," she called over her shoulder, "thanks for the Coke."

Robin smiled when Guy caught her eye. "May I take lunch now, Mrs. Parker?"

"Go ahead," she replied. "The counter is quiet enough for me to handle."

"Let's eat in the Atrium," Guy suggested. "It's even better than a window table in the breakroom. If you'll grab my lunch bag from the refrigerator, I'll get a Coke for each of us."

They settled on an alabaster bench in the sunny atrium. Robin unwrapped her sandwich and Guy opened both Coke bottles. "Guy, I'm glad that you're cool with just being friends. I'm not up for the responsibilities of a relationship. The plans I have for this summer just don't leave enough time for one, and at the end of the summer, I'll be a thousand miles away. I don't want to complicate college with a long-distance relationship. Honestly, I'm not sure I'm ready for a relationship under any circumstances."

"You don't need to explain, and you don't need to worry. I'm not interested in a relationship either. I'm glad I ran into someone who's intelligent and quick and fun to spend time with, but I'm not looking for a girl..."

"You have the same challenges that I do," she replied. "You'll be going back to school at the end of the summer, and…" Robin's sentence trailed off when she realized that she'd interrupted him. "I'm sorry. You weren't finished."

Guy hesitated, looking perplexed,

Frustrated, Robin spread her hands. "What am I missing?" When he didn't answer immediately, Robin replayed his last sentence in her head and smiled, "You're trying to tell me something."

Guy sighed. "I need to tell you something and I'll understand if it makes you uncomfortable. It's not something you can just assume someone will understand… or accept, for that matter."

"First, don't worry about whether I can understand or accept it. Accepting isn't a problem. It doesn't change that you're bright and funny and a gentleman. You'll have to help me with the understanding part. I don't have a single point of reference, but I also don't have any preconceived notions that you'll have to dispel. That should make your job easier," she concluded.

"Well," Guy said, obviously having no clue where to begin.

Robin giggled. "I didn't mean you had to start at the beginning. I just wanted to let you know that you can be comfortable telling me things you think I need to know. Oh, and I want you to be okay with my questions. Please don't think I'm prying."

Guy looked around and lowered his voice. "Robin, I'm gay. And, that's the *only* reason I'm not looking for a relationship. If you were a guy, you can *bet* I'd be interested. A guy as cool as you would be a great catch."

"Hmmm… interesting, and not what I was expecting… but you gotta admit that it's convenient. We get to be friends and I don't have to dump you. You didn't decide to be gay just so I'd stick around, did you?" Robin grinned.

"I must admit," Guy said with relief, "that wasn't as difficult as I expected. I hoped that telling you my secret wouldn't blow our friendship. You're cool and you have one helluva sense of humor."

"Seriously, Guy. I'm fine with it." Robin assured him. "Does your family know?"

"Yeah, they know. It wasn't their first choice, but they're OK with it, at least my mom is; my dad tries hard, but I know it's a struggle for him. We keep it secret. Even though Illinois is the only state in the US that doesn't have a law against homosexuality, it has the potential for being a problem. We all agree that sharing works best on a *need to know* basis."

"I'm glad you decided that I needed to know."

Robin stretched as she came into the kitchen at 8:30 on Saturday morning. "It felt good to sleep in. How long have you been up?"

"Unfortunately, my internal clock doesn't recognize weekends. I'm up at six 'most every morning. Coffee's hot. Pour yourself a cup and tell me what you'd like for breakfast."

"Whatever you're hungry for is fine with me," Robin replied. "Gram, do you think that Mom will be able to pull off the shopping trip next Wednesday? She did seem excited about it, but I hate to get my hopes up if you don't think it will happen."

"I've not seen Aileen that animated in years. Your interest in a relationship is a special treat for her. I'm banking on her not wanting to give that up. I think she'll do everything she can to make the visit next Wednesday happen."

"It was being with Katie's family that made me realize how much I wanted my mother back in our lives. I wrote to Katie to tell her that we reached out to her. I knew it would make her happy since family means the world to her."

The doorbell startled them. Gram went to the door with Robin close behind. "Yes?" said Gram to the man standing on her front porch. "Can I help you?"

Removing a business card from a clipboard and handing it to Gram, he replied, "My name is Carter... Benjamin Carter. I represent Carter Construction, the primary contractor on the Old Town Renovation Project. You are..." he checked his clipboard, "Mrs. Maureen Kelly?"

"I am," replied Gram, without smiling.

"May I come in, Mrs. Kelly? I'd like to tell you about the project."

"Mr. Carter, does this conversation include notice that my property will be involved in the renovation?"

"Well, yes. Yes, it does, but we're not ready to announce the date for that phase of construction," he explained. "Procuring the property for the project takes time, and Carter Construction believes that property owners who are involved should have plenty of time to explore their options."

"What, exactly, are the options for a homeowner to consider?"

Robin listened, smiling inwardly. "*That man has no idea that Gram's testing him. If he doesn't give her a straight answer to that question, he won't have a prayer of being invited inside.*"

"I expect that you would prefer a conversation to a cursory response, Mrs. Kelly. Could we, perhaps, go inside and sit while we talk?"

Robin grinned. "*He passed. This should be interesting.*"

"I would, indeed, Mr. Carter." Gram invited him in with a sweep of her arm and led him to a settee in the small living room. She and Robin settled into the two comfortable chairs facing him. "So, Mr. Carter, the options?"

"Well, the options vary depending upon the length of time before construction begins. A property owner can, at any time, sell the property on the open market for whatever a buyer is willing to pay. Property values in this neighborhood have been depressed for several years. The owner might find it difficult to make enough to purchase a comparable dwelling elsewhere. Early in a project such as ours, the contractor usually offers a premium price. The reason for offering more than market value is to provide owners with an option that is too good to pass up.

The amount of the offer never goes up over time, only down. I will be honest with you, Mrs. Kelly. When the government is involved in city improvements, keeping one's property is ultimately not an option. The City will condemn the remaining properties through eminent domain and the property owner will get whatever compensation the City offers. That last option is really a lose/lose situation because the owner gets less than the contractor offered, and the delayed negotiations reduce the contractor's profit margin."

"How will I know that the contractor's first offer is his best offer?" Gram asked.

"It has to be," explained Mr. Carter. "If property owners found out that the contractor raised his initial offer, everyone would hold out until the last possible moment, and that would defeat the purpose."

"So, when is all this happening?" Robin chimed in. "When will Gram know what you're offering and how long will it be before she has to move?"

"You've summed up the situation perfectly, young lady," Mr. Carter said, "however, I don't have a definitive answer to either question. I would be willing to go out on a limb and say that you should have an offer within three to six months." He stood and extended his hand to Gram.

She took it, rose from her chair, and walked with him to the door. "Thank you for the information, Mr. Carter. I feel sure that I will be ready with an answer when you return."

"If either of you has a question, please don't hesitate to contact me at the number on my card." With a nod to both women, he went down the steps and turned toward the next house on the block.

Robin poured two cups of fresh coffee. "So, what are you thinking, Gram?"

"I haven't had time to think," Gram laughed. "But it's not like I didn't know this was coming."

"If you moved to Dallas, Mom would have a safe place to live, even if she's too frightened to think about it right now. We have time to convince her she could have a better life."

"Robin, please don't put all of your eggs in that basket. The plan sounds logical, but *we* aren't the ones at risk. Aileen has been living in fear for years and it's the only life she knows, even if she feels trapped. And to top it off, she still thinks he loves her. Time makes a situation like that worse, not better."

"It doesn't make sense, Gram."

"Sometimes knowledge and logic are not the determining factors in decision-making. This is one of those times."

Dejected, Robin pleaded, "But you'll come to Dallas when you sell the house, won't you? You'd love it there, and we'd be together."

"I'm not sure I could leave Aileen with nowhere to turn."

"But that makes no sense. You hadn't seen her in years until this week, and then it's only by sneaking around. You'll never be able to enjoy being a normal mother and daughter."

"When you're a mother, you'll be able to see through my eyes. It's not a logical position; it's a perspective that you're not able to understand yet."

"What if I never get married or never have children? Does that mean I'll never understand?"

"I think you'll grow to accept my position, even if you don't share it. When you were small and you disagreed with me, I told you that when you were older, I would share my opinions with you, but would respect you enough to let you make your own decisions. In an adult relationship, neither person is in charge. Each one must respect the decisions the other makes or the relationship won't last. No adult wants to be controlled by someone else... influenced, of course, but not controlled. Compare our relationship to Aileen and Harold's and then decide which one is healthier."

"You always make sense," Robin said. "That used to make me so mad when I was a kid! I *knew* you were right, but admitting it always felt like I was losing an argument. Anyhow, please keep Dallas in mind. I wouldn't want to make you choose between Aileen and me, but I know you'd love it there, and I would love to have you nearby. Promise me you'll keep it in mind."

Gram nodded. "You might want to get ready for work. Then we can visit until you have to leave. It's Saturday; you'll have lots of opportunities to practice your crowd control techniques."

"Right! I'll be right with you Ma'am. Thank you for your patience, Ma'am."

Robin looked up from the register and a frisson of apprehension sped through her body when she caught a glimpse of Jake wandering aimlessly around the store. He stopped frequently, casting glances in all directions as he inspected item after item. Robin thought, "*He's not a sophisticated thief. His whole demeanor screams, 'look at me. I'm up to no good.'*"

She looked down as he turned in her direction. "*Don't come near me, Jake. Stay far away. You don't want to make this my business.*"

A customer captured her attention. When the sale was completed, Jake was gone. Robin let out a long, slow breath. "*I should tell security.*"

Guy's voice broke into her reverie. "You look like you're a million miles away. Can you take a break?"

She looked for Mrs. Parker who was nowhere in sight. "I guess not. I'm not sure where Mrs. Parker went or when she'll be back. Can you have lunch with me? Gram and I baked cookies and she insisted I bring some for you."

"Lunch it is. I wouldn't miss cookies. I'll stop by for you."

Guy turned to leave, and she reached for his arm. Jake was wandering around the perfume counter, lifting the bottles, ostensibly checking the prices.

"What?" Guy asked. "What's wrong?"

Robin whispered, "That guy at the perfume counter… the one in the ratty jeans… he's trouble. He's the leader of the losers I ran around with in high school. He's casing the store. He told me he lifts expensive stuff and sells it. If I say anything now, he'll know it was me and I don't trust him. He could do something bad to Gram or the house without batting an eye. Besides, I don't want anyone to know that I even *know* someone like him."

"He *looks* like trouble. Security keeps an eye on people like that because they don't fit the profile of a Marshall Field shopper. Stay away from him, Robin, and let Security handle it."

"I'm glad you said that. It's what I want to do, but I felt kinda guilty not stepping up and reporting him."

"If you haven't seen him take anything, you really don't have anything to report. I'd report him, but I'd end up having to tell Security that you told me about him."

"Can we go to the Atrium? I want to talk to you about something else," Robin asked as she and Guy grabbed their lunches. She hesitated, then said, "I'm not sure how this question is going to come out, but how did you figure out that you're gay? When did you know?"

Guy looked around skeptically, then shrugged. "I'm not really sure," he replied. "I'm not like the guys who have always known they were different and struggled their whole lives. I never thought about it seriously until junior high when my friends started making a big deal over girls and I realized I didn't feel at all like they did."

"Thanks, I know this is personal, but I'm trying to figure myself out. The only boyfriend I've ever had was that friggin' creep I pointed out to you earlier, and that was only because I was being rebellious. It was a miserable mistake and I'm still trying to make it up to Gram for not listening to her. What I want is a relationship like Katie's and John's; she calls him her soulmate. They've been sharing their secrets since they were little. I've never had a friend like that, male or female. I don't have time for a romantic relationship and I'm not sure I'm even interested in one. It could be that I'm just focused on school and work, but I think it may be more than that. I appreciate your listening to me. Close as I am to Gram, this is not a conversation I can imagine having with her."

"I'm glad you trust me with your secrets. I'm probably not the best authority on the subject, since the whole relationship thing is a mystery to me, too, but it's nice to be able to talk about it. Maybe we can be soulmates like Katie and her John."

"I like that idea."

"Want to join me and some friends after work some Saturday? No special plans yet, but we usually get together over drinks and music and just shoot the shit. But one thing we need to agree on upfront – when you come, I'm paying for the drinks. I know you're saving every penny and I don't want you to say *no* because it's a waste of money."

Shaking her head, Robin gave Guy a cheery grin. "No deal. You *are* a gentleman, but I budget for entertainment. Dutch treat."

"Gram let's take our coffee and sit on the porch," Robin suggested. "We should take advantage of the gorgeous weather before the summer gets hotter'n hell. In case Mom gets cold feet at the last minute, we'll catch her before she heads back for the bus."

"Definitely," Gram agreed. "If she looks hesitant, one of us can tackle her and the other can drag her back by her hair."

Robin looked perplexed, then burst into laughter. "Gram, you're amazing. You always know how to make me laugh."

They sat in the old, squeaky rockers, occasionally glancing toward the bus stop. "I love the sound of these old chairs. It reminds me of when we'd sit together in one chair and read to each other. They were old and squeaky ten years ago. I can't imagine why they haven't fallen apart by now."

"What's wrong with *old and squeaky?*" Gram retorted. "Would you like to bring your coffee and come sit in my lap? We could read the paper… or would you prefer *Little Women*?"

"It looks like I missed a funny joke," Aileen said, surprising them into silence as she climbed the porch steps into their circle of laughter.

Robin jumped up, her chair skittering backward. "You came! I wasn't sure you would."

Aileen replied nervously, "I wasn't sure I could do it, but in the end, I didn't want to waste the opportunity. It's so good to see you."

"Come inside, you two. There's fresh coffee."

"We were just laughing about the porch chairs. They squeak. Gram offered to read me *Little Women* in memory of old times." Robin's nervous chatter accompanied the three women to the kitchen table. "Those chairs squeaked when Gram brought me here. I wondered how they could still be holding together." Her tumbling narrative ground to a halt.

Gram poured coffee into the mismatched cups on the table. "We made cinnamon rolls this morning to celebrate the occasion."

"I've been looking forward to today," Aileen said, her soft voice shaky. "I couldn't sit still. When I told Harold I was going shopping, he bombarded me with questions."

"What did you tell him?" Robin asked.

Shrugging her shoulders, Aileen replied, "I said I had cabin fever and needed to get out of the house for a bit. I wasn't sure he'd buy it because when I go somewhere, it's usually because he tells me to. My neighbors are afraid of Harold so the only time I get to visit is when I run into a neighbor and it's too awkward *not* to ask me in."

"That's awful. What would he do besides rant and rave? Would he hit you? I remember him yelling and screaming in a drunken rage and pushing you around."

Aileen's shoulders sagged and her smile faded. "He shoves me to make a point, but only when he's drunk. He's really a good man, but he can't help himself when he drinks. He's always sorry afterward. That's just the way he is."

"But Mom, how can you live like that? What kind of life is it when you can't do anything?"

Aileen sat a bit straighter, but her mousy voice conveyed the truth. "Well... I keep the house clean. Harold likes a clean house. That's a good thing. Of course, I have meals to cook. Harold likes a hearty breakfast, and he sometimes surprises me and comes home for lunch. I always keep the makings for a big submarine sandwich on hand. When I have time, I watch some television."

"You must be a good cook, then?" Robin questioned.

Aileen's smile brightened, then faded. "Not really. There are certain meals that Harold likes, and I prepare them *just so*. I don't get to experiment. Occasionally, if I see something interesting on TV and if he's in the right mood, I might ask him if I can try it out."

Exasperated, Robin asked, "What do *you* like? I mean, do you read? What kind of books do you like; what kind of music; what movies? Do you go to the movies?"

"Well, no. I do like movies, but matinees are usually around lunchtime and I have to be home in case Harold comes for lunch. Regular movie prices are higher and Harold wouldn't approve of that. The library's too far to walk and buying books and magazines is too expensive. A neighbor used to lend me books." A smile crossed Aileen's face and was quickly replaced by a frown. "Once she lent me John Steinbeck's *Of Mice and Men*. It was so beautiful and so sad. Harold told me I wasn't to fill my head with such crap and to quit borrowing books. After that, she lent me *Lady Chatterley's Lover* and I hid it because I knew Harold would have a conniption fit. I was right. I put the book on the table near the door and Harold came home for lunch before I had a chance to take it back."

Robin's eyes widened as she listened. "What did he do?"

"He wasn't happy, that's for sure! He screamed and hollered for a bit. Then he threw the book at me and stormed out of the house. He didn't even stay for lunch. I'm just glad he didn't tear it up. I have no idea how I could have replaced it. After that, I just figured reading wasn't worth the hassle."

Aileen interrupted when Robin started to protest. "Robin, you have to understand. Harold works hard to take care of me. We have a house and he pays all the bills. He just expects me to be grateful for what he does. What would I do without him? I love him and he loves me in his own way."

"I'm trying to understand, Mom. I just can't imagine living like you do. I need to take care of myself and make my own decisions. What makes no sense to me is that I learned that from Gram. You're her *daughter*. How can you not be anything like her?"

Completely deflated, Aileen whispered, "I wanted those things once. In my junior year in high school, I was like most kids my age, angry and rebellious and sure that I knew better than my old-fashioned mother. I was determined to show her how grown up I was. I met Harold at a bar where I wasn't supposed to be, and I was flattered when an older man, Harold was 23 and I was 17, told me how lovely and mature I was. We started hanging out and I skipped school on his days off. He was domineering, but to me, it seemed mature."

"What made him so special?" Robin couldn't imagine.

"He was handsome, in a tough guy kinda way. He worked construction and still does. I think I admired most that he was on his own. He didn't even graduate from high school, but he made enough to be independent. Harold was proof that Mother was wrong about education. He was doing just fine without school. Honestly, at that point, I didn't care about much of anything but being grown up and being with Harold."

Gram refilled coffee cups and replaced cinnamon rolls as her daughter and granddaughter absently sipped and nibbled.

"Things didn't turn out exactly like I expected," Aileen said. "We married before the end of my junior year and I just never went back. My grades were so bad by then I wouldn't have passed anyhow. From the start, Harold made all the decisions, and it didn't take long for me to resent having no money of my own and not being able to come and go as I liked. Every time we argued about it, he told me I could go and do whatever I wanted, but if I wanted *him* to keep a roof over my head and food in my mouth, he had every right to be in charge. It made sense at the time, and I guess it still does.

"I thought when we had a baby, things would be different. I would have a child to take care of and he would be the provider. We'd both have something important to do."

"At least you were married when I was born."

"That's true. I was. We'd been married 15 months before you came along. I was excited when I got pregnant. I couldn't wait to tell Harold, so I was totally unprepared for his reaction. I couldn't believe my ears when he ranted about having a brat in the house and another mouth to feed and all that extra expense. I promised him I'd take care of the baby and not ask him for help, and he'd hardly know there was a baby in the house."

Aileen sighed. "I kept my promise, but it took all of the joy out of being a mother. You were adorable and such a good baby. Even so, it was hard to keep you quiet and out of sight. I was so exhausted from doing what I could to keep my promise to Harold that I didn't have any energy left to read to you or play with you, and the only toys and nice clothes you had were what your grandmother brought when she visited.

"Your grandmother took you to the park and the zoo, and she's the one who taught you to read. But the older you got, the more resentful Harold became. I think he was jealous of the time I spent with you. He complained about how your grandmother spoiled you, and as you got older, he yelled at you and threatened punishment for anything you said or did. I was frightened, but I couldn't confront him or he'd take it out on both of us. I was relieved when Mother took you. I knew it was best… for you AND for Harold and me."

"Mom, that's pathetic. I can't think of any other way to put it. It turned out for the best, for sure, but you let me go without a fight… without a word. Even now that I know the story, I can't understand how you could do it."

"It was my fault for having a child without asking him first. How could I expect that he'd behave any differently? Harold is a good provider, and he doesn't hurt me often."

"Waaait a minute," Robin interrupted. "What do you mean by *hurt you* and what's *not often?* Are you telling me he beats you?"

"No, no, no, Robin. It's not like that. He doesn't beat me. He only shoves me around when he doesn't know what he's doing. He would never hurt me intentionally. When he sobers up, he always tells me how sorry he is. I just wish he were sober more. He gets a few drinks with the guys after work so he's well on his way to drunk by the time he gets home every night. On weekends, he gets up late and starts drinking before noon."

"Mom, you deserve better."

"Perhaps," Aileen murmured, without conviction.

Robin said, "then consider a different life! You are an adult and can make up your own mind. You don't need him. You could leave him and be safe with us."

Aileen shook her head. "I used to think about it, but I knew I could never make it on my own. I don't have any money and I don't have any skills. I have no transportation and no place to go. And the truth is, if I did leave, he'd find me, and life would be much worse. Honestly, Robin, I stopped dreaming a long time ago."

Robin looked at Gram who nodded permission to continue. "Mom, maybe you can start dreaming again. Gram and I have something we want to discuss with you."

"I can't imagine anything that could possibly make a difference." Aileen sighed.

"Well, this will. Gram's going to sell the house because this whole area is being renovated. A man came by over the weekend to explain the plans for the project, and it's going to begin within a few months. I want Gram to move to Dallas. Everything about Dallas is better for her than Chicago."

Aileen's eyes went wide, and her mouth fell open. "Mother, you can't leave. I need you here. With you gone, I'll be completely alone."

"That's quite true, Aileen, but I've been here all along, and it hasn't made any difference at all."

"But…"

"What *would* make a difference," Gram continued, "is your coming to live with me far away from Chicago where Harold can't interfere. I can't see him spending his money or the energy to track you down."

"Mother, I couldn't", Aileen replied without hesitation.

"And why is that? You didn't spend one instant thinking about what I said."

"But…"

"No, Aileen. It was an invitation, not a request for an answer. My hope is that you will think about it seriously and share your questions and concerns so that we can consider them together."

"Mom," Robin pleaded, "please take Gram seriously. Don't let the past slam the door on our future. Coming to Dallas is the right thing to do. After all, Gram has been right about everything, hasn't she?"

Aileen sighed. "Yes. Yes, she has. But I'm just not sure I can do this. He loves me."

"No decisions now," Gram insisted. "Just think about it and we'll discuss your concerns. This is a big decision. It's only fair to give it the time and consideration it deserves."

"Mother, I hope you know how much I appreciate you, even though I've not shown it. I promise I'll think about it. It's time I got home. This morning was a treat. "

"Can we visit tomorrow, Mom? I'm off. You could come back here or we could come there and sit in the park."

Gram interrupted. "Instead of *we*, how about the two of you spend some time together? Robin, you and Aileen could sit in the park or walk the neighborhood. Take her to lunch if she can work that out. You need some time together."

"Mom? Can we?"

Aileen stood and glanced from her mother to her daughter, her look more serene than either had seen before. "Let's meet at the park at 9:30, Robin. I'll see what I can do about lunch."

Chapter 5

R obin jumped from the bus and hurried toward the park. *"Mom will see how great it will be for all of us to be together in Dallas."* Her smile faded as she scanned the empty park benches. *"Did she get cold feet? Could she be stuck because that shithead's still at home?"*

She started off in the direction of her mother's house, then stopped in her tracks. *"What am I doing? I can't show up there."* Robin reversed her steps, then dropped dejectedly onto a bench. She fidgeted for nearly an hour, then rose and trudged toward the bus stop.

"Wait. Robin, wait." Aileen called out and hurried to catch her. "I was so sure the bus would come before I could stop you," she panted. Noting Robin's surprise, she blurted, "You didn't think I chickened out, did you? I wouldn't do that. I want to be with you and Mother."

Robin's eyes widened. "Really? You'll do it? You'll come to Dallas with us?"

"I want to, Robin. I really do. But I'm not sure that I can. Harold was late leaving this morning. He just dawdled and watched me, like he had something on his mind. I can't imagine that he suspects, but he made me uneasy. Let's go back to the park and visit. Then we'll have lunch at this little café just a few blocks away. There was enough money in the grocery jar for me to treat. How about that?"

Robin smiled, heartened by her mother's enthusiasm. "First, lunch is my treat. You've got to trust me and Gram to take care of everything. We won't let anything happen to you."

"Listening to you and Mother gives me courage. We have about an hour before the café opens. What's your favorite lunch? I suppose you've outgrown frozen dinners."

Robin laughed. "Gram wouldn't have such a thing in her freezer. Too much money for not enough flavor, she'd say. She's a great cook and a good money manager. I've always been amazed at how she can make a feast out of hamburger meat or hot dogs. But today, I think I'll splurge on a club sandwich. What's your pleasure?"

Aileen frowned. "It's been so long since I've had lunch out that I don't have a clue. I'll just enjoy reading the menu and see what captures my fancy."

At 11, they made their way toward the café. "It's just a block or so past our house," Aileen explained, as they approached her corner. Suddenly, eyes wide, she grabbed Robin's arm and took in a sharp breath. "Oh, no, Robin, he's home for lunch. I have to go before he gets inside and discovers I'm not there. I'm so sorry."

Stunned, Robin watched a Chevy pickup cruising for a parking place. As soon as it turned the corner, her mother dashed across the street and through the door without a backward glance.

Robin's shoulders sagged. "*That rotten bastard…, Mom has got to get out of that hellish life and I'm going to find a way to rescue her.*"

Robin's eyes widened when she glanced up from ringing up a customer's purchase.

"Is everything alright, Miss?" said an elderly lady wearing a Jackie Kennedy pillbox hat with a loose net draped down over her forehead. The woman's eyes were hidden behind large sunglasses. "Miss?"

"Oh, yes ma'am. Robin blinked, startled back into the present. "Everything's just fine. I do apologize. I thought I recognized someone from my past. Here is your receipt. Will there be anything else?"

"You are too young to have a past, My Girl."

Robin smiled at the woman. "Have a good day, ma'am." She watched the woman waddle away, stuffing the receipt into her handbag. *"She's too old for that hat and those sunglasses. She looks like she was built the same year as the Model T."*

Robin watched as a familiar figure approached. "Hello, Cindy. That *is* you, isn't it? Cindy Smith? As I live and breathe! I thought there for a moment I saw a ghost. May I help you, Ma'am?"

"Hi Robin," Cindy chuckled. "Working in a swank place, aren't ya?"

"Yes, for the summer. What's been going on with you this past year?

"Oh, just hanging."

Robin glanced around and lowered her voice. "I haven't seen you since the day I left for school last year, the day Jake stole those cigarettes from the drug store while we stood on the corner. I could have lost my scholarship if he'd been caught. I hope you aren't hanging around that loser anymore."

"Jake's not a loser," Cindy insisted. "He's a pretty neat dude in his own way. You sure were all about him in high school. What's got your panties in a wad, anyway? Jake takes care of his own, you know."

"Cindy, I can't believe you said that. You're better than that. You and I were friends and the only reason we hung out with Jake was because we couldn't tolerate the rich bitches. I thought by now you'd have figured out what a scuzz he is."

"Jake's okay, Robin. Besides, he sorta looks out for me these days. He and I got tight once you were out of the picture. I'm his girlfriend now; that is, as long as you don't make a play for him."

"No chance of that! I saw him in here the other day casing the place. He is up to no good."

"Can you take a break with me or something," Cindy asked, "so we can catch up?"

"Yeah that would be cool, let me check with my boss," Robin said nodding toward the other counter.

Mrs. Parker scanned the department. "Seems quiet. Go on, but no longer than 15-minutes," she said and glanced at her watch.

In the customer snack lounge, Robin and Cindy grabbed Cokes.

"So, what are you up to? Are you enjoying being out of high school?" Robin asked.

"Well… I don't do much of anything these days. Try to avoid being at home, so I hang out at Simpson's or the hamburger joint with the gang. They don't run us off so long as we buy something every now and then. Not much has changed since you left. Same group, doin' the same old stuff."

"Does that ugly fellow still hang out with you, the one we called Lurch? Jake called him Sluggo." Robin cocked her head. "What *is* his name…," then snapped her fingers. "Ah, Charlie Slagger. How could I forget?"

Cindy giggled. "Yeah, he still shadows Jake most of the time, and he hasn't gotten any prettier… or any smaller."

"What a jerk." Robin said, "with that hulking physique and ugly face, you'd think he'd get a job as a bouncer somewhere." She laughed. "What am I saying? I can't imagine any of those losers getting a job anywhere." Robin's eyes narrowed. "Can you believe that?" she said as Titus Smithers slid into a booth. "There's another loser. That guy is a summer employee like me and he's here in the customer lounge so no one will catch him loafing. He's out of his department more than he's in it."

"Cool if you can get away with it," Cindy commented.

"Not cool," Robin shot back. "If you're getting paid to do a job, you *do* it!" Cindy shrugged and Robin continued, "So, do you still live at home?"

"Yeah, no money to move out. Thought about maybe getting a job as a waitress, but there aren't any decent restaurants left in our neighborhood. Wonder if I could get a job here?"

"I worked all last year at school waitressing in a steak house for spending money and to pay for my trips home. My boss gave me a great reference letter that helped me get the job here," Robin said. "I'm working as much as I can this summer, so I won't have to work as much during the school year. I need the time to study."

"You seem happy. In high school, you never smiled. You were always upset about something."

"Well, my life changed when I went to college. I have loads to smile about. I have three cool suitemates. I'm going to be a nurse, and I like Dallas. The weather is a major improvement over Chicago."

"That's cool... Ah... Jake thinks you might help him with a project he has in mind. That's why I'm here."

"No way in hell.! He told me what he's doing, and I told you that Jake is a no-good loser. I have no intention of letting him anywhere near my life. Cindy, he'll drag you down if you stay with him."

"I kinda get what you're saying, but he does look out for me. Besides, he doesn't want you to *do* anything. He just wants you to be his eyes and ears so if Security is around you can give him a heads up. That isn't much to ask, right?"

"Wrong! Stealing is a crime no matter what part you play in it. Cindy, I can't believe you fall for his crap. That asshole would somehow manage to get off scot-free and you and I would land in the slammer in a heartbeat. I won't take any part in his shenanigans under any circumstances. In fact, if I see him trying to steal, you can bet I'll report the bastard"

"That could be a problem, you know?" Cindy said.

"Problem how? He's no part of my life anymore. I'm going to be a nurse and Jake is *not* going to jeopardize that for me. Cindy, it's been good to see you, but I have to get back to work."

"It was wonderful seeing you again, Robin. Think about it, though. Jake can get a little unhinged for no reason these days. Don't make him your enemy."

Robin stood. "Bye, Cindy. Get away from him. Take care of yourself."

"Robin, your mother called this morning," said Gram. "She was concerned that you might not still want to see her after she rushed off and left you standing there when Harold came home unexpectedly for lunch last week."

"You told her I do want to see her, didn't you?" Robin interrupted.

"Of course, I did. She said that Wednesday will be perfect for you to visit because Harold's crew is working in Schaumburg, and that's too far away to come home for lunch."

"Did she sound excited… like she really wants me to come?"

"She certainly did. You've brought your mother the first joy she's experienced in years. She could never have anticipated that you would want to reconnect. I don't think it ever occurred to her how happy that would make her."

"Let's take lunch over. You can make her favorite dish. It will be a celebration."

"Not this time. I have some things to do on Wednesday, so the day will belong to you and your mother. We'll make cinnamon rolls first thing that morning. Aileen always loved them right out of the oven."

"We baked these especially for you." Robin thrust the plate of warm sweet rolls at Aileen as soon as she opened the door. "Gram said that you love them… and they're still warm. Today is a celebration!"

Aileen reached for the plate. "Then, let's celebrate." She led Robin to the kitchen where a percolator burped and hissed. "Coffee is almost ready. We can sit in the living room and visit."

Robin was surprised by how little the place had changed in all the years since she'd lived there. The dirty brown couch had grown worn and shabby, but the TV in the corner was brand new. "*The house is spotless, no photos, and no clutter of any kind... a morgue.*"

"Come sit and let's enjoy these rolls. Tell me all about school, your friends, the job, and why you want to be a nurse. I want to know everything about you."

Robin leaned forward, took a deep breath, and eagerly began, "I have three suitemates. Leslie's all about sports, Frannie's my roommate and a bit of an airhead but ya gotta love her. Katie... you'd think she was an Indian princess. She's beautiful and she really *is* an Indian. Her family is Choctaw and she lives on a farm in Oklahoma. I spent Thanksgiving with her last year and it was terrific. Spending time with her family made me want to see if you, Gram, and I could be a family again."

Aileen smiled, "sounds nice... I'm grateful to your Katie and her family."

"Before Crestmont University offered me a full scholarship, I hadn't been sure what I wanted to do; then I settled on nursing because it's such a flexible profession. I'll have loads of opportunities when I graduate. I finished my first year on the honor roll."

"I'm so proud of you, Robin. What about your friends here in Chicago?"

"I don't have any friends here. I ran around with a bad crowd my last two years in high school and I don't want anything to do with them anymore."

"Oh, my. That sounds a bit like the beginning of my story. Thank heavens you realized that mistake in time."

"I was resentful of the spoiled *rich kids* in school. I didn't want to be like them, so I kinda went overboard in the wrong direction. I'm doing my best to make it up to Gram for being so ungrateful my last two years at home. Gram is the best!"

"She certainly is. I do wish that things were different here and that I could make things up to her, too. Let's stay here for lunch. I want to hear more about your friends. You can stay until three-thirty and then leave before the buses get too crowded. I'll need time to be sure there's nothing here that might catch Harold's attention. Now, tell me more about school."

Robin shared her freshman year stories until Aileen noticed the time. "Let's move into the kitchen. You keep talking and I'll fix lunch."

"Mom, things could be like this all the time… if you'd come to Dallas with Gram and me. You would be safe, and you deserve to be happy; we all do. You could work and have money of your own. There is no future here for you and there's every reason in the world to come with us."

"I've thought a lot about that, Robin, and I believe that you're right. I can't stop imagining what it would feel like not to be afraid. I *would* like the chance to make something of my life, not to mention being able to enjoy my own mother and my daughter. I know that I make excuses for Harold, but what choice do I have? As volatile as he is, he's never really hurt me. He's rough, but he's not violent and he does love me. But now, with you and Mother back in my life, it's hard to imagine giving you up again. It's harder to make excuses now."

"Then it's settled!" Robin exclaimed. "We have plenty of time to think of *everything* and work out all the details. Just think, Mom… you and Gram could live near Crestmont. You could work at *Rob Rory's Steakhauz* if you wanted. I know Mr. Davis would give you a job. He's the best boss in the world. Or, you could work at Nieman Marcus, or wherever… that's the best part; you can do whatever you want."

"I'm a good cook, Robin. I wonder if your Mr. Davis would let me work in the kitchen. What fun that would be! On the other hand, a department store could be exciting. It would be nice to dress for work every day. I could have a wardrobe and it would matter to someone what I look like. I don't think Harold even *sees* me. He only cares that I don't gain any weight. He insists he won't be married to a fat slob."

"Mom, that's pathetic! He has no right to treat you like property."

"It's not too bad, Robin. If I keep the house spotless and stay out of his way, I'm usually OK. Except when he's drinking," she paused, "but he drinks most of the time. When he's drunk, he flares up and gets ugly with no provocation at all."

"All of that is going to be ancient history. Before you know it, you, Gram, and I will be together in Dallas and you'll be safe and *happy* for the first time in years. We'll *all* be happy."

"I'm already happy, Robin. Just thinking about being with you and Mother makes me want to wiggle my nose and be in Dallas immediately. Unfortunately, real life isn't quite *Bewitched* and there are other things to consider. It could be dangerous. There are so many ways that it can go wrong. This might not be the best decision. Harold might hunt me down and kill me."

"Mother, stop!" Robin interrupted. "Coming with us is absolutely the best thing you can do. You deserve to be happy. We have the rest of the summer to think of everything. You'll be safe with Gram and me."

"But..." Aileen hesitated.

"No! No *buts*! You know it's the right thing to do! The man from the construction company said he expected Gram would get an offer on her house within six months. We have plenty of time to cover all the bases. Just think... you, Gram, and I will be together and happy and safe before next summer."

"It's almost too good to be true. I haven't been able to think of anything else. I just hope that it's the right decision."

"Gram will tell you it's the right thing to do. I know she wants to go to Dallas, but she said she couldn't abandon you. You *have* to come so that we can all be together. We need to figure out how to keep in touch in the meantime. Do you think that there's any way Harold will let you be in touch with Gram? After all, she's your mother. He never has to find out about me."

"For now, we'll just leave things the way they are. There's no reason to stir up trouble. I need time to think and plan. There are loads of details to consider. I can manage to contact Mother if I need to. In the meantime, let's enjoy the rest of our afternoon."

A door slammed. Heavy footsteps echoed through the house, then stopped abruptly.

"Aileen? AILEEN! Where the hell ARE you?"

Aileen stared wide-eyed at Robin. The color drained from her face and terror replaced excitement. She looked frantically around the kitchen as if searching for a place to hide. Then Robin realized that Aileen wanted HER to hide.

Harold's brawny shape filled the kitchen doorway. "You BITCH!" he shouted. He glared at Aileen, ignoring Robin. "I *knew* you were up to something! What made you think you could put something over on me?"

Robin stood to block his path as he moved toward Aileen. "Just a minute. I can explain…"

Before Robin could continue, Harold back-handed her out of his way. The blow took her breath away and her hands flew to her face. She back-pedaled, tripped over her chair and crumpled to the floor with blood running from her nose and her face on fire.

Without a glance in Robin's direction, Harold stormed toward Aileen who stared transfixed. He grabbed her upper arms and yanked her out of her chair. Holding her off the ground, he shook her like a rag doll. He lowered his face toward hers, and growled, "I've told you before, You Bitch, *no strangers in this house*! How dare you defy me!" He gave her another violent shake and continued, "Who pays the bills around here? If it weren't for me, you'd be on the street." With disgust flaring in his eyes, he flung her away from him. Aileen's arms flailed as she sailed backward. Her head hit the floor with a crack that nearly stopped Robin's heart.

"You bastard," Robin screamed as she crawled to Aileen who lay still, her eyes closed. "Mom, are you OK? Mom, please answer me."

There was no response.

Robin screamed, "Call an ambulance, you bastard!"

66

Harold moved unsteadily toward the living room, mumbling, "The bitch had that coming. A wife needs to do what her husband tells her. She shoulda listened to me."

"Call an ambulance!" Robin screamed a second time.

Harold turned his gaze toward the sound and seemed to notice Robin for the first time, showing no sign of recognition. He growled, "Who the hell are you?" Without waiting for a reply, he shouted, "*Get out of my house.*"

Robin ignored him. "Mom, wake up!"

Harold loomed above her. He yanked her to her feet and pulled her across the kitchen and through the living room. Still gripping her arm, he pulled open the front door, shoved her out, and slammed the door.

"Help!" Robin shrilled as she burst into the grocery store, the first occupied place she encountered as she ran in search of help. "Someone call an ambulance. My Mom could be dead. The drunken bastard threw her across the room like a rag doll." Her eyes were desperate as she swiped at the trickle of blood from her nose."

Several customers stared wide-eyed as Kevin Gardner, the owner, approached rapidly from the rear of the store.

"Please help," she pleaded.

Mr. Gardner reached for Robin's hands, making eye contact. Her panic eased as she sensed his concern. He led her to a chair beside his desk. "Sit here," he directed as he reached for his phone. "Tell me who your mother is and where she lives."

She inhaled and her words tumbled out. "My mom is Aileen Hart. She lives down the street that way," Robin pointed.

"Do you know the house number?"

Robin's eyes widened as she tried in vain to recall the address. She opened her mouth. "Uh…" she stuttered, her panic returning.

"It's okay." Mr. Garner's voice was soothing. "They'll find it. We'll be waiting in the yard." He turned his attention to the phone and called for an ambulance, then dialed the police and repeated the story. "Come. They won't be long. You can tell me what happened on the way."

Robin 's words tumbled over one another as she recounted the story. "She might be dead. The drunken bastard didn't even know me…" She took a breath. Sirens wailed in the distance.

When they reached the house Mr. Gardner instructed, "Stand right here and hail the ambulance and police. They'll be here in just a minute. I'll see about your mother."

As he pounded on the front door, the ambulance turned the corner, followed immediately by a police cruiser. Robin waved furiously and both vehicles pulled to a stop in front of the house. Four doors flew open and a uniformed man and woman jumped from each vehicle. The medical team rushed to unload a stretcher, and both police officers joined Mr. Gardner on the top step.

The male officer shouted, "Police. Open up, Sir." There was no response to his first three requests. Then from inside, "What the hell do you want?"

"We need to come in, Sir. Please open the door."

"You ain't comin' in MY house. Get off my steps!" His words were nearly incomprehensible.

"Sir. Open the door, or we'll force our way in. There has been a report that someone has been injured. Where is your wife, Sir?"

The door opened. "She's in the kitchen where she belongs," Harold mumbled. Then, more forcefully, "Now get the hell off my steps." Harold spotted Robin and pointed, reaching for the door frame to steady himself. "That bitch had no right to be in my house. My wife knows better than to let strangers in here. She got what was comin' to her." He reached to shove the officer out of the doorway.

The officer grabbed Harold's arm and twisted it behind his back while the second officer pulled handcuffs from her belt and snapped them onto Harold's wrists. "Calm down, Sir," she said gently. We're here to investigate a report. If you don't cooperate, we'll have to take you to the Station."

The officer propelled Harold to a chair in the living room. Robin rushed into the kitchen, the medical team right behind her. She dropped to her knees by Aileen. "Mom?" Her voice was desperate. "Mom, please wake up."

When Aileen made no response, the medical team eased Robin aside and assessed the unconscious woman. "She's completely unresponsive," the man said.

"Her left pupil isn't responding," observed the woman.

"Please tell me she's going to be alright," Robin pleaded. "He's a beast! He had no right to hurt her."

"We need to move quickly. You can come with us," the woman assured Robin while she helped her partner maneuver Aileen onto the stretcher. The man pushed and the woman guided the stretcher to the ambulance while Robin trotted beside them, holding her mother's hand. Before the ambulance pulled away with Robin and Aileen, the police took Robin's name, address, and phone number and instructed her to call the station to provide details of the incident as soon as she could.

Robin watched Aileen's stretcher disappear as an emergency room clerk led her to a desk and began to ask questions. "Wait." Robin stopped her. "I need to call Gram. She needs to be here. She'll have the information you want. I need a phone."

The woman pushed the phone toward Robin. She dialed the seven digits, the phone dial rotating with agonizing slowness between each one. Gram answered on the fourth ring, and Robin's words tumbled over one another. "Gram! I'm at Grant Hospital in the Emergency Room. Please come. Harold came home and… Gram, he hurt her. I can't answer all their questions. She was unconscious and…"

"Robin Hart" echoed through the waiting room.

Holding the phone, Robin jumped from her chair and waved her hand. "I'm here. Gram, they're calling me. Please hurry." Robin thrust the receiver at the clerk and hurried toward a gentleman in a white coat as quickly as the crowded room allowed.

"I'm Dr. Aaron," the physician reached to take Robin's hand. "We need permission to take your mother to surgery." Glancing at the clipboard in his left hand, he continued. "This says that her husband is unavailable and that you are 19. You're old enough to give consent, and we have no time to waste. Unless we can relieve the pressure on her brain, she will not regain consciousness. As it is, there is no guarantee that it's not too late."

Robin drew a quick breath and blurted, "That bastard is most definitely *not* available. He's the reason she's here and I hope the police threw him in jail. Please don't let her die."

Robin scribbled her name on the consent form on Dr. Aaron's clipboard without reading a word. "Hurry," she said, her eyes pleading.

Dr. Aaron patted her hand, then took the clipboard. "In the meantime, get someone to look at your nose," he said. Robin watched the double doors close behind him, then walked slowly back to the intake clerk's desk.

"You did well," Gram reassured Robin as they sat arm in arm, waiting for word from Dr. Aaron. "I'm glad your nose isn't broken. What an awful day you've had!"

They had been huddled together in a corner of the waiting room for more than an hour. "Gram, it's so unfair. We had a great morning. Aileen was going to come with us to Dallas. I know she meant it. She said she couldn't stop thinking about it and she would have time to work out all the details. We talked about her working at the SteakHauz or at Neiman's and she was excited. We were going to be a family again, safe and happy, far away from here. Then he ruined *everything*! I don't know how he knew. I hope he rots in hell."

"I do hope he gets what he deserves," Gram asserted. "After this, Aileen may have legal protection from Harold. She can come live with me while we decide about the future. Once the developers make an offer on the house, we will be able to make plans."

Robin jumped to her feet as Dr. Aaron approached. "How is she? Did she wake up yet?"

Dr. Aaron reached for Gram's hand. "You must be Mrs. Hart's mother."

Gram took his hand and pulled herself from the chair. "Yes, I'm Maureen Kelly, Aileen's mother. Thank you for helping her."

"She had a large hematoma, a collection of blood in her brain. We were able to put in a shunt to reduce the pressure, but she is still unconscious and is not breathing on her own. There is no way to know when or if she will respond."

Gram reached for Robin's hand. "When can we see her?" she asked, her voice quivering. Robin had never seen her grandmother this shaken before.

"It will be at least another hour before she's settled in the intensive care unit. They usually allow only one visitor at a time, but I'm sure they'll allow both of you to see her briefly."

Gram nodded and Robin said, "Thank you. Where should we wait?"

"You'll be more comfortable in the ICU waiting room on the third floor. Someone will come for you when it's time to visit. In the meantime, you might want to get something to eat. The cafeteria is to the left through those doors." He nodded and turned to leave.

"Dr. Aaron?" Robin's voice cracked. "Will she be OK?"

Dr. Aaron turned back; his eyes filled with concern. "There's no way to know," he said softly. "We just have to wait and see."

"Gram!" Robin squeezed Gram's hand and gestured toward a nurse standing in the doorway, scanning the ICU waiting room.

The nurse's kind eyes settled on Robin and Gram. "Are you the family of Aileen Hart?" she asked. "You can see her now. Her vital signs are stable, but she's still unresponsive and a machine is breathing for her."

"But she'll be okay, won't she?" Robin asked.

Robin's chest tightened at the nurse's hesitation and the worry in her eyes. "We'll have to wait and see," the nurse replied gently. "She experienced severe trauma. Every patient is different, so it's difficult to make predictions. We'll watch her closely. The ICU visiting hours are limited, but you'll be able to visit for an hour twice a day. You can sit with her from 1:00 to 2:00 pm and from 7:00-8:00 pm. We have limited space, so it would be best if you took turns. You can talk to her. Sometimes patients can sense the presence of loved ones, even when they are unconscious."

They followed the nurse from the subdued waiting room into a cacophony of monitor beeps, whooshing air, and soft voices that overloaded Robin's senses. She and Gram stood on silently on either side of Aileen's bed. Aileen lay in an endless spaghetti snarl of drip lines and wires. The beeping monitors traced green patterns on black screens, and a fat, clear tube from a ventilator disappeared down Aileen's throat.

Gram smiled with sad, tired eyes. Tears streaked Robin's face and she bit her lip as she gingerly touched her mother's hand. Gram lay a hand on Aileen's shoulder and leaned in close. "We're here, Aileen. Sleep well tonight and we'll be back tomorrow."

"That scumbag will pay for this," Robin seethed. "He'll rot in jail and we'll all be together in Dallas."

Chapter 6

Robin's application for the Lead Trainer position had been submitted. Mrs. Parker had added her recommendation, identifying Robin as a stellar employee and Robin expected that she had earned the promotion.

She pulled the envelope from her employee mailbox in the break room. *Miss Jennifer Lynn Hart* was printed in courier typeface, just like her weekly paycheck. But this wasn't payday. She crossed her fingers, ripped open the envelope, unfolded the letter, and read…

Dear Mr. Smithers,

We are pleased to offer you the position of Lead Trainee. Your salary increase of 20% will begin with the next pay period and…

"*WHAT? No way!*" Robin stopped reading. She had been promised a 10% increase if she got the position. "*This makes absolutely no sense. This guy is in the break room more than he's on the floor. What could they be thinking?*"

She crammed the letter back into the envelope, wanting to scream and cry at the same time. Mostly, she wanted to punch Titus Smithers the Third in his rich, entitled, smug face.

She rechecked the envelope to make sure it had been addressed to her. "This is pure shit!" she growled, then glanced around the room when she realized she had said it aloud. She sighed with relief when no one turned in her direction. *"If I got his letter, that means he got mine. That suck-ass will be laughing at me all the way home."*

Robin thought about storming into Mrs. Hall's office and demanding an explanation. How could she choose Titus Smithers the Turd over her when she knew that Robin worked circles around that idiot? *"He brags about not having to work as hard as everyone else and I've overheard Mrs. Hall reprimanding him repeatedly about overextending his breaks and lunch."* Robin took a breath. *But... Mrs. Hall could fire me, and I need this job."*

She stared at the envelope, then at her watch. *"I have time to make a copy. Anyone who sees me will think I'm making copies for Mrs. Parker."* Robin managed her frustration for the remainder of her shift, then all the way home she imagined belting Titus in an unladylike fashion, like maybe with a baseball bat.

As soon as the dinner dishes were washed and dried, Robin went to her bedroom, pleading a long, tiring day. Idly she picked up *The Exorcist* from her nightstand. It was the most popular book of the summer and she'd been fortunate to find a copy at the library. She read three pages and tossed the book aside, realizing that she couldn't remember a word she had just read. *"I want to exorcise that Titus Smithers the TURD right off this planet. Who does he think he is getting my job?"*

She punched her pillow, imagining it was Titus' head. *"I'll talk to Guy. He might have an idea about what I can do, or maybe Mrs. Parker can fix it."*

Robin arrived at Marshall Field the next morning before the employee doors were unlocked, armed with the atrocious letter over the signature of the owner of Marshall Field and a pit bull attitude. She paced back and forth, clenching and unclenching her fists. She scarcely acknowledged the security officer when he opened the door and doffed his hat.

Robin marched to the locker room, then pounced on Mrs. Parker the moment she walked through the door. "Look at this," she demanded, holding out the letter. "It's not right and it makes no sense. That jerk does less around here than any other summer hire and look what they did!"

Mrs. Parker raised a hand to stifle Robin's tirade. "Let me put my things away," she said as she stowed her lunch in her locker and pulled out the blue cover jacket she wore when she worked in the back or the loading dock. The clock on the wall clock ticked as Robin paced and employees stared in silent fascination. Mrs. Parker picked up her briefcase and said, "Let's can find a private place to talk."

Robin's face turned crimson when she realized that everyone was watching. She followed Mrs. Parker, concentrating on her shoes, still gripping the letter as if it were Titus' neck. They stopped in a quiet alcove.

"Now," said Mrs. Parker, "Tell me what has you so upset this morning."

"Yesterday this letter was in my mailbox. It's addressed to me, so I read it, but it's not for me. Read it," she said, thrusting the crumpled envelope toward Mrs. Parker. "It's awful."

Mrs. Parker scanned the envelope, then pulled the letter out. Robin bit her tongue to remain silent while Mrs. Parker read the letter.

"Hmmm." Mrs. Parker shook her head. "That's unfortunate. I know that you were hoping to get that position. We need to take this letter to Mrs. Hall so that she can get it to the right person."

"But it's *wrong!*" Robin insisted. "He goes on breaks all the time and laughs at not having to work to earn his pay. He doesn't deserve to be a lead *anything*, except maybe *lead jerk*! And that's not all. His starting pay is more than mine and we were hired at the same time. Oh, and one more thing: I was told that I would get a 10% raise if I got the position, and he's getting 20%. How is any of this fair!"

"Robin, take a deep breath and get control of yourself. Life is not always fair, and men dominate the business world. In our culture, men are considered the breadwinners. Women leave to get married and have babies, while men are stable employees who need to provide for their families. That's just the way it is."

Robin's mouth gaped, "I can't believe that is happening, this is 1971, not 1950!"

"Things may be changing, but culture changes slowly, and this store is old-fashioned in that way. If you insist upon complaining to Mrs. Hall, keep in mind that she is part of the Marshall Field's culture and the confrontation may not turn out well for you."

"I'm sorry, Mrs. Parker. I appreciate that you're looking out for me. I'll bite my tongue if I have to, but this just isn't right."

They walked to Human Resources and stopped outside of Mrs. Hall's office. "Jenny," Mrs. Parker asked Mrs. Hall's secretary, "is she available to meet with us this morning?"

Jenny smiled. "She's always available for you Mrs. Parker. Go right on in."

"Good morning, Brenda," Mrs. Parker said. "Robin and I hope you might have a moment to visit with us?"

"Certainly, please have a seat."

Mrs. Parker handed the envelope to Mrs. Hall. "This was addressed to Robin, but it clearly was intended for someone else."

Mrs. Hall unfolded the letter, then looked up. "Robin, I know you must find this upsetting. Although it is true that you are an outstanding employee, Mr. Smithers *was* selected for the job as the letter indicates."

Robin sat on her hands to help keep her temper in check. She took a breath and said, "I know it was a mistake that I got the letter but, there is more," she paused, "...wrong with this than just the letter to the incorrect person. Titus and I started working here the same day, so I don't understand why his salary is higher than mine. I have heard him say that he doesn't have to work to get his check and he takes more breaks than anyone else. To top it off, you said that the person who got the job would get a 10% raise, and he got 20%. How is any of that right?"

"Robin, I know this is not what you want to hear, but life is often unfair. It's possible that the committee offered Mr. Smithers the position thinking it might influence him to remain with Marshall Field when he graduates.

"Or they may have considered that his father is on the Board," Robin thought but remembered her promise to Mrs. Parker to be discreet. "Will you tell me what I did wrong not to get it, and why I am not making the same salary as he is?"

"You did nothing wrong. I know you're disappointed and I want to assure you that we consider you a valuable employee. The committee's decision, however, is final. Is there anything else I can help you with this morning?"

"No," said Robin, still sitting on her hands, and not trusting herself to say anything more.

As they left Human Resources, Mrs. Parker squeezed Robin's shoulder. "I agree that it's unfair, but you have to accept that things are the way they are here. Go on to the counter. I'll be working with inventory most of today, and I'll check with you later this afternoon."

Robin nodded. *"Marshall Field is way more old-fashioned than I thought. A store as fine as this one should be setting an example. Women should not have to put up with discrimination… not at this store… not anywhere!"*

"Hey there, eating lunch means that you have to actually take a bite of that sandwich," Guy said. "Mind if I join you?"

Startled, Robin looked up. "Oh, sit down," she groused. "You men are all alike, always making jokes and getting your way."

"Whoa, what's *that* all about? Something ugly crawl out of your cereal today?"

"Yes, it did," Robin said, still seething over the injustice.

"Want to tell big brother, Guy, all about it?" He teased.

"This isn't funny. I've been waiting to tell you what happened."

Guy shrugged his shoulders when Robin finished her story. "Life sucks sometimes; then you have to get over it." He took a giant bite of his own sandwich.

"You're kidding! Doesn't anything ever phase you? Men are all alike. You... you *fair-haired boy*... isn't that what you said about yourself? You get a job every summer without even trying, just because you're a man. Women have to fight for a job if a man is available, then work twice as hard for a lower salary just to keep it. Do you think that's *fair*?"

"Nobody's saying it's fair, but you can't fight city hall, right?"

"Who says I can't!"

"Are you going to eat that cookie?"

"Here!" She threw the cookie at him. "Guy, listen to me! I'm serious about this not being right."

"Even though you have a point, there's not much you can do about it if you want to keep your job. For now, suck it up and put a pleasant smile on that lovely face of yours. Remember this is the world of, *how may I help you* and *please* and *thank you, Ma'am*. Besides, now's not the time to take on a fight against the world; you have other things on your plate, like your mom in the hospital. That's more important than a summer job and fighting over the likes of Titus. Besides, his family is tight with the owners of this place and his father is on the Board."

"Okay, you made your point," she heaved a sigh, "but just for now. I don't plan to put up with shit like this for long."

"We have to get back to work. Neither one of us is a Titus Smithers, the Third."

She slugged him on the shoulder as they walked out of the lunchroom.

"Ouch, what was that for?"

"For being a man!"

Robin nestled a ring into its box. "It's lovely," she said, matching the smile on her last customer's face. "I can imagine how pleased your fiancée will be."

"Thank you," the young man replied, grin still in place.

Robin closed out her register and turned to Mrs. Parker. "Thank you for letting me leave in time for visiting hours." She grabbed her purse and hurried to catch the bus.

"She just HAS to get well. With that bastard in jail, it will be easier to get her out of Chicago and settled with Gram and me in Dallas." Robin rocked from foot to foot, waiting impatiently for the bus to wheeze to a stop. She hopped on before the doors were fully open.

"You're in a hurry," commented the driver as Robin fumbled coins into the farebox.

"Gotta make it in time for visiting hours at Grant," she replied. "Wish this bus had wings."

"No wings, I'm afraid," the driver replied, "but traffic is light, and it won't take us fifteen minutes." Robin dropped into a seat.

"This whole ordeal could be a blessing in disguise. Now that Harold's out of the way, Aileen can stay with Gram until the house is sold. I wonder how fast we can bring her home from the hospital." Robin sat lost in her daydream.

"Young lady." The driver's voice startled her. "This here's your stop."

"Thanks again," she said as the bus doors closed behind her.

Robin darted across the street, pushed through the lobby doors, and strode directly to the bank of elevators. There were only twenty minutes of the visiting hour left and no elevators were on the lobby level. Robin tapped a foot, then spotted the *Exit* sign. With a satisfied grin, she pushed open the door, sprinted up three floors to the ICU, and joined Gram by Aileen's bed.

"Is she awake?" Robin panted, catching her breath. "Can we take her home soon?"

Gram lifted her eyes to meet Robin's and the sadness in them burst Robin's bubble of enthusiasm. She cocked her head, and whispered, "What is it? Tell me."

Still holding one of Aileen's hands in both of her own, Gram began, "Nothing is certain," she sighed, "but they want us to know that they are not hopeful. Aileen's condition has not improved at all, even after they put in the shunt to relieve the pressure. They said that they almost lost her twice during the procedure."

"But she *could* wake up, right?" Robin asked.

"She could," Gram conceded. "We'll just have to be patient and hope for the best."

Robin moved to the other side of the bed and lifted Aileen's hand gently. "Mom listen to me. You have to wake up. You're going to be safe and happy and we're going to make up for all those wasted years. Just think about that and come back to us, *please!*"

They passed the last few minutes of the hour in silence. Aileen lay still except for the rhythmic rise and fall of her chest in sync with the hiss of the ventilator. Robin's gaze remained fixed on Aileen, watching for the slightest voluntary movement, the flicker of an eyelid or the flare of a nostril. *"Please, Mom,"* Robin pled silently. *"Let me know that you heard me."*

"Visiting hours are over now," the nurse said softly from the doorway. We'll watch her closely and you can come back tomorrow afternoon. I'm so sorry that I don't have better news for you."

Gram thanked the nurse while Robin leaned over Aileen and whispered, "Remember what I said. You have to wake up. Everything is going to be perfect from now on."

Chapter 7

Robin watched Jake move from counter to counter. *"If he takes anything, I'm going to tell Mrs. Parker. If I don't report him, he could claim that I helped him. That's NOT going to happen."*

Jake approached the jewelry counter furthest from the register where Mrs. Parker was occupied with a patience-testing customer. When he snatched a watch and turned to leave, Robin grabbed his arm, and hissed, "You asshole, put that back, or pay for it now!"

He whirled, jerked his arm from her grasp and balled his fist, ready to strike her. Robin stood tall and glared at him. He glanced around and lowered his hand. "Listen up, Girlie," he growled. "You'll help me, or I'll make your life miserable. I'll come after your snooty Gram and you know damn well that I can. Don't make a scene, or you'll regret it."

Robin's cheeks flushed as her temper flared. "Put it back and I won't say anything."

Jake looked around, then grabbed Robin's arm and muscled her against the counter. "I own you, Bitch. Don't mess this up for me."

"Back off, Asshole. You're hurting me." Sweat trickled down Robin's spine. "You don't own anyone, and you certainly don't own *me.* I told you before that if you steal, I'll alert security. Either put the watch back or I'll do just that! You're the one making a scene, not me."

"Is there anything I can help you with, Sir?" asked Mrs. Parker, interrupting the tense confrontation.

Jake dropped the watch on the counter and replied with a smirk, "No thanks. I don't think I'll buy this today." He flashed a venomous look at Robin, a surly grin at Mrs. Parker, and sauntered to the exit.

"Are you alright?"

"Yes, ma'am. That guy was being a jerk. I thought if I came out from behind the counter, I could calm him down."

"Customers can be a bit testy sometimes. You seemed to handle it well. Now that the Department is quiet, I need your help inventorying those gold necklaces that arrived yesterday. Then will you arrange them in the display case?"

"Yes, ma'am. I'd be happy to help." Robin took a deep, calming breath, and slowly unclenched her fists. She turned so that Mrs. Parker couldn't see that her hands were shaking.

"Robin, you haven't touched your lunch or said a word. What's going on?" Guy took another bite of his tuna sandwich. "Robin?"

"Huh... oh, sorry, Guy. I was thinking about something. What did you say?"

"You're not yourself and you're pasty white. Are you sick?"

"No, I'm... well kinda..." Robin's shoulders slumped, and she grimaced. "That jerk from high school I pointed out to you the other day just tried to steal a watch. He expected me to let him walk out with it. He threatened me. He even said that he would hurt Gram if I didn't help him."

"No wonder you're white as my mother's morning gravy. Did you tell Security?"

"No, I was afraid he was serious about hurting Gram. We live in the area where he hangs out and I wouldn't put anything past him. He scared me. His glare was like a laser burning through me, and I don't frighten easily."

Guy reached across the table and took her hand. "Robin, you have to report this, or it will come back to haunt you. He won't stop until he is caught, and I suspect you know that as well as I do. Bullies like that think they are invincible. They don't care who they hurt."

"I know you're right, but what if I report the bastard and he takes it out on Gram? He didn't actually take anything, so I don't really have anything to report."

"But you know he will. He's not done with this. He expects that you'll come around, right? After all, he's the tough guy, and you're the defenseless damsel."

"Now you are just pissing me off."

"Good. Maybe you'll get angry enough to do what you need to do. If you want, I'll go to Security with you right now. They should know to be on the lookout for him."

Robin swallowed, then sighed. "Okay. Thanks."

Their chairs scraped as they stood to leave. Robin tossed her uneaten sandwich into the trash and flashed Guy a grateful smile.

Guy and Robin approached just as Mrs. Parker finished with her last customer. "Mmmay we speak to you?" Robin stammered.

"Of course. You're back early." Frowning, she added, "What's wrong?"

Robin hesitated and Guy gently pushed her closer to Mrs. Parker.

"Well... remember that scruffy guy in the bell bottoms who decided not to buy that watch before we went to lunch...?"

"Yes. I remember."

"He... he stole that watch. I saw him take it and confronted him. I threatened to report him if he didn't put it back. I know him from high school. I can't believe I didn't realize then what a thug he was. He expected me to let him get away with it. Then you came over and he had no choice but to put it back and leave."

"I see… is that all?"

"He threatened to hurt my Gram if I ratted him out. I think he is serious about hurting her. I can take care of myself, but I can't protect Gram when I'm not with her. Mrs. Parker, I am so sorry. I don't want to lose my job. I really like working here. What should I do?"

"Robin, you were right to come to me. Let me call Guy's supervisor to see if he can cover our counter while we visit with Security."

Guy put his arm around Robin's shoulders. "You're trembling. Try to relax. You did the right thing."

Robin took Guy's free hand in both of hers. "Thanks for sticking with me. I don't think I could have done it on my own."

"If he comes back, Security will be ready for him. If he steals something, he'll be dealing with the police. There is no way that scumbag could convince anyone that you were any part of his scheme."

"I hope you're right…"

"Guy," Mrs. Parker said as she placed the phone in its cradle. You can manage the counter until we return. Robin, come with me. You can tell Security everything you told me. I'm proud of you for reporting that man. I know that wasn't easy."

"Thank you, Mrs. Parker. "Do you think I could lose my job?"

"Oh goodness no. You have done Marshall Field a favor. Everyone will be grateful for that. Theft is more common than you might expect; that's why we have plainclothes security throughout the store."

Robin relaxed for the first time since Jake snatched the watch. She repeated her story to Chief O'Shaughnessy. He assured Robin that Security would pay special attention to the jewelry counter. "I suspect he'll be back, Miss Hart. He thinks he has you scared and expects that you'll help him. With your description of him and the girl, Cindy, you said may be working with him, we'll be able to spot them easily enough."

"Mr. O'Shaughnessy, I don't want Cindy to get in trouble. She fears Jake and hangs with him because she thinks he's all she has. He'll blame everything on her. Can you help her out if he tries that?"

"We'll keep that in mind, but she *is* responsible for her own behavior. She should be smart enough to know that helping him steal can get her into a world of trouble."

Robin hung her head, "I know, but Jake is scary. It's easy to believe that he will do the things he threatens."

"We'll be looking out for you here in the store, but if he threatens you anywhere else, you should contact the police. It's not wise to let him get away with that behavior; it just makes scum like him feel powerful."

"Okay…" Robin hesitated, "but if I call the police, he could hurt Gram to get back at me."

"I understand why you're concerned," Chief O'Shaughnessy said. "Perhaps we can manage this so he has no idea that you are involved. If you see him in the store again, ignore him and alert Mrs. Parker so that she can contact us. We'll arrest him as soon as he steps outside of the store if he steals anything. You will not be involved at all."

Robin brightened.

He continued, "You were brave to come to us, Robin. He's sure to steal again, and we'll catch him. He'll go to jail and that will be the end of it."

Robin's steps were lighter as she returned to the jewelry counter with Mrs. Parker. She flashed Guy a *thumbs up*. Despite her satisfied expression, her hands continued to tremble. She wondered what she would tell Gram, and worried that she could not protect her from Jake.

As soon as Mrs. Parker let her leave, Robin hustled to the hospital to meet Gram.

"Mrs. Kelly. Robin. I'm glad I caught you," the nurse beckoned as soon as they entered the ICU. "We'll be moving Mrs. Hart to our skilled nursing unit on the second floor in the morning."

Robin's eyes widened. "Does that mean she's better? Did she wake up?"

The nurse shook her head. "There's been no change at all in her condition and she can't breathe without the ventilator. She's been with us for five days and her condition has stabilized. She no longer needs the intensive level of care we provide in the ICU. The nurses on 2-West, our skilled nursing floor, will concentrate on preventing the skin breakdown and muscle wasting that can occur when a patient remains unconscious for an extended period. The good news is that you'll be able to spend more time with her there."

The nurse handed Gram a business card. "Her doctor would like to speak with you tomorrow. When you arrive, ask someone on 2-West to page him. He'll be expecting you."

"Thank you. We'll sit with Aileen for a while now." Gram took Robin's hand and they walked to Aileen's cubicle.

"I heard once that sometimes people who are unconscious are aware of what is going on around them and even remember what they heard when they wake up. Do you think it's true?"

"Anything is possible, Sweetheart. We have to hope for the best and behave like that is exactly what will happen. It certainly can't hurt to think positive."

"She *has* to wake up. That monster is in jail so there's nothing stopping her from being free and happy. Think how great it will be. We'll all be together - a real family. You've waited a long time for that, too."

"I have, indeed," Gram agreed, lifting Aileen's hand and giving it an affectionate squeeze. "We'll just hope for the best."

Robin leaned over the bed rail and held Aileen's other hand. She chattered non-stop, hoping that what she'd heard about unconscious people hearing and remembering conversations was true. "You'll love Dallas, Mom. The weather's great compared to here. Summers can be beastly, but the rest of the year makes up for it. You'll never have to freeze through a Chicago winter again."

Gram's smile never wavered, but her eyes betrayed her fear as she watched Aileen's chest rise and fall with each cycle of the respirator. Beyond that, there was no movement at all.

"What happened?" Robin exclaimed, eyes wide. Gram was stretched out on the couch, both legs propped on pillows with an ice pack on her right knee.

"I'm fine," Gram replied, reaching for Robin's hand. "Just a little bruised is all. I was in Simpson's drug store and that hoodlum Jake bowled me over on his way out. I can't imagine why he was in such a hurry. He didn't so much as stop to see if I was hurt. Dick Simpson brought a chair for me and tended to the scrapes. He wrapped this Ace bandage around my knee and told me to put ice on it as soon as I got home. He was about to call the cops, but I wouldn't hear of it. There's nothing they could do. The poor guy has no help in the store. When he's in the pharmacy, there is no one upfront to look after things. He said that Jake and his buddies have been stealing from his store. He's the one in danger. Jake and that gang of his could do more than just steal."

Fighting tears, Robin stood. "Let me get more ice."

She returned with a plastic bag of ice wrapped in a dishtowel and settled the package gently on Gram's knee. Robin winced when Gram moaned. "This is all my fault," she said. "I need to tell you about Jake. He hurt you because of me."

Gram's eyes widened. "Because of *you*. How can that be?"

"You know Jake is an evil person. Well, he came to Marshall Field and demanded that I help him steal from the store."

"Robin, that's ridiculous."

"Of course it is, Gram, and I would never do that. I ignored him as long as I could, but the other day I saw him take a watch and I confronted him. He threatened to hurt you if I didn't help him. Mrs. Parker interrupted him, so he made up an excuse about deciding not to buy the watch. The look he gave me when he turned to leave was like an ice pick in my chest. I had to tell Mrs. Parker the truth."

"What happened? What are they going to do?"

"Security is going to watch for him. They said they would keep me out of it, but I'm not sure I can count on that. Jake won't give up and he'll hound us just to be spiteful."

"You did the right thing, Robin. Let them take care of Jake. He'll get what he deserves. No good will ever come of him."

"I finally figured that out right before I left for Crestmont. I told you what he did that day."

Gram nodded, "I remember. I just wish you had felt you could talk to me. Well… we can't undo the past, but we are certainly in charge of the present. We can stand up to bullies like Jake, and we will."

"Gram, he's evil and I know he won't leave us alone. That's another reason to move to Dallas with me. It's not safe for you here."

"The police will take care of Jake and I'll be fine. This is my home. When I have to sell, I'll consider my options. I most certainly will not run away from the likes of Jake Zidder!"

Robin gave Gram a warm hug. "I love you so much."

Patting Robin's back and holding her tight, Gram said, "We can't solve all this tonight. It's time we fixed some dinner."

Chapter 8

"Mrs. Parker, how can I alert you when Jake comes in the store?" Robin asked.

Mrs. Parker looked thoughtful, then snapped her fingers. "I have it! We'll tape a red and a green sales tag back to back and set them here on the register. The green side will signify that all is well. When you see Jake, turn the tag over and the red will signal me to alert security."

"Awesome! A traffic light for a jewel thief; green for go and red for *stop him in his tracks*. Cool idea, Mrs. P."

"A senior staff member will be here with you at the counter at all times. I expect that Jake will be back sooner than later, and we want you to feel secure."

"I appreciate that Mrs. P. I want to do the right thing."

"You *are* doing the right thing," Mrs. Parker assured her.

For several days Jake was a no show and Robin stopped shuddering each time she caught sight of the red and green tag on the cash register. She began to think that Jake had changed his mind after coming so close to getting caught. "*I hope I never see him again.*"

The huge sale on Saturday attracted a crowd and neither Mrs. Parker nor Robin had time for even a short break. At noon, Mrs. Parker sent Robin to lunch. "I'll manage here..." Before she could finish her sentence a gaggle of young women began to explore the items on display at the counter. Mrs. Parker shrugged. "Sorry, Robin."

As Robin turned to help the women, a man with his back to her captured her attention. She squinted "*...could be Jake, but he never wears a hat.*" Robin glanced at the *traffic light.*

She rang up a purchase and handed the woman her receipt. "Thanks for shopping at Marshall Field and have a nice day." When she turned to the next customer, Jake's eyes met hers. He sported a twisted grin and wore a coat inappropriate for summer. Jake mouthed one word, "Gram."

Robin's heart pounded and sweat beaded on her upper lip as she rang up another purchase. As she handed the woman her receipt, she flipped the *traffic light* to red. She turned and walked toward a group of women, each step feeling like a single frame in a slow-motion movie. "*Please, Mrs. Parker, see the tag; he's here!*"

Jake approached the watch counter. "May I help you, Sir?" Robin said a little louder than she'd intended.

"Shut the fuck up, Bitch," he growled through clenched teeth. "You'll ruin everything. Wait on someone else and stay away from me. If I get caught, you and your Gram will pay big time!"

"Jake, please don't do this." Robin crossed her fingers below the counter, hoping that Mrs. Parker had seen the red tag and activated the plan.

"I got what I came for," Jake growled. "You just act natural and nobody gets hurt."

Robin backed away from him and turned toward another customer. Her face was white and her heart raced; she felt as if she couldn't breathe.

"Miss, how much is this bracelet?" said one woman.

"Miss, can you help me with this ring?" said another customer.

Robin's world dissolved into slow-motion agony. *"He's going to get away. The shit is actually going to walk out scot-free."* Robin's heart thudded as Jake pushed open the door and left the store. Before she could look away, a burly man fell in step with Jake. Her face broke into a smile when she recognized Jim, a Marshall Field security officer. *"She pulled it off! Mrs. Parker saw the red tag."* Then tentacles of fear squeezed her heart. *"He'll blame me and hurt Gram, just for spite."*

On the sidewalk, Jim's knee pinned Jake to the ground. Jake yelled, "Robin, you Bitch, you'll pay for this, I promise you!" he repeated over and over.

"Settle down," Jim commanded as he dragged Jake to his feet and pushed him up against the plate glass window. Jake pulled his index finger across his throat before Jim grabbed his arm and cuffed his wrists behind his back. Jake continued yelling, "You're dead, Robin. Your Gram is dead!"

Robin fell into a chair in Chief O'Shaughnessy's office. He said, "You will have to give a statement to the police. With all the threats the thief made during his arrest, they're certain to understand your concern for your grandmother's safety and your own. I commend you, Miss Hart. As a representative of Marshall Field, I am grateful for what you've done."

Robin's smile of appreciation didn't reach her eyes. *"This isn't the end of it. He'll be back to haunt me."*

The calm atmosphere on the 2-West Skilled Nursing Unit the next morning was a welcome change from the air of urgency and the constant noise of medical equipment in the ICU. Patients greeted one another as they walked the corridor with the help of attendants or propelled wheelchairs from one end to the other. One nurse pushed a medication cart from room to room and another popped her head into each room to ask if the patient needed anything.

Robin scanned the hall as if she expected to find Aileen walking with an attendant or sitting in a wheelchair. Gram reached into her purse for the doctor's business card. "How may I help you?" asked a nurse in a crisp white uniform, perky white nursing cap, and buffed duty shoes.

"We've come to visit Aileen Hart."

"Ahh, you must be Mrs. Kelly, and Robin," she said, nodding toward Robin who was still studying the patients in the hallway. "We've been expecting you." I see you have Dr. Bailey's card. He asked me to page him when you arrived. I'm Kathleen Evans, the day charge nurse on this unit. Here we care for patients while they improve to the point that they can manage at home. You'll be able to visit with Mrs. Hart any time between 9 am and 9 pm. She is in room 237, the third door on your right. We keep our ventilator patients close to the nurses' station because we check on them often."

Aileen looked tinier in the larger, quieter room than she had in ICU. Her chest rose and fell rhythmically, though the rest of her body seemed to be made of stone. Robin's heart sank at the realization that Aileen might not awaken from this nightmare.

A white-coated man entered the room and cleared his throat. Robin and Gram turned in unison. "I'm glad I caught you before you settled in to visit." He reached for Gram's hand and nodded to Robin. "I'm Dr. James Bailey, Mrs. Hart's neurologist. I'd like to discuss her condition with you. There is a small conference room by the nurses' station where we can talk."

Dr. Bailey leaned forward in his chair. "As you know, Mrs. Hart has been unresponsive since the incident. We did some follow-up testing before transferring her to this unit. The shunt has reduced the pressure on her brain and all her vital signs are stable, but there is no brain activity and none of the indicators suggest that will change. Our only option is to keep her stable, protect her from the damage that immobility can cause, and wait to see what happens. I am sorry that I don't have better news for you, but experience has taught me that families are better prepared to make good decisions when they know the truth."

"I'm grateful for your compassion, Dr. Bailey. I know that you are doing everything you can," Gram said.

"She could respond at any time, couldn't she?" Robin interrupted, her tone challenging. "You're not telling us that it's over, are you? That it's time to pull the plug?"

"I am providing information to help you understand your mother's condition," Dr. Bailey said gently. "Theoretically, anything can happen, but the longer a patient remains unresponsive, the more likely it is that the body's systems will begin to fail."

"But we can wait as long as we want to see how she does, can't we?" Robin insisted.

"Since Mrs. Hart is unresponsive and her husband is unavailable, decisions regarding her care rest with you, Mrs. Kelly, as her mother and next of kin. Please be assured that we are here to give her the best care possible, and to support whatever decision you make."

"Gram, you know that she'll wake up, don't you? She will. I'm sure of it. Now that she has a chance for a real life and happiness, she has to wake up!"

"Sweetheart, no one loves Aileen or wants to see her happy more than I do, but wishing doesn't make it so. We must be thankful that Dr. Bailey can be open and honest with us. We won't make any hasty decisions. We'll watch, wait, and pray for her recovery. The rest will have to be up to her."

"Gram promise me you won't give up. We're going to be together, all three of us, and make up for all the lost years that we should have been happy together. Promise?"

"I want that as much as you do, but you must promise me something."

Robin leaned forward.

"You must promise me that you will use both your heart *and* your head when we discuss Aileen."

"But, Gram...."

"Can you promise me that, Robin?"

"This nightmare is unfair. I'm positive that she decided to be with us. After all, she's gone through, and all the time you've waited for her, this can't be happening. I hope that scumbag rots in hell for what he did! No one should get away with ruining other people's lives."

Dr. Bailey put his hand on Robin's arm. "Mrs. Hart is fortunate to have a caring family. Spend all the time you can with her, and we'll hope for the best." He rose and reached to help Gram from the chair. "Please have the nurses contact me any time you have questions or need to speak with me."

Gram nodded. "Dr. Bailey, I am grateful for your concern and for your honesty. I know that Aileen is in good hands."

The new room had a large window. Robin was sure that this bright environment with concerned nurses would help Aileen improve. She and Gram took turns talking to Aileen and holding her hand. Robin left for work feeling more hopeful than she had since the incident.

Cindy moved slowly toward the jewelry counter. She reminded Robin of a tired sweater. "Are you okay?" Robin asked. "You don't look so great?"

"No," Cindy replied. "I am not okay. My insides are in a constant battle over what is happening with Jake. I can't eat and I can't sleep. I'm definitely not okay. Can we go someplace and talk?"

"Mrs. Parker, may I go to lunch now?" Mrs. Parker nodded, and Robin said, "Thanks. I'll be back in 30 minutes."

"So, what's up?" Robin asked as she slid into the booth in the Snack Lounge.

"I don't know where to begin," Cindy sighed. "Jake ordered me to find a bail bondsman to get him out of jail. He is horrifically mad at you, Robin. Even if he stays in jail, you and your grandmother aren't safe. I won't be safe either if I don't do what he wants. The police interviewed me, and they expect me to testify against him. Can you believe that? Jake will kill me."

"Were you involved in what he did?"

"Well, kinda. I knew what he was planning. I watched him take the watch and I saw you talking to him. I was pretty sure you were in on whatever got him caught, but I didn't see you do anything but watch him leave."

"What did you tell the police?

"I told them I didn't know anything. I figured fessing up wouldn't help Jake and it would get me into a world of hurt. I just couldn't risk getting thrown in jail."

"I didn't see you in the store that day. I was too fixated on what that creep was doing, and how helpless I felt. I admit that I'm frightened for Gram. Did you know that he roughed her up in Simpson's Drug Store? He pushed her to the ground and banged up her knee."

"Yeah, he was bragging about that to the gang. He was egging Lurch on, saying that he needed to get with the program. He's been threatening to make you sorry you wouldn't help him, and he's got the whole gang riled up. I haven't seen him since he was arrested, but he used his one phone call to tell me what I have to do."

"You're an idiot if you don't put some distance between you and Jake. He's a bully; he'll twist you into a knot if you let him. You know that nothing good can come of that relationship. Cindy, wise up! He was caught red-handed outside Marshall Field with two stolen watches worth hundreds of dollars. He won't get away with it. He's gonna fall hard and he'll take you down with him. I can't imagine that you're willing to get thrown in jail for the likes of him!"

"But, if I don't help him, who will? We've been dating. He's my boyfriend. I can't just drop out on him."

"Are you out of your friggin' mind? Listen to yourself. You're afraid of getting in trouble, but you feel sorry for the asshole who's about to put you in jail. You sound just like my mom, and you know full well her life sucks."

"You're scaring me, Robin."

"I certainly hope so! This is your life, Cindy. You have to take control. No one can do it for you. Do it *now* or you'll be paying for a bad decision for the rest of your life. You know I know what I'm talking about."

"If I help Jake, I could go to jail as an accessory. If I don't help Jake, he'll get the gang to make me pay, and when he gets out, he'll kill me. I'm screwed no matter what I do."

"You're not poor white trash, Cindy. You come from a good home and your parents will support you if you make the right decisions. How can you even consider letting that fucking bastard ruin your life?"

Cindy took a deep breath. "I know what I need to do. I'm just not sure I can *do* it."

"We both have to tell the police everything we know. If you have to testify against him, that's what you'll do. I know this is scary shit. I'm scared too. But I have to live with myself when all of this is over, and so do you. We can stick together and do the right thing. Do your mom and dad know about this?"

"Not much. They don't like Jake, so I don't spend much time at home. It's not going to be easy telling them that they were right, and I was wrong. Any chance you could come with me and help explain. When you and I were friends in school, they liked you. I think I can do this if I don't have to do it alone."

"You've got to tell them, Cindy. You'll be surprised how happy they'll be when you admit they're right. They can afford to hire somebody to protect you from Jake if it comes to that. Besides, from what you told me, if you don't testify against Jake, you'll wind up in the slammer right alongside him, so what are your options?"

Cindy hesitated.

"One option, Cindy. You have only one option. You work with the police and help them put Jake behind bars where he belongs."

Cindy held Robin's gaze and took a long sip of her drink. She sat up straight and squared her shoulders. "You're right, Robin. I just hope I have the strength to do it."

"I know you think I have my shit together, but I don't have all the answers, either. I just got pissed enough about Jake and all his crap to realize that I have to do something, or I'll never have my life back. That's where you need to be, too. Unless something has changed, you could whup any of those creeps in Jake's gang one-handed. Remember how we scared them shitless that night they thought they could bully us? They found out in a hurry that two little broads could whup-ass. They're losers."

Cindy chuckled. "You sound like old times, taking no crap off anybody."

"Well then, are we going to handle this or are you going to wimp out on me and ruin your life?"

Cindy took a long sip of her drink. "You're on, Robin. We'll come up with a plan and we'll make it happen!"

"Right on! You can do it, and I'll bet it won't be as hard as you think. When I fessed up to Gram, she was grateful, not angry. And as for the strength to take him on, when Jake pushed Gram around in Simpson's, it made me so angry I could have done him some real damage."

"Robin, thanks for believing in me."

Robin and Gram sat on a bench in the police station and waited to meet the detective in charge of Jake's case. "This bench could have come from the church I grew up in, except for the lewd comments scratched all over it," Gram mused.

"No, one gets this nervous in church," Robin said. "I wonder how long we'll have to..."

"Miss Hart? Are you Robin Hart?" asked a burly man with shirt sleeves rolled to his elbows."

"Yes, Sir. I'm Robin," she said, standing, "and this is Gram... er... Mrs. Maureen Kelly, my grandmother."

"I'm Detective Nelson, Andy Nelson." He extended his arm to shake Gram's hand. "Let's visit at my desk. It's not private, but this lobby is like Grand Central Station." He escorted them up one flight of stairs and through the open bullpen where detectives were engaged in discussions with a rag-tag lot of nefarious-looking people. Robin wrinkled her nose and moved closer to Detective Nelson whose *Brut* cologne helped to mask the whiff of vomit and body odor coming from one corner of the room.

They reached Nelson's desk at the far end of the floor. Nelson offered Gram his visitor's chair and pulled another from the adjacent desk for Robin. At least we have more privacy than they do," Detective Nelson said, motioning to the hubbub they had just walked through. Can I get you something to drink?"

"No, thank you," Robin and Gram said with one voice.

"I won't keep you long. I understand you knew Jake Zidder before you began working at Marshall Field. Let's start with that and then move to the incident. I'll take notes and I may interrupt you with questions. What is your relationship with Jake Zidder?"

"I met Jake in high school. I was his girlfriend for about two years, which I regret now." She told the story of Jake's theft of cigarettes from Simpson's Drug Store. "I couldn't get away from him fast enough. Just knowing him could have gotten me in trouble." Gram reached over and squeezed Robin's hand and Detective Nelson's warm eyes welcomed her to continue. She relayed the details leading up to the day of the theft including Cindy's role. "Cindy is my high school friend and she became his girlfriend after I left for college. She told me I needed to do what Jake said because he was serious about hurting me or Gram. I told her that wasn't happening and in a few choice words, I told her what I thought of Jake and suggested she distance herself from him and his gang of losers. Even though she could end up in jail, she may not be capable of standing up to Jake."

Detective Nelson flipped a page in his notebook, then looked up. "You're doing fine, Robin. Do you want to take a break or need something to drink?"

"No, I'm good." Robin took a deep breath, grateful to be getting the whole story off her chest. "Jake knocked Gram down in Simpson's drug store to send me a message."

"Mrs. Kelly, can you describe that incident?" asked Detective Nelson.

"Of course. Out of nowhere, Jake rushed by and shoved me, then raced out of the store without a backward glance. When I crashed to the floor, I knocked over a display of *Dippity-do* and the racket brought Dick running. That's Dick Simpson, the owner. I twisted my knee and scraped myself up a bit. I didn't realize at the time that the incident wasn't an accident."

"Thank you, Mrs. Kelly," said Detective Nelson. "Robin, let's move on to the next time you saw Jake."

"Hmmm... that would be the day he was arrested. He knew I saw him steal the watches and he made it clear that he'd make trouble for me if I reported him. I turned the green tag by the register over to red to signal Mrs. Parker and prayed that she would see it. When I watched him leaving the store, I thought he was getting away with it, but then security seemed to materialize from nowhere to catch him. When Jake saw me through the window, he sliced his finger across his throat and kept yelling that Gram and I would pay."

"Thank you, Robin and Mrs. Kelly. I'll contact you if I have more questions."

"Will I have to go to court?" Robin asked.

"It's likely that you will need to testify."

"I'll only be in Chicago for the summer and then I go back to school. I can't afford to fly back and forth to Chicago."

"Let's take it one step at a time." He stood and handed his card to each of them. "I'll walk you back downstairs. Call me if you think of anything else you need to tell me, and thank you for coming today."

Robin and Gram walked arm in arm out of the police station and into the sunlight...

Chapter 9

Robin walked the short distance from the train station to the courthouse in a shroud of gloom that matched the overcast sky. Halfway up the courthouse steps, she halted, wide-eyed gasping for air.

"Robin, for pity's sake, we can't dawdle; it's nearly 9 now." Looking closer at her granddaughter, she said, "Slow down and take a deep breath. Everything will be fine."

"But what if it's NOT fine?" Robin panted. "What if Jake has his hardass buddies hurt you when I'm back in Dallas. If I testify, he could really hurt you worse than knocking you down. It won't be safe for you in Chicago. I can't do this." Robin turned and started back down the steps. "I can't let anything happen to you. Let's go."

Gram pulled Robin to a stop and hugged her to her chest for a long moment. Then she held her at arm's length and looked directly into her eyes. "Jennifer Lynn Hart, I did not bring you up to run from filth like Jake. You're a fighter. You've never run from anything in your entire life. Whatever happens to that despicable man is his own doing. You're here to do the right thing. Besides, I wear granny panties, and no one messes with me!"

Robin grinned slowly, and Gram pulled her in for another long hug, then propelled her up the steps.

Assistant District Attorney Hammerschmidt was waiting for them on a bench outside the courtroom. "Good, you're here. Do you have any questions about how we'll proceed today?"

"I think I'm okay," Robin said, drawing in a slow, deep breath. "We've been over this so many times I could testify in my sleep. This whole ordeal is a nightmare."

"It will be over soon. Just be yourself and remember not to embellish when you answer the attorney's questions. You'll be fine."

Cindy pushed through the door at the far end of the hall followed by her parents. Mrs. Hammerschmidt stood and greeted them. "We're all here now. Cindy, they will call you first and Robin will follow. The time spent with each witness varies, but both of you will testify today."

Cindy said, "Do I have time to go to the bathroom?"

"Yes, of course. The ladies' room is down the hall to the left.".

"Robin, will you go with me?"

When the door closed behind them, Cindy said, "I don't need to go but I do need to talk to you." She peered under the stalls. She was trembling when she turned to Robin. "Lurch cornered me the other day and said if I don't straighten up and do what Jake says, he'll kill me. I'm scared, Robin. What am I going to do?"

"Cindy, take a deep breath and listen to me. We knew this would get nasty. Ms. Hammerschmidt promised that they'll do what they can to protect us. We just need to let her know about the threats. Besides, Charlie doesn't have the balls to act without Jake beside him. Jake is in jail and we have to testify to make sure he stays there. We're doing the right thing!"

Cindy slumped against the sink and rubbed her temples. "I don't know..."

"Cindy!" Robin's voice was sharp. "Suck it up! Get in there and tell the truth, or you'll be cleaning up after Jake your whole life... IF you don't end up in jail along with him."

"But, I... I... didn't do anything bad, not really."

"You're wrong! Knowing about criminal behavior and not reporting it makes you complicit, and that's a crime. It will be even worse if you perjure yourself on the witness stand. That will land you in jail, for sure. Are you willing to go to jail for that asshole?"

"No, of course I don't, but I am afraid of Jake and what he can do, even from behind bars."

"Listen to yourself. You have the chance to take your life back and you're talking about throwing it away. Nothing will make you safer than putting Jake behind bars. Do it! We're in this together. Now, get in there and show everyone what you're made of."

Cindy stared at Robin, then squared her shoulders. "I can do this. Can you come in when I testify?"

"They won't let me in until it's my turn, but maybe they'll let you stay when you're done."

The girls linked arms and returned to Gram and ADA Hammerschmidt.

"Wait here and the bailiff will call you. Any last-minute questions?" She nodded when neither girl spoke. "Mrs. Kelly, When they call Robin, you may go in with her. The prosecution table is on the right. Look for an empty seat on that side."

Gram and the girls sat in silence, people-watching as the bailiff closed the courtroom doors. Robin concentrated on quelling the butterflies in her stomach. It was half an hour before the bailiff came for Cindy.

Robin reached for her hand and whispered, "Stand tall, Cindy. I know you'll do fine!"

Robin paced the hall, stopping by the ladies' room twice, then fidgeted on the bench. The butterflies multiplied. "It seems like hours since they called Cindy. What time is it, Gram?"

"It's only been 25 minutes," said Gram. She reached for Robin's hand. "I'm sure it won't be long now."

Then the bailiff pushed open the courtroom doors, looming above her and calling her name. She sat wide-eyed and glued to the bench until Gram rose and pulled her up.

The bailiff held the door open for them. Robin spotted Cindy immediately. Her face was ashen, but she sat tall in her seat. She slid over to let Gram sit beside her.

Robin followed the bailiff, her eyes glued on ADA Hammerschmidt, avoiding even a glimpse of Jake at the defense table.

The bailiff swore her in, then nodded to the witness chair. Robin climbed the two steps on rubbery legs, then perched on the edge of the large wooden seat.

"Your Honor. May I approach the witness?" ADA Hammerschmidt began.

"You may."

Robin relaxed a bit when she realized that Ms. Hammerschmidt completely blocked her view of Jake, shielding her from his murderous glare.

"Miss Hart, let's begin with your name."

"Robin Hart," Robin said. "...I mean, my name is Jennifer Lynn Hart. Everyone calls me Robin."

With Ms. Hammerschmidt's gentle probing, Robin relaxed and answered each of the questions about herself, her relationship with Jake, her job at Marshall Field, and the entire sequence of events leading up to Jake's arrest.

"Thank you, Miss Hart." said the ADA. She gave Robin an encouraging smile. "Your witness," she said to Jake's lawyer as she returned to her seat at the prosecution's table.

"Miss Hart," the defense lawyer said. Robin turned to face him, and her breath caught in her throat when her eyes locked on Jake. Her gut twisted at the satanic expression on his face. She looked away quickly and silently recited the mantra that kept her focused:

"Jake is pond scum weak,
Grannie panties strong,
Don't let him get in your head."

She scanned the room. Gram caught her eye, smiled and gave her a thumbs up. *"I can do this,"* she reminded herself, sitting up straighter and focusing on the attorney, studiously avoiding Jake's spiteful glare.

When Jake's lawyer began his interrogation, Robin realized how well the ADA had prepared her for his tactics. She didn't lose her cool when the lawyer made too much of her relationship with Jake and hammered relentlessly on the possibility that it was she who instigated the plan to steal from Marshall Field. Playing her mantra over and over in her head, she stood her ground and finally the defense attorney had no more questions.

"Thank you, Miss Hart," said the judge. "You are excused."

As she left the courtroom, Gram, Cindy, and Cindy's parents rose to join her. When the double doors closed behind them, Gram swept both girls into a hug. "I'm so proud of both of you."

"You did an awesome job, Robin." Cindy said, "I wish I had the guts you showed in there. I couldn't lift my eyes from the floor the whole time I sat in that chair."

"Thanks, Cindy. I wish I could have been in there for you. I won't pretend it was easy. The looks Jake gave me nearly stopped my heart."

"You girls deserve a treat. Let's get burgers and milkshakes at the diner down the street." Cindy's parents nodded their assent.

As they descended the marble steps of the courthouse, Robin spotted Lurch moving to intercept them. Before he could speak, Robin closed in on him. "Stay away from us, Lurch," she commanded. "Jake's gonna get thrown in the slammer, and If you know what's good for you, you'll put as much distance between you and him that you can, otherwise, you'll end up in jail with him. And stay far, far away from me and my family. Do you understand me?"

Though he towered over Robin, Lurch cringed and backed away. When he'd put several yards between them, he pointed a menacing finger at her and growled, "Don't think this is over Girlie. You ain't heard the last of Jake." Then he turned and hurried away.

Chapter 10

The sky outside the hospital window was growing dark while Gram sat quietly in Aileen's room. Aileen lay immobile and nearly invisible among the tubes and wires. "*I wish I could have done more for you, Aileen.*"

Gram startled when the young nurse said, "Mrs. Kelly, you really should go home. Get some rest and eat something more satisfying than hospital food. I'll take good care of Mrs. Hart and you come back in the morning."

"I suppose you are right; I'll leave in a bit. It's hard to leave her this way. I want to believe that she'll wake up if I stay."

The nurse squatted down beside the chair and took Gram's hand. "If there is any change, I'll phone you immediately."

Gram patted the young nurse's hand and with her eyes lowered said, "I know... I know... Thank you."

Gram stood and leaned over to tuck a wisp of hair behind Aileen's ear. "I'll be back soon," she whispered. "You rest now." She kissed her daughter's bruised cheek and a single tear slid down her own as she turned and left the room.

The hooded figures followed Gram as she crossed the street and turned toward the train station. They closed in from behind and the tallest one snaked an arm around her neck and covered her mouth with a meaty hand. He pulled her into an alley and slammed her against the building, scraping her face. The massive figure twisted her head and growled in her ear. "You scream, Lady, and you're dead; d'ya hear me?"

Too frightened to reply, she nodded.

"Good. NOW, you and that traitor of a granddaughter have been warned. You'll both pay for what she did. Be VERY afraid, Old Lady. We've got eyes on you night and day. We can get to you whenever we want." He ripped her purse free from her arm and threw it to one of the shadowy figures. "Take the cash." He twisted Gram's head again and placed his mouth to her ear. "One word to the pigs and this little warning will seem like a walk in the park. Understand, Bitch?" Before she could respond, he knocked her against the wall. "Ya hear me, Bitch?"

Gram nodded.

His punch to her ribs would have crumpled her, but he held her pinned to the wall. "I asked you a question, Bitch. I want to know you heard me loud and clear?"

Through tears, Gram gasped, "Yes."

He shoved her to the ground and the four figures fled.

Breathless from the blow, and aching from cuts and scrapes, Gram clawed the wall and inched her way to her feet. She leaned against the wall until her head cleared and her balance returned. *"That was the boy from the courthouse steps that Robin called Lurch. I'm sure, but I can't prove it because I never saw his face. I never saw any of their faces."*

Numbly she gathered the remnants of her purse, lipstick, a broken compact, her empty wallet, but no train ticket. Then she remembered... She slipped her hand into her dress pocket and breathed a sigh of relief. She'd put the ticket there so she wouldn't have to rummage in her purse for it. She leaned against the wall until she felt steady enough to walk. *"At least I'm still alive and I have a way home. Banged up and bruised, but nothing broken. I'm counting myself fortunate. I need to get home and get cleaned up. I can't be looking like a train wreck when Robin gets in from work."*

"That looks like Gram," Robin thought, as she watched a figure limping along nearly a block ahead of her. When Robin caught up, Gram was holding tight to the railing and pulling herself slowly up the steps. "Gram, what..."

Robin gasped when Gram turned to face her. "My God, what happened? Who did this? Are you okay?" Her words tumbled over one another.

"I'll tell you when we get inside, but first I need to clean up and just sit for a moment."

"Jake did this! Somehow this is his doing, I know it. I'm gonna kill that bastard! Gram, tell me what happened."

Holding her palm up like a traffic cop, Gram insisted, "Robin, I'm fine. We can talk in a while."

Robin recognized her own Irish stubbornness reflected in Gram and knew that Gram wouldn't talk until she was good and ready. "Okay," she conceded, "I'll fix us some supper while you clean up. Do you need any help?"

"I'll be fine, Robin. I promise."

When Gram came to dinner, her color was better, and she was steadier on her feet.

"You look much better." Robin took a bite of her sandwich while Gram sipped her tea. "Now tell me what happened."

"When I left the hospital that boy you called Lurch pushed me into an alley and scuffed me up is all. There were three others with him. They all wore hoods, so I won't be able to identify them, but I recognized Lurch's voice from the courthouse steps. He's the one that roughed me up. The others emptied my purse. The angels were definitely looking out for me today. My train ticket was in my pocket, and I was only a block from the train station."

"Gram we need to call the police and report this now!"

"Yes, of course. I needed to get home first to make sure you were safe. I'll make the call right after we finish eating. A few minutes won't make a difference. I'm afraid the police won't be able to do anything since I couldn't see their faces, but I'd have no trouble picking Lurch out of a "voice lineup."

"Gram, you absolutely *have to* move to Dallas. We need to get away from this nightmare."

"Perhaps, but I can't leave until Aileen has recovered and is out of the hospital. You have to understand that. I'll make that call to the police now. We'll make sure that they can protect us. In the morning, I am going back to the hospital to be with Aileen. We may need to have someone walk with us to and from the train station for now."

"Gram, I..."

Gram interrupted. "I'll make the call to the police station; why don't you go upstairs and call Katie. I think that would do you a world of good."

"I should be with you. I'm not leaving you."

"Jennifer Lynn Hart, you'll do as I say. When the policeman arrives, he and I can discuss the matter without you. If he needs you, I'll come get you. In the meantime, when he comes you call Katie."

Robin dried the last dish and was putting it in the cupboard when the doorbell rang. She sighed and looked at her reflection in the window. *"What a mess I've made of things. I had no business ever being with Jake and look what came of that stupid decision! Gram's right; I need a good talk with Katie."* She joined Gram and the policeman in the living room, her eyes pleading with Gram to let her stay.

Gram introduced Robin to the officer and the officer nodded in acknowledgment. Gram nodded toward the stairs and Robin grudgingly ascended.

"Grayfox residence."

"Hello Mrs. Grayfox, this is Robin. Is Katie there?"

"Oh, Robin, how nice to hear your voice. Let me get her." Robin could hear Katie running down the steps.

"Robin, it's been forever since we talked. I read your letters over and over. I just wish I could be there with you."

Katie's voice unleashed the flood of tears that Robin had held at bay for so long, and she couldn't say a word.

"Robin, are you okay?"

"I'm… I'm okay," Robin choked out between sobs. "Katie, I don't know what to do. I feel like I'm against the world. I don't have a handle on anything. Right now Gram is talking to a policeman because one of Jake's thugs beat her up and it's all my fault that my drunken father put my mother in a coma just because I wanted her in my life again. Katie, I can't fix anything," she said, dissolving into sobs.

"Robin, listen to me," Katie insisted. "You're not against the world. You've done the right thing about Jake and your mom, and your Gram is proud of you. Jake and your father are the criminals here, not you."

"Katie, you are such a rock. What would the Nurseketeers do without you? What would *I* do without you?"

"Well I don't know about being a rock, but I do know that you have always been there for us, too. Frannie might have died without you. As for Jake, he's getting what he deserves, and hopefully, so is your father."

"I wish I could be sure of that. I don't trust Jake for an instant. It's more important now than ever to get Gram to move to Dallas. Katie, I'm going to make her see the light. She *has* to listen. When Mom gets better, she'll stay with Gram and they'll come to Dallas together. Her brute of a husband will be out of the picture."

"That sounds like a great plan. We'll all enjoy having your family close to the campus."

"Katie, I've missed you so much. I want to talk all night, but this call is going to cost Gram a fortune."

"Good night, then. Write me soon and keep me posted. You and your Gram are in my heart and in my prayers. I love you. Bye for now."

Chapter 11

"Gram, if there's a chance that Mom will wake up, how can anyone know when it's the right time to stop hoping? I couldn't live with myself if I thought we decided to let go too soon."

"Sweetheart, that's a question with no right answer. When we decide, whatever we decide, we'll be sure that we're doing the right thing based on what we know, what we expect, and how we feel about it."

"But how will we *know?*"

"We won't. We'll decide upon a course of action because we feel sure that it is the best decision we can make. Then, we'll commit to it without regret. If we were to second-guess every hard decision we make, we'd spend our lives mired in uncertainty. Avoiding the hard questions would leave us in the same unacceptable situation.

"Well, I'm definitely not going to give up on her. It would be a triple tragedy if she died. First, she's happy for the first time in forever, and second, she'll be safe with us in Dallas. Lastly, she deserves the chance to make up for all those miserable years. If she can't count on her mother to believe in her, who CAN she count on?" Robin stormed out of the kitchen.

Robin paced, throwing pillows across the room, one after the other. *"Gram expects Mom to die. Well, she's NOT going to die. Gram needs to help me fight this battle for her."* She grabbed her teddy bear, shook him, and ripped one ragged arm from the limp body. *"NOOOOOO,"* she moaned, hugging the remnants to her chest. He'd been Gram's present for her eighth birthday. Exhausted, she collapsed onto the bed and sank into a fitful sleep.

On her way to her bedroom, Gram peeked into Robin's room and took in the small form sprawled across the bed, fully clothed and sound asleep, clutching her teddy bear. She touched the bear gently, then pulled a quilt over her sleeping granddaughter.

Robin awoke at nine the next morning. She clutched the ruined teddy bear to her chest, and a tear trickled down her cheek. *"I can't believe I shouted at Gram. She's suffering, too. She spends all day with Aileen, sitting and hoping with every breath that there will be a sign of improvement."*

She showered and found Gram at the kitchen table, staring into a cup of cold coffee. She looked gray and haggard.

Robin knelt beside her and took her hand. "I'm so sorry. I don't mean to be such an ungrateful bi... twit. Please forgive me for being selfish. I wish I were like you. I always think of myself first and you always put others first. All of this with Mom has got to be killing you, and I only think of my own pain."

Gram managed a small smile and placed her other hand on top of Robin's. "These are hard times. We're grappling with a monstrous situation and there are no easy answers. I'm as exhausted as you are. I know how desperate you are for Aileen to enjoy a new life with us. I'd love for that dream to come true, too... but we'll have to keep on living even if that doesn't happen." Worry clouded her face. "When I watch her lying there without moving a muscle, I pray she isn't in pain. I wonder if she's suffering because she knows we're here and she wants to reach out to us, but she can't. I can't imagine what she's experiencing… or if she's already gone. There is just no way to know for sure. It's understandable that neither of us is at our best right now."

"Gram, I can't imagine what I would do without you, or who I would be if you hadn't been the one to raise me. Can we go to Grant to see Mom? I need to be at work at 1:00. Just so you know, I'm not expecting that she'll be different, but I AM hoping. I know you are, too."

"Mrs. Kelly," Kathleen called as Gram and Robin passed the nurses' station. "Mr. Henderson from the Finance Office left this for you."

Gram thanked the woman and opened the envelope. "Oh, my," she murmured.

"Is everything okay," the nurse asked.

"There seems to be an issue with Aileen's long-term care insurance. I'll have to stop by his office and see what this means. Gram folded the envelope into her purse and asked for directions to the Finance Office.

"Let me call to be sure that Mr. Henderson is in. It won't do to send you down there for nothing."

"Thank you," said Gram.

"He's in," Kathleen said, placing the receiver in its cradle. "You'll find his office in the corridor right behind the information desk in the first-floor lobby."

Gram and Robin found the office and Mr. Henderson stood to greet them, gesturing toward chairs in front of his desk. "I'm afraid we have a situation to discuss," he began. "Mrs. Hart's insurance doesn't include long-term care. I wanted to be sure that you were aware of this right away so that you'll have ample time to explore options. Her policy covers our skilled nursing floor for 30 days. If she remains unresponsive, we must transfer her to long-term custodial care, and without insurance, your options will be limited. The expense of a private facility may be prohibitive. In cases like Mrs. Hart's, there's no clear indication of how long the stay will be, which makes it difficult to project the cost of care."

"I'm grateful that you thought to discuss this with me," Gram said. "I haven't had time to get my bearings."

"We can provide information about the long-term care facilities to which we transfer patients. That will give you some time to investigate and decide what will work best for you."

"Thank you, Mr. Henderson."

"If she wakes up soon," said Robin, "this won't be a problem at all. This whole thing sucks!"

Robin pushed open the door to 2-West in time to see a group of people moving quickly down the hall, led by a nurse pushing a machine into Aileen's room. She and Gram found the room crowded with people intent upon managing whatever was happening. Robin looked around wildly for someone to ask for an explanation.

Kathleen separated herself from the crowd and shepherded Robin and Gram into the hall. "The team has everything under control," she assured them. "Mrs. Hart's heart began to beat erratically, and they are working to stabilize her."

"Tell me what that means," Robin insisted. "They'll fix it, won't they?"

"That's difficult to answer," Kathleen replied softly. "What happened is troubling. The abnormal heart rhythm means her stability is failing."

"We can't let her die!" Robin insisted.

Gram's shoulders sagged and she reached for Robin's hand.

Kathleen caught Gram's eye, then turned to face Robin. "I'm told that you are a nursing student, so I feel sure that you will understand. The shunt that was put in immediately following the incident relieved the pressure on your mother's brain, but it didn't reverse the damage that had already been done. Your mother has demonstrated no voluntary muscle activity and no reaction to pain. These are cardinal signs of brain death."

"NO!"

Kathleen waited until she was sure Robin was listening, then took her hand and held Robin's eyes with her own. "Robin, your mother's body is living, at least for the time being, but her brain is not. With no signals from the brain, even the best of nursing care can't prevent her organs from failing. It is a slow process, so there is no rush to make decisions. However, brain death is an irreversible process."

Robin squared her shoulders, biting her lip to maintain control. "I do understand your assessment, but I'm not ready to give up. You're taking great care of her and she has every reason to want to live. She deserves that chance."

"That's a reasonable response," Kathleen said. "Facing losing someone close is difficult under any circumstances. We understand that everyone processes that challenge in their own way. I've given you all the information I have. I'll come get you when we're done."

"Robin, you look upset. Is it your mother?" Mrs. Parker asked.

"It was a rough morning. Thank you for asking. I'm glad we're busy and the customers will keep me occupied."

Robin's break time came and went, unnoticed, while she managed a steady stream of customers. She was surprised when she heard, "Dinnertime, Robin." She looked up to see Guy smiling at her. "That is, if Mrs. Parker can do without you for half an hour."

"Actually, you can have 45 minutes. You've been working non-stop since you got here," Mrs. Parker said.

"Thank you," Robin said, taking a deep breath. "We've been so busy I hadn't noticed the time."

"So, two questions," Guy said. "First, can I buy you dinner? I know you came straight from the hospital. Second, what's up?"

"For once, I just might take you up on that offer. It's been an awful day and I need to talk about it."

"Hea-vy!" he said, concerned. "It's got to be important if you didn't put up more of a fight than that. Let's run through the line and sit in that corner. What's your pleasure?"

"Just a salad and iced tea, please. I don't have much of an appetite."

"You have to consider that piece of chocolate cake," he said, pointing "Everyone needs chocolate after a tough day."

Robin grinned. "You're good for me. Today has been the worst day of my life and I'm smiling. Go figure."

They sat next to one another so they could both look out the window. Guy ceremoniously placed Robin's salad in front of her, and the chocolate cake by her iced tea. "Now let's have it," he coaxed, "from the beginning."

"I think I need to start at the end. I'm... I'm afraid Mom's going to die... and my dream of her moving to Dallas with me and Gram will never come true. It's not fair!"

"Oh my God! What happened?"

"Today when Gram and I got to the hospital, the emergency crew was working on Mom because her heart rhythm went hay-wire. She's stable now, but her nurse said that there isn't much hope that she'll recover. She's only been back in my life for a couple of weeks after all those years, and now... I want to kill that bastard. He had no right to ruin all of our lives!"

"At least you know he's going to get what's coming to him."

"What's more," Robin continued, "I wanted so much to believe that Mom would get better that I didn't pay attention to how hard this is on Gram. Last night I threw a temper tantrum like a selfish bitch and accused her of not having faith in her daughter."

"Robin, this is an awful time for both of you. I know your grandmother understands."

"She does, but I'm kicking myself for making things hard for her. She never calls me out or loses her temper. She is amazing and I don't deserve her."

"Your grandmother wouldn't want you feeling like this. She knows how hard this is for you and she wants to be there for you just like you want to be there for her. Quit thinking about what you did wrong and concentrate on doing the best you can now. I hate that you're going through such an awful time and I wish there were something I could do." Guy paused as a wan smile turn up the corners of Robin's mouth.

"You're a good friend, Guy. I needed to say all that out loud. I'm not ready to give up yet. I want to believe that Mom can make it, but you're right about facing forward. Being angry and feeling sorry for myself isn't helping. I need to quit acting like Gram's committed a crime whenever she mentions the possibility that Mom might die. Time to *man up*! I'm acting more like Frannie and I'd never let her get by with this crappy behavior."

"Frannie? Your ditzy roommate?"

"Not ditzy, really; she's just spoiled." Robin laughed out loud. "Boy, if *that's* not the pot calling the kettle black! I think I just got a dose of my own medicine. You *are* a good friend!"

After work the next day, Robin hurried to 2-West, hoping for a miracle. As she passed the nurses' station, Kathleen called her name.

"Robin, your grandmother is in the chapel on the first floor. I'll give you directions if you'd like to join her."

"Thanks. I'll just look in on Mom first."

Aileen lay motionless in the bright room, only the hiss of the ventilator interrupting the stillness. Her sallow skin blended in with the bedding. A chill passed through Robin; it felt as if the room were empty. She reached to squeeze Aileen's hand. "I'll be back in a bit, Mom."

Gram was alone in the Chapel. She knelt in the first pew, chin resting on her clasped hands, her eyes closed. Soft music came from somewhere behind the altar. Gram felt Robin's presence and patted the upholstered kneeling bench beside her. Robin stood for another moment, the music and soft lighting calming her. Then she knelt slowly beside Gram who snaked an arm around her shoulders and pulled her close.

"I thought about stopping by St. Michael's this morning," Gram began, "but I was anxious to get to the hospital and see if there was any change. Aileen had another spell of erratic heartbeats during the night and again about mid-morning, while I was with her. They rushed that machine in again to help her. One of the nurses suggested I come here, while they were sorting it out. It's peaceful and the music helps me think. The constant hiss of the ventilator in her room won't let me clear my mind."

"I understand what Kathleen told us yesterday, but I keep coming back to believing that there's no harm in waiting," Robin began. "Why be in a hurry to pull the plug? Mr. Hutchinson said that she can stay here for thirty days. We can wait at least that long, can't we?"

"I suppose that's an option. My concern is for Aileen herself. If I were sure that she is completely unaware of what is going on, I wouldn't worry that she is suffering and can't do anything about it. If she's awake inside, but can't communicate, she could be in agony. I can't imagine being in pain and not being able to ask for help. Even if there were no pain, not being able to move a muscle or communicate in any way would be agony."

"That's an awful thought, Gram. Do you think it's a possibility? I was thinking about what the doctor said could happen to her body… to her skin and muscles. The nurses exercise her arms, legs, feet, and hands at least a couple of times a day. Probably more when we aren't here. Dr. Bailey said that, even with the exercises, her muscles will get weak and her joints will stiffen up if she stays in a coma too long. How long is too long?"

"No one knows. Would you like to go back upstairs for another hour or so?"

Robin helped Gram up from the bench.

"Kneeling in church was a lot easier when my knees were younger," Gram said. "But, I'm grateful to be as spry as I am. I watch patients on 2-West struggle every day, and most of them are younger than I am."

Robin hugged her grandmother. "You're the youngest old lady I know, and I love you."

Two nurses were with Aileen when they returned to her room. One said, "We'll turn her every hour instead of every two. It won't do to let her skin break down."

"What does that mean?" asked Robin, approaching the bed.

"You know how it feels when you sit too long in one spot?" the nurse asked. "You get uncomfortable and you shift your body into a better position. That's because when pressure builds up, it restricts the flow of blood to the tissues and makes you uncomfortable. When someone can't move, the pressure begins to damage the skin and muscle. We need to reposition your mother frequently because her skin is showing signs of pressure damage. See this reddish area here? We need to keep pressure off this area and make sure that no other areas become reddened. We'll do that by repositioning her often."

The green lines on Aileen's cardiac monitor jumped wildly and the alarm sounded. One nurse raced for the machine they kept by the nurses' station and the other lifted the phone by Aileen's bed and said, "Dr. Bailey to room 237, STAT!" Then she asked Gram and Robin to wait outside.

Gram stood quietly with her head bowed. Robin paced up and down the hall angrily, "Everything is going wrong at once. It's like Mom is falling apart in front of our eyes. Gram, do you think she wants it to be over? Do you think that maybe she thinks that dying is better than running away and being scared he'll come for her?"

"Maybe, Sweetheart, but it's possible that the end was decided the instant that Harold destroyed her brain, and we just had to go through the motions until we understood that. There's no way to know. Now we just have to hope that they can manage this crisis and give us a bit more time."

"Time to realize that it's over?"

"Time to take it all in... to ask questions and get all of the answers they can give us.

They stood in silence until Dr. Bailey came out of the room. "Mrs. Kelly, Robin... Mrs. Hart is stable for the time being. We were able to convert the irregular heartbeats to a normal rhythm."

He made eye contact with each of them. "It has been nearly two weeks since the incident and she has begun a steady decline. Today the nurses noted the first signs of skin breakdown. We can prevent serious damage, but we can't reverse the brain's process. It will become harder and harder to maintain her equilibrium as her systems begin to fail. I wish I could hold out some hope for recovery... but I can't."

"Thank you, for your honesty." Gram whispered.

Robin shook her head from side to side, saying nothing.

"Watching your mother slip away is more painful than I could ever have imagined," Gram began, "but, she is slipping away, and I can't convince myself otherwise. Every day has been the same or worse than the day before. There has not been one good day, and I cannot bear to see her deteriorate."

Robin interrupted, "I'm so sorry, Gram. I didn't want it to be this way, and I thought that if I stuck to my guns, a miracle would happen."

"You're a fighter, Robin. Aileen was proud of you. You turned out to be the person she would have liked to be. You made her happy for the first time in her adult life. You'll always have that memory."

"What do we do now?" Robin asked, her chin dropping to her chest.

"I don't think there's anything we *can* do, except let them know that we understand there's nothing that anyone can do. I think they will guide us from there."

"Gram, I feel so empty." Tears slipped down Robin's cheeks. "There's nothing left inside me."

"Robin, you are the best thing your mother ever did. Let's be grateful that she finally got to see that for herself."

Robin's tears fell and her mind wandered. Snippets of Aileen whirled like a carousel behind her eyes... *Mom cowering from that shithead while I shivered behind the bedroom door... Mom laughing at Gram and me sitting together in one porch chair... Mom's brilliant green eyes wide with terror when Harold's car appeared on our way to lunch... Mom enjoying our last day together... before Harold came home."*

Robin brushed away the tears and faced Gram with her back straight and her chin high. "Gram," she said. "I need to tell her one last time that we're a family and Harold's gone and she's not alone. Then I'll go find Kathleen."

Gram nodded and gathered Robin into a hug. They stood in the hall wrapped in one another's arms.

"What do we do now?" Robin asked Kathleen. "I mean, where do we go from here? How long will she live without life support? We want to be with her. We don't want her to be alone. Can we stay even if it's after visiting hours?"

When Robin paused for a breath, Kathleen took her hand and led her to the conference room where Gram sat, waiting. "Let me answer your questions one at a time. First, you may stay as long as you like. Visiting hours will not be an issue.

"Mrs. Hart can't breathe on her own. Without life support, she can't live for more than an hour. I know you want to be with her, but I must tell you that it can be difficult. On one hand, time creeps by slowly, and at the same time, you realize that there is little time left. The erratic process and symptoms of dying can be misleading. She may not breathe for a period, and just when you think she has passed away, she will take another breath or two. This is common as the heart and lungs fail. The monitor will give us an accurate indication of what is happening."

"Kathleen, what will we do when it's over?" Gram asked softly. "What happens then?"

"We'll contact the funeral home of your choice and they'll guide you through the process from that point," she said.

"Gram, do you know who that is? We haven't talked about any of this."

"Yes, I do. Kathleen, we'll need some time to make these arrangements. Can we wait until tomorrow to make the final decision?"

"Certainly. In the meantime, we will continue to provide the best care for Mrs. Hart."

"But what if she dies before we're ready? Before we have everything set up?" Robin asked.

"We'll take care of her until you've made your arrangements. It's late and I know you want to see her before you leave. We'll watch her closely tonight, and you can contact the funeral home in the morning. Remember that you can reach out to me at any time." Kathleen gave Robin's hand a reassuring squeeze. "I'll see you tomorrow."

Robin stood on the stoop, watching Gram unlock the door. "Gram, it's nearly midnight. You must be exhausted, but I don't want to go to bed yet. My head feels like a merry-go-round."

"How about a cup of hot chocolate and you sleep with me tonight? When you were little, you slept with me when you didn't feel well, or climbed into my bed when you had a nightmare. It's been a long time since we've helped each other through a difficult night."

"Perfect," Robin sighed. "What funeral home will you call?

"My parents were friends with the Doyles. It was their funeral home that took care of all the burial services for our family. They even took care of your Grandfather when his body was shipped home from the War... but that was before your time."

"I'm almost 19 and I've never been to a funeral. In high school, there was a boy who died in a car crash, but they had a private service and none of us attended. What can I do to help?"

"Doyle's will take care of everything. We'll write a nice notice for them to put in the paper, and we'll make a list of the folks we'd like to invite to the funeral, like Mr. and Mrs. Simpson and Mrs. Hornsby, and our neighborhood friends." Gram smiled wryly,

"Old folks never like to miss a funeral. Guess it makes them feel good not to be the guest of honor."

"You make me smile even now."

"Would you like your friend, Guy, to come… and Mrs. Parker? It's nice to have the people you care about with you at times like this."

"I hadn't thought beyond us. It would be nice to have friends there, even if they didn't know Mom. I wish Katie, Frannie, and Leslie were here. I didn't realize how much I'd miss them over the summer. Maybe Cindy will come."

"Let's take the rest of the hot chocolate upstairs. I'll call Doyle's first thing in the morning; then we'll go to the hospital to be with Aileen."

A kaleidoscope of images of Aileen, Gram, and Robin on Gram's porch, in the park, in Gram's kitchen, and in Dallas passed behind Robin's eyelids, then faded. She opened her eyes slowly, confused by the unfamiliar surroundings. She squeezed her eyes shut and opened them again. This time they settled on the photo of Aileen on Gram's dresser and the day came slowly into focus. Her first instinct was to close her eyes to stop this day from beginning.

Robin's nose twitched at the nutty aroma of coffee that wafted into the room. "A good cup of coffee will make it easier to face today," Gram said, placing a cup and saucer on the bedside table.

Robin couldn't help but smile. She sat up and reached for her cup while Gram settled on the bed beside her.

Robin sipped, then sighed. "What do I do now, Gram? I wanted my dream to come true so badly that I never considered an alternative."

"First, I'll call Doyle's. They'll help us with most of the decisions we must make. If we concentrate on the things we need to do for Aileen, we'll make it through today."

Chapter 12

R obin sat holding Gram's hand, eyes fixed on Aileen's simple coffin resting on a frame above the open grave. "I'm glad Mom's at peace," she whispered. "We were right to let her go, even if it's not fair, not even a little! We would have been happy together as a family."

"She was happy for the first time in years," Gram replied. "You did that for her, and that's what you need to remember." She nodded toward the women sitting in folding chairs and the men standing respectfully, spilling out from under the canopy that shielded the gathering from the summer sun. "Aileen was loved even if she didn't know how much."

"You're right. It's perfect that the day for Mom's funeral is so beautiful and all of these people came to say goodbye." Robin glanced around, caught Guy's eye, and mouthed *thank you for coming.*

Resplendent in his vestments, Father Gilroy, the elder priest from St. Michael's who had baptized Robin, faced the group and cleared his throat. "We gather today to commit Aileen Kelly Hart, beloved daughter and mother, to her final resting place..."

Gram offered pitchers of iced tea to accompany the plates of food that everyone brought to the house after the graveside service. Robin found Guy on the porch, visiting with Mrs. Parker and Mrs. Hornsby.

"Mrs. Parker has been telling me how pleased she is with your work at Marshal Field this summer," Mrs. Hornsby said. "Knowing your grandmother, I knew you would be an excellent employee. I'm glad it's working well for you there."

"Thank you, Mrs. Hornsby. I love my job and Mrs. Parker is a terrific boss."

"Well, thank you, Robin. Please excuse me, Eleanor," Mrs. Parker said, "I see Mrs. Simpson over there and want to catch her before she leaves."

"Mrs. Parker recommended me for the lead trainee position," Robin told Mrs. Hornsby. "We both know that I deserved it more than the jerk who was selected. Can you believe that he started out making more than me, and then he gets rewarded for spending more time *not* working than paying attention to business!"

"You'll learn that it's still a man's world, Robin," Mrs. Hornsby said softly. "As much progress as women have made, men are still privileged in the business world. But, Robin, with your work ethic and your drive, you'll be twice as good as your competition, and eventually, it will be impossible to ignore that."

"Thank you. I intend to make a difference."

"I have no doubt that you will." Mrs. Hornsby said.

Guy asked, "Would you like to stretch your legs? It's been an intense day."

Robin jumped at the offer. "Yes, a walk would be great."

They walked in comfortable silence for several blocks. Robin swept her arm to indicate the neighborhood. "None of this will be here for long."

"What makes you say that?"

"This is the next phase of Carter Construction's project to renovate Old Town. Our neighborhood is slated for high dollar housing. It's sad since Gram's lived here forever, but I guess it's good in another way since the whole area's so run down. Gram's hoping that they'll spare St. Michael's with that impressive spire, those gorgeous stained-glass windows, and the lovely old chapel where we had the funeral today. It would be a crime to tear it down. After all, rich folks go to church, too. Don't they?" she declared, and an alarm bell clanged in her head. "I'm sorry, Guy. That was rude. I put my foot in my mouth again."

Guy laughed. "Yep. You'll be happy to know that there are God-fearing rich folks out there, and my family is among them. I've been going to the same church as long as I can remember, and I'd be crushed if someone thought about tearing it down. Don't beat yourself up. I know better than to take offense at anything you say off the cuff."

"I don't intend to be rude, but I let my feelings draw a line in the sand, then my mouth barks it out and the fight is on. I can't tell you how many things I've screwed up by not being will-ing to consider the middle ground. I rebelled in high school by running with the *bad* crowd. I didn't even particularly like them, but they accepted me. I became Jake's *girl*. It was a status thing, not a romantic relationship. I had nothing in common with the rich kids, and Jake's crowd made me feel superior.

"I was a surly brat who didn't lift a finger to help around the house. The only thing I did right during those two years was keep up my grades and get the scholarship to Crestmont. I can't even take much credit for that. I didn't have to study hard for good grades, and the rich kids didn't need scholarships to get to college. Guy, I could have blown everything!"

"But, you didn't blow it," Guy reminded her. "When it counted, you made the right decision. I think your Gram knew that you would. That's why she was willing to wait and let you figure it all out for yourself."

"That's not the worst of it. It was my stubbornness that ruined any chance of a relationship with my mother before this summer. When Mom let Gram take me away without any resistance, I chose to hate her because she opted for The Brute over me. Now it's too late to fix anything." Robin's shoulders slumped. "I wish I could undo all the damage I've done..."

Guy interrupted. "Believe me when I say that everyone wishes they could undo something. You're fortunate because there's no permanent damage. First, you didn't ruin your mother's life. Your Gram would never have let that happen. Even she couldn't get through to your mother. She did the best thing she could have done for her daughter by raising you as well as she did. What you need to remember is the time you got to spend with your Mom this summer. I'm sure *that* made her happy."

They had reached St. Michael's without realizing how far they'd walked.

Robin's eyes welled with tears. "But I..."

"Let's sit in the courtyard. It's quiet and you can cry if you want to. It might do you a world of good to just let go."

"Crying never makes me feel better. It's just that sometimes I get so frustrated I can't help it," she sniffled.

Guy pushed her gently down onto a bench. He sat beside her, reached into his pocket, and handed her his handkerchief. "The best thing about a pity party is coming out of it with the resolve to deal with whatever it is that's eating at you. I'm glad that you're talking about how you feel, but that's only worthwhile if you can put it in perspective and look forward, not backward."

They sat in companionable silence while Robin gathered her thoughts.

"I can tell you're not done talking," Guy said.

"Are you a mind reader? I was just thinking about something else I've wanted to ask you. I haven't come up with a good way to start."

"Just spit it out. I'll do my best to keep up."

Robin opened and closed her mouth a few times. "I need to ask you about being gay. How do you know? What does it feel like? When did you figure it out? *What* did you figure out?" She stopped. "I'm sorry, that was too many questions and the whole topic may be too personal for me to be asking."

"Of course, it's personal and I'm glad that you feel comfortable enough to ask me those questions. I don't know too many people who can handle that subject. My mother manages, but my father just can't. I think he's convinced that if he ignores it completely, it will go away. So, tell me why you're asking. I know that it's not idle curiosity."

"I think I may be gay. I... I've been curious about myself for a while, but I never considered *gay* because I'm not interested in girls... at least no girl has ever made me think like that... romantically, I mean." Robin hesitated.

"Go on."

"It's more that I'm not interested in guys. Jake never tried more than kissing. I was grateful because boyfriends and girlfriends tend to do more than kiss and I didn't want any of it. Even kissing was gross because he was a sloppy kisser." She curled her lip and shuddered. "When I read love stories it's like a spectator sport. I don't get it." Robin paused, slowly raising her eyes to meet Guy's.

"Everyone is different and there are no right ways to feel. You are who you are, and you don't have to know everything about yourself right this minute. The whole relationship game is an evolution and there doesn't seem to be any clear explanation to the way people's sexuality develops." Shrugging his shoulders, he said, "There's no reason for me not to have a traditional approach to sexuality. There are six people in my immediate family, and I'm the only outlier in that department."

Robin glanced up when he paused.

"I've told my parents but never shared with anyone my true feelings about this before. Feels good to know someone who will listen and not judge. So, the crowd I hang around with here is straight, and they're not necessarily the most open-minded people in the world.

"Go on," Robin encouraged.

"As a kid, I was just like everyone else. I didn't like dolls or dress up in girls' clothing. I liked sports, but individual sports like tennis, golf, and swimming, not football or soccer. Then came puberty. When my friends started fixating on girls, I daydreamed about guys. I've never been attracted to girls romantically or sexually. The first things that grabs me about a guy is *kind eyes*. I can't tell you what *kind eyes* look like, but once the eyes have me hooked, the rest of the man comes into focus. I like confident men who speak well, dress well, and take care of themselves. There are no smokers or loudmouths or slob in my dreams."

"That's no surprise," Robin smiled. You're looking for a guy like you. Makes sense to me."

"Well, I haven't met *my guy* yet, but when he comes along, I'll know it. You don't have to have all the answers."

"Thanks, Guy... Just realizing that it's okay *not* to know is somewhat of a relief. But you're so normal."

"Well thanks, I've always thought of myself as normal."

"I didn't mean that. I meant that you're gay, but you still fit in with the heterosexual world."

"I don't have much choice. Even though it's legal here in Illinois, most folks won't tolerate it. So, the only safe way to be gay is to be 'normal' as you say. That's something you'll learn quickly. For the most part, you need to keep that information to yourself. As I said, most people can't tolerate homosexuality and you can't un-tell someone when you discover it was a mistake to let them know."

"Okay then, I'm making the executive decision to concentrate on getting through this summer and back to school. I'll figure out the personal stuff when I need to."

"I'd say you've enough on your plate for now. When you get around to those other questions you can always call me collect. Guy held her gaze and said, "Friends for life, pinky swear?"

"Pinky swear."

Chapter 13

"It's been a quiet week," Robin said. "After all the stress this summer, it feels good not to be waiting for the next shoe to drop."

Gram poured coffee into their favorite mugs. "I like it when you work the later shift on Saturday. Spending time with you in the morning makes my day special."

"After breakfast, let's take a walk. I'm curious to see how far they've come with the first phase of construction. It's moved faster this summer than I would have imagined. Wouldn't it be grand if you could be in Dallas before Christmas?"

"I've lived in this house for more than forty years... It's hard to think about leaving."

"I understand. There is a lifetime of memories here, even for me."

"I'll bet there are things in drawers and closets...," Gram's eyes widened. "Oh, goodness... and the *attic*! I'd completely forgotten about the attic."

"I don't leave for school for three weeks. I can help you sort through everything before I go. It would be fabulous fun for us to go through the house together. I love your *before-I-was-born* stories."

"I can certainly use your help," Gram agreed.

"It might be fun to go through the attic. I haven't been up there since I was maybe 12 or 13. I played dress up in your old clothes. We laughed at how funny and out of date the clothes looked...."

"Who knows what we'll find this time!"

"I'll have plenty of time to do the actual packing after you leave. The idea of closing the door on three generations of my lifetime... Well, you'll have to be patient with me."

"Think about it. You get to decide what will be part of your new life. My stuff needs to be sorted, too. We can help each other decide what we want in Dallas and what we can give away. It won't be long before we're together again. You can't imagine how I missed you last year." Robin spread her arms as wide as she could. "Chicago seemed as far away as Pluto."

"I missed you, too. It wasn't easy letting you go, but your scholarship was a blessing, and Crestmont is a fine school."

"As soon as I get back on campus, I'll ask the Davis's to help me find a place for you to stay until you decide where you want to live. The neighborhoods around Crestmont are lovely and it will be grand to have you close to campus."

"Let's go for that walk and see what we can find out about the construction project. There should be something on the signs around the site to give us an idea about their progress."

"Can you believe how busy this construction site is on a Saturday?" Robin said. "They're in a helluva hurry to get this project completed."

"Look," Gram said, pointing to the top of the large construction map. "They've added Phase II. It looks like the streets in our neighborhood will have townhouses, and I see at least three apartment buildings." Gram's voice rose and her finger waggled in the direction of North Avenue and Cleveland. "And there's St. Michael's, right where it belongs. It looks like they're going to let it stay."

"Fantastic!" Robin gave Gram an enthusiastic thumbs up.

"Do you see anything about a time schedule?" Gram asked.

"Mrs. Kelly, is it?" Startled, Robin and Gram turned as one.

"Yes, yes, it is," Gram replied, nodding at Mr. Carter.

"Can you tell us about the schedule for Phase II?" Robin asked.

"It's a nice coincidence that I ran into you," Mr. Carter said. "I had intended to stop by on Monday to give you an update. Demolition will begin on Phase II in late fall, around November first. I'll be delivering an offer to purchase your home by the end of next week. As I explained earlier, our first offer will be our best, and it will be valid for a limited time. In the meantime, you might want to check on the current market value of your property. I think you'll find our offer generous."

"Thank you, Mr. Carter. We appreciate the information. It appears that St. Michael's will not be demolished. Is that correct?"

"Yes, that property is owned by the diocese and is not included in our project. The church will remain where it is. If you don't have any more questions, I'll be by with a contract for you next week."

"You might call first to be sure it's a convenient time for me." Gram said with a hint of frost in her voice, "I don't recommend your just showing up unexpected like you did last time."

Mr. Carter hesitated, then reached to give Gram's hand a firm shake and left with a satisfied smile.

"Wow," Robin said as Mr. Carter walked off. "That was quick."

Gram eyed him suspiciously as he walked away. "I'm glad that the church will be spared," Gram said. "I may not be quite ready to move but I'm a practical woman and the property values around here have declined steadily for years. If the offer is as generous as Mr. Carter insinuated, then this whole renovation may be for the best."

"Housing in Dallas is less expensive than in Chicago and the weather is lots more enjoyable. I know you'll be happy there."

"I expect I will, but it's not easy to dismantle a life at 60, even when you're planning to build a new one. You'll have to give me some time to adjust to the idea." Gram said. "On Monday, I'll call a friend of mine whose husband is a realtor. He'll be able to give me an idea of the market value of our home. We'll see how Mr. Carter's idea of *generous* compares."

They'd walked in silence for several blocks when Gram reached for Robin's hand. "Robin, I just thought of something. There are two boxes of Aileen's in the attic. She packed them away right before she married Harold. Just think, she was younger then than you are now. I remember her asking if I would keep them until they got settled. I left the boxes in her room for months, then took them to the attic. They've been there, forgotten, ever since."

Robin's steps grew faster and she pulled Gram along. "Let's go see. I wonder what she wanted to save. How sad that she never came back for any of it."

"Perhaps there will be something you'd like to keep. However short it was, your reunion this summer was a happy time for both of you. That's the memory you'll want to savor."

"Tell me where to find the boxes," Robin said, her words tumbling over her shoulder as she ran up the stairs to the second floor. "I'll bring them down. The attic's way too hot in July. We can use my room for sorting stuff. Let's get started before I have to get ready for work. I can't wait to see what Mom saved."

"They should be easy to find. I wrote *AILEEN* on each box and stacked them in the far corner on the right."

Robin tugged on the cord that lowered the wooden attic stairs and clambered up as soon as the bottom rung touched the floor. She disappeared into the darkness. Moments later, a yellow light etched an angled pattern on the carpet below. "Found them!" came her disembodied voice. She reappeared at the top of the steps; arms wrapped around the first box. She carried it into her room, then scrambled back up to get the second one.

"You do the honors," Gram handed Robin a knife. The boxes sat between them on Robin's bed. "Careful," she warned as Robin attacked the tape.

As soon as the flaps were open, Robin squealed, "Look. Mom had a teddy bear just like mine."

Gram's eyes glazed, looking thirty years into the past. "She called him *Cubby*," she whispered. "I'd almost forgotten that."

"May I have him? I'm sorry I ruined my bear, but Cubby will be safe with me. I promise never to take my temper out on him." Robin squeezed the bear to her cheek. "Cubby, I'm glad to meet you."

"Of course. I'm sure you'll be good to him. Let's see what else is in here."

"I guess Harold didn't like music," Robin growled, lifting a stack of 45 rpm records from the second box. "Otherwise, why pack these away? What a shit!" She raised both hands. "I'm sorry, Gram, but he brings out the worst in me!"

"He's gone from our lives, Robin. Don't waste your anger on him. Look at this." Gram held a book with a padded cover and a small key attached to a pink ribbon. "I didn't know that Aileen kept a diary." She tightened her grip when Robin reached for the treasure.

"Gram, she was a teenager. She was a mystery to you then. Don't you want to know what she was thinking? I sure as heck do!"

Gram relaxed her grip and Robin set the diary in her lap. She fitted the tiny key into the lock and the book sprang open, stuffed with mementos and pages covered with Aileen's pretty script. "It starts in her junior year," Robin said, "right after she met Harold. Listen to this."

"He's gorgeous and so mature. I can't believe he's interested in me. Mom would shit a brick if she knew that Lisa and I sneaked into a bar. She's so old-fashioned it's pathetic. I'd be grounded forever if she found out. But, what a night! It was so worth it. I hope he calls me like he said he would. Oh, Shit! What if he DOES call? What if Mom answers? I need a story."

Robin looked up and caught Gram's pained expression. "I'm sorry. I never stopped to think that you raised *two* rebellious teenagers. How did you manage to put up with me after what you went through with my Mom? I could always tell when I had hurt you, but you never punished me… not more than an occasional grounding."

"I was nearly 20 years older and wiser by the time you were a teenager. I'd learned some hard lessons by then. When your mother clung to Harold, I realized that I was partly to blame. I was so intent upon raising her that I gave her ultimatums, not choices. I didn't take the time to listen. When you rebelled, I knew you would have to make your own decisions, so I concentrated on keeping my door open and giving you no reason to feel that you couldn't come home whenever you were ready."

"I'm grateful for that. I'm sorry for Mom and for the choices she made, but I'm grateful for all you've done for me." Robin closed Aileen's diary and put it on the nightstand. "Let's make a plan for sorting through the house. If we get started now, you'll have everything ready by November."

"Hey, Cindy," Robin said into the phone, "Want to meet up at Simpsons' for root beer floats?"

"Groovy!" Cindy said, "Meet you there in 20."

"Perfect, I need to grab a few items for Gram. See you in a shake."

The bell tinkled when Cindy pushed open the door. "Your timing is spot on, Girlfriend," Robin said, pocketing the receipt for her items. The girls climbed onto two red vinyl bar stools at the soda counter. "These have been here as long as I can remember," Robin said. They looked at one another in the blue mirror behind the counter. "What've you been up to since the trial? That was one bad-ass day."

"I have great news. I'm going to start taking classes at the community college next month. I've saved money waitressing, and Mom and Dad said they would help me with my tuition."

"That's fantastic! What are you taking?

"The basics like English and general math the first semester, then the fun begins with Bookkeeping 101 and Accounting 101. I can't wait to get started."

Bookkeeping sounds right up your alley. You're great in math. Cindy, I am proud of you for taking control of your life. It took guts to leave that shithead behind, and you did it!"

"You were right. Jake is a jerk. I needed to get him out of my life." Cindy shrugged. "I'll admit that it helps that he's behind bars because I'm still afraid of him."

"He can't do anything to either of us anymore. The judge pretty much threw away the key when he ordered the maximum sentence. Jake will be off the streets for ten years. I'll bet that put the fear of God in his goons. Nobody left in that lifeless gang has any balls. After we filed the police report for what they did to Gram, we haven't heard a peep from them." Robin said.

"You won't want to hear this, but sometimes I miss him. He was nice to me."

"Oh good grief, Cindy! Don't ever forget that the only person Jake cares about is Jake. If he was nice to you, it's because there was something in it for him. Don't look back. You need to follow the instructions in that song from "*South Pacific*," and *wash that man right outa your hair!* Soon you'll be in college and you'll meet loads of guys... decent guys. You have a future now. Forget him and all of his crap."

"I will... I promise. So, tell me about you."

"I'm helping Gram sort out the house cuz she'll be moving to Dallas soon. I'm still working at Marshall Field. I need to bank up as much cash as I can this summer, so I can work less during the school year. I need the time to study. There are four of us in my suite. We're all in the nursing program so we study together. We call ourselves the Nurseketeers. I've missed them this summer."

"That sounds way cool. Maybe I'll be able to transfer to a real college after a couple of years."

"Why not? You'll have to write and keep me posted on your new adventures."

The bell over the door tinkled and both girls sat up straighter as Lurch sauntered over to the counter. "You two did Jake wrong, you'll pay for that."

Robin and Cindy were off their stools and in his face in a flash. Robin poked his chest with one hand and shoved him with the other. "Listen up, you jerkwad. Jake is in jail and you'll be right there with him if you keep this up. We didn't take any shit off him and we aren't taking any off the likes of you!"

"But I..."

"But? But WHAT, Dimwit? The cops have you in their crosshairs after what you did to Gram. Make no mistake; they know it was you! Get a job! Get a life! Do something with your worthless self, Charles Slagger." Robin continued poking his chest as he stumbled backward.

The bell tinkled as he backed out of the drug store, and both girls laughed until tears came.

"What's going on up here?" asked Mr. Simpson, coming from the back.

Catching her breath, Robin managed to reply, "We ran off an undesirable customer. We politely suggested that Charlie Slagger get a job."

"Maybe we weren't so polite," Cindy said, still laughing.

"Good for you. I can do without the likes of him in my store. Must admit, I have a hard time picturing that lazy boy working. Look there. You two have about polished off those root beer floats. How about a refill on the house?"

"Guy, will you have dinner with Gram and me before I leave," Robin asked as she slid into the chair next to his. "Gram wants to know what's your favorite meal. She's a great cook, so you won't be disappointed."

"No chance of being disappointed. Anyone willing to make me shepherd's pie and whipped Jell-O gets five stars on my "favorite places to eat" list.

"We both get off early this Thursday. How 'bout come home with me after work and take the train to your house from there? It'll be a late night, but you can sleep in on Friday since we work the late shift."

"You're on! But only if it's lime Jell-O."

Robin nodded. "Lime Jell-O it is!" She glanced out the window. "I can't believe that summer's almost over. Gram's getting an offer on the house next week. It had better be a good one or she's gonna rip that sleazy Carter guy a new one. We've been sorting through the house, deciding what Gram should bring to Dallas. Once I leave, she'll just have the packing left to do."

"Do you think she'll need help moving boxes around? I wouldn't mind coming over to help her until I leave for school."

"That's an amazing offer, Guy. She'll say she's fine, but I know that she'd appreciate it."

"She's quite a lady, that Gram of yours."

Robin nodded. "I can't imagine where I'd be today if it weren't for Gram. She's a rock!"

"I'm sure that she grew into who she is. I have absolutely no doubt that you'll grow into one helluva woman, too. I just hope we can stay in touch so I can enjoy the venture."

"I'd like that, Guy. I do want to keep in touch. I wish we'd had more time this summer for me to get to know your family. Who knew that so much would happen in just three months? The Jake thing was drama enough, but my mom... I still can't believe that bastard killed her!"

"It's cool that your Gram is moving to Dallas. But that means you won't be coming back to Chicago. I was looking forward to your being here over Christmas. Working at Marshall Field won't be nearly as much fun with you gone. Hmmm, unless Mrs. Parker hires some really hot dude..."

Robin cuffed him on the shoulder.

"That was the best shepherd's pie ever," Guy beamed at Gram, "and the desert...," he said, licking his spoon, "none better!"

"My pleasure," Gram said. "Robin said it was your favorite. Now you two run along while I tidy up the kitchen."

"Thanks, Gram. I want to show Guy what they're planning for our neighborhood. C'mon. You won't believe how ritzy this place is gonna be."

They walked in the direction of the construction zone. "Can we talk more about being gay?" she blurted. There won't be anyone to talk to once I leave. I need to figure out if I'm gay or just weird?"

"I'll vote for weird," Guy chuckled. Robin punched his arm.

"Seriously, Guy... I do need to figure it out."

"I'm happy to listen, Robin, but I can't answer your question. There's no litmus test for gay. Besides, you don't have to decide. I told you before to keep an open mind and pay attention to your feelings."

"How did you know? When did you figure it out?"

"Well..." his reply was tentative. "It was more of an evolution than an event. "I couldn't get into it when my friends started going nutsola over girls and every conversation was about boobs and booty," Guy sucked in a breath. "Sorry, Robin. That was crude."

"No, seriously, keep talking. I get it."

"I liked girls who were smart and friendly... the same girls I'd always liked. That didn't change when I hit puberty. It took me a while to realize that I was the weird one; the other guys fit the mold. Once I figured that out, I felt like you do now... confused and curious and a bit worried."

"That's it *exactly!*"

"When I realized that I was the one who was different, I spent a lot of time watching my friends and comparing my thoughts and feelings to theirs. I certainly didn't let them know that I was interviewing them, but that's exactly what I was doing. I'd say things like "*she's hot, right?*" to see what they'd say so I'd understand what they were thinking. I wanted to know how they thought, even if I didn't think like that myself. I can't believe how analytical I was, but in the end, it was clear to me that I'm gay and I'd have to figure out what to do about it."

"What did you do next?"

"I took the easy way out. I kept my mouth shut and waited to see what would happen."

"AND?"

"Nothing. I'm good at acting like a straight guy. I say the right things and keep my secret a secret. I figure that it's the safest position to take until I have a reason to stand up for myself. I haven't met him yet, so here I am, walking gingerly in the straight world waiting for my opportunity to plunge into the gay one."

"I'm glad I asked you." Robin sighed. "In a way, you gave me the perfect answer to my question. If you felt that way and now, you're okay with who you are, then I can be okay, too. I'll give it time and trust that I'll figure it out myself."

"Well, that was easier than I expected," Guy grinned. "You're a sharp cookie, Robin. I predict that some girl is gonna make you mighty happy... if she's smart and can keep up with you." He jumped back and cradled his arm. "*OUCH!* Keep punching my arm and I'll be crippled for life." Guy laughed. "This counseling is dangerous business."

"It's Mr. Carter, Gram." Robin peeked out the living room window when the doorbell rang a second time. "He looks mighty impatient."

"He'll settle down. It won't take him long to see that pushy doesn't sit well with me," Gram said on her way to the door. When she opened it, Mr. Carter was about to ring a third time. "One ring would have been sufficient, Mr. Carter. It's polite to give folks a chance to reach the door."

Mr. Carter stammered. "I, uh, wasn't sure that you'd heard the bell."

"I'm not deaf, Mr. Carter, and the bell works just fine. You can hear it loud and clear, even from out on the porch. Were you planning to come in?"

"Uh... uh, yes, please. I have an offer for you."

"Let's go into the living room and see what you've brought."

"You'll be pleased, Mrs. Kelly. It's a generous offer."

"We'll see how pleased I am, Mr. Carter. As you recommended, I've done my homework on property values. I have been advised by a credible source on what to expect."

With a smug grin, Mr. Carter presented Gram with a sealed envelope with the lot and block number of the property; there was no address. Gram frowned. "My address is 322 West Schiller Street. I have no idea of what property this contract refers. Can I assume that I will recognize my home on the documents inside?"

"Well, uh, I'm not sure." He took the envelope from Gram, ripped it open, and unfolded the letter, checking each page. "Yes, yes... here it is on page three... 322 West Schiller Street." He sighed with relief but remained perched on the edge of his seat.

Gram reached for the letter and read it slowly. "I see that you expect me to vacate the property by October 15th."

"As I told you the other day, we'll begin demolition the first part of November. We will be disconnecting the utilities during those last two weeks of October."

Robin watched Gram's eyes move from left to right and back as she read through the document, her frown deepening as she turned the page. She nodded and smiled faintly when she reached page three. "Well, it seems you finally got to the offer," she said sarcastically, "...which, I might add, is thousands lower than I was expecting." Her eyes pierced Carter like a stiletto. "When you assured me that your offer would be generous, I expected to recover at least the market value of the property. A reputable realtor assured me that I could sell it myself for more than you're offering."

"Oh, but Mrs. Kelly... selling your property is a difficult and time-consuming project, and there are expenses associated with the sale. In the end, you rarely get what you're asking. This offer is an ironclad guarantee of sale, and there are no hidden expenses. You'll walk away with the total amount offered."

"Thank you, Mr. Carter," Gram said formally as she folded the letter and began to rise. "My realtor will take the listing and assured me thousands more than your offer. He is prepared to purchase the property himself, and he's not in business to throw money away. Shall I see you out?"

"Sit, sit, Mrs. Kelly. I'm sure we can work this out."

Gram stood, looking down at him, her face stony. She waited for him to continue. Robin turned toward the kitchen to hide a broad grin. *"Go, Gram! He's squirming just like the slippery eel you said he was."*

Looking up at Gram, frustration etched into his expression, he continued. "I'm sure the company has built-in some leeway, Mrs. Kelly. If we consider the expense associated with resorting to eminent domain, we can increase our offer. I feel sure that I can add four thousand. That's more than fair."

Still glaring down at him, Gram retorted, "Fair isn't the issue, Mr. Carter. It's not *fair* that you are commandeering my home in the first place. It's even less *fair* that you're prepared to pay less than market after assuring me I could expect a generous settlement. *Fair* isn't a word I'd toss around lightly, Mr. Carter."

"Eight thousand, Mrs. Kelly," he interrupted. "I'll add eight thousand to the offer in that letter. You'll get a check for the full amount and there will be no hidden expenses... no realtor's fee or legal fees or closing costs. The money will be all yours, Mrs. Kelly." He took a deep breath while Gram continued to stare down at him. He stood. "What do you say? That's as good as you can expect from your friend, and without the hassle of a sale. Just let me change the amount in the letter and we can both sign it to seal the deal."

"Please initial the change," Gram said, "for now. You can leave this signed document with me and bring by a clean copy of our contract for both of us to sign. Contracts with changes and scribbles can become problematic should they be challenged in the future."

"Yes, yes, of course." Mr. Carter used the arm of the chair as a desk, changing the dollar figure and signing the last page. "See,

I've initialed the change as you requested. I'll bring a clean copy for your signature. You'll have no need for a realtor."

"Thank you, Mr. Carter," said Gram as she took the signed letter from him. Without a smile, she turned toward the front door and he followed. "When you return, one ring of the doorbell will be sufficient."

Robin laughed out loud. "That was masterful. I wish I could have captured that whole thing on film. It would be a box office bonanza."

"That should do it. Whatever I've left behind will have to wait until you come to Dallas," Robin said as she stuffed Cubby into a corner of the suitcase open on her bed. "I may have to sit on this to get the locks to close."

Gram surveyed Robin's room. "You're not leaving much behind. I doubt there are many teenagers with so little stuff. I'll bet you're the most organized of all your suitemates."

"You're right, and Frannie is the least organized human being I know." We make quite a pair."

We did a fine job of sorting through the house. I couldn't have done that without you. Packing will be a piece of cake now. I'll have plenty of time to get it all done and find a home for what I'm leaving behind."

"Just think, in a few months we'll be together for good. You gave Mr. Carter a run for his money, and you got what you deserved for the house. I can't wait for you to come to Dallas."

"I have lots to do before then, Sweetheart, starting with getting you to the airport so you don't miss your plane."

Chapter 14

"I'm heeeeeeeere! Where is everybody?" Robin called as she pushed into the suite and threw her arms wide open.

Katie and Leslie tumbled out of their room and the three friends hugged.

"How can it be that the summer flew by, but it feels like a century since I've seen you?" Katie said, and hugged Robin again. "Come on. You gotta see this."

"Amazing!" Robin whooped as she stepped into the room she shared with Frannie. Frannie rushed out of the closet, a jumble of dresses in her arms. "Absolutely amazing," Robin continued. "You're already here and I actually have a bed, a chair, and a dresser. I expected a mountain of crap on every surface. Roomie, there's hope for you yet."

Frannie beamed. "Look at the closet. I only took *half!*"

"We're off to a good start, Frannie. Wanna help me put my things away?"

"We're nearly done in our room," Katie said. "We'll be back to help in a jiffy."

"Frannie, if you hand me stuff, I'll figure out what to do with it."

Frannie dumped her dresses onto her chair and lifted a pile of neatly folded clothes from Robin's open suitcase. "Mother and I spent the summer in Atlantic City. We rent a house on the beach. Daddy came weekends, then for one whole week. Look how tan I got. I hope it lasts. How long do you think a tan will last? I had to buy all new makeup because my regular shades were way too light."

"Enough about tanning, for pity sake! You look great. Can we talk about something meaningful? Did you do anything this summer but lie on the beach?"

Crestfallen, Frannie stammered, "No, not really. Mother and I did get in a lot of shopping and I read a few romance novels."

Robin rolled her eyes.

Leslie interrupted. "Katie and I are done. What can we do? We need to hurry this up so we can run over to the cafeteria and find out who's here and what's cooking with everyone. Summer was great, but it's good to be back. I missed the Nurseketeers."

"Hand me closet stuff." Katie held out her arms. "Leslie and I have extra hangers."

"I left her *lots* of hangers," Frannie insisted. "She has a whole *half* of the closet."

"So she does." Katie winked at Robin and disappeared with an armload of Robin's things.

"Voila!" Frannie announced as Robin snapped her empty suitcases shut. "We're done!" "Let's grab our suitcases," said Katie, "and we'll stow them in the basement on our way to the cafeteria."

"I didn't miss the food." Robin wrinkled her nose at choices in the cafeteria line.

The girls scanned the crowd, looking for their friends. "Frannie, over here!" Missy called, arms waving frantically.

Frannie beamed, "C'mon, there's room at her table." Missy and Frannie rushed into a bear hug, both squealing and talking at the same time. The others smiled at the love-in reunion. "You weren't supposed to be here until tomorrow," Frannie said.

"Ooooh, Sweeeeet Thing, my dad had some ol' business trip he had to make, so I got to fly in. It was so cool. I just got here an hour ago. I've been waiting for my honey bear to show up. You haven't seen J.R., have you?"

"Well, maybe…" Leslie said pointing to the entrance where two tall stocky guys stood scanning the room.

Missy shot out of her chair, waving wildly. "J.Rrrrrrrrrrr."

J.R. folded Missy into an embrace as soon as he and Mike reached the table.

"It looks like we're all accounted for," Robin said. "J.R., Mike… why don't you guys see if there's anything edible left in the line."

Robin watched Leslie follow Mike with her eyes. *She's got the hots for Mike. You go, Girl. It's time you freed yourself from Paul. Vietnam should help him grow up some, but even so, he's not for you.*

"Ooooh, girls you have to hear the scoop on Stephen," Missy said, once they were all seated again.

"That shit!" Robin said. "I hope he's up to his ass in alligators."

Raising her eyebrows and grinning from ear to ear, Missy said, "Oh honnney, he is! He won't be back to Crestmont ever! He is in *jail*. Not only was he picked up for possession, he was dealing, and, can you believe it, right here at dear ol' Crestmont."

Robin bit her lip to keep from saying, *"I told you so, Frannie,"* before Katie had a chance to shoot her a warning glance. Robin gave Katie a *thumbs up, and Katie smiled her approval.*

"His sidekicks, Greg and James, are still here in the dorm," said J.R. "They just missed being roped in with him. Seems they ratted out their best friend to avoid going to jail themselves. They're not quite as cocky as they were last year when the three of them thought they were invincible."

"Frannie, what Stephen did last year was unforgivable and there's no making that right, but he's in a world of hurt now and he deserves every iota of it," Mike said.

Leslie reached over and squeezed Mike's hand.

Robin, Katie, and Leslie struggled with the seating arrangement of large chairs in the sitting room of their suite, while Frannie continued rearranging her closet for the umpteenth time.

"This Kirkwood suite feels bigger than our suite in Hadley," Robin said.

"Hmmm, I think you're right," Katie said, "but I liked the layout in Hadley better. I think we've finally found the best arrangement for the furniture in here..." She flopped into her designated chair.

"I'm going to get my schedule and check on Frannie," Robin said. "She may never finish if I don't prod her." Robin walked into her bedroom. "Frannie, what's all the crap on my bed? You were fine with the way we left the room before dinner."

"I'm taking out the winter stuff to make more room. That's all that's on your bed. I'm going to pack it back into my trunk and I'll have your bed cleared in two shakes. Will you help me take my trunk down to storage when I get done?" Frannie asked.

"Oh, good grief! Yes, I'll help if it will get you to hurry up. Give me your class schedule. We're checking to see if we all have the same classes again this year. I'll be in the sitting room when you are ready.

"Frannie's being Frannie," Robin announced slumping into her chair. "She's rearranging again."

"You have to quit letting her get under your skin like that," said Leslie. "Chill out or you'll get an ulcer."

"Good advice." Katie ran her finger down her class list. "I have Western Civilization Literature on Monday, Wednesday, and Friday at 8 and right behind that is Western Civilization History. Drats, the two classes are all the way across campus from one another."

"Yep, that sucks, but I have those same classes and so does Frannie. We'll have to hustle to get to that history class on time." Robin said.

"Then it's back to Sheppard Hall for General Psych but we have an hour between history and psych. That's not enough time to do much of anything," Leslie said, "but it does let us stop at the dorm to drop off our books so we don't have to schlep them all morning."

"Shit. On Wednesdays, we have Chapel right after History, so no time for swapping books," Robin said.

"But we won't have to hustle anywhere. Isn't History in that auditorium in the basement of the chapel? We're already in the building." Katie offered.

"You're right," said Robin. "That's definitely a plus."

"Tuesday, Wednesday, and Thursday we gotta get lunch at noon. That's the peak time in the cafeteria, so we'll have to move our butts to be on time for our 1:00," Robin noted. "What about your Tuesdays and Thursdays?"

"I have Gym at 8 then Anatomy and Physiology at 10. Thank heavens for the break there. I'd be embarrassed to show up in A&P without a shower." Katie said.

"Agreed," Robin said. "And that matches mine and Frannie's schedule too."

"Leslie, do you have the same classes?" asked Katie.

"Everything but gym. I'm in the sports program, so I don't take gym."

"I think we lucked out." Robin said, "The Nurseketeers can study together again!"

"I have basketball at 2 pm on Monday, Wednesday, and Friday, so I won't make the Nurseketeers study sessions until 3:30 or so."

"I need to work my schedule at the *Steakhauz*," Robin said. "It would be nice to work lunch on Monday and Friday, but the evening shift generates more tips. I'll go tomorrow and see what's what."

"We're done and still no sign of Frannie," Robin shrugged. "I could stock the whole jewelry department quicker'n she can organize her clothes."

"I heard that," said Frannie. "It didn't take me that long. I'm done and you promised to help me get my trunk to the basement. By the way, what is A&P?"

"It stands for Anatomy and Physiology, Dimwit," Robin said. "We'll need a shower *after* A&P from what I hear. I'm not sure you'll need to worry what you smell like from gym, Katie. Tuesdays and Thursday afternoons might not be my best days for working dinner at *Rob Rory's*."

"I'm not a dimwit. I just didn't know what the initials stood for. Besides, I thought you were going to quit being mean."

"Okay, okay. Let's take care of the trunk."

Chapter 15

The aroma of good food and controlled chaos enveloped Robin as she pushed open the door to Rob Rory's Steakhauz. She waved as she approached Maddie at the hostess station. "Can I assume I still work here, boss?" Robin saluted. "I'm present and ready for duty."

"Lemme think about it," Maddie quipped, then pulled her into a hug. "Welcome back. You definitely work here, and I hope you're ready to start your first shift 'cuz we're short-handed. Look at this crowd! The summer help left last week and you college brats are just returning. Mom and Dad will be glad to see you. Seriously, can you stay?"

"Sure. I'm presentable enough," she assessed her skirt and blouse. "I just need to let the girls know I won't be back for dinner. I'll go say hi to your dad and use his phone."

"Mom is in the kitchen. Stick your head in on your way; it will make her day to see you're back. She's been meeting herself coming and going all week. How did your summer go?"

"I've got oodles to tell ya, but the best news is that Gram is coming to live here. I hope your mom and dad will help find a place for her to stay."

"We have a guest room and I know Mom would invite her to stay in a heartbeat."

"She's coming for good. We had to sell the house and..." Robin stopped when a couple approached the hostess station. "I'll fill you in on all the details later."

"Welcome back," Maddie said, and turned to seat the couple at one of the few remaining empty tables.

Mr. Davis looked up when Robin rapped on the doorframe, and a broad grin spread across his face. "Robin! You're a sight for sore eyes. Come in and sit down ...but not for too long. I hope you're here to work because we're short-handed. Did I mention that it's nice to have you back?"

"I can stay if I can use your phone to call the dorm."

He pushed the phone toward her, and Robin dialed. She relayed her change of plans to Leslie. "Can you let the front desk know that I'll be late getting in tonight. I don't want to get locked out my first night back." She hung up and pushed the phone back in place. "Mr. Davis, I have something to ask, you."

"Yes?"

"I was hoping that you and Mrs. Davis might help me find a place for my grandmother to stay when she gets here. She'll buy a house once she's settled, but in the meantime..."

"We'll be glad to help. Roberta knows lots of people with garage apartments. We'll talk more about it later. Right now, I need you on the floor. If it's this busy at 4:30, imagine what it will be like by 6:00."

The next evening, Katie said, "We need a *welcome back* celebration. The College Diner fits our budget, so how about it? Let's have dinner out."

"Let's do it," Robin replied, and the girls took off for their evening out. They chatted ceaselessly from the time they left the dorm 'til they were settled around a table at the College Diner.

A startled cry behind Robin captured her attention and she turned to see their waitress glaring at a scruffy young man at the next table.

"What's wrong, Taaaahnya?" He squinted at her nametag. "Can't I get a little piece of black ass with my burger? After all, I'm paying a pretty penny for it."

Tonya spun on her heel and marched toward a man standing beside the register. He had been watching the spectacle, but made no move toward Tonya.

"Get someone else to serve the jerks in booth eight. I don't need to put up with that crap."

"Come on, Tonya, they're just guys. Suck it up and get back to work. They're paying customers, so cut them some slack."

"You're shittin' me! My job description doesn't include groping and racial slurs."

"It does if you want to keep working here," he growled. "They didn't mean any harm. If you can't take a bit of ribbing, that's your problem. You want this job, you'll get back to work."

Teeth clenched, Tonya considered her options. She squared her shoulders and returned to the table, stopping well out of reach of the occupants. Her voice dripped with sarcasm. "What can I get you, Gentlemen."

Robin watched the interchange, mouth agape. When Tonya approached their table, she couldn't hold back. "That's bullshit! No one should get away with that kind of behavior. What was your boss thinking?"

Tonya replied bitterly, "He thinks I'm a black bitch working for minimum wage and the customer is always right… as long as he's white!" Tonya looked past Robin at the rest of the girls and her shoulders sagged, "I am so sorry. That was out of line. I wasn't thinking. What can I get you folks?"

Robin huffed, "You don't need to apologize."

Katie and Leslie nodded their agreement. Frannie sat wide-eyed and silent.

"*DOES she*, Frannie?" Robin glared at her roommate. "Tonya doesn't need to apologize for being upset about being treated like a second-class citizen."

"I… I guess not. I don't know any Negros. I don't know what kind of citizens they are."

"Jeeeeeeeeeez, Frannie. We're *Americans*. Everyone is supposed to be equal, no matter what color their skin is or where their ancestors came from. And… Negro is an old word. Tonya's *black* and she's a human being, just like you and me. What would *YOU* do if that guy groped you and called you names?"

"I don't know. Nobody ever did that to me."

"*That's* your problem. You live under a rock and you have no clue what's going on around you. Well, Tonya *is* the world around you, so wake up and stick up for her. No one at this table is eating in a restaurant that treats people like those asswipes at the next table or the total bastard that's running the place do. *Are we?*" Robin looked to Leslie and Katie for confirmation.

"Let's leave," said Katie. "If we can't do anything else, we can at least let them know that some of their customers won't put up with bigots."

"Please stay," Tonya said quietly. "I can't afford to get fired. I need this job, crappy as it is. I just transferred to Crestmont and I'll have to drop out if I can't make tuition. Don't leave. I'm used to guys like that and I didn't expect my manager to do anything. I should have known better."

Robin looked to her suitemates. Katie and Leslie nodded; Frannie sat still, dumbfounded. "We'll stay. The last thing we want is to get you fired. I'd like a hamburger medium rare with fries crispy. Frannie, quit staring and tell Tonya what you want to eat."

Tonya smiled her appreciation and left to fill their orders, giving table eight a wide berth.

"We can't continue to put up with behavior like that," Leslie said. "We need to stand up and make a difference. I'm going to get active in the Student Nurses Association. Sam is the president this year. You remember her, don't you?"

"Of course," Katie replied. "Joining SNA again this year is a fine idea, as long as it doesn't take too much time from studying. It won't do any good to get active in support of women and nursing and then not graduate."

"Good point," Robin added. "We'll have to get good at keeping lots of balls in the air. I have to work, so it'll take some juggling to fit SNA into my schedule, but I'd like to do that with you."

"SNA's sorta like a sorority for nurses. Do they have parties?" Frannie asked. "They'd have to hook up with some fraternity cuz J.R.'s the only guy in nursing at Crestmont, as far as I know."

"Geez Louise!" Robin cried, then saw Katie shake her head. She took a calming breath and shot Katie a *"got it"* smile.

"Frannie," Leslie said, "let me explain. SNA is the organization for student nurses. We participated some last year, remember? I'm sure they have social activities, too, but their purpose is to foster professional development by introducing standards of nursing practice, professional ethics, and the variety of opportunities available to nurses. I see joining SNA as a chance to be part of nursing before I graduate and get my license. I was hoping that we'd all join. After all, we *are* the *Nurseketeers*."

Tonya arrived balancing all four plates on her arms. "Let's see. This one is yours," she said as she set Frannie's plate in front of her."

Frannie pulled her plate close. "Thanks, I'm Frannie."

Katie and Leslie introduced themselves as Tonya deftly placed their orders on the small table.

"I'm Robin, and I'm impressed. It looks like you've done this before."

Tonya smiled at the compliment. "I've been waiting tables since I was old enough to carry a tray. When my dad died, mom went to work at a restaurant in our neighborhood and I practically grew up there. After I graduate, I pledge never to lift a tray or take another food order as long as I live."

"Ditto that!" Robin agreed. "I work at Rob Rory's. I'm grateful for the job and the Davises are great bosses, but waiting tables is nowhere near my idea of a career choice." Robin's eyes widened,

"Wait a minute.... Rob Rory's is *nothing* like this dive. I mean, the Davises would *never* tolerate diners treating their employees like those guys treated you. Why don't you see if you can work there? Mr. Davis does most of his hiring at the beginning of the semester."

Tonya shook her head. "I don't think so. I can handle this place."

"But you shouldn't *have* to put up with that. It would never happen…"

Tonya interrupted, "I'm fine, Robin. But thanks for thinking of it. I need to go." She gave Robin an apologetic smile and hurried toward another table where the manager was seating six people.

"Hmmm," Robin muttered. "That was weird. As soon as I mentioned working at Rob Rory's, something changed… or it could be my imagination."

"For a restaurant with a crappy personality, they make pretty good food," Leslie commented, "and the prices aren't bad either. Rob Rory's isn't outrageous, but it's too rich for my budget."

"That might be why Tonya prefers to stay here," Katie suggested. "It's probably more like what she's used to."

"Maybe," Robin mused. "Tonya does seem to know how to look out for herself. It's just unthinkable that she should have to protect herself from jerks. No restaurant should tolerate disrespectful behavior, and a manager should support his employees when they're right. *The customer is always right* should only apply to customers who *deserve* it."

"Spoken like a true idealist," Leslie laughed. "Let's eat."

Robin stopped at the empty hostess station and searched the nearly full restaurant for Maddie. On the far side of the room, Maddie stood by a table in animated conversation with two good-looking young men. Her hand rested on the shoulder of the one closest to her and she was leaning in to hear what the other one was saying. Robin watched for a few moments, smiling. *"Maddie has a boyfriend after all. Maybe they met over the summer."*

When Maddie returned, Robin said, "Sooooo, is there something you want to tell me?"

"About...?" Maddie looked confused.

"Like maybe you have a boyfriend I don't know about? Gotta admit that guy is cute... *if* you like cute guys," she said.

The comment seemed to take Maddie by surprise. She eyed Robin quizzically, then shook her head and replied, "Nope, definitely not a boyfriend," she said. "Just guys I've known since I was a kid. They're...." Maddie hesitated, then asked, "Are you up for section four this evening? We're going to be busy."

"Hmmm. I wonder what she was going to say." Robin glanced at Maddie's friend, then back to Maddie, "Sure thing," she replied and picked up an order pad.

"Maddie's good-looking, bright, and fun to be around... yet no boyfriend... and what was she going to say about the guys before she changed her mind. Hmmm... I wonder if Maddie could be gay... wouldn't that be cool! if I ask and she's not, I don't think she'd be upset with me."

The shift passed in a blur and Robin didn't have a chance to think any more about Maddie. On her way back to the dorm, she weighed her options. *"If I ask Maddie about being gay and she's not, what's the worst that could happen. Shit, I wish Guy weren't so freakin' far away; I need someone to talk to."*

Robin lay seething, then got up and turned off Frannie's alarm. "Wake up, dammit," she insisted, shaking her roommate's shoulder.

Frannie pulled the covers over her head without opening her eyes. "Later, Mother. Come get me later."

Robin yanked the covers from Frannie's head. "FRANNIE," she said, hoping she hadn't awakened Katie and Leslie. "I'm not your mother. Get up NOW or you're on your own. Getting up first was *your* idea. Personally, I don't care if you sleep all day."

Frannie opened her eyes, struggling to focus. "Is it morning already? I was dreaming about the beach. Why didn't my alarm go off?"

Robin took a deep breath. "Just get up. When you said you wanted the bathroom first, I thought this year would be different. You have exactly thirty minutes before I kick you out of the bathroom whether you're done or not. We planned just enough bathroom time for Katie, Leslie, and me to get ready. Today's our first day of classes and we're not going to be late. MOVE."

"I'll be ready, you'll see," Frannie promised, then slid out of bed and stumbled into the bathroom.

Robin chuckled. The outfit that Frannie had taken thirty minutes to choose the night before was laid out on her chair. *"She's making an effort."*

Katie stuck her head in the door. "I heard the shower. I just wanted to see if it was actually Frannie in there."

"Amazing, isn't it? She slept through her alarm, but it didn't take too much coaxing to get her out of bed."

"Well, I'm impressed. Come have a cup of coffee while we wait for the bathroom. Leslie brought a coffeepot for our baby kitchenette."

"Way cooool."

At 7:00, loaded with oversized Western Civ Literature and History texts, the *Nursketeers* left for the cafeteria. "Frannie, you should be proud of yourself," said Katie. "You made a promise and kept it."

Frannie beamed at the compliment.

"Now you need to figure out how to hear your alarm. I'm not getting up thirty minutes early every morning," Robin said.

Deflated, Frannie replied, "I didn't hear it at all."

Robin relented. "We'll figure something out."

When the girls entered the crowded cafeteria, Missy stood, arms waving. "Over here," she called. "We saved seats for you."

Gratefully, they dropped their books, got in line, and filled their trays. Mike saved the seat beside him for Leslie. Robin looked up to see Tonya balancing books and a tray, frantically searching for a place to sit. "Look, Tonya from the diner is here and she's looking for a seat," she said. "I'll go get her."

Robin returned with Tonya and introduced her to Missy, J.R., and Mike. "We met Tonya at the College Diner the other night. She's a helluva waitress. She carried all four of our meals out at once like it was nothing."

"Lots of practice," Tonya smiled. "I've got Western Civ Lit at 8:00 so I'm gonna wolf this down. I spent the night at my mom's and the bus was late. It didn't leave me much time."

"That's where we're going," Robin said. It's cool that we have a class together. What's your major?"

"So far it's general business. I want to own my own company, but I'm not sure what it will be. All I know is restaurants, and I'm positive that it will *not* have anything to do with food service. I figure part of my education will be figuring out what I'm interested in. I'm keeping my options open."

"That sounds reasonable," Robin said. "We're all nursing students, except Missy and Mike here… J.R.'s the only guy in the nursing program; at least he was last year. Hey, J.R., maybe you set a good example and more guys enrolled this year. I think guys have a lot to offer in nursing. After all, nurses aren't handmaidens anymore."

"I've never thought about nursing," Tonya said. "Could be an option."

Leslie piped up, "Let's eat or we'll be late for class. If we hurry, we might all be able to sit together."

"We made it in plenty of time," Katie said as they approached the Chapel for their second class. "It didn't take as long to make it all the way across campus as I thought it would. I enjoyed Western Civ Lit. I hope Western Civ History is as interesting."

The group found seats together in the third row. "Lucky us," Robin said. "Not quite front row center, but almost. I like being able to see over the people in front of me."

"Welcome to Western Civilization History." Mrs. Rockford stood beside the podium, not behind it. *"That's a good sign,"* Robin thought. *"Maybe she won't spend the hour lecturing us.* "She looks enthusiastic," Robin whispered to Tonya.

"Just last week," Mrs. Rockford began, "we celebrated the fifty-first anniversary of an important milestone in our country. On August 26, 1910, the 19th Amendment was ratified. It gave women in America the right to vote. Last week, to commemorate that event, Congresswoman Bella Abzug submitted a resolution to Congress to designate August 26th as *Women's Equality Day.*"

There were some audible groans. "Gentlemen, make no mistake... women's equality is important for men as well. Along with recognition and freedom comes responsibility. Men no longer bear the weight of running the country alone. Competition for employment makes the workforce stronger and motivates individuals to be prepared to compete for the positions they want."

Leslie stood. "But isn't it true that women still have to be twice as good as men to compete?"

"Yes, that's sometimes the case, but a substantial change in culture never happens quickly. Despite the progress that women have made in becoming educated and broadening their employment options, women are still perceived as homemakers and men as breadwinners. More noticeable is our gender-specific vision of employment. Compared to men, there are proportionally fewer women doctors and lawyers and business executives, and there are even fewer male nurses, secretaries, or teachers in the primary grades."

"We seem to be making even fewer strides in racial equality," Tonya said. Hers was the only black face in the class.

Mrs. Rockford waited to see if any student would break the uncomfortable silence.

"Tonya, *you're* here," Robin said into the void. "That's a good start."

Students called out, "Right!" and "Go, Girl!"

"Our country has a long way to go in turning our intentions into reality," Mrs. Rockford agreed. "The important thing about history is that it prepares us to create our future. This Western Civ class is all about making that connection. I think we're off to a good start."

Robin and Leslie walked back to the dorm, side by side. Waves of heat made the sidewalk shimmer. Katie and Frannie walked ahead. "I thought Dr. Rockford was right on about the rights of women," Leslie said. "The guys in class squirmed the whole time she was talking."

"Yep, she's got her head screwed on right. I would love to have been on the front lines at that *women's strike for equality* she talked about. I didn't even know it was going on, I was so caught up in my own problems at home." Robin said. "Yet again that scum father of mine and asshole Jake made my life a living hell… I need to keep creeps like them out of my life."

"There was a *NOW* conference in March last year and there should be one this coming spring. Who knows, we could become part of that movement and make a real difference," Leslie said. "We could lead our own March across campus to bring attention to the issues here."

"There's an idea! You mentioned that you wanted to get involved in SNA," Robin said. "Maybe the members would be interested in women's rights and that would be a great platform for you. We could mobilize the nursing students, then get support from the sororities… and maybe even some of the faculty, like Dr. Rockford. You were talking about running for an office in SNA for next year. All that would certainly help you get known and elected down the road."

"Wow! You have a point; getting known for quality work is key to being recognized. I'll have to develop a plan to get others motivated to join the fight for right!"

"That sounds like your campaign slogan: *Join the Fight for Right!* We all have friends who are involved in activities outside of nursing. They can help us gain support for the rights of women across campus and promote your success in the long run."

"Hey," Robin called to Katie and Frannie. "You two, hold up a minute," The four girls gathered under the ancient oak tree between the Chapel and Kirkwood hall, and Robin described what she and Leslie had been discussing.

Katie didn't hesitate. "I'm in all the way. In high school, I put up with kids calling me names because I'm Indian. It would be great to help stop that kind of behavior. It's not just men who think they're entitled. The racial divide is as big an issue as the gender gap."

Finally finding her voice, Frannie said, "I don't know, this could get us into trouble... marching across campus like that."

"Good grief, Frannie, for someone who's had her own round of trouble with a man, it seems like you would be on track with this plan," Robin said.

"I... I... I would but I... I... like guys, I wouldn't want someone to think I am... fruity...you know," she said, flipping her hand.

"Shit! You didn't hear anything Dr. Rockford said in class today." Robin asked. "She didn't say anything about feminist activities being related to lesbians. She didn't mention sexuality at all. She talked about the rights of women."

"But..." Frannie began.

"You're an idiot! Women didn't even get the right to vote until 1920 and that was after the Suffragettes were abused and thrown in the friggin' jail for fighting for the rights that you take for granted."

"I..."

"Don't bother! We're going to be late if we don't get to the dorm for our psych books." Robin said.

The Nurseketeers hurried to the dorm and gathered their books. On the way to their psych class, Leslie said, "Frannie, I understand your concerns about getting in trouble for demonstrating. We need to organize our thoughts about our mission and determine how we want to convey our ideas to others. This is a huge issue and certainly one we can all get behind."

"We need to check out the NOW organization and see if our goals fit well with their mission. They might be set up to support local initiatives." Katie offered.

"Someone in the library should be able to help us figure out how to contact them," Robin said. "Maybe Mrs. Rockford would be interested in helping us. She obviously supports women's rights, or she wouldn't have been so passionate about it in class today."

"You're right," Leslie said. "There are activist events scheduled all the time on campus. We just need to find out how to get approval for whatever we plan. I think we can make this happen."

"Right on! We are women!" Robin said. "We are the *Nurseketeers*! We can do anything we set our minds to do!"

"Let's get to the library straight after lunch so we can get a study room on the fourth floor where we can talk without being shushed," Katie said.

"Good idea," said Leslie and Robin at the same time.

"I'm going to spend the afternoon with Missy," Frannie announced. "We have to catch up."

"You don't waste any time making bad decisions, do you, Dimwit? Now is the time to be creating good habits. If anyone should have learned that, it's you."

"But there's hardly anything to study. We've only had one day of classes. How much time can it take to review one day's assignments? Geez!"

"Go! I forgot how important gossiping with Missy is to your future… and how could I have forgotten what a *terrific* student you are?" said Robin.

"Robin's right, Frannie," Katie said soothingly. "Setting a study schedule at the beginning of the semester is the right thing to do. You, of all people, should know how hard it is to catch up. We're the *Nursketeers* after all. We're in this together."

Frannie brightened. "I'll tell Missy that we'll have lots of time over the holiday weekend to catch up.

"Good," Robin said "You're catching on."

At 3:15, Robin gathered her books. "I'm going to work early so I can talk to Mr. Davis. He said they would help find a place for Gram to stay. I'll see you guys tonight."

Robin dropped her books in the dorm and hurried toward the Steakhauz.

"Tonya, wait up," Robin yelled at a figure nearly a block ahead. "*At least I think that's Tonya.*" The figure turned around and waved.

"Where are you off to?" asked Tonya. "It's too early for work."

I was going to ask you the same thing. "I'm going in early so I can talk to my boss. My grandmother is moving to Dallas this fall and I need some help finding her a place to stay. How about you?"

"Heading home. Do you have time to wait for the bus with me? It won't be here for another twenty minutes."

"Sure. We were all glad that you spoke up in Western Civ this morning. Leslie wants to organize a women's march and I'm all for it. If she gets permission, would you be interested in helping with it? Racial equality is just as important as gender equality."

"That would mean a lot to me, but I work five days a week and can't sacrifice any study time. I'm here on scholarship and I'm determined to have an A average. There aren't many scholarships that send black kids to upscale white schools and I can't let anything mess that up. Getting my degree at Crestmont means everything to me"

"Makes sense to me. We'll keep you posted and hope you can join us. It must be tough having to take a bus to school when you have early classes. I thought you lived on campus."

"Actually, I live just a couple of blocks from here. I have an efficiency over the flower store on Hall street. The scholarship includes meals, but it doesn't include housing. I guess they figure inner-city kids have a roof over their heads but not enough to eat. I'm grateful for the cafeteria cuz I don't have much of a kitchen. I save by not having to buy food and the jerks at the College Diner let me eat there when I work. It's about the only nice thing they do. Right now, I'm going to my mom's house."

"Are you coming back to work tonight?"

"I work all weekend, so I have two days during the week off. Usually, I study until the library closes, but today my mom has a doctor's appointment and I want to go with her. It's just Mom and me."

"I hope she's okay. It's just Gram and me, too, so I understand you might be concerned. I take Gram's health for granted, I guess, cuz she's never been sick."

"Yeah. We'll see. She just doesn't feel well, and I couldn't talk her into seeing a doctor. Then a friend of hers recommended a guy she thinks walks on water and doesn't charge an arm and a leg, so she agreed to go. I'm going to make sure she doesn't change her mind."

The screech of the braking bus startled them. "Wow, that was a fast twenty minutes. I'll see you Wednesday morning." Tonya waved as the bus door huffed shut.

"Come on in." Mr. Davis waved Robin to the chair by his desk. "So, tell me about your grandmother. When is she coming and how can we help?"

"She needs to be out of the house by October 15th."

"Let's get Roberta in here; she's the real estate queen."

"Did I hear my name and royalty in the same sentence? Someone must appreciate my talents," Roberta Davis grinned as she sank into a chair. "So, Robin, what's this I hear about your grandmother coming to town? How terrific! Now you can work the holidays instead of abandoning us for Chicago."

"Our whole neighborhood's being demolished and it's gonna turn into something we can't afford. Gram got a good price for the house from the construction company. You should have seen her manage that shyster who thought he could low-ball an offer. He learned in a hurry you don't mess with Gram! Anyhow, she'll be here by mid-October. Do you think we can find her a place by then? I figure she'll buy a house after she's lived here a while and gets to know Dallas."

"I have several friends with garage apartments. Do you think one bedroom will be enough? Storing her furniture won't be a problem; we own a building with plenty of space. Let's see... we have about six weeks to find just the right place, and if we don't find one in time, we have a guest room."

"Thank you so much. With school and working, I wouldn't have much time to search, and I don't know Dallas at all."

"Ahhh, but helping you is helping us," said Roberta.

As soon as the suitemates entered the A&P lab, Robin wrinkled her nose and Frannie pinched hers shut. "What is that awful smell?" Frannie asked.

"You'll see."

"Come on in, ladies and gentlemen," said the gray-bearded man standing at the front. "When you're settled in, there should be two students at each station."

The suitemates paired up: Robin and Frannie, Katie and Leslie. Robin saw J.R. in the back of the room, sharing a station with another classmate.

"Yuck," Frannie said, pointing. "That's a dead cat!"

"What did you expect, a plastic mannequin?"

"Well, no, but I didn't know we would be cutting up kitty cats."

"Give me strength..." Robin sighed.

"Welcome to Anatomy and Physiology lab. I am Dr. Matthew Hixon. Over the course of the semester, each team will dissect the cat at your workstation, layer by layer. You must be careful with your dissection because your final exam will require that you point out the various anatomical structures."

Dr. Hixon recognized a raised hand on the far side of the room. "Shouldn't we be wearing gloves and masks to cut up this cat?"

Frannie nodded her head in agreement.

"That isn't necessary. The cats have been in formaldehyde for some time and that will have killed any pathogens. Buck up, folks."

"*Prissy Frannie is gonna croak,*" thought Robin.

"Anatomy lab provides a three-dimensional view of the body. The small case on each table holds a scalpel or knife and two pairs of forceps or tweezers, one rat-tooth and one smooth. There are two hemostats; those are the instruments with finger rings that clamp shut. There is also one pair of scissors and a metal probe in each case. These instruments are your tools for the semester. The instruments are numbered to match your station. Do not abuse them. At the conclusion of each lab session, I expect you to clean the instruments with these wipes," he instructed, holding a package up for the students to see. "There is a package at each station. The graduate assistants and I will take it from there. We'll do the final cleaning of the instruments and store your cats for the next lab session."

"The schedule has instructions for planning for each lab. I expect you to come prepared. Safety is always our first priority. Remember that you are using sharp instruments and do try to avoid cutting yourself or those around you."

"Today we will make a skin incision in the anterior abdominal wall. Follow the directions in your workbook. As you dissect through the tissues make sure you can identify each layer as it is identified in the diagram. Later, we will explore the nervous and vascular systems as well as the larger organs of the body. Listen carefully as I explain how to make the first incision."

"I'm not touching that thing," Frannie whispered sliding the knife towards Robin.

"Good Lord!" Robin huffed. "Give me that thing. It's going to be your turn next, so suck it up, Frannie. You'd better pay attention and do a good job. I'm not failing this course because of you."

Robin wielded the scalpel and Frannie pointed to the pictures in the manual. They began to identify the first layers of skin, fascia, and muscle. "This is actually pretty cool. Look at this, Frannie. It's the fascia," she said, pointing out the layer with the probe she had just identified.

"Yep, it looks sorta like this picture," said Frannie.

By the end of the class, Frannie had lost some of her initial trepidation and they were both engrossed in the dissection. They tidied up their station and joined their suitemates. J.R. came up behind them, "Y'all heading to dinner? Can I tag along?"

"You bet," said Robin, and the group walked toward the cafeteria, chatting about their experience in the lab.

They carried their trays to a large table of nursing students in the back corner of the cafeteria. Two people at the next table got up and moved to the other side of the room. Frannie waved frantically to Missy who had just passed the dessert station. When Missy leaned down to give J.R. a hug, she grabbed her nose and backed up. "Uck. Y'all stink. What is that smell, Honey Bear? You certainly don't smell like honey right now. You reek like something died," she said and backed away from the table.

The nursing students teared up, laughing hysterically. "The formaldehyde must have fried our sense of smell," J.R. said, reaching for Missy as she continued to back up.

Wagging her finger at him, she said, "Oh no you don't. You won't be coming near me until you shower. You might have to soak for a loooong time to get rid of that awful smell."

"But ..."

"No buts about it! I'm sitting on the other side of the room with my sorority sisters. Let's hope y'all's perfume doesn't drift our way. I'll meet up with you later in the game room *after* you shower with LOTS of soap." Missy backed away holding her tray and her nose at the same time.

Chapter 16

" Welcome to the Sophomore Nursing Seminar. I'm Ms. Judy Langston. I'll be leading the class and with your participation, we'll have a semester of engaging dialogue. This is my fourth year at Crestmont. Pediatrics is my specialty and I have a special place in my heart for children who must endure the trials of illness."

Frannie's attention was riveted on Ms. Langston. Frannie perked up at the mere mention of kids, and Robin knew she would lap up everything Ms. Langston said. *"This is one class she'll take seriously this year."*

Robin scanned the circle of chairs. *"Looks pretty much like the same group as last year. J.R.'s still the only male nursing student."*

"We'll begin our seminar with a discussion of the Crestmont University Student Nurses Association, the SNA. I have the privilege of serving as the Faculty Advisor for the chapter this year. I encourage you to join because involvement in nursing professional organizations is essential to your growth as a professional. The SNA will introduce you to emerging trends in healthcare and legislative issues that affect nursing practice. The members are the voice of the future of nursing. Participating in the organization is an opportunity for you to become leaders and gain recognition for your contributions. We also have social activities that promote your engagement with one another and with the community." Ms. Langdon acknowledged Frannie's waving hand.

"Wasn't the Halloween party for the children last fall sponsored by SNA?"

"Yes, that's right. Please tell me your name. It won't be long before I know all of you, but in the meantime, please introduce yourself when you speak."

"I'm Frannie Braun. I had a great time at the Halloween party last year. I hope we do it again this year. There was a special little girl I met, and I'd love to see her again."

"Well, you're in luck, Frannie. The children's Halloween party is an annual event. The Freshman Seminar class helps to sack and distribute candies. Our Sophomore class will help the SNA members set up and take down the decorations. Like last year, we'll wear costumes and engage with the children. Many of these children have had traumatic experiences like family violence, the loss of a parent, or a hospitalization. We can ensure that their impression of nurses is positive. The older ones may even ask you questions about becoming a nurse."

Ms. Langston acknowledged Robin's raised hand. "I'm Robin Hart. You mentioned that some of these children may have come from abusive homes. Would the SNA consider sponsoring an event to advocate for women's and children's rights? A group of us were considering a March across campus to bring attention to these issues."

"That's an excellent question and certainly a proactive move. There have been campus Marches in the past that made the news, at least locally. I recommend that you come to the SNA meeting tonight. This year our meetings will be held on the second Wednesday of the month at 7 pm in one of the conference rooms in the Student Union. You can present your idea at the meeting. In the meantime, I'll find out what's involved in getting permission to conduct such an event."

Leslie winked at Robin.

"During the year we'll participate in a variety of community service initiatives, including food drives and CPR classes for the community."

Robin was concentrating on the March potential. She snapped back to the present when Leslie said, "Asking Ms. Langston about a March was a groovy move. Do you think we can convince the powers that be to let us have our March across campus?"

"Why not?" Robin said. "All we need is a good plan and a leader and we have you! You know the Nurseketeers are behind you all the way. I think we should include women's rights along with violence since often it's women and children who are abused. I'm glad I don't have to work tonight so I can go to the meeting. You'll need to present the idea so that people will associate the project with you."

"I suppose you're right. I do want to get involved in SNA and I'm sure I'll want to run for office for next year. Will you help me with what I should say?"

"You bet. We can use some of our study time before dinner to plan."

"It looks like most of the sophomore nursing class showed up," Robin said as the Nurseketeers signed in for the SNA meeting. I hope they'll all be interested in the March."

"Glad I caught you," said Ms. Langston. "Dean Abbott, the Dean of Student Affairs, is the person you will need to see to arrange for the March. If the SNA members vote to back the initiative, you'll have a better chance of gaining his approval."

"Thank you, Ms. Langston," Leslie said. "I'm going to take the lead and introduce our idea to the group this evening."

"The Nurseketeers are here to support the proposal," Robin said.

"I'm supporting this motley team, too," said J.R. who'd walked up while Leslie was speaking. "I think it is a fantastic idea."

Frannie leaned in and gave him a big hug. "You're wonderful!"

"Let's get seats or we'll wind up standing against the wall in the back," Leslie said as she marshaled the group to seats near the front of the room.

"Welcome everyone," Samantha began when the hubbub subsided. "My name is Samantha Kensington, but please call me Sam. I am the Crestmont University SNA President this year. I'd like to begin our meeting by introducing the other chapter officers who are seated in the first row."

"Cool," Robin whispered to Leslie. "Sally Adams is Secretary/Treasurer. She was our Hadley dorm resident assistant last year. Knowing two people on the Board might help us move this initiative forward."

"True," Leslie whispered back. "That and Ms. Langston's support gives me hope. I've got a case of the nerves!" Leslie's hands were twisted in knots and her thumbs twirled in circles.

Robin covered Leslie's fidgety hands with her own and whispered, "You'll do fine, we're here for you."

When Sam reached "New Business" on the meeting agenda, Robin poked Leslie in the ribs and Leslie raised her hand.

"Leslie," Sam said, "what do you have for us?"

Leslie stood as she'd seen the others do before speaking. "I... I'm Leslie Bleu. I represent a group of Sophomores who are interested in organizing a campus March against Violence to demonstrate our support for that initiative. Many of you participated in the Halloween event for the Children's Home last year. Some of those kids come from violent home settings, so we're already on board with the concept. We've considered including other initiatives such as women's rights and racial equality since they are closely related, and all involve equal rights and respect for all individuals. We request that SNA back the event and help gain support for it from other campus groups. If you agree to support the initiative, we will seek Dean Abbott's approval. We ask for your vote in moving forward with the activity." Leslie exhaled as if she had been holding her breath, then flopped down into her seat, spent.

Sam acknowledged Sally's raised hand. Standing and turning to face the audience, Sally said, "I am in favor of SNA's supporting this initiative. I move that we form a planning committee for a March against Violence and that Leslie be the committee chair."

A "second the motion" came from the back of the room and Sam recognized a variety of individuals who asked questions or made suggestions. When there were no more hands waving for recognition, Sam asked, "Are we ready for a vote on the motion?"

A chorus of *You bet*, *For sure*, and *Right ons*" made Sam smile. "All in favor…"

The motion is passed unanimously. "Sally," Sam said, "we'll need you on the committee since this event wasn't in our budget and we'll need your advice to address the expenses." Sally nodded and Sam continued, "Leslie, you'll be chairing this committee?" She raised her eyebrows and added, "You *did* renew your SNA membership for this year, didn't you?" That drew chuckles throughout the room.

"Where do we sign up for the committee," J.R. asked. Hands flew up around the room indicating an overwhelming readiness to serve.

"Looks like you'll have loads of help, Leslie. Perhaps those who are interested can stay and meet with you after the meeting. You can collect names and contact information and follow up with them."

The group gathered to meet with Leslie. "Thanks so much for your support," she said. "We'll have a planning meeting next week. Will Wednesday afternoon meetings work for everyone?" Everyone agreed and Leslie added, please stop by the sign-up table on your way out to leave your name and a contact number."

"Works for me," Robin said when Leslie rejoined the Nurseketeers. "We get out of *Seminar* at 2 pm and if we meet at… say 2:30 or 3 pm, I could still work a shift."

The group agreed and Leslie said, "Sounds like we have a plan. I'll find a room and let Sally know so we can get the word to everyone."

"Leslie's peacock feathers were preened tonight," Robin said to Katie as they left the room. "This is going to be fun."

Robin thumped Leslie on the back, "Way to go girlfriend! You are a firecracker!"

"I'm proud of what you did tonight, Leslie," said Katie. "I don't think I could have stood up in that group with so many juniors and seniors."

"Well, I have sweated through the pits of my blouse. I couldn't have done it without all of you. Now I have to make an appointment with the Dean."

"I wonder if he has office hours like faculty or if you schedule an appointment like a doctor's office," said Frannie.

Leslie laughed. "I have no clue. I'll go by the Administration Building after my run tomorrow, about 9:00. Will y'all go with me?"

Three heads nodded in unison and Katie gave her roomie a *thumbs up*. "Looks like the Nurseketeers are once again *all for one and one for all!*"

"You'll be fine Leslie. We'll be right there with you," Robin said as the Nurseketeers cut across the oval past the fountain with the Crestmont Coyote peering down from atop the tall four-sided pedestal.

"Maybe I need to run through it one more time," Leslie said.

"No!" All three of her suitemates said in unison.

Robin said, "You've practiced for hours and we all know it by heart. *Dean Abbott, we would like your permission...*"

Throwing up her hands, Leslie said, "Okay, okay, I get it. Let's do this." She squared her shoulders and led the Nurseketeers up the steps and through the double doors of the Administration Building.

They found the Dean's office listed on the information board in the lobby and rode the elevator to the top floor. "We have an appointment with Dean Abbott," Leslie announced when the secretary raised her head.

She nodded. "He's expecting you. Please have a seat and I'll let him know you're here."

A tall man with graying temples and a full head of salt and pepper hair beckoned them to his office. He was about five inches taller than Leslie's 5'9." From Robin's 5'5" vantage point, he seemed like a towering giant. He sat with them at a conference table in a corner of his office. Through the window, Robin looked down on the Crestmont Coyote they'd just passed.

"Thank you for meeting with us. Dean Abbott, my name is Leslie Bleu, and these are my suitemates." Leslie introduced each in turn. "Ms. Langston, our SNA Advisor suggested that you were the person from whom we should obtain approval for a project to organize an event. The SNA has voted to take the lead in organizing a campus March Against Violence to focus attention on the issue."

The Dean nodded for Leslie to continue.

"We have formed a committee to plan the event. We intend to include all other campus organizations. We would like your permission to proceed with the event and your recommendation for the best time to hold the March. We thought that spring would give us adequate time for planning and promotion." Leslie finally took a breath.

Dr. Abbott nodded. "Ms. Langston has advised me that you have the beginnings of a plan for this initiative. The concept is certainly in alignment with the university's community service mission and we would be delighted to support you and the SNA in this endeavor. Have you talked to any other organizations?"

"Not yet. We felt that we needed your permission first. We have contacts with a couple of the sororities, and we believe they will get behind our initiative," Leslie said.

"We also think we can get some of the businesses near the campus to help us with advertising and possibly donations for the cause as well," Robin said.

"Spring would be a good option... I recommend the week before Spring break. Let me check the calendar to be sure there are no conflicts." He moved to his desk, flipped through a desk calendar, then looked up. "Let's plan for Wednesday, March 15th." He carried a document back to the table. "Leslie, this is the form that you will need to complete. You must have the support of at least two other campus organizations. The presidents of SNA and those two organizations must sign here on the back. Additional organizations will strengthen the effect of your initiative. I will place the event on the university calendar when you submit the form, but you have my permission to move forward with planning your project."

"Thank you so much, Dean Abbott. I'll get this form back to you as quickly as possible. This is marvelous!"

Outside the building, the Nurseketeers were a bubble of chatter. Leslie heaved a sigh. "I'm glad that's over! I can't keep this up. I'm sweating through every nice blouse I own."

"What a night! Funny how quiet it seems in here after everyone has left," Maddie said. She and Robin relaxed after closing for the night. "We were busier than ever, and you did a great job on tables."

"Thanks, Maddie. I love working here, but tonight my feet are so tired, they're numb. I'm going to sit here until I can feel them again. Want a pop?"

"I'll get us both one since I can still feel my feet. Hostessing isn't as exhausting as waiting tables, though it can be challenging. Making people feel good about waiting 45 minutes for a table takes finesse."

"And you do it well." Robin laughed. "We sound like a mutual admiration society."

"We do, don't we," Maddie smiled.

"Maddie," Robin said after they'd sipped their sodas in companionable silence for a few moments. "Can I ask you something? It's personal and I hope you don't take offense."

"Now I can't say *no*; I'm too curious," Maddie leaned forward in her chair.

Robin took a deep breath and blurted. "Are you gay?"

Maddie sat up a bit straighter and her eyes widened. "What made you think that?"

Robin's response tumbled out. "Well… you're pretty, terrific, you don't have a boyfriend, and you looked at me funny the other day when I said, *if you like cute guys,* if you remember." Maddie nodded and Robin rushed on. "I hope you're gay because I need to talk to someone and if you *were* gay, you'd understand," Robin ran out of breath and sucked in air. She closed her eyes, praying that she hadn't ruined a friendship.

A knowing smile spread slowly across Maddie's face. "Robin, you can talk to me."

Robin breathed deeply. "I was hoping you were gay so you could tell me about it. I want to figure out if I'm gay. I think I am, but I don't know for sure. There was this great guy I worked with this summer. He's gay and that was a good thing because I wasn't interested in a relationship and we probably wouldn't have become friends if I thought he was looking for a girlfriend.

"That got me thinking," Robin explained to Maddie that her high school relationships had been confusing and admitted the bad decisions she had made. "I told Guy – he's the one I worked with this summer – all about my conflicted feelings and he seemed to understand. Anyhow, the part I'm most confused about is that I've never been interested in a girl, either."

Maddie sat quietly until she was sure that Robin was finished, then began, "Robin, gay isn't a black and white phenomenon. It's broad and unwieldy. Gay is more a description of what you're *not*. Gay means you're not straight, but it doesn't define any more than that. Gay has lots of variations, including not being sure exactly where you fit in. It's not necessary to have all the answers. You know the most important thing: you're not straight. You can figure out the details as time goes on."

"Do you have a girlfriend?"

"No. I don't have all the answers for myself yet, either. I met a girl who's a few years younger than I am. She's bright and self-assured. I didn't know she was gay, but she somehow knew that I might be."

"How did she know?"

"I have no clue. But then, you thought so, too."

"Did you two hook up?"

"For a short time we tried, but it didn't work out. Everything about us was different and our relationship just didn't fit with the rest of our lives. It was more of a problem for me than for her, but it takes two to tango, as they say. It was too much of a juggling act for me; I had to break it off."

"Do your parents know?"

"I think they'd suspected for a while, but I sat down and told them when my friend and I were together. Honestly, that was part of why it didn't work out for us. Mom handled it pretty well, but it made Dad uncomfortable. He talks a good game, but he keeps hoping I'll grow out of it. That's not going to happen, and I suspect that he'll come around. We've always been close, and I don't think he could let his frustration damage our relationship."

"Didn't they like the girl?"

"They never met her. That was also part of the issue. I didn't want to bring her into my life at home with Mom just getting used to the idea and Dad so uncomfortable with it. She was confident about being gay and thought I should be stronger. I just couldn't. I chose my family over my relationship. It was the right decision. I don't think that she was the right life partner for me, and my folks needed time."

"I'm sorry it didn't work out, but it sounds like you did the right thing. What's going to happen when you *do* meet the right girl?"

"When I know it's the right girl, my parents will learn to live with it, and I'm sure they will. They want me to be happy and they wouldn't interfere with that. They'll just need time to adjust."

"Once I'm sure, I'll have to tell my roommates. I have no clue how that will go."

"You don't have to tell anyone anything. You'll know in your heart whom you can trust and if you're not sure, then stay quiet. It's a lot less complicated to keep your secret than to deal with the reactions from the people around you. Being gay is illegal and can get in the way of achieving something that's important to you, like getting your nursing license. It's not unusual for narrow-minded people to throw up major obstacles, and the more influential the person, the more trouble they can make for you. My advice is to stay quiet. The best time to let the world in on your secret is after you've accomplished your goals, when it's too late for anyone to interfere with your success."

"I understand what you're saying, but I don't like secrets. I can't imagine being able to keep one so important, and for so long."

Chapter 17

"Robin," Roberta Davis called when Robin arrived for work. "I've got some good news. Come into the office so I can tell you what I've found."

"Be right there," Robin called.

"Rory and I have a dear friend who's a widower. He lives close by and he has a two-bedroom garage apartment that is currently vacant. I didn't think to ask you earlier about climbing steps. Garage apartments are typically above the garage. Would a flight of steps be a challenge for your grandmother?"

"No, Ma'am. Gram's healthy and she walks a lot. The bedrooms in our house in Chicago are upstairs, so she's up and down the steps all the time."

"Then Richard's apartment will be perfect. It's larger than most and close to the school. He'd be pleased to have your grandmother stay as long as she'd like. The rent's reasonable, and they are a delightful family. Richard has a daughter about your age who is a student at Crestmont. There are two older boys, but they are out on their own."

Robin's eyes widened as she listened to Roberta's description. "Mrs. Davis, is your friend Richard's last name Phillips?

My suitemate Leslie is good friends with Barb Phillips. They're both in the athletics program. Last year we made cupcakes for the first home game in Barb's kitchen and it sounds like you're describing her family."

"My goodness, he certainly is Richard Phillips," exclaimed Roberta, "and his daughter is Barbara. It never occurred to me to ask if he knew you."

"This is perfect. The Phillips' home is super convenient. It's a ten-minute walk from the campus. Thank you so much. I can't wait to tell Gram."

"The apartment is furnished, so we'll store your grandmother's furniture in our warehouse. It can stay there as long as necessary."

"The timing is perfect, too. Gram has a couple of weeks before she has to be out of the house. That will give her plenty of time to decide what to pack for the apartment and what she'll store in your warehouse."

"How about calling her now. Don't worry about the long-distance charges; this is a special occasion."

"Thank you so much. Will you stay nearby in case Gram has questions? She might want to talk to you."

"Of course, I'll be at the hostess station; just call if you need me."

Robin misdialed twice in her excitement. Then she tapped the desk impatiently waiting for Gram to answer. The phone rang four times and Robin's disappointment was growing when Gram picked up the phone.

"Hello."

"Gram, you're home. I thought you weren't going to answer. You won't believe the good news. Mrs. Davis found you the perfect apartment and it turns out it belongs to a family we know."

"Robin…"

"Barb is Leslie's friend and it's only ten minutes from campus, and…"

"Robin… ROBIN," Gram got Robin's attention. "Slow down. Start from the beginning."

"Sorry... it's just so perfect!" Robin took a breath. "The Davises are good friends with Barb Phillips' dad. Barb is Leslie's friend. Anyhow, the Phillips have a two-bedroom garage apartment and it's available and it's only ten minutes from campus and Mrs. Davis says the rent's reasonable." She took a breath.

"This does sound like wonderful news. Is the apartment furnished?"

"Oh... yes. Mrs. Davis said it was furnished... but I didn't ask her about a washer and dryer. It's also up one flight of stairs. It's a garage apartment. Do you want to talk to Mrs. Davis? I didn't think to ask her for any details."

"That might be a good idea. I do have several questions."

"Just a sec. I'll get her, but don't hang up when you're done talking. I want to say goodbye."

Robin called Mrs. Davis. "Gram has some questions for you. I thought she would."

"Mrs. Hart? Is it Mrs. Hart?"

Gram chuckled, "It's Kelly... Maureen Kelly... and please call me Maureen. I have a few questions that will help me decide how to pack."

"Of course... I'm sorry, I should have asked Robin your name, she always calls you Gram. If I can't answer your questions, I'll get the information and call you back." When their conversation was over, Roberta handed Robin the phone.

"Gram, I can't wait until you get here!"

"I'll make flight reservations today and let you know when I'm coming.

"You'll love them, Gram. You'll love Dallas, too. Gram, I love you."

Gram walked straight into Robin's open arms. "My, what a welcome," she said, taking in the sea of smiling faces.

"Everyone wanted to be here to welcome you to Dallas," Robin said, giving her another hug. "I can hardly believe you're finally here. Let me introduce you to…"

Gram raised a finger, "Wait… I'll bet I already know each of you." She reached to squeeze each of the Davises' hands. "I can't thank you enough for all you've done." Then she turned to the Nurseketeers and hugged each in turn. "Katie, Frannie, Leslie… I hope I will see lots of you. Robin tells me I'm just a short walk from the campus, so I can fix dinner for you occasionally. I'm looking forward to getting to know you."

"The girls will help you get settled, then we'll see you at dinner at the SteakHauz, our treat, of course," said Mr. Davis. "The apartment is fully furnished, and Roberta has the kitchen and bathroom stocked with the basics. There's a market nearby for anything you need. We put shelves in the warehouse so you can organize your belongings when they arrive from Chicago. Robin, you and your grandmother ride with Roberta and me; Leslie and the girls can follow."

"Thank you so much, Mr. Davis," Gram said.

"It's Rory, Mrs. Kelly, and Roberta. You and Robin are almost family. Let's get you settled."

"I'm Maureen," Gram said with a smile.

Chapter 18

"Hold up guys I want to check the mail before we go. Leslie spun the combination dial, retrieved two letters, handed one to Frannie, and tucked hers into a book. They got the last available study room in the library and settled in for the evening.

Robin said, "Before we get started, Gram invited us to dinner on Tuesday. We can walk over after we clean up from A&P lab. That will give us time to visit and have an early dinner. There will still be time for the library if we need it."

"I'm definitely up for real food," said Katie.

"Me, too," Frannie added.

"She wants to make something we all..." Leslie's gasp stopped her in mid-sentence.

"What's wrong, Les? What happened?" Robin asked.

Leslie sat open-mouthed, shaking her head slowly from side to side, and staring at the letter in her hand. "No... no... that couldn't happen..."

"*WHAT* couldn't happen?" Frannie asked.

"Paul. Paul's dead. His entire squad was killed in a bomb run. I can't believe he's gone. I was *glad* he went to Vietnam because he was doing something worthwhile with his life, and he wasn't making me miserable. He was so lost when he didn't get a scholarship, and angry that I accepted one so far from home."

No one uttered a word. "I haven't thought about him in months," she continued. "We were so busy last semester, and summer was a blur. I hardly noticed he wasn't around. He was a huge part of my life in high school and we expected to be together forever, but then it turned out we had nothing in common." Tears streamed down her cheeks as she stared at the letter.

"You didn't turn your back on him." Robin insisted, "You did everything possible to include him in your life. When he came for homecoming last year, he wasn't interested in joining in; he wanted you to ignore everything and pay attention to him. It was all about Paul. You two were finished before he left."

Katie added, "We all knew he didn't want to be part of the life you chose for yourself. He only wanted you to be part of *his*. Of course, you feel bad that he died, but you aren't responsible for his choices nor for what happened to him."

"*Petey* could die," Frannie blurted. "Nobody cares if Paul is gone, but what would I do if my brother didn't come back? I couldn't live if Petey died in Vietnam."

"Frannie! That's a horrible thing to say," Robin shook her head.

"I... I didn't mean it that way. I just meant that Paul isn't part of any of our lives and Petey's my only brother and..."

Robin cut her off. "What *I* mean is that Petey's fine and this isn't about you, it's about Leslie. It's not the time to dwell on *what-ifs* and how *you* would feel. We're focusing on Leslie. Try being less selfish for a change."

"I *do care* about how Leslie feels, but she doesn't even *like* Paul anymore."

"It's okay, Robin," Leslie spoke up. "I'm okay now. It was just unexpected. I haven't thought of him for ages, and now this." She took a deep breath. "I'm sorry for his family that he won't be coming home but going to Vietnam was the right thing for Paul to do. Petey, too, Frannie. Serving your country is an honor. You should be proud of Petey and I hope that everything goes well, and he'll be home for Christmas like he said he would."

"Mom, Dad," said Katie, after giving each of her parents a hug, "this is Mrs. Kelly, Robin's grandmother.

"Please call me Maureen." Gram squeezed each of Katie's parents' hands in turn. "I am grateful for your kind invitation. Thanksgiving is such a grand holiday, and even more special when it's shared with friends. Robin loves your farm and I'm looking forward to the weekend.

"I'm Mary," said Mrs. Grayfox, "and my husband is Jim. We're pleased to have you."

Mr. Grayfox hoisted three suitcases into the truck bed. "Katie, there are blankets for you and Robin to get comfortable, and your mother brought two quilts. You'll need them to keep warm."

"How did your move go?" Mrs. Grayfox asked when they were settled in the pickup.

"I lived in my house for nearly forty years, so I shouldn't have been surprised at the mountain of belongings I'd accumulated. If Robin hadn't helped me sort it all out over the summer, I'd still be there packing. I'm looking forward to some peace and quiet after that frenzy. Even after five weeks in the lovely apartment Roberta found for me, I'm exhausted."

"I can't imagine living anywhere but the farm," Mrs. Grayfox said. "We've been there since before the boys were born. It's the only life I know."

"The countryside is gorgeous here. I haven't been outside of a crowded city for longer than I can remember. And I can't get over the weather. It's already Thanksgiving and still so pleasant. It was 43 degrees in Chicago today, and likely it'll drop below freezing overnight. I'm glad that Robin chose a college in Dallas, and that she and Katie are suitemates."

In the truck bed, the girls chattered. "It's super of your folks to have Gram and me for the holiday weekend. I had a groovy time last year. Do you think we can go to the fair again? I bet Gram would appreciate the Indian crafts. Oh, if we run into that bitch from last year, I'll do her some major damage."

Katie laughed, "I don't think she'll mess with this Squaw Girl again."

"John and his dad are having dinner with us tomorrow."

"How's his dad doing?"

"Mr. Brown's recovery has been amazing, considering what a terrible tractor accident that was. He still has a limp, but it doesn't keep him from doing anything he needs to do, and he's gotten all his strength back."

"That's terrific! So, how about John and school?"

"He says that Freshman year hasn't been much of a challenge for him. He's taking an extra course each semester to make up for starting late because of his dad's accident. He and I were A students, but I had to study and he hardly cracked a book. He's looking forward to his pre-vet courses like we're anxious for our nursing courses to start."

John and his father were on the Grayfox's porch when the truck pulled into the yard. They hurried to welcome the guests and help with their bags. "Mr. Brown," said Robin, "it's nice to see you're good as new."

"That I am, young lady," Mr. Brown replied. "Gonna be a terrific holiday with you kids home from school. First time I've seen John since summer. And it's nice to meet you," he said to Gram. "I hear that you've settled in Dallas. This Thanksgiving will be a true celebration. Each one of us has something to be thankful for."

"Can I pour anyone another cup of coffee?" asked Mrs. Grayfox. Robin, Katie, and Gram lounged at the kitchen table covered with the remnants of a hearty breakfast. The men had been out hunting for hours and Naomi, Katie's younger sister, was still sleeping.

"I thought Robin and I might go for a walk after we do the dishes," Katie said.

"The farm is such a peaceful place," Robin said. "It's a world apart from the congestion of Chicago… and from the chaos of the campus."

"You girls go ahead. I can get these dishes done easy peasy, while Maureen and I visit," said Mrs. Grayfox, shooing them out the door.

"Come on, I'll take you to John's and my *secret place*," said Katie, leading the way along the fence rail.

"Secret place?" Robin arched her eyebrows. "Is there something I should know about you and John?"

"Oh, good heavens, no. Our secret place is a special corner of my world on the farm. John and I played there as kids and still meet there to visit in private," Katie said. "You might say it's my safe place." She chuckled. "John and I thought no one knew about our secret hideout, even though everyone knew where to find us anytime we went missing." She chuckled, "We never let Naomi tag along with us. When she was old enough to be out of mom's sight, we'd sneak away without her. It became a spot just for John and me."

"The trees are huge," Robin said, as they continued along the well-worn path.

"This grove of oak trees shaded us in the summer and protected us from the winter wind when we built forts and snowmen… *and snow women.* The ones I made had to have a girly look or I wasn't happy with our little family of snow people."

Pointing back towards the fence row, Katie said, "See how that ridge hides my house and John's."

"I like the feeling that we're the only living souls around," Robin said.

"John and I played cowboys and Indians here, and in our world, the Indians were always the good guys. I am full-blood Choctaw and John's half and half; his mom was Choctaw, too. We grew up sharing our happiest times and our darkest moments… right here in our special place.

"I remember once Dad found a small sick rabbit. John and I tried to nurse it back to health, but it died," said, pointing to the grass under one of the trees. "See *Skeeter* carved into the trunk near the base? The morning after the rabbit died, John and I dressed in our Sunday best. I pressured him into it, and he did it for me. He lugged a shovel and I carried Skeeter in a shoebox. While he dug the grave, I carved Skeeter's name into the tree. We buried the rabbit and John said, *Rest in peace, Skeet*er. By then, I was bawling my eyes out. He took my hand and didn't say another word."

"A friend like John makes a tremendous difference in how we handle grief," Robin said.

"You're right. When the white bullies at school got to me, this is where I'd come. Just telling John made me feel better."

"I've never had a close friend like John. Gram's always been my "go-to" person for secrets, but the ones I couldn't share with her, I just had to keep to myself."

"That's got to be tough."

"One thing I never talked about was Mom because I didn't want Gram to think I was ungrateful. I was furious with Mom for sitting there doing nothing when Gram took me away. It's not that I didn't want to go. I was afraid whenever my father was home. I wouldn't trade my years with Gram for anything but spending time with your family last year made me see how much I'd missed not having Mom in my life. When we finally got back together this summer," Robin's voice rose, "that BASTARD took her away from me!" Robin choked back a sob.

"She was trying to see me again, Katie, and it meant a lot." Robin placed her hand over her heart. "I miss her. She was gone from my life for so long, and she was finally in it again." Robin pounded her chest with her fist. "It's like a knife stabbing my heart over and over." Robin began to cry, tears turning into sobs. Katie shifted closer, wrapped an arm around her, and held her quietly.

Robin sniffled, swiped at the tears, and stared into the distance. "Gram remembered two boxes that mom had stored in the attic right before she got married." She looked into Katie's compassionate eyes, then back into the distance "Gram picked up a strip of faded evergreen grosgrain ribbon and held it, rubbing her thumb back and forth." Robin unconsciously made the same motion with her own hand. "After a bit, she told me it came from a dress she'd made for Mom for a Christmas party when she was ten. Mom loved that dress and tried it on over and over. Then, on the day of the party, she tripped on the steps and ripped the dress. Mom was a basket case. Gram took the dress, made buttonholes at the bottom of the skirt and ran the ribbon through it. Mom was speechless. She ran to Gram and hugged her and the dress. Gram said she didn't know how much that dress meant to Mom until she found the ribbon in the box.

"Katie, I was just getting to know Mom for the first time this summer. Now I've lost her forever." Tears streamed down Robin's face again. She pulled her knees to her chest. "I feel like I am hurting all the time. Telling that story hurts, but it feels good too. It's like Mom existed... she was significant... I don't know..."

"You know, Robin," Katie said, "it's okay to feel what you feel. I appreciate that you told me the story. My People tell stories a lot, particularly about our history and the people who have gone before us. I think it's in the telling of stories that healing begins, but I also cherish the memories. You are a special woman and your stories have meaning. Thank you for trusting me."

Robin held her friend tight until there were no more tears.

"That turkey was the best I've ever eaten," Gram said. "There's no comparison to one that you buy from the supermarket."

"Thank you, Maureen. Nearly everything on the table is farm fresh. The bread and pies are homemade and the cranberry sauce recipe has been in our family for generations. Thanksgiving is a day of gratitude for just about everything in our lives. You and I can sit and visit, while the kids enjoy themselves. We can clean up later after everyone has let the meal settle.

Robin and Katie ambled down the farm road with John between them. "It feels good to be home," John said. "The hustle and bustle of Stillwater gets to me; I miss the peace and quiet of the farm. I haven't found a spot yet on the OSU campus to hide from the hubbub. Don't get me wrong. I love the school, but I'm a farm boy at heart. Soon as I can get my DVM, I'll be back here to set up shop. Old Doc Benally's bound to retire by then. "

Katie smiled. "You've been talking about being a vet as long as I can remember."

"That's really cool," said Robin. "It's great that your Dad has done so well and you're off to college, making your dream come true."

"Never wanted to be anything else," John said. "And I never wanted to be with anyone else. You could consider nursing animals instead of people, Katie. You've always been great with them. We could set up shop together."

"Don't think so," Katie laughed. "I always imagined myself at the clinic in Atoka, but I expect school will broaden our horizons and most of us will end up in a specialty that never crossed our minds. Nurses work in every health care setting. There are school nurses, industry nurses, nurse administrators, researchers, and educators. There are nurses that work in other countries with underserved people.

"Wait a minute. You're not thinking of joining the Peace Corps, are you?"

"No," Katie laughed. "I'm just saying that I'm going to keep an open mind and learn all I can before I settle on a specialty."

"I...," John began, then stopped.

"What?" Katie asked when he didn't continue.

"Nothing. I was just thinking we should get on home before your mother and Robin's Gram clean up everything by themselves."

"You're amazing, John," said Robin. "I didn't think men ever lifted a finger in a kitchen."

Chapter 19

Mrs. Rockford ended the Western Civ History class with a unique assignment. "We're going to study major events in the last five years that have had a significant influence upon perspectives and behaviors in our country. Pair up and choose an event. Your assignment will be to present the event to the class and demonstrate its influence on our culture. You will have two weeks to develop a fifteen-minute talk. I'll have a sign-up sheet for presentation slots on Monday. The most economical medium for delivering your material would be the overhead projector, but you are free to use whatever approach you'd like. For those who choose to use the overhead, I will provide transparencies. Take the last few minutes of class to choose a partner and get started."

The eight friends huddled. Missy was the first to speak up. "J.R. and I will be partners." She poked J.R. who grinned in assent. "Leslie, how about you and Mike?"

Leslie hesitated, but Mike said, "I'd like that. Les, is that alright with you?" She agreed and a blush crept up her cheeks. "Cool. It's a date."

Robin stifled a grin. *"They make a cute couple."*

Missy continued, "That leaves Katie and Frannie and Robin and Tonya."

Katie looked at Frannie and said, "I expect you to take this seriously. A good grade in the course depends upon it, and I, for one, plan to get an A."

Frannie looked blank but nodded slowly.

Robin turned to Tonya. "Okay with you to be partners?"

"Sure," Tonya replied. "I can suggest an event right now. The 1969 Stonewall riots in New York City had a huge effect, at least on one segment of society in America. The incident virtually launched the gay rights movement."

The choice caught Robin by surprise. She stammered, "Sssure. That sounds interesting."

Tonya nodded. "I hoped you'd like the idea. I've got to go. See y'all on Wednesday."

"She picked that for a reason. Could she know? No, there's no way. Maybe she's gay. That's not so far-fetched. She's independent and kind of a loner... and I've never heard her mention a guy, even in passing. Hmmm... Interesting..."

"You're right about the riots," Robin said as Tonya dropped into the chair next to her. "The cops' response opened the door for gays and lesbians to speak out publicly." Robin had chosen a spot in the far corner of the library's fourth floor. "We'll work until you have to leave for the Diner, then I'll hook up with the girls and study until I have to leave for work." She stacked the material she'd collected about the Stonewall riots on the table. The more she thought about Tonya and their topic, the happier she was about partnering with her on the project.

"We have fifteen minutes to present," Tonya began. "I say we spend five minutes describing the riots themselves and then ten on the gay and lesbian movement and how the riots launched it."

"Good idea," Robin agreed. "I think Mrs. Rockford is more interested in the effect on our culture than in the event itself. I can't believe that I didn't know anything about the riots before you suggested the topic."

"New York is a long way from Dallas, and if you have no connection to the gay community, there's no reason they would be important to you," Tonya explained.

When Robin reached to turn the page, Tonya's hand closed over hers, sending a pleasant thrill through her body. Startled, Robin pulled her hand away.

"Sorry," Tonya said and smiled as she continued reading.

"That was weird... but okay, too. It was probably an accident... or maybe not," Robin thought. She continued to review the moment and decided, *"I hope it wasn't an accident."*

The project came together nicely. They read, took notes, and outlined the presentation. "We can sign up for one of the early presentation slots," Tonya said. "I'll bet we'll have this done by the end of the week."

"That would be cool," Robin agreed. "We wouldn't have any more work to do for this class for the rest of the semester, except to study for the final. We need to remember to ask Dr. Rockford for transparencies."

"Sounds like a plan."

They were gathering their belongings when Tonya asked, "What time's your shift at the SteakHauz? We could walk to work together."

"Not until 5:00, but they don't mind if I come early. There's plenty to do before the dinner crowd, and that means extra bucks in my paycheck. I need to let the girls know I won't be studying with them before work. Let's go."

Robin couldn't stop thinking about Tonya's touch. She kept space between them as they walked to the dorm. *"How embarrassing it will be if this is all my imagination."* She glanced at Tonya who seemed to be watching her think. *"I'll be disappointed if Tonya's not gay after all. I want her to like me, but I don't have a clue what I'd do if it turns out that she does. If I let her make the first move, I'll be sure. If she doesn't, I'll be disappointed, but at least I won't be embarrassed."*

On Wednesday they made progress on their project. Tonya gave no indication that she might be interested in a relationship. Robin was disappointed, but relieved at the same time. "We'll be finished by Friday, for sure," Tonya predicted. "Can you start your shift early again today?"

"Sure," Robin said, pleased just to be spending time with Tonya.

On Friday, they finished the project with an hour to spare, stacked their transparencies, and slipped them into a folder. "Let's drop these by the dorm. We can have a pop and relax before we have to be at work."

"Okay by me," Tonya said.

Robin got two sodas from the fridge and dropped into her usual seat in the sitting room. Tonya took Katie's chair and they sipped their drinks. Robin broke the silence. "How did you come to be at Crestmont? Where were you freshman year?"

Tonya didn't answer immediately. Robin wondered. *"It's an easy question."*

"I did my freshman year at El Centro downtown." She hesitated, then continued. "But I didn't go to college straight from high school. I had to work that first year to save money for tuition."

"If I hadn't gotten my scholarship, I would have done the same thing. Did you work in a restaurant?"

"I've been in a restaurant my whole life," Tonya said. "My dad died before I turned three and my mom had to work. She has two spinster cousins, Lulu and Elva, who own Luva's, a restaurant in our neighborhood, and I grew up there. Once I could carry a glass of water without spilling it, I helped out. We practically lived there. Mom and I were either at Luva's or at church. We didn't do much more than sleep at home. Mom used to tease me and say that she couldn't be sure I did all the right things unless she kept me where she could see me. I loved being wherever she was."

"That's kinda cool," Robin said. "Your mother sounds like my grandmother. I lived with Gram from when I was eight, and except for my last two years of high school when I was practicing being a perfect shit, I spent all my time with her. How did you get from El Centro to Crestmont?"

"That's a long story and I need to get moving. I told them I'd be in early today so I can leave early. I need to help Mom and my aunts cater a party tonight. Can you go in early?"

"Sure"

Tonya stood and started to reach for Robin's hand to pull her up from the chair. When she hesitated, Robin reached out. Tonya pulled her up and they stood facing one another. Tonya smiled, then she gathered her things and started for the door.

I think she's okay with me, Robin concluded. *I wonder if she's waiting to see what I do.*

As they walked, Robin said, "Tonya, can I ask you something personal?"

Tonya hesitated, then startled Robin by saying, "I'm not sure that's a good idea."

"You don't even know what I want to ask."

"I think I do."

"Then why isn't it a good idea? If you didn't want me to know…"

"That's not it. I'm glad that you know, but you're thinking about a relationship with me, and I'm not the right person for you, that's all."

"That's silly. You're the *only* person. Until this summer I didn't know anyone who was gay. As a matter of fact, *gay* never crossed my mind. Then I worked with a cool gay fellow at Marshall Field and I realized that *gay* hadn't occurred to me because I'd never met a girl who made me think that way… until now. You make me curious and interested. I feel different when I'm with you."

Tonya nodded. "How about we talk more about it? We can use our study time next Monday to talk. Don't let anyone know that we're finished with the project."

While her suitemates studied in the library, Robin and Tonya curled up with sodas in the sitting room. Robin leaned forward anticipating Tonya's story. "So, start from the beginning. I need to understand this better. Oh, and thanks for trusting me with your secret. That means a lot to me."

"I haven't been gay all my life like lots of gay folks describe. The only difference between me and the kids I grew up with is that my mother was focused on education and my future. I come from a poor neighborhood and most of those kids are going nowhere. Instead of playing in the streets after school, I studied and worked in the restaurant. I'm comfortable with women because there's never been a man in my life. My dad was never in the picture and the guys who came into Luva's weren't the best role models. Mom, Lulu, and Elva always kept them away from me."

"How did you get to be gay?"

"When I started high school, I studied for a couple of hours after school with a friend. It was easier to study at her house than at the diner. It kinda just happened. We never came out to our folks or anyone else, and the only people who knew were a few other gay kids at school. We were together until Spring of our junior year when her dad got a job in Indiana."

"Did you stay in touch?"

"For a little while, but our relationship wouldn't have lasted after high school. I knew I'd go to college and she didn't have much ambition. Then, after high school, I worked in a restaurant and one of the waitresses I liked came on to me. It was an easy relationship. She was working to save money for school, too, and ended up going to school out of state. We talked about my going with her, but I didn't have the money and I didn't want to leave Mom."

"Speaking of your mom, does she know?"

"She knows. She's not happy about it. She's been accepting, but she's hoping that someday I'll see the error of my ways." Tonya smiled, "That isn't going to happen."

"Last year I went to El Centro and I ran into a couple of girls who were interesting, but neither of them turned into a relationship. Then I fell for a white girl, which is why I say I don't think you and I would work out. You remind me of her, and I think we'd run into the same problems."

"What are you talking about?" Robin said.

"Our world just isn't ready for a two-tone lesbian couple. It isn't ready for gay *or* black and white, let alone both at the same time. Well, that's what happened to us. It was just too much to deal with. Her family owns a restaurant and I met her when they catered an event at El Centro. I was in charge of food... no big surprise since I've spent my whole life in a restaurant. I worked the event with her. We hit it off and spent about six months seeing each other. But... her family wasn't happy about it and it turned out that she wasn't committed enough to me to find a way to make it work. It won't be any different for you. Picture yourself having to choose between your Gram and me. Seriously, Robin, think about everything you'd have to deal with, not to mention the legal challenges."

Robin started to protest but stopped. "I have no clue what Gram will think or feel. I've been concentrating on my own feelings. Gram's open-minded and not at all judgmental, but she has mega traditional values. I don't think she'd be okay with it, at least not at first. It'll be too much of a stretch from her beliefs, and if she finally does come around, she'll worry about all the things I would have to deal with. I suppose that's what *you're* telling me to do."

"Exactly," Tonya said. "You need to think long and hard about what it means to keep a secret that important and to be sure it doesn't interfere with your other hopes and dreams. I think the black community has an easier time with it. They're more accustomed to adjusting to whatever comes along. Blacks face so much bullshit already, this is just one more thing."

"I wish we had more time to talk. I have a zillion questions."

"We can talk on Wednesday if we pretend, we're still not done with our project."

"Okay. Do you want to meet in the library? We can go back to the dorm if no one will be there."

"That's fine. In the meantime, think about if it's wise to tell your Gram."

"I have to tell Gram," Robin thought. *"There's no way I can keep a secret this important from her. She'll know something's wrong and Tonya nailed it, I could wind up having to choose between her and Gram. I need to figure this out."*

Robin pushed the door to the restaurant open and Maddie waved from the hostess station. "Glad you came early," she said. "There's a party of 20 coming at 7:00 and the kitchen needs help with the prep."

"No prob. Glad to help." Robin added, "The bigger paycheck will be much appreciated."

As she prepared vegetables for twenty salads, she replayed Tonya's story over and over, trying to decide how she would manage the challenges that Tonya described. Suddenly, her eyes widened, and she sucked in a breath. *"Maddie could be Tonya's white ex-girlfriend! That would explain why Tonya shut down completely at the diner when I told her she should be working at Rob Rory's. I need to convince Maddie to confide in me."*

Robin hustled out of the kitchen and checked with Maddie to get her assignment. She liked working the back section that had smaller tables for intimate dining. There was the same amount of seating, but customers at the larger tables sometimes got rowdy. They weren't inappropriate, but they could be annoying. Friday nights were always busy, and Robin was in no mood to deal with rude people.

For a while it looked like her section might slow down, but the tide changed. Maddie said, "we need to move these tables together to accommodate a group of 10 that just showed up."

With a heavy sigh, Robin helped Maddie create a table for ten. Ten men who had been drinking heavily filled the table. Maddie handed them menus. Robin shot Maddie a pleading look and Maddie shrugged her shoulders and made her way back to the hostess station. Robin filled ten glasses with water and began to distribute them.

"Hey, Red, got anything stronger to drink in this dive?

"I'll get you the wine list, sir, as soon as I empty this tray." When Robin turned to take another glass of water from her tray, the man slapped her on the rear. "Get it now, Red!"

The tray tilted and the remaining glasses of water tumbled into the man's lap. Furious, Robin screamed, "My name's not Red and you can't hit me, you asshole!" She stormed out of the section.

In the kitchen, she jerked a mop from a bucket and took it back out to the table. The man was standing over Maddie, his shirt and pants dripping. He yelled, "I want her fired! Look at this mess."

Maddie took the mop and motioned Robin toward the office where Mr. Davis was standing. "I'll take over here," she said and began to pick up glasses, ice cubes, and the glass shards setting the mop aside for the moment.

The man continued yelling, "You ruined my suit, Bitch. I'll be suing you and this pathetic restaurant for everything you've got!"

Robin bit her lip and followed Mr. Davis into the office, expecting to be fired on the spot.

"Sit down, Robin." Mr. Davis said.

"I'm so sorry, Mr. Davis. I shouldn't let dopes, uh… men like that get to me, but he *hit* me. I was going to clean up the mess., Maddie didn't have to do it for me. I…"

Mr. Davis held up his hands and said, "Hold on, Robin. Yes, you are right about his behavior, but I want to talk to you about your response. "I saw what he did, and I won't tolerate that type of behavior from any of our patrons. However, your behavior was equally inappropriate. Yelling and name-calling placed you on his level. The fact that he behaved poorly first doesn't excuse your response. Can you think of a way you might have made your position clear while diffusing the situation rather than escalating it?"

"I'm sorry, Mr. Davis. It was an automatic reaction. The jerk slapped me on the butt for God's sake." She dropped her head, shut her eyes, and took another deep breath. "Maybe I can start again?"

He waited.

"I could have held my temper and backed away from him. I could have said that assaulting a waitress is unacceptable behavior in this restaurant and I don't appreciate being treated that way.

"Well, that is an appropriate response. Do you think you can manage that should it happen again?" Mr. Davis asked.

"Yes sir, I definitely can."

"What about the loaded tray? Your reasonable response still wouldn't have prevented the mishap with the water."

Robin paused, "I think that, before speaking, I should recognize a disaster in the making. I could have set the tray down before I told him I wouldn't tolerate his behavior."

"Yes, now you're thinking like the mature individual you need to be if you're working with adults. Robin, in all reality, anyone taking care of that table would have encountered a similar situation. He wanted a fight and you obliged him."

"Right after I told him I wouldn't tolerate his behavior, I would come to you and you'd kick him out, right? You'd believe me even if you didn't see it with your own eyes?"

"That wouldn't be my first response. Remember that we began this conversation by discussing ways to diffuse the situation, not escalate it. First, I'd do something that would encourage him to behave properly. For example, after what happened, I would assign Bryan to serve that table. He's a huge burly guy, and that loudmouth is too cowardly to consider taking him on. Likely, his friends would corral him. He would shut up, eat his dinner, and they would leave without any further disruption. Robin, I want you to think about controlling your temper. Sometimes your quick temper shows up when you deal with the staff."

"But I..."

Mr. Davis held up his hand to her, "distancing yourself just a little when you're facing confrontation can be a good choice.

Try to think before speaking. Changing behavior takes practice, but improvement is worth the effort. I do want our wait staff to be able to take care of themselves and not have to call me each time they face a difficult situation; however, tonight that might have been a wise option. In work and life, we pick our battles. The goal is picking the ones that matter, not the ones that get up your nose."

"I'll try, Mr. Davis" Robin said, "Do I still have a job?"

"Yes, Robin, your job was never in jeopardy. Go back out and check in with Maddie, I suspect she has Bryan waiting your tables and has a new assignment for you by now. Go on, get back to work, the team needs you out there."

Chapter 20

"Leslie, did you realize that Robin hasn't joined us in the library for more than a week?" Katie asked. "I know she's been working on the Western Civ project with Tonya, but that's only one class and finals are coming up fast."

"I was thinking about that this morning," Leslie replied. "She's got something on her mind."

"Yeah. That's obvious. I hate to think something's bothering her and she isn't telling us about it. The Nurseketeers stick together. She knows we'd be happy to help with whatever it is."

Leslie cocked an ear. "We're alone, aren't we? Frannie's off with Missy somewhere, right?"

"I'm sure she is," Katie said. "Why do you ask?"

"Because I want to talk to you about something that isn't for Frannie's ears." Leslie leaned closer to Katie. "I think maybe Robin is dealing with something she isn't ready to talk about; something she's trying to figure out for herself."

Katie cocked her head, "What do you mean?"

Leslie took a deep breath. "I think that Robin and Tonya are developing a relationship." Katie started to speak, but Leslie raised her hand. "Wait. Before you say anything… this may just be my imagination. I certainly don't have anything to back up what I'm thinking."

"Why would Robin's liking Tonya be a problem? I like her, too."

Leslie fidgeted in her seat. "I mean..." She took another breath. "I mean an unconventional relationship." When Katie's confused expression didn't change, she added. "I think Tonya is gay."

Katie processed this, then said, "Do you think Robin is gay, too?"

Leslie nodded. "I think that's what Robin is struggling with... maybe not *being* gay but considering that she may be."

For a few moments, they sat lost in their own thoughts. When Katie looked up, Leslie explained, "Unconventional relationships aren't all that uncommon. They're just kept private. Once you've been involved with someone who's gay... I don't mean *involved*... I mean when you're in on the secret... you can recognize it." She paused, waiting for some indication that Katie understood what she was trying to say.

Katie nodded. "Go on. You don't have to walk on eggshells. I want to hear what you're thinking."

"In high school, there was a girl on the team I liked. I thought it would be cool if she had a boyfriend and they could do stuff with Paul and me. I tried to fix her up with friends of Paul's and finally, she told me her secret. I guess she knew she could trust me, and my trying to find her a boyfriend put her in an awkward position... always having to find an excuse. We were good friends in school, but I wasn't part of her private life. She didn't run around with me and my friends outside of school... but I liked her, and I didn't care that she was gay. Tonya reminds me of Gail."

"Was Gail black, too?" Katie asked.

"No, but she was independent and had a strong personality like Tonya does. Remember when we first met her in the diner... when that guy pinched her butt, or whatever he did?"

"I do."

"Tonya did just what Gail would have done. She'd have decked him if she weren't so self-controlled. She knows how to take care of herself without drawing a lot of attention. I was impressed. Anyhow, the more I'm around Tonya, the more I think of Gail."

"If you're right..." Katie paused. "If Robin *is* gay, what do you think will happen? I don't know anything about gays. We never discussed it at home, which probably means that my parents don't consider it a topic for conversation. My mother was fine with teaching my sister and me about things like menstruating and what happens if you're not sexually responsible." Katie laughed. "I've always known where babies come from. After all, I grew up on a farm. But seriously, *gay* never came up."

"I can understand that. If I hadn't known Gail, I doubt I'd ever have thought of it either."

"Now that we're talking about it, I think that homosexuality had a place in Indian culture a long time ago. Homosexuals were thought to be people of two spirits and were considered special, but even then, it wasn't considered normal. It's definitely not well accepted now."

"Well, if I'm right, it's going to be a bit sticky for the Nurseketeers. If she doesn't want us to know, we'll just have to respect that. If she tells us, I know you'd find a way to come to terms with it. It's Frannie I'm worried about."

"I agree. I can't imagine that Frannie's black and white view of the world will leave any room for compromise. It would be convenient if you're wrong."

"How true. I could just as easily be wrong as right, but something's up, for sure."

"Whatever it is, we'll deal with it. At least I hope we will."

Leslie put her finger to her lips. "Shhhh. I hear Frannie and Missy in the hall."

Robin and Tonya were the first in the class to present. They took turns speaking. Tonya placed their first transparency on the overhead. "This is the Stonewall Inn in New York. Two years ago, in June of 1969, an incident occurred there that had a significant influence on American culture. The police raided the Stonewall Inn using a liquor license issue as an excuse. They didn't have to hurt anyone, but the Stonewall Inn was a gay bar and dance club and the police were brutal. They beat up the people they arrested and for the first time, the community fought back. Confrontations took place over the next six days."

Robin changed the transparency and said, "Illinois is the only state where it's legal to be homosexual. Originally the laws were intended to protect individuals from non-consensual encounters, but today the laws are used to discriminate against homosexuals. The gay community decided to fight for their right not to be hassled just because they were different."

Tonya and Robin took turns telling the story of the six days following the incident, using their transparencies to stay on track instead of note cards. Robin concluded, "Gay communities around the world took courage from the people in New York who fought back. That's how the Stonewall riots in New York in 1969 launched *Gay Pride* worldwide."

"That went well," Tonya whispered to Robin while the class applauded.

"I wonder if the clapping was because we had the guts to go first," Robin whispered back, "or because we did a good job. Either way, I'm glad it's done."

"Nicely done, girls," Dr. Rockford said. "Your presentation met the project objectives. Class, do you have any questions or comments for Tonya and Robin?"

"I'm from New York," said one young man, "and I remember when that happened. It was all anyone talked about that whole week. My Civics teacher had our class study the history of homosexuality in modern times. I admit that I didn't know anything about homosexuals before then. Now I know several and they're just regular people."

"It was astute of your teacher to take advantage of the opportunity to use real-life events for teaching important concepts."

Another student raised her hand. "We studied the riots in Civics, too," she said. "My class wrote a letter to the editor of our hometown paper about everyone's right to make their own decisions about private matters like that."

"But it's *wrong*," Frannie blurted out. "They shouldn't do that. It's just *not right*." She grimaced. "Men and *women* do that; not men and *men, or women and women,* either. That's disgusting!"

Gasps punctuated the silence in the classroom.

Frannie looked around, confused. "What? What's wrong? How can you think it's okay for people to act that way? My mother says it's illegal and the police should have put all of those people in jail."

Dr. Rockford's voice echoed in the stunned silence. "Frannie, people differ in many ways, and one aspect of maturity is developing tolerance for people and ideas that are different from our own. The objective for this class is to study the political, cultural, and social history of western civilization and explore the ways in which our history has shaped our current environment. It's important to maintain objectivity and avoid being judgmental."

"But it's just *wrong,*" Frannie insisted in an undertone. "It's *not right!*"

"You two nailed the assignment," Leslie said to Robin and Tonya before the four suitemates left for their psych class. "There were lots of good comments from the class."

Tonya's smile morphed into a frown when Frannie grumbled, "That doesn't make it right."

Tonya shrugged her shoulders. "Gotta run."

"Frannie, some things are personal," Katie said. They can be right for some people but not for others."

"But Katie, couples are men and women. That's the way it's supposed to be."

"THAT'S ENOUGH," Robin shouted as she rounded on Frannie. "Why waste your time in college if you already know everything? I can't believe I'm living with a narrow-minded bigot. What gives you the right to decide what's right or wrong for other people. That's the whole point of a democracy. EVERYBODY counts; not just YOU. GROW-UP!"

Robin and the Nurseketeers joined Leslie's planning team meeting in the large conference room in the Student Union. Leslie had managed to garner the support of every sorority, fraternity, and student organization on campus. There were barely enough seats for one representative from each organization to serve on the leadership team.

Leslie rapped the table with her knuckles and the group quieted down. "Thank you for serving on the leadership team for the March against Violence. Each of you has a list of the committees that the SNA thinks we need to organize the event. Tonight, we can make any changes this group recommends, and then each of you can volunteer to serve on one committee."

"The *Promotions* committee will be responsible for getting the word out with window signs in local businesses, posters, placards, t-shirts, and anything else the committee can dream up. We also have *Crowd Control/Motivation*, *News/Publicity*, and *Coordination/Communication*. We have enough work to keep every participating organization busy. Are there any other committee functions we need to add?" Leslie asked.

"This needs to be a coordinated effort. My proposal is to divide and conquer. Let's spend some time filling the committees, then each committee can select a chair. The chairs will coordinate the committee's efforts with the other committee leaders."

"Seems to me like you have covered all the bases," Missy said. "Put Theta Rho Xi down for the *Promotions* committee. I love making signs and dreaming up slogans. My sorority sisters will be good at that."

"I'm in there with you," said Frannie. "Put me on Missy's committee."

When each organization had selected a committee, Leslie said, "Gather your team members and pick a corner of the room or step out into the hall. Take 20 minutes to identify a chair and choose a date and time for your group to meet. Save a little time for brainstorming on the tasks your committee will undertake, then we'll all meet back here, and the chairs can report on each committee's plans and progress."

"I'll join *Crowd Control/Motivation*," Robin said. "I can bark orders with the best of them."

"Oh, so true," said Frannie, prompting a laugh from the Nurseketeers.

Crowd Control/Motivation selected a chair from one of the fraternities. He assigned someone to record the committee members' names, organizations, and contact information, then finalized a meeting date for the following Wednesday.

"*Timing is perfect. The meeting is after Nursing Seminar and before dinner so maybe I could have time with Tonya before going to work.*" Robin thought.

Each chair reported to the group and gave Leslie a copy of their committee's roster. Leslie said, "Plan to have at least three committee meetings between now and February when we should start meeting more frequently. If I can book this room, we can meet here on December 15th at the same time. I have your phone numbers, so I'll let the committee chairs know, one way or the other. Until then, if there are no objections, this meeting is adjourned."

The Nurseketeers helped Leslie pack up from the meeting. Robin said, "Jason Rodriguez, the guy who's chairing *Communications and Motivation team,* said he thinks he can arrange with campus security to let us borrow walkie talkies for the event. "Wouldn't that be cool?"

"Wow!" said Katie. "That will definitely help keep everyone informed and coordinated during the event. It sure beats having runners carry messages from one end of the March line to the other."

"We need to decide the route for the March... where we'll start and where we'll finish," Leslie pondered, "and, do y'all think we should have the rally before or after the March?"

"If we gain more supporters and gawkers as the March progresses, a rally at the end would be better attended," Robin said, and the end is a better time to emphasize key takeaways about violence."

"A band at the end would provide entertainment and could space out any boring speeches," Frannie said.

Katie said, "That's a good idea, Frannie. Maybe we can find a local band that wouldn't charge us anything. I think there are several student bands right here on campus that might be interested."

"Do you think any of the local politicians might get behind this? We could invite them to speak if they'd agree to keep their talks short," said Robin. "If they get long-winded, we'll have to give them the hook or we would lose the crowd. Having locals participate might increase community participation."

"I keep thinking about what we want to accomplish," Leslie said. "We haven't talked much about what that might look like. Dean Abbott asked us that question and I know he expects us to have an answer. Besides, we need to define our objectives so we can determine how to measure how well we're doing."

"We want to increase awareness, isn't that what we told Abbott?" Frannie offered.

"We did, Frannie, but Leslie is trying to define the goal in measurable terms so we can tell if we achieved it with the March," Katie said. "It's hard to measure awareness."

"Yes, exactly," Leslie said.

"We can count the number of campus organizations that participate in organizing the event," said Robin. "We started with one, the SNA, and now we have every organization on campus involved. If they all follow through, that would be a pretty impressive accomplishment."

"Every business that supports the March with a sign in their window is another hard number," Katie said. "The number of actual marchers is a good measure of support."

"Perfect," Leslie said, "We can also count the number of newspaper articles and radio announcements. You know… if we found out what the paper's readership number is and how many listen to the radio stations that support us, we could learn a lot about our actual reach for this initiative, right?"

"We're doing all of this without funding and that makes support for the event impressive," Robin said. "Leslie, you should feel pretty good right now. You ran with the idea, then you came up with a plan to make it memorable and measurable. The *Nurseketeers* rock!"

Robin studied the cat on the lab table while Frannie fiddled with the scalpel. Robin snatched it from Frannie's hand. "Give me that. Class will be over before you make the first cut. You're awfully slow for someone who knows everything." Robin glanced at the lab manual, then sliced into the carcass.

Frannie winced. "I just don't like hurting animals."

"This is an anatomy and physiology lab and this cat is dead; it's not hurting. If you're not here to learn, why ARE you here?"

"Why are you being so mean?" Frannie asked, near tears. "You say something nasty every time we're together or you don't say anything. You promised you'd be nicer this year."

Robin didn't look up from the cat. "It would be easier for me to be nicer if you were trying to improve. You're spoiled and you avoid every opportunity to grow up. You're positive you have the answer to everything, but you don't know *anything!*"

"Are you still mad that I didn't like your presentation in Western Civ? You're the one who said everyone is entitled to her own opinion. How come I'm not entitled to mine?"

"That's the point, Frannie. You don't have an *opinion* about anything. People with *opinions* accept that it's okay for other people to disagree with them. You have a *position*. Whatever *you* believe must be right for everyone. For your information, *it isn't!*"

"That's not fair. My parents told me that what those people do is wrong."

"Fair!" Robin glared at Frannie. "What's *fair* about your deciding what another person can and can't do in his private life, especially if his life has nothing to do with you in any way? Who gave you that right?"

"But, I...."

Robin interrupted. "What you don't get is that someone who disagrees with your belief is not automatically a bad person."

"That's silly."

"No. It's NOT silly. Silly means absurd or foolish and there's nothing silly about what I'm telling you. Now, are you going to help with this lesson, or do I have to ask for a lab partner who wants to learn something?"

Frannie sat on her bed, winding her alarm clock. "Robin, are we going to be friends again?"

"That's completely up to you," Robin said.

"I fixed the things you wanted me to. You don't have to wake me in the morning, and I can get ready in time to leave with the rest of you. I never leave anything on your bed or your chair anymore. You haven't talked to me for days."

"We're all grateful for small miracles, Frannie. It's the important things that make or break a friendship."

"Like what? Tell me what to do."

"Grow-up!"

"What? What does THAT mean? I'm older than YOU!"

"That's what's so pathetic!" Robin shrugged. "When someone says *grow-up*, they're talking about how you *think* and how you *act*, not how old you are. Children think in absolutes. Everything is either right or wrong, good or bad; children don't understand that there are a zillion shades of gray in between. Adults call that "the gray area" respecting an individual's right to have her own opinion. Because people and circumstances are so different, one dress doesn't fit every woman."

"What does this have to do with dresses?" Frannie squealed, her face a mask of confusion.

"You're shittin' me. You *really* don't know what I'm talking about?" Robin took a slow, calming breath. "Okay… okay… let's start with the kindergarten version."

"I hate when you do that." Frannie sniffled. "Just because I don't understand, you have no right to make fun of me. How is that respecting other people? You'd have a hissy fit if I made fun of someone just because they didn't understand."

Robin slumped. "You're right. Sorry. Let's start again."

"When I say that a child's perspective is black and white, I mean children see things as right or wrong… period. Children aren't sophisticated enough to recognize all the factors that can make what's right for one person NOT right for another. That sophistication is called maturity and you develop it during the process of growing up. Are you with me so far?"

"Yes, but there are lots of things that ARE either right or wrong," Frannie insisted.

"When adults decide if something is right or wrong, they take into consideration the circumstances; that means they think about the people involved and what effect the decision may have on others. Here's a simple example: is being late to class right or wrong?"

"Wrong! Where's the gray in that?" Frannie answered with hesitation.

"If I'm late to class because Katie fell down and hurt herself and I helped her back to the dorm, is that wrong? Should I have said, Sorry, Katie, gotta run. Take care of yourself? Should Dr. Rockford give me an F for the day because I helped her? Was it wrong for me to be late?"

Several times Frannie opened her mouth to speak, then shut it.

"You see. Being late isn't right or wrong. You have to decide based on the circumstances. That's the difference between thinking like a child and growing up."

Frannie nodded without speaking.

"If you want us to be friends, you can't act like there is only one right way to think. You're allowed to think what you want, but you have to give other people the right to do the same."

Frannie began to nod. "You're talking about the two-men instead of a-man-and-a-woman thing, aren't you?"

Robin nodded. "Can't you even SAY *lesbian,* or *homosexual,* or *gay?*"

Frannie cringed, "Ugh. Do we have to talk about that?"

"*THAT* is exactly what I'm talking about. You are entitled to feel the way you feel. What you're NOT entitled to do is demand that everyone else feel the same way. And you're not entitled to be obnoxious to people because they're different from you."

"But it's illegal. My parents told me that it's against the law to be that way."

"Frannie, if blue eyes were illegal, what would you do?"

"That's silly."

"It's no sillier than making it illegal to be Jewish or Protestant or Black or mentally ill, and there *have* been laws like that. Sometimes it's the *law* that's silly."

"There's nothing right about two men acting like a couple."

"You're entitled to that opinion. But those men are none of your business. They have nothing to do with you, and you have no right to make that decision for them. Besides, being homosexual is only one part of who they are. They may be kind, brilliant, thoughtful, and talented. Does being homosexual instantly make all those good qualities not count?"

"But even the *Bible* says it's a sin." Frannie took a breath intending to continue her rebuttal.

Robin interrupted. "Enough. It's late and I need some sleep. Just think about it."

Frannie winced.

"I don't mean think about homosexuals." She snapped off the light. "I mean think about giving people the right to make decisions for themselves when their decisions have nothing to do with you. I promise I'll be nicer if you can promise to do that."

"Come on you guys, if we don't get to Barb's, we won't get the cupcakes baked. The SNA is counting on us to get them made for the home game festivities." Leslie said. "Robin, you did say Tonya was meeting us there, didn't you?"

Robin nodded. "She's probably on her way now. Frannie, get your rear in gear. The Leslie bus is leaving and if you don't want to walk to Barb's, get moving."

The Nurseketeers piled into Leslie's car, Nellie, with the supplies they had purchased. "The one nice thing you can say about Nellie is she has loads of room to haul our stuff around," Leslie said.

Katie said, "You bet, and we're grateful you have a car and you're willing to share."

Barb and Tonya were on the porch steps when they arrived. The six girls hauled grocery sacks into Barb's kitchen

"So," Leslie said, "Here's the plan. We'll work in pairs: Robin and Tonya, Frannie and Katie, Barb and me. We'll do a conveyer-belt thing. Robin and Tonya get the cupcakes ready; Barb and I manage baking; Frannie and Katie can be clean-up until the cupcakes are cool enough to frost. At the end, all of us will be frosting cupcakes. What do you think?"

"Maybe we should call you "General" cuz you're such a good strategist. You always manage to get us all together working as a team. You rock!" Robin said.

Frannie said, "I'm in as long as I get to lick the batter bowl and the frosting beaters."

"Oh lord," Robin laughed along with the others. "That part of being a child I can deal with."

"Turn that up! It's Cher's *Gypsies, Tramps, and Thieves*" and they all chimed to sing the lyrics.

Leslie paced back and forth in the sitting room fidgeting with her blouse. "What is up with you Leslie?" Robin asked. "You're as nervous as you were the day we went to see Dean Abbott."

"Uhhhh… Mike asked me to go with him to the bonfire tonight. I'm excited and I'm nervous at the same time. I like him, but, well, you know, I have responsibilities with the booth for SNA. I'll be at the booth for several hours. There might not be enough time to spend with him."

"For heaven's sake, let him sell cupcakes with you. He can be your gofer. He idolizes you; just let him hang with you and he'll be on cloud nine."

"You think so?" Leslie asked. "I signed up to work the extra time before he asked me to go with him."

"He knows you're working, doesn't he?"

"Yes, I've told him often enough about what SNA is doing and my part in tonight's activities."

"And he asked you anyway. Let the puppy dog tag along and you'll both have a super time." Robin said with a smirk, "You like him, don't ya?"

Leslie threw a pillow at her. "Yes, I like him."

"We've known that for months, and it is about time you two got connected. Is he picking you up here?"

"Yes, but I'm afraid I'll make a fool of myself or drop the cupcakes. I don't want to look stupid in front of him."

"Too late for that. Besides it's time you two shared something other than sweaty, bouncy-ball games." Robin said. "He's a guy; you're a girl; there's more to life than sports."

Katie and Frannie came into the sitting room carrying boxes of cupcakes. "Let's go out the back door. It's a shorter walk to the booth," Katie said.

Leslie hesitated before picking up her box of cupcakes and Robin said, "Uhhhh, Katie, we need to go out through the lobby."

Katie nodded and Frannie blurted out, "Why on earth would we do that? It's shorter out the back."

"Well…, it's because we have a little love-bird activity going on," Robin said nodding toward Leslie, "and I don't think you'll want to miss it."

Frannie jumped up and down, jostling her cupcakes. "Wow, Mike finally asked you out! Way cool!"

"Careful with those cupcakes, Girl," Katie said, "though I agree that a celebration is in order."

Leslie looked perplexed. "Did you already know about this? Did Mike tell you he was going to ask me?"

"Yes, we knew, and no, Mike didn't tell us. Mooning like love-sick puppy dogs kinda gave it away. It was just a matter of time before one of you got brave enough to make a move." Katie said.

"I don't believe this! Okay, okay, let's go" Leslie said.

Mike was waiting in the lobby. He beamed when Leslie appeared. Leslie's face flushed the color of Robin's hair.

Mike reached for Leslie's box of cupcakes and she blushed again as his hand touched hers. "Thank you," she stammered when she finally found her voice. "Uhhhh, let's get moving," she added, pleading with her eyes for the girls to move along.

Katie cleared her throat. "We'll see you there," and hurried Robin and Frannie along.

Chapter 21

Tonya rose from her chair and stretched. "I'm going to the Student Union for a coke. Anyone want anything?" she said to the Nurseketeers. "I need a break. Our Western Civ Lit final is next week, and my mind is wandering."

"No, thanks," Katie answered. "I'm on a roll."

"Me, too..." Leslie said. Frannie pushed back her chair. "Frannie," Leslie said, "we finally got you to the library with us, so please stay here and study."

"I'm in," Robin said, pushing her chair from the table."

Katie glanced at Leslie who responded with a hint of a smile.

Outside, Robin spoke softly. "I still don't have answers to any of the hard questions, but that doesn't change who I am and what I feel. Knowing that Gram will have a hard time with this doesn't stop me from wanting to be with you. It means I have to figure out how to deal with it. The tough stuff isn't going to go away, so why pretend?"

"That's easy to say now, since you haven't dealt with any of it yet, but you're right about it's not going away."

"Can we be friends? I mean, can we be more than friends?"

"We're already more than friends," Tonya chuckled.

Robin's chest tightened and a shiver ran down her spine.

"What?" Tonya asked, noting Robin's reaction.

Robin shook her head. "I've just never felt this way before. It was like my body heard what you said."

Tonya bumped Robin's shoulder as they walked. "You gotta watch that, Girl. A body can get you in a heap of trouble."

They were laughing when they got their sodas in the Student Union. "Too bad we have to go back to the library," Robin smirked. "I'm imagining the trouble I could get into if we didn't have to study for finals."

"All work and no play aren't good for you either," Tonya bumped Robin's shoulder again. "We'll figure something out. In the meantime, you need to think about how being a lesbian is going to play out for you. You won't be happy if you have to give up things that are important to you."

"That's true," Robin said, "but life is full of compromises."

"You need to keep yourself from getting blindsided. Think carefully before you put yourself in a position where you don't have time to come up with a plan. Even if things don't go according to your script, you'll come out ahead if you've thought it through."

"I was hoping you'd help with that. You've already had to face telling your mom. I could use some advice."

"Sure, I'll help. You're stubborn and hotheaded… personally, I like that in you… but with this, you can't just blurt out the first thing that comes to mind. The subject is controversial; there's no getting around that. You're butting up against a solid wall of prejudice. If people could deal with this, we wouldn't be having this conversation. How you handle it has a lot to do with how things turn out for you. You need to have your thoughts in order so you can keep a conversation from becoming confrontational and degenerating into a *who's wrong and who's right* argument. When that happens, everybody loses."

Robin thought back to her conversation with Frannie about *growing up*. "Tonya, I can do this. I waited all this time to figure out who I am, and I'm determined to work it out. I'm not great at keeping things from people I care about, so I need to talk to

218

Gram, Katie, and Leslie. Talking to Frannie will start World War III because there's not one mature cell in her brain. She's been programmed in black and white. Ultimately, if this destroys our relationship, so be it. I can't spend my life helping her grow her up, and I'm sure as hell not letting her keep me from living *my* life. I can't imagine that the rest of the world needs to know."

Chapter 22

"Hurry up Frannie, we'll be late if you don't haul ass." Robin hissed.

"I'm coming, I'm coming, don't get your panties in a wad," Frannie retorted.

Robin left the suite with Katie and Leslie, and Frannie caught up to them on the steps. "I said I would be right there. You could have waited."

"If we waited for you every time you said that, we'd never make class on time," Robin said.

The girls entered Montgomery Hall. Robin passed her usual seat and sat between Katie and J.R. instead of next to Frannie.

Conversations faded away as Ms. Langston began to speak. "In today's seminar, we'll discuss the stages of grief. Understanding the grieving process can help us, as nurses, work with patients and families who are dealing with death or loss, either their own or a loved one's. I asked you to prepare for this class by writing down your own thoughts about someone passing away in your life. I hope that capturing your reflections on paper helped you see how important expressing your feelings is in the grief process.

Although it is not mandatory, I encourage you to share those thoughts with us.

"The five stages of grief are *denial, anger, bargaining, depression,* and finally, *acceptance.* Some suggest that these stages represent a linear transition, one stage moving into the next in this order. I disagree. I believe that individuals move back and forth among the first four stages until they reach acceptance. The order of steps and the length of time the process takes is unique to the individual. Some who grieve may not ever reach acceptance." After responding to a series of questions, Ms. Langston explained that when *denial* is used as a coping mechanism, *anger* is a step in the direction of taking back control.

Robin sat mesmerized, she felt like two people, one listening to the lecture and the other watching from a distance, reliving the experience of her Mom's death.

"Bargaining is the third stage." Ms. Langston continued.

"I held on to denial so long that I didn't have much time to think about Mom's death. I pleaded with God to let her wake up because her life was going to be so much better."

Ms. Langston reached the fourth stage, *depression.*

"Some days, I feel like I'm in the middle of a giant cloud and can't see anything around me except gray. Maybe depression is where I am now. I go to work, class, and I study, but concentrating is harder than last year; I can't keep focused. I'm functioning in a daze most days. I don't sleep well; I toss and turn trying to figure out if I could have done something different. I'm short-tempered with Frannie even when I don't want to be."

Several students shared their stories of grief. Robin tried to listen, but each story tore at her heart, and with each one her fists clenched tighter. There wasn't a dry eye in the room except for Robin's. *"I'm not depressed; I'm pissed as hell! I'm going to explode. I need to get out of here,* NOW!"

Ms. Langston had barely finished when Robin bolted from her chair and was the first one out the door.

"Leslie, would you take my stuff back to the dorm," Katie asked. "I'm going to go check on Robin."

Katie spotted Robin across the oval, pacing back and forth in front of a bench, pointing as if she were talking to an unseen person. She approached slowly and stopped well back, giving Robin time to notice her.

"Leave me alone, Katie. Why did Ms. Langston have to bring all of this up!"

Katie sat down on a nearby bench, waiting patiently while Robin continued to rant. Finally, spent, Robin plopped down on the bench she had marched in front of, buried her head in her hands, and began to cry.

Katie waited until Robin had cried herself out, then got up and went to sit beside Robin. She snaked an arm around Robin's shoulders and pulled her close. Robin dropped her head onto Katie's shoulder, an occasional sob punctuating the silence.

"I feel like I am going crazy. One minute I want to punch someone's lights out and the next I'm sorry for whatever I just said or did."

Katie lifted Robin's chin and looked into her eyes. "Robin, feelings *happen* to us because of the things we experience, and we can't turn them on and off like a water faucet. Grief is awful. The only thing good about it is that eventually, you'll get to acceptance. That certainly doesn't mean you'll be okay with it; it just means that you won't hurt as much."

Sniffling, Robin said, "It's taking forever. This roller coaster is driving me nuts."

"You're doing better than you give yourself credit for. We each experience pain in our own way, and whatever way that is, it's *our way*, which makes it the *right* way. Now, do you want me to stay or go?"

"I'm better now. Thanks for pulling me back from the ledge, but I need a little alone time. I'll imagine that I'm in your secret place on the farm. Besides, I'd eat Frannie alive right now if she even thought about opening her mouth."

Chapter 23

"Come on Frannie, Leslie will kill us if we miss the start of the game," Robin yelled as Katie paced the sitting room. "I'm coming, I'm coming."

"Leslie was super excited about this game," Katie said. "She thinks the coach is going to let her start. That's unusual for a Sophomore, don't you think?"

Frannie rushed into the sitting room dressed in Crestmont colors, purple slacks and a white top with a purple and gold coyote plastered across her chest. "Where is your coat?" Robin snarked at Frannie. "It will be cold out by the time we come back."

"Oops, I was concentrating on my new outfit."

Robin shrugged, "Will we survive her?"

They hustled to the gym. "Bet you're glad you have that coat," Robin said. "The front's coming in faster than we thought. I won't be surprised if the rain gets here before the game is over."

They settled into their seats in front of Missy, J.R., and Mike just as the Lady Coyotes ran onto the court.

"Look," Katie said. "Leslie's starting! There she is, right in the middle of the pack."

The entire Coyote section leaped to their feet, whooping and hollering as the team gathered in front of them. Mike's rich baritone led the Coyote chant. They hardly heard the announcer introduce the starting Ravens, but they cheered wildly when Leslie was announced among the starting Lady Coyotes

Mike said, "She's the best!"

Robin laughed, "You bet she is!"

The game was intense, and the teams remained neck and neck. The Coyotes sank a three-pointer near the end of the first half, and the Ravens sank one of their own just as the buzzer sounded. "If this keeps up, I'll have a stroke before the game is over," Robin said, taking a deep breath.

It was the third quarter before the Coyotes began to pull ahead. "I don't know what the coach said to them, but Leslie and the team are on fire!" Robin said.

Mike explained, "He shifted some of the players' positions. Leslie started as a power forward because of her height, but she's playing point guard now. That was a good move."

Mike's explanation was cut short by a shout erupting from the Coyote crowd and a collective moan from the visitors when one of the Ravens fouled out.

Leslie was calling signals for her teammates and the Coyotes scored on most of their possessions. "*She is an awesome piece of work; a born leader!*" The Nurseketeers and their friends chanted, "Les-lie, Les-lie" and the Ravens began to lose their momentum.

Mike's game was next, and he left to suit up. Robin next saw him with the men's team at the edge of the court, cheering on the Lady Coyotes. Moments before the final buzzer, Leslie led her team down the court and tossed the ball to another player who sank it for a three-pointer. The cheering was deafening, and the men's team swarmed onto the court to congratulate the ladies. Mike lifted Leslie and swung her in a victory twirl.

Frannie went with J.R. and Missy to get popcorn and sodas for the break between games. Leslie arrived breathing hard. "Whew. I didn't want to miss any of Mike's game," she said as she plopped into the seat beside Robin.

"You're amazing!" Robin said.

"Thanks. That was a first. I got to play the whole game. Did you see I got to play point guard for the second half?" Leslie gushed.

"Yeah, Mike explained how the coached shifted your position. It made a huge difference, too, even though I don't understand basketball. What's the difference between one guard and another?" Robin asked.

"Well, the point guard leads the plays, like a quarterback in football. I've played *point* in practice but never in a game. That was so cool!" Leslie stood as the men's team poured onto the court. "There's Mike!" The stands rocked with the cheers.

The men's game was as intense as the women's had been, each team forging ahead then falling behind.

"This is making me a nervous wreck," Leslie said. "They need to get far enough ahead for some breathing room." The game stayed tight and the score was tied, when, a few seconds before the final buzzer, a Coyote snatched the ball and passed it to Mike who charged in for a layup and sank the ball for two points. The fans held their collective breath as the ball swished through the net and Mike and the Raven defender crashed to the floor, a kaleidoscope of purple and gold and black and red.

Robin heard the crack and saw Mike's expression morph from elation to pain. Leslie was on her feet, but Robin grabbed her arm. "The trainers will take care of him, you know he's in good hands."

"I know, I know!" she said twisting out of Robin's grasp.

The Nurseketeers huddled protectively around Leslie, all eyes riveted on the scene below. The trainer helped Mike to his feet, but his ankle crumpled as soon as he tried to walk. The trainer and another player chair-carried Mike to the locker room.

The victory had been costly, and the collision subdued the crowd. The girls hurried down the stairs and onto the court where Leslie all but tackled one of Mike's teammates. "How is he, Bud? How is Mike?" Leslie pleaded.

"Wait here. I'll be back in a minute."

The Nurseketeers huddled outside the locker room for what seemed like an eternity before Bud returned. His troubled eyes made Robin reach for Leslie's hand. "They think he broke his ankle, but they won't know for sure until they get him to the hospital."

"Which hospital?" Leslie pressured him.

"I suspect it will be Parkland."

"I need to get to him," Leslie said and hurried toward an exit.

"We'll go with you," Robin said. "Wait up."

Leslie paced from one end of the Parkland ER waiting room to the other. When the Coach came through the door from the treatment rooms, she raced to him. "Coach, how is Mike? Is he OK?"

"He'll be fine, but the team will miss him. He's a helluva player and he'll be out for the rest of the season. His ankle is broken and he needs surgery. He'll need time to recover then to train." The coach smiled and patted Leslie's shoulder. "Maybe you can help him with that, huh?"

"Thanks," Leslie heaved a sigh, then squared her shoulders and said, "Yes! I can."

The coach returned to the treatment room. Leslie sank into a chair and burst into tears.

"What are you crying for?" Frannie asked. "He said Mike is going to be okay."

"Shut up, Frannie," Robin said. Katie wrapped her arm around Leslie's shoulders and Robin held her hand. Frannie stood, her face a mask of bewilderment.

Through tearful hiccups, Leslie said, "I want to see Mike before he goes to surgery. Do you think they'll let me see him?"

Robin shrugged her shoulders. "Nothing ventured, nothing gained. Let's go ask."

Leslie scrubbed her cheeks. "May I see Mike Hampton, please?" she asked at the nurses' station.

"Are you family?" Asked the clerk.

"She's his sister," Robin said before Leslie could answer. "She's been waiting to see him all this time." Leslie's mouth remained open and her face paled."

"Just a minute." The clerk scooted her chair back and picked up a phone. After a brief conversation, she said, "Two of you can go back for a few minutes. They'll be going to surgery soon, so you won't be able to stay long."

"Ok, thanks," Robin said and hustled Leslie back to where Katie and Frannie waited. "She's in but only one of us can go with her. They think she's Mike's sister."

Katie's mouth dropped open and Frannie giggled. Leslie grabbed Robin's hand, "You're going with me. You cooked up this scheme, and if I get caught, you're going down too."

Leslie and Robin pushed through the double doors and found the nurses' station. Leslie asked, "Can you tell me where to find Mike Hampton?" When the clerk began to shuffle through the charts at her station, Leslie said, "He's the basketball player from Crestmont."

"Oh, of course. He's in the last cubicle on this side. Surgery will be coming for him shortly." The girls hurried down the hall.

"I'll say out here," Robin said.

Leslie took a deep breath and slipped behind the curtain. As she approached the stretcher, Mike's eyes fluttered. "Mike?" she said softly. His eyes flew open and a gigantic smile lit up his face. He reached for her hand.

"I'm so sorry this happened... You played a fantastic game... and that was a groovy final shot. I'm so sorry it ended like this. Does it hurt much?"

"It was hell at first, but they filled me full of happy juice and now it hardly hurts. I managed to bugger up my ankle. They're gonna make me a bionic one with plates and screws. That should give me an edge on jump shots." He laughed aloud.

"Shhhh... You sound like you're drunk."

"Yep, this is cool stuff. And you're here, so I got everything I need."

"They think I am your sister, so we need to be quiet."

"SSSister? Hell no, you're not my sssister, you are my giiiirl!"

She put her finger to his lips "Shhhh. You're gonna get me kicked out of here."

Robin peeked around the curtain and whispered, "You guys better be quieter. That nurse at the end of the hall keeps looking this way."

Mike grabbed Leslie's other hand and snickered, "I love you."

Robin watched the blush climb from Leslie's neck to her forehead.

A young man in surgical scrubs halted his stretcher at Mike's cubicle and stuck his head inside. "Mr. Hampton, Mike Hampton?"

"Yep, that'sss me." Mike slurred.

"I'll be taking you to surgery. I hear you need to get that ankle fixed up."

"Right on man. Let's git this shindig on *go*. Lemme give my sisssster a kiss first." Mike pulled Leslie toward him. He planted a sloppy kiss, missing her lips completely.

Chapter 24

R obin woke early on Christmas morning to the smell of coffee. Gram stood in the bedroom doorway holding a steaming mug. "Merry Christmas, Sleepyhead," she said and sat on the edge of Robin's bed.

Robin took a sip and sighed. "No one makes coffee like you do," she said. "Our first Christmas in Dallas has begun with perfection. What's first? Breakfast or presents?"

"My, my… we must be growing up. It's the first time you've ever considered the possibility of breakfast first."

"That was just a courtesy," Robin said laughing. "Let's open our presents."

Their small tree was aglow with lights and decorated with ornaments collected over the years. "Gram, you've only been here two months and this apartment is as cozy and familiar as if you'd been living here for years. The kitchen smells like home."

Robin surveyed the room. "I'm glad you're happy here. I love having you close and not missing you for months on end. This apartment is cute and convenient. Maybe Mr. Phillips wouldn't mind if you traded out some of his furniture for your own."

"I'm fine. I'll bet it was Mrs. Phillips who originally decorated this apartment. It's tasteful and the furniture is nice. I'm happy to be near you and surrounded by lovely people like Richard and Barbara and the Davises. I don't think I'll be looking for a house any time soon. This apartment is comfortable and convenient, and as long as the Davises don't mind storing my furniture, I'm going to take it easy right here."

"I love that you're so close to campus, and I have to admit that the four of us look forward to having dinner with you every couple of weeks or so. It makes me feel special to share you with the Nurseketeers." Robin hugged Gram, then a fist clutched her heart ... *"and Tonya... I have to tell Gram before she meets Tonya. I wish we could talk today, but it's Christmas and I don't think Gram will consider my news a great present."*

"Shall we see what Santa has for us?" Gram said, her eyes twinkling as she knelt to choose a bright silver box with red ribbon and a *Robin* tag.

"Wait," said Robin. "Let me choose one for you and we'll open them at the same time." Robin retrieved a small box with a huge bow and handed it to Gram. "Okay, now!"

Gram carefully untied and folded the gigantic bow. "Such a lovely bow."

"Keep going, Gram," it will all make sense when you see what you got." Robin grinned at Gram's perplexed expression.

"Oh, my," said Gram, holding a television set designed for a dollhouse. "Can I assume that we won't be watching Jeopardy on this one?"

"You can, indeed," Robin said. "The bow will fit much better on the real thing. Mr. Phillips will set it up for you after lunch." Robin raised her hand to forestall Gram's comment. "And don't say I shouldn't have spent so much. I didn't have to buy a plane ticket to Chicago, so we're celebrating being *here* for Christmas."

"You're amazing and I hope you know how happy I am to be in Dallas with you."

Robin opened her present. "Oh, Gram, it's beautiful," Robin said after opening her present. The box held a diary bound in silky white material with a robin embroidered on the cover. A red silk ribbon sewn into the binding marked a page. "I have mom's diary in my dresser drawer, and I've thought lots of times about keeping one of my own. Thank you."

"Open it."

Robin gave Gram a quizzical look and fitted the tiny key into the lock. The book opened to the page marked with the red silk ribbon revealing a folded sheet of paper. Robin read. *"I love you, My Darling...."* then tears filled her eyes as she read the rest silently. *"Capture your thoughts and feelings. Write them down and own them. They are important, for how you manage them will determine your future."*

Robin recalled Katie's words about feelings and was overcome by the realization that she had people who cared about her deeply. "I love you." Robin knelt in front of Gram's chair and gathered her into a hug, feeling warm and happy and more hopeful than she had since Aileen died.

"Let's have breakfast," Gram said. We'll have Belgian waffles with whipped cream and strawberry jam. What a lovely day – our private time in the morning, lunch with the Phillips, and dinner with the Davises. How thoughtful everyone has been to include us in their festivities. They're beginning to feel like family."

They sat quietly in the kitchen, waffle crumbs on empty plates. *"I've got to tell Gram, but how to begin?"*

"Let's do the dishes and you can tell me what's on your mind."

Startled, Robin said, "What do you mean?"

Gram replied, "Sweetheart, I can tell when something is bothering you. Christmas is as good a time for talking as any other."

"Oh, I wish it were that easy!" Robin gave her a wan smile and said, "You always were a mind reader. I would hate to think that the whole world can read me like you can."

"Not to worry. I know you better than most."

Robin's shoulders slumped and Gram hugged her and chuckled. "Let me help you out. Repeat after me: 'I have something to tell you. I know you're a reasonable person and you'll listen carefully, so this is what I want to say.' Gram spread her arms wide, giving Robin the floor.

"I have something I want to tell you…," Robin giggled, then became serious. "I know you're a reasonable…"

Gram laughed, "You can skip to the important part." Her Mona Lisa smile gave Robin courage.

"There is someone I want you to meet. Her name is Tonya. She's a junior who transferred to Crestmont this year. She's getting her degree in Business Administration. We met at the beginning of the semester when the girls and I had dinner at the College Diner where she works. She and I were paired up to do the presentation on the Stonewall Riots for Western Civ History I told you about and we've become friends."

"I remember, and you did quite well on that project, right?"

"Yes, we did." Robin smiled at the memory of getting to know Tonya during that project.

"What makes Tonya special?" Gram asked.

"Well, two things actually." Robin paused, then blurted, "She's gay and she's black." Robin held her breath and waited for Gram's reaction.

Gram nodded, "I can understand your concern. You aren't sure how I feel about blacks or lesbians because we've never discussed them before."

Robin nodded, waiting for Gram to continue. "I've not thought much about either, but I can assure you that I judge people by their behavior, not by characteristics over which they have no control. Your friend Guy was charming and the black families who moved onto our block in the past couple of years were quite pleasant, though I didn't get to know any of them well." Gram paused, then asked, "Does that help?"

Robin's head bobbed up and down. "I expected you felt that way. But this is different. Tonya and I are friends. I mean we're more than friends."

Gram's breath caught in her throat, but she recovered quickly.

"I can't do something this important without telling you." Robin held her breath, then her words gushed in a torrent. "I'm gay like Tonya, I'm sure of it. Being with her is totally different from Katie and Leslie… and Frannie. They're great friends, but being with Tonya makes me feel like Leslie sounds when she talks about Mike… and Missy when she's around J.R. It's hard to explain, but there's a *specialness* when I think about her." She paused and a blush crept up her cheeks. "I finally understand the lovers in the books I've read. All those sensations that made no sense at all make sense to me now." Robin knew she was rambling. She looked into Gram's eyes, beseeching her to understand, yet dreading what she might say.

Gram remained silent, her expression showing that she was struggling with her response. She took a deep breath and said, "I don't know what to think or say. I never considered that option for you. It never crossed my mind, so I'll need a bit of time to adjust. I have to admit that I'm not happy about it, but I presume that you're struggling a bit, too."

"I'm not struggling with the decision, but it's true that I don't know how I'm going to manage it."

"Placing yourself in a position that is at odds with the world you live in is a serious matter. It's only wise that you consider all the potential consequences. It's illegal, you know. You are independent and outspoken, so it's not unlikely that you could end up in jail."

Robin's chin dropped to her chest. She said softly, "I know, but it doesn't change the way I feel inside. It doesn't change that it's Tonya who makes me feel alive. What does someone like me do? I don't want to go through life alone, now that I know what it's like to want to be with someone." Tears of frustration welled in her eyes.

"Don't cry, Darling. I'm not turning my back on you. Just because I'm not comfortable with your decision doesn't mean I love you any less. Of course, I wish you'd change your mind, but I also know that isn't likely, at least not for the time being."

"Probably not ever."

"The important thing right now is not how I feel. I'll have to work that out for myself. Let's focus on the practical implications of your decision."

"Practical?" Robin asked. "What do you mean?"

"I mean that you have no choice but to guard your secret carefully. You will be in jeopardy of losing something important to you every minute of every day. Making your way in the world is a competitive process, and it's rarely smooth sailing. Almost every milestone, like getting a job or a promotion, depends upon influencing other people. Anyone who knows or even suspects that you are a lesbian can interfere with your education, your profession, your job, even your personal life."

"It's not right that other people can tell you what you can and can't feel. And who else's business is it anyhow? That's just not fair!"

"As cliché as it sounds, life *isn't* fair. It's a constant challenge. Keeping your secret is not something you will be able to control. Even if no one betrays you intentionally, an overheard conversation or an unintended comment can unravel your secret. Your life will be a juggling act, balancing your public life with your private one."

"I know that."

"What is even more challenging is *inuendo*. People make assumptions and those assumptions become their reality. If someone sees you as unconventional, they may create their own truths about you. For instance, it is not unusual for a narrow-minded person to conclude that a woman who does not have a boyfriend or who does not marry is a lesbian. That conclusion becomes their reality and it influences their behavior and their decisions. You will encounter prejudiced people and I'm concerned that your decision will make your life difficult and cause you a great deal of pain."

"If I can manage Frannie, I can manage anybody," Robin grinned to lighten the weight of Gram's words. "But I'd rather face off with a jerk than never have a special relationship with anyone. I have to figure out how to make this work. Other people have figured it out, so there's gotta be a way."

"I didn't mean that you're in an impossible situation; it's just a particularly challenging one. You need to think it through and acknowledge the obstacles as well as the benefits. Recognizing the challenges you'll face every day will help you prepare to meet them."

"I'm glad you understand."

"I do understand, but that doesn't minimize my concern. You're young and still have time to learn about yourself. This is a decision that will affect the rest of your life. I've never been one to make decisions for you, but I hope you will keep your options open. You may even meet someone who makes you feel differently about intimacy, so keep an open mind."

Gram opened her arms and Robin melted into the hug. After a few moments of silence, Robin said softly, "Most kids aren't lucky enough to be raised by someone like you. Even when you're disappointed, you stick by me."

"Robin, if I'm disappointed it's because I see the challenges you will face and the pain you may experience. I would be happier if you chose otherwise, but... when you force a loved one to choose between you and something else, there always the chance that they'll choose the *something else.*

Maddie rang up the last customer's bill, then joined Robin in the dining room. "Let me give you a hand setting up for tomorrow's lunch crowd."

"Thanks. I was hoping you could stick around a while after we're done." Robin said, "I need to talk to you."

"Is everything okay?"

"Yeah. I just want to talk."

By the time the restaurant was ready for the next day, everyone else had clocked out. Maddie said, "Let's grab a coke and curl up in the break room. If my feet need a rest, yours must be begging for mercy."

They settled into chairs and Robin began, "I met someone."

"A girl? Does that mean you're not wondering anymore? You're sure now?"

"I'm sure. So sure, that I told Gram. I couldn't *not* tell her something so important. Besides, she's a mind-reader and somehow, she'd figure it out for herself. I learned years ago that the worse the news, the more important it is for me to tell her before she finds out on her own."

"How did it go?"

"She's not happy about it, but it's because it will make my life difficult, not because she has a problem with gays, though she's not wild about my decision. First, it's illegal and if anyone reported me, even if they only suspected, it could prevent me from getting my nursing license or land me in jail. She said that Texas is one of the least tolerant states and that I'll come up against prejudiced people who can keep me from accomplishing things I want."

"She's right about all of that. There's nothing easy about the challenges we face. The world isn't ready for us, though it's certainly time they were."

"In Western Civ, Tonya and I did a project on the Stonewall Riots. I learned about prejudice against homosexuality preparing for that assignment. It's hard to believe that there are that many imbeciles in the world. I mean, what makes people hate something that doesn't concern them? And what makes them think that violence is the answer to everything?"

"I told you I had a relationship with someone I liked, but it didn't work out."

"I remember," Robin said.

"The reason it didn't work out was that I couldn't manage the complications. I couldn't resolve the challenges, like my parents not being okay with it and the effect it would have on the restaurant if someone were to make a stink. My folks are too much a part of my life to keep something that important a secret. My family is a big part of our local culture because of the SteakHauz, and it's hard to hide in plain sight."

"I can understand that, but your folks are terrific people. There has to be a way to work it out. You can't go through life being half a person."

Maddie laughed. "This is all new to you, Robin. You're feisty and you meet issues head-on. This one calls for subtlety because missteps can be fatal, both figuratively *and* literally. A mistake can cost you the future you've been working for, but rape and murder are also common. Crazies think that raping a lesbian will introduce her to the glory of heterosexual intercourse and she'll realize she's made the wrong choice. For the same crazies, intolerance also leads to murder."

Robin sucked in a breath and put her hand to her chest. "That's so wrong! It's hard to believe that people can be that out of control."

"It's not as uncommon as you'd think. If you're gay, you stay vigilant all the time. It's as important to avoid suspicion as it is to keep your secret. People act on their suspicions as if they were the truth."

"Gram said that, too," said Robin, shaking her head.

"Even if the accusation weren't true, it would still cause damage, because there are people who will continue to believe it. We can't change who we are, but we certainly have to pay attention to the responsibilities that come along with it.

"To make the situation more challenging, my friend was black," Maddie continued, "which isn't a problem for me or my family, but society makes it an issue. There are as many people out there as prejudice about race as they are about homosexuality. Fortunately, being black isn't illegal. But can you believe that it's only been legal for blacks and whites to marry since 1967? That's less than five years!"

"Wow. I never realized that. It's amazing how we can be completely unaware of something so important because it doesn't affect us personally? My friend's black, too, but that doesn't seem to be an issue. When we first met her, Frannie made some stupid-ass comment about black people being maids and janitors, but Frannie never lived in the real world before she came to Crestmont. Tonya's a good student and everyone seems to respect that."

"My friend didn't have a problem in my world. I was the one who was uncomfortable. She grew up in a neighborhood where no one cared about education or planned for a future, but her mother made sure that she studied and worked. She learned to live in both worlds. She's confident and capable and doesn't let being treated like a second-class citizen get to her. I can't do that. It grates on me when that happens. On the other hand, folks in *her* world resent *me*. People who have nothing and nowhere to go assume anyone more accomplished, especially a white girl, is a *rich bitch*. I never felt welcome there."

"She could just visit her neighborhood without you, couldn't she?"

"I'm a family person. I want my partner and me to be a real couple, including being part of one another's lives. She's close to her mother and visits her frequently, but her family isn't happy with her choice of lifestyle, so bringing me to visit was awkward. And it's no more comfortable with my family. I'm just not ready to deal with the complications."

"I hear what you're saying, but I don't want to stop. I've always had friends, but I've never felt so *connected* before, so *alive,* and *special.* It's like I've always been a spectator, and for the first time, I'm a player." Robin cocked her head. "Am I making any sense?"

Maddie nodded, "Yes, you are. That makes it even harder to face the reality of the world we're stuck with."

"She's different from anyone I know. But it's more than that. *I'm* different when I'm with her, and I like the way that feels. "I don't want to have to choose between Tonya and the rest of my life. I want her to be *part* of my life."

Maddie hesitated for a few moments, then said, "My friend's name was Tonya."

"What a coincidence."

Maddie remained silent. Then Robin's eyes widened. "Noooo. Not *my* Tonya? Not Tonya *Jackson.*"

Maddie's shoulders sagged. "Uh-huh… Tonya Jackson."

Chapter 25

"We can go to my place," Tonya suggested. "It's close and we'd have some privacy. It's a 15-minute walk, but we can make it in less if we hoof it."

Robin smiled, "Great idea. I'd like to see your place."

"It's not much, but it's clean and convenient. There's no real kitchen, but I hardly eat anything but breakfast there. If I have a Sunday off, I spend it with Mom, and we eat at Luva's."

Let's stop by the dorm and I'll drop my books and change so I can go straight to work from your place," Robin said.

"Sounds like a plan," Tonya replied. "We'll have a couple of hours together. Think we can put them to good use?"

"Hmmm… we'll think of something," Robin bumped Tonya's shoulder.

"Want a pop," Robin asked as she opened the door to the suite?

"Sure," Tonya replied and dropped her books on the sitting-room table.

"Grab one from the fridge for each of us."

Tonya set the sodas on Robin's dresser and watched as Robin unbuttoned her blouse. "Need help with that?" Tonya teased.

Robin grinned. "Might be faster with both of us working."

Tonya finished unbuttoning the blouse, then pushed it gently off of Robin's shoulders. She moved closer to Robin as the blouse slid to the floor. Pleasure traveled from Tonya's touch to every part of Robin's being. She purred as Tonya kissed her shoulder. Robin shuddered as Tonya pulled her into an embrace. "I know what we can do with our couple of hours," Tonya whispered into Robin's ear.

Robin couldn't find her voice. She held Tonya tighter.

Tonya eased back from their embrace. "C'mon. We gotta get a move on."

Robin dressed hurriedly and they picked up their sodas and Tonya's books on the way out the door.

"You're sure about this?" Tonya asked. "It's a big step and you need to be sure."

"I haven't thought about much else. Gram is being reluctantly supportive of my decision. I know it hasn't been easy for her."

"What about the Nurseketeers? We can't spend time together without disrupting your study routine and they can't help but notice. They're bound to ask questions."

"One thing's for sure; I won't lie about it. I'm not good at lying. I learned from Gram that lies always catch up with you, no matter how careful you think you're being. I've always gotten a lot better reaction from her when I tell the truth than when she catches me in a lie. So, no lies here."

"What are you going to tell them?"

"No clue! There's got to be a right way to handle this, but I haven't figured it out yet. I have to tell Katie and Leslie, but Frannie can't know. She is unreasonable and the secret wouldn't be safe with her. All she can say is *it just isn't right!*" Her parents didn't do her any favors by raising her with such an uncompromising view of the world."

Tonya stopped at the flower shop. "If you're sure, here's my place." She took the last swallow from her soda and reached for her key.

"I'm sure," Robin replied, anticipation and trepidation tightening her chest.

Tonya welcomed Robin in with a sweep of her hand.

"I like it," Robin said, taking in the cheerful room.

Tonya arranged her books on a card table near the kitchen alcove. "If you want another coke, there should be one in the fridge."

While Robin retrieved a can from the tiny refrigerator, Tonya went to the single bed that doubled as a couch, with a patterned throw and a row of brightly-colored pillows lined up against the wall. She tossed the pillows onto the single upholstered chair beside a lamp table. "Not a lot of room for two, but it will do." She spread her arms wide. "Come cuddle. I want to hold you."

Robin's breathing quickened and she hurried to sit beside Tonya on the bed.

Tonya's arm encircled her shoulders and Robin leaned into her. "Are you sure?" Tonya said softly.

Robin reached to trace Tonya's cheek with her hand. "Yes, and no," Robin said softly. "I'm yours."

Tonya reached to cup Robin's face in both hands. "Slow is best," she whispered, "at least at first." She drew Robin toward her and placed a feather-light kiss on each cheek, then one on each closed eye.

Robin shuddered and pulled Tonya close, feeling that if she let go, she might float away. Tonya began to unbutton her blouse and the now-familiar ripple of delight coursed through her. When Robin's blouse slid down her arms and onto the bed, Tonya whispered, "Now mine."

Robin fumbled with the buttons of Tonya's blouse while Tonya stroked her bare shoulders. Robin arched her back as Tonya traced Robin's bra across her back.

When the last button escaped its buttonhole, Tonya shrugged off her blouse and drew Robin closer. She looked into Robin's eyes and murmured, "Just do what I do." Their gazes locked on one another, Tonya stroked Robin's face tenderly then moved onto her neck, arms and back. Electricity coursed through Robin with each touch.

Robin caressed Tonya tentatively, then mirrored her movements. Tonya responded with a purr. They took turns exploring one another, Robin taking her cues from Tonya, needing neither sight nor words.

They unsnapped bras and slowly pushed down bra straps, sending rockets of emotion as breast touched breast. In time, they worked each other's slacks loose and lay together, separated only by bikini panties.

The sensations intensified and concentrated in Robin's core. She pressed her lips against Tonya's and pulled her close, their bodies coming together.

Then Tonya pushed her away gently and kissed both of Robin's cheeks. "We don't have time today," she said softly.

Robin moaned, then slowly released Tonya, though her body had not yet adjusted to the change in plans. She lay still as the trembling subsided into longing.

"She's still avoiding me," Robin lamented, glancing at Maddie at the hostess station. *"Whenever I manage to catch her eye, she looks away."*

The restaurant was crowded, and it wasn't until the last guests left that Robin had a chance to approach Maddie, who was gathering her things to leave. "Can you wait until I clear my tickets? I'd really like to talk to you."

"I thought I'd get out of here on time for a change. I need some downtime," Maddie said over her shoulder as she walked away.

Robin shrugged, disappointed. *"I need to fix this. I'm starting to dread coming to work."* She went to the register to collect her tips.

Two weeks later Robin cornered Maddie. "Are we ever going to be friends again?" Robin asked.

Maddie shrugged. "I can't help feeling jealous every time I see you. I was sure I made the right decision but, listening to you made me wish I'd been more courageous. It seemed like such an overwhelming proposition at the time that I had no choice but to back away. Then, listening to you so eager to plunge into a relationship made me realize how lonely I've been and how unlikely it is that will change."

"But..."

Maddie interrupted, "I know it's not your fault and I'm sorry I've been taking it out on you." She raised her hand to stop Robin from interrupting. "And, I'm still concerned for you. Being a lesbian is like walking a tightrope without a net; disaster is only one tiny slip away, and you rarely get a second chance. You're so eager. You've got to be careful."

"Are we gonna be okay? I mean, I know you can't just turn jealously on and off like a lightbulb, but I don't want to have to choose between you and Tonya. Besides, I can't work here if we aren't friends. It would be awkward"

"Robin, I made my decision about Tonya and I'll live with it. I'm sorry I've been a twit." Maddie laughed. "I'd say, *Let's kiss and make up,* but that might be kinda tricky."

"Let's just shake on it," Robin grinned and put out her hand. "Is there any chance that all three of us can all be friends?

Maddie took a deep breath. "You're asking a lot, Girlfriend, but I'll manage. There's no reason that Tonya and I can't be friends, as long as she doesn't hold my decision against me."

"I haven't told her I know about you two. Is it okay to tell her? When she told me about the relationship that didn't work out, I didn't get the sense that there were any hard feelings. She sounded disappointed but understood why you made the decision. She warned me that we weren't right for each other because I reminded her of you, though, of course, she didn't tell me who you were. She said that I would face the same challenges that made the relationship too difficult for you to manage.

"We'll be okay. Lesbians are a small community, relatively speaking. We have enough problems with the rest of the world; we don't need problems among ourselves."

Robin nodded. "We'll act okay and we'll be okay. Gram taught me that if I act as if I things are the way I want them to be, it increases the chances of having them turn out that way. I'm going to make reservations for dinner to introduce Gram and Tonya. This time we'll go somewhere else. I don't want Tonya to be uncomfortable either and she doesn't know yet that I know you were a couple."

"Gram, I'm going to make reservations for dinner so you can meet Tonya."

"I wouldn't mind cooking. It's been a while since we've entertained."

"I knew you'd say that, but at a restaurant, there's nothing any of us has to do but enjoy one another. I have to find out when Tonya's free. Is there a time you'd prefer if she can make it?"

"My evenings are generally free. I think we should defer to Tonya's schedule. You said that she works a lot of hours."

"She does. She has a scholarship that covers school expenses, but she takes care of everything else. You'll be impressed with how responsible she is. I've never met her mom, but she sounds like someone you'd appreciate. She did a great job of raising Tonya in a place where success in life is rare. When Tonya talks about her, it sounds like she's talking about you.

"Do you know how her mother feels about her being gay?"

"Not really. I get the impression that she hopes Tonya will grow out of it. I don't know if Tonya talked about it while she was still living at home. We don't get to spend much time together. I only saw her over the holidays when we met for a few minutes before work, and we don't have class together this interim semester, so I hardly see her at all. I did enjoy working with her on that project, and we may have a class or two together spring semester. She's a transfer student, so there are required courses she has to pick up. Sometimes we meet up to walk to work together."

"Friendships that develop slowly usually last."

Chapter 26

"We've been studying hard all week," Katie said, looking up from her book as the suitemates lounged in the sitting room "What do you say we take ourselves out to dinner tonight? I, for one, am *not* up for cafeteria mystery food this evening. Sally recommended a Moroccan restaurant they went to after the last SNA meeting. I've never had Moroccan food."

Frannie leaped out of her chair, "I'm game. What do you wear to a Moroccan restaurant?"

"What you have on will be just fine."

"Oh." Frannie slumped back into her chair.

"Sounds like fun," Leslie added. I've never eaten Moroccan food, either. Wonderful idea, Katie. The four of us can each order something different and share."

Leslie parked Nellie down the street from the restaurant, and the girls piled out of the car.

"Do you think this is a safe place to eat? This neighborhood is creepy, and the restaurant looks like a dive." Frannie said.

"We may just be early for the dinner crowd." Katie said, "Sally said it was great, so I think it's worth a try."

Inside they were seated on pillows at a table no more than a foot off the floor. A young man uncovered a tray stacked with warm, wet cloths and passed one with tongs to each girl. They looked at each other, then at him, and he pantomimed using the cloths to wash their hands. Giggling, they complied.

As the girls studied the menu, the restaurant began to fill and soon a line of waiting customers snaked past their window. "Look at that," Robin pointed. "I'm glad we got here when we did, or we'd be standing out there in the cold."

"Yeah, the restaurant is small, but that crowd must mean the food is great. I won't live it down if it turns out that none of you like it." Katie said.

"Aaaah, we'll give you credit for the fun and adventure. Let's enjoy ourselves," Robin said.

Frannie's nose wrinkled as she read the menu. "Here's a dish with lamb or beef and *prunes*. That sounds awful. Who eats meat with prunes?" Frannie said.

"Obviously Moroccans do. Probably to keep their bowels up to speed," Robin deadpanned, and the girls laughed.

"Some of these meals look big enough to share," Leslie said. "Maybe we don't need four dishes after all."

A waitress knelt beside their table. "You are correct, Madam. The meals are served family-style so everyone can taste a bit of everything. Three orders should be more than enough for the four of you." She placed a basket in the center of their low table. "This is *khobz*. It is a traditional Moroccan bread. We use it to scoop food from the plate to our mouths."

"Do we eat the meal with our fingers?" asked Katie.

"Yes, offering the cloths to begin the meal with clean hands is a tradition" the waitress explained.

The men at the next table were getting rowdy. "I hope they get a grip," Robin said. "Why is it that guys without women just don't know how to behave?"

"Maybe they'll quiet down when their food comes," Katie said.

The girls settled on three dishes. The first was couscous with vegetables. The waitress explained their second choice. "Chicken Bastille is a savory pie cooked with saffron, ginger, pepper, and cinnamon, layered with a crispy *Warga* pastry, an herb omelet, and fried almonds, then scented with orange flower water. The last dish is called tagine, a slow-cooked, popular Moroccan stew."

The girls had debated over one additional dish made with chicken, preserved lemon, and olives, but finally decided that was too close to food they recognized. "Tonight's an adventure, after all," Robin concluded.

At the next table, there was an endless flow of bottles of wine and the men grew louder by the minute.

The waitress returned with four towels on a tray and offered one to each girl. "These are for your hands and to protect your clothing. Some keep them on the table; others tie them at the neck like a bib." Giggling the girls each took a towel and fashioned a bib as suggested.

Determined not to let the noise from the next table interfere with their dining, they dug in when their food arrived. They enjoyed their meal choices, messy fingers and all. At the next table, one of the drunks rose unsteadily from the floor, wine sloshing from the glass in his hand. He lost his balance and wine cascaded down Katie's back. All but one of the men howled in amusement, slapping one another's backs and pointing at Katie.

The waitress rushed over to apologize, but Katie was already on her feet. She punched the stumbling man's shoulder. Startled, he turned and stared as if he were looking at a bug.

Without preamble, Katie said, "You dumped your wine down my back, you imbecile. I expect you to pay for my dress."

The whole room stopped buzzing, intent on the interchange. "Gentlemen," Katie said as if it were a dirty word, "Your behavior is deplorable. You are rude, crude, and disrespectful of everyone in this restaurant. You owe everyone in this dining room an apology, especially the kind waitress who has tolerated your reprehensible behavior all evening. And YOU," she said, facing the man still wobbling beside her, "You owe me for my dress!" Katie turned on her heel and marched to the ladies' room with Leslie and the waitress close behind her.

The men paid their bill and, on their way out, the youngest of them, the one that hadn't laughed handed Robin a couple of folded bills. "For your friend."

Robin took the money. "Do you really think this makes it right? Your friend was way out of line and the lot of you made royal fools of yourselves. I am proud of Katie for putting that jerkwad in his place."

The younger man's face flushed. He stammered, "I'm sorry" and hurried to catch up with his colleagues.

Katie said, "Let's finish our meal and get some dessert. I need a sugar fix right now."

The waitress draped a towel around Katie's shoulders.

"I am so proud of you, Katie. You've grown a pair!" Robin said.

"He was the last straw. We've committed to a March against Violence and that kind of male chauvinistic behavior is part of the problem. I just couldn't let it go. I kinda exploded." Katie said, flushing.

"Never be embarrassed when you stand up against something so wrong. You rock! What you did wasn't just for yourself, you did it for women everywhere, and for the *Nurseketeers*!" Robin said.

"Tonya doesn't have to work this Wednesday, so we can have dinner and you can finally meet her. Where would you like to eat?" Robin asked Gram.

"I think we'd all be more comfortable eating somewhere that Crestmont students are less likely to frequent. There is a lovely place not too far from here where Roberta and I had lunch last week. I believe it was called The Sailmaker."

Robin paused, then smiled at Gram's observation. "I'm not used to considering what other people might think when I make plans. I guess that responsibility comes with the territory."

Gram nodded. "You've chosen a path that demands vigilance. I wish it could be easier for you, but..."

"It won't be," Robin finished Gram's thought. "I know I have to be careful, but it's not fair for anyone to be able to dictate another person's private life. I know," she added before Gram could respond, "it's not like you haven't reminded me forever that life isn't always fair."

"We'll have a delightful evening, just the three of us, and not give a second thought to what anyone else might be thinking. I'm looking forward to meeting Tonya and nothing is going to spoil that. I'll make reservations if you tell me what time you think will be convenient for her."

"I'm sure that 5:00 would work, but I'll check with her and tell you tomorrow."

Tonya was window-shopping at a nearby bookstore when she saw Robin and Gram. She waved and walked to meet them in front of The Sailmaker. "I'm Tonya, Mrs. Kelly," she said, extending her hand. "I'm pleased to meet you."

"Likewise," Gram said, clasping Tonya's hand in both of hers. "I'm looking forward to a lovely evening."

"The hostess squinted at the trio as they approached, then recovered quickly. Will anyone be joining you?"

"No, it's just us," Robin replied coolly.

"Then follow me." The hostess led them to a corner table at the back of the room. Handing them each a menu, she said, "Your waitress will be with you in a moment," then strode back to her station.

Tonya shook her head ruefully. "That wasn't too bad. She almost pulled it off."

Gram smiled and said, "Let's consider ourselves enlightened and not let others' narrow-mindedness spoil our evening. I believe our country is ready for meaningful relationships among our diverse cultures. Women's place in the social structure is certainly different from when I was young."

Tonya said, "Women are doing better than blacks, that's for sure. I'll give our hostess credit for trying to hide her reaction to the three of us eating together."

"That's all part of the March against Violence that we're planning for Spring. We can't sit back and do nothing and expect that society will change."

"True," Tonya replied. "I'm looking forward to the March. I must admit that I was surprised at the response from the campus organizations. From what I've heard, every one of them has chosen to participate. I think you're right, Mrs. Kelly, about society moving forward."

"What I would like," Gram said, leaning forward, "is to get to know you, Tonya. Robin tells me that you are pursuing a business degree."

"That's right. My goal is to own my own business. I'm not sure what kind it will be, but I guarantee that I'll be an equal opportunity employer. I want my business to be known for promoting the success of minorities in the workplace."

"That's an impressive goal."

Their waitress, a young black woman, placed a glass of ice water in front of each of them. She gave Tonya a quizzical look, then asked Gram if they had made their dinner selections.

"Not quite yet. Give us a few moments."

"Well, girls, what will you have?" Gram asked. "The grilled halibut has caught my fancy."

"Crab cakes for me," Robin chimed in.

"And for me as well," Tonya added.

Gram signaled the waitress who returned to their table. "What would you like to drink?" she asked.

"Water for me," Gram responded

"A Coke, please," said Robin.

Tonya added, "Sweet tea for me."

"I'll be back with bread and your salads," the waitress said as she tucked her order pad into her apron and shot Tonya another quizzical look.

"Even our waitress was surprised to see me eating with you two."

"One small step for mankind," said Robin with a smirk, or should I say "womankind?"

"Perhaps it won't be long before we're the status quo and the bigots are the outliers." Gram concluded.

The girls gave Gram an *OK* sign.

"Look how dark it is already," Gram said, nodding toward the window. I think we'll take a cab home. I enjoyed the walk over, but I don't think I'd enjoy it as much in the dark. Then the driver can take Tonya home and drop you at the dorm."

"Gram, we need a car."

"But I don't drive."

"You can learn. Dallas isn't like Chicago. The bus doesn't stop on every corner. Besides, I'd love for us to be able to explore on weekends. There are lovely places in the Hill Country and East Texas according to friends on campus, and they're close enough to explore in a day or at least over a weekend. Don't you think that would be fun?"

"Hmmm," Gram tilted her head. "I hadn't thought about a car, but you have a point. It would be nice not to have to rely on Roberta or Richard for transportation. They've been wonderful to me, but a car would be convenient. Learning to drive would be an adventure."

"I don't have to buy plane tickets anymore. We can buy a car together. I'm sure that Mr. Davis will have a recommendation."

"Tonya, are there weekends that you have at least one whole day off?" asked Gram. "Robin says that you spend all your time either studying or working. Perhaps you and your mother could join us for a day in the country."

"What a lovely idea. My mother hardly ever gets out. I know she'd love it. I work as many shifts as I can get, but I could arrange time off. I was fortunate enough to get a scholarship to

Crestmont, but I have to cover all my living expenses and Mom doesn't have the money to help with that."

"Robin, we'll have to give your car idea some serious thought. A drive in the country would give us plenty of time to visit."

The three lingered over their meals, then dessert. "Tonya, I think your mother and I have similar attitudes toward education and hard work. I expect that we'll have a lot to talk about if she'll join us on a drive."

"Does that mean we're getting a car?" Robin beamed.

"Not so fast. I have to do a little looking into it before I make a decision."

Robin laughed. "Why am I not surprised?"

When Gram asked for the check, Tonya reached for her purse. "Not tonight," Gram said with a smile. "It's my treat. I've had a wonderful evening."

"Me, too," Robin and Tonya said at the same time and burst into laughter.

Chapter 27

"Gender identity? This is garbage!" Frannie snorted as the girls left Psychology of Exceptional Children. "Girls are girls and boys are boys. It's pretty obvious, don't you think?"

"Not if you were listening in class," Robin shot back. "Do you *ever* listen to an idea that's different from what you think you know?"

"Of course, I do. Not knowing if you're a boy or a girl just doesn't make sense. How can you not know? You just have to look at your... well, you know. Why did you pick that for our presentation?"

"Because it's fascinating and I'm interested, and you need to allow one or two new ideas into that Fort Knox of a mind of yours." Robin put up a hand. "Don't say it. I am *not* picking on you. I'm encouraging you to take advantage of your college education. You're interested in children. Why wouldn't you want to know about the problems they face so that you can understand and be of some help? Hell, if you had all the answers, you sure wouldn't be *here!* You'd be in some genius think tank. So, listen and learn, for Pete's sake."

Frannie frowned. "I want to take care of kids and you're right; it would be awful not to know if you were a boy or girl, or worse to think you're one and everyone else thinks you're the other."

Robin's grin spread from ear to ear. "Lemme look. I think I see a crack in your skull. It sounds like you actually let in a new idea."

Frannie brightened. "This *could* be interesting."

"I hope the library has something for us to review. It's a pretty new topic. They should be able to help us find what we need wherever the resources might be."

"You did manage to pick an interesting topic," Katie remarked. "Leslie and I picked learning disabilities."

"I was thinking there might be a good reason that I'm such a lousy test-taker," Leslie said. "I'm not stupid, but I've never done well on tests. How cool would it be if we discovered the reason and I could do something about it!"

"I think getting a choice of projects makes studying interesting," Robin said. "If I'm gonna put all that work into a project, I want it to be something I care about or that will do me some good. I picked our topic for me *and* Frannie. It's a new specialty in pediatrics and it could give Frannie a leg up when we graduate if she knows more about it than other pedi nurses."

Robin smiled at Katie's wink.

"I can't believe you really picked the topic for me." Frannie was pleased and surprised. "That was thoughtful, Robin, and I promise I'll do my best. I like the idea of helping boys and girls be happy about who they are. You know what's sad? When parents want a girl and they get a boy or the other way around, and they kinda remodel their kid into what they wanted in the first place."

"You're catching on, Grasshopper. There's hope for you yet."

Chapter 28

R obin glared at Greg and James as they stumbled into the
Steakhauz with two girls. Higher than a kite, they giggled and
bumped other patrons as Maddie seated them in Robin's section.

"*Oh Lord, give me strength. This is all I need… as if that asshole from the other night wasn't enough. My patience will be tested
tonight.*" She took a deep breath, filled a tray with four water
glasses, and set one in front of each of them.

Greg looked up. "Well, I'll be dammed if it isn't Robs, everybody. Didn't know you worked here."

"How's your little blond buddy… Frannie, right? Stephens'
ditzy plaything," James said with a smile that said he knew it all.

Robin swallowed hard, holding her rising temper in check.
She took a deep breath, bit her lip, and handed them menus. "I'll
be back to take your order." The four of them broke into peals
of laughter earning disapproving looks from the other patrons
as Robin walked away.

Robin sat in a stall in the employee bathroom with her head
in her hands. "*I have to get this in check, or those assholes will get
me fired. I can't lose my temper.*" She allowed self-talk for a few
more minutes, then rose. "*I can't hide in here all night. They are*

not my only customers." She squared her shoulders, then scrubbed her hands as if she could wash the anger away. Resolved to control herself, she picked up a breadbasket and approached their table, pad in hand. When their raucous laughter subsided, she asked, "May I take your order?"

"Oh, Robs, don't be such a tight ass. All I did was ask about Frannie" Greg said giving her a creepy grin and a shiver ran up her spine.

"Frannie is fine," Robin said through clenched teeth. "What would you like to order?" She held the order pad tightly enough to bend it in half and her fingers turned white as she gripped the pen. The girls giggled as they placed their orders. Greg and James ordered burgers and fries. Robin pushed through the swinging doors of the kitchen and approached Mr. Davis who was talking to the chef.

"Excuse me, Mr. Davis, might I have a word?"

Mr. Davis signaled her to wait but changed his mind when he saw her expression. "I'll be right back, Chef."

They moved to a quiet corner and Robin began, "You remember that jerk, uh, man that I spilled the water on that night?"

"Yes."

"Well, there are two major jerks from Crestmont with dates at one of my tables. They're either drunk or so stoked on pot that exhaling might make our customers high. They're goading me about an incident last year involving a despicable friend of theirs and my roommate, and it's all I can do to keep from taking them on.

"I see."

"Mr. Davis, I don't know if I can keep my cool with those guys."

"Hmmm, let's see what we can do. Do you have any suggestions?"

"Well, Bryan isn't working tonight, so trading with him isn't an option. Honestly, I don't know if anyone could get those bullies to behave like human beings. They're so rowdy, everyone around them is giving them dirty looks and..."

Maddie burst into the kitchen, "Dad I need help out here!"

Maddie, Mr. Davis, and Robin hurried through the double doors. All three stopped short, shocked to see Greg and James having a food fight with the basket of bread. Patrons at nearby tables were becoming innocent battle casualties.

Robin and Maddie stood rooted in place, but Mr. Davis marched without hesitation to the table. "Gentlemen," he said, "please follow me, NOW!"

"Whoa, Big Daddy," Greg slurred. "Cool your jets. We're just having a little fun. Don't be so uptight."

Mr. Davis stared at Greg and said in a cold, measured voice, "Come with me *now*, Sir, or the police will remove you forcibly from the premises and you'll end up in jail."

"Oh, don't get your panties in a wad, Daddy-O," Greg rose shakily from his chair. "Who wants to eat in this crappy joint, anyway. Come on you guys, let's blow this place." Greg wobbled to his feet, knocking over his chair.

James and the two girls stifled their giggles and had the decency to duck their heads as Mr. Davis escorted them out of the restaurant, followed by the chef and the burly dishwasher.

Mr. Davis returned to a standing ovation. He raised both hands and modestly nodded. "Enjoy your meals," he said and walked toward the kitchen, motioning for the wait staff to follow him.

"We will not tolerate behavior like that at the Steakhauz," he said. "However, none of you need to deal with unruly customers alone. Thank you, Chef and Romero, for helping me escort them out without incident. Let's all get back to work. Offer the guests free beverage refills on the house." Robin turned to go.

"Robin, I am proud of you," he said. "Reporting the problem before it got out of hand was the right thing to do."

The Nurseketeers stared wide-eyed as Tonya stormed into their study room in the library and slammed her books onto the table.

"What is it?" Robin asked, alarmed at the furious expression on Tonya's face.

"You're not going to believe what happened in my civics class! And this is 1972 if you can believe it! The professor picked me to captain one of the debate teams, and the guy who didn't get picked told his buddies, in a whisper loud enough to hear in Chicago, that no black broad who got here on a *gimme grant* should get picked over a white guy who's paying his way. You coulda heard a pin drop."

"No way!" Leslie said. "I can't believe someone would say that out loud, even if he believed it. Did the class crucify him?"

"Interestingly, not really. Professor Davidson did a great job of managing the moment. The only reason I'm so hot right now is that on the way out of class, the jerk elbowed me and said, "You might think you're hot shit, Nigger, but my family's gonna hear about this and you're gonna find yourself outside looking in, which is exactly where you belong."

"That sucks," Robin said. "Who is this jerk?"

"His name is Simmons. I heard something that made me think someone in his family is a Crestmont muckety muck. It really would suck if the Crestmont Board could prevent minorities from getting scholarships. There's no other way a student like me can get a good education, and that's our only shot at a decent future. It doesn't matter how smart you are, if you want to get ahead in our society, you need one of two things, money or a good education. Without scholarships like I got, there's no way out of the ghetto, even for the smartest kids."

"We need to build *against prejudice* into the March theme," Leslie said. "It's connected to women's rights, and it's too important to ignore."

"Tell us the whole story," Katie said. "I want to hear what your professor did."

Tonya sat and everyone leaned in to listen. "Professor Davidson said, 'Mr. Simmons, that's an interesting position to take in this era of affirmative action. You also seem disappointed that you were not chosen to captain this debate. Well, here's what we can do about that. Our next debate will address opposing views on the interpretation and implementation of affirmative action in today's society. You can captain one team.' Then he asked me if I would prefer to captain the opposing team or keep my position as a captain of the current debate."

"What did you pick?" asked Frannie, grinning. "If you were Robin, I wouldn't even bother to ask."

Tonya grinned back. "You got it, Girl. I said, 'I choose to debate my attacker into the dirt.' You could tell that the class wanted to laugh, but everyone was sitting on eggshells waiting to see how it would all shake out. Professor Davidson was stifling a grin. He said, 'If you prepare well, you will have the opportunity to do just that, Miss Jackson. Remember, though, that Mr. Simmons has the same opportunity.'"

"Was there anyone willing to be on the jerk's team?" Leslie asked. "I can't imagine standing behind him after he made such an ass of himself."

"There were a few who admitted their families felt much the same way, even though they didn't have the same strong convictions. The professor reminded us that a debate is the presentation of opposing views supported with evidence, not a popularity contest. Basically, he coerced his skank friends to be on his team. There were loads of volunteers for my team, so the professor selected two students who were also the ones most actively waving their hands.

"He sounds amazing," Robin exclaimed. "I hope we get him next year. Can I help you prepare for the debate? The reading should be fascinating."

"I wish I had time to help," Leslie lamented. "It's all I can do to keep up with my classes and sports. What would be cool would be to get to watch the debate. We don't have class that hour. Do you think Professor Davidson would allow spectators?"

"Hmmm. This would be far out! I don't know when he'll schedule the debate, but he'll give us at least a week to prepare. He'll set the date next week and I can find out then. In the meantime, I need to get my act together and you guys need to get back to your studying. Thanks for listening. I won't be able to concentrate on anything but having a chance to crush Simmons."

"I was serious about helping," Robin said.

"You're on!" Tonya said

"Ms. Jackson, Mr. Simmons, are your teams ready?" asked Professor Davidson. "There has been a great deal of discussion about this debate. The topic is obviously of interest to our students. I'm sure you've noticed that we have quite a few visitors." He grinned. "It's a professor's dream to teach to a standing-room-only crowd."

The audience chuckled and Professor Davidson continued. "Before we begin, I want to remind you that how you conduct yourselves will affect your score. Respect for one another as well as for the rules of debate will affect the outcome." The six debaters nodded their understanding and Edgar Simmons shot Tonya a sadistic grin.

Pointing to a group of five professors sitting together, Professor Davidson continued, "We have a panel of professors who will determine the winning team based on your adherence to debate criteria and the compelling nature of the arguments."

"Miss Jackson, heads or tails?" Professor Davidson asked as he bounced a quarter on his palm.

"Heads," she responded solemnly.

He tossed the coin and examined his palm. "Heads," he said. "Will your team go first or second?

"Second," she replied.

Edgar Simmons approached his podium. "Culture doesn't change overnight," he began. "This country was founded on a hierarchal model. Our European forefathers invested their resources in developing a new continent, and part of that investment was bringing people over from Africa to help with the work. That's what they're here for... to help with the work that needs doing to make our country prosperous."

"My esteemed colleague," Tonya said, nodding to Edgar, "seems to have forgotten that our American Pledge of Allegiance concludes with… 'liberty and justice for all.' The Africans brought to help develop the new continent were freed from bondage and empowered to continue to help build our country as free and equal Americans. Some of our citizens of European origin have chosen to ignore the Emancipation Proclamation and continue to deny American citizens of color the education that would empower them to contribute to the growth and development of our country."

The audience took a collective breath when Edgar Simmons chimed. "My esteemed opponent must understand that culture doesn't change overnight."

"I humbly suggest," Tonya nodded to Edgar, "that my colleague seems to be a slow learner. The Emancipation Proclamation was signed nearly a century ago. American Culture has had more than thirty-five thousand nights to get the point."

"Okay," Professor Davidson said, standing and pointing an index finger at each of them in turn. "That will do. I understand the polar nature of this topic but addressing diverging topics is the essence of debate. Both of you know the rules of debate and one more infraction will disqualify your team."

The audience exhaled and Professor Davidson raised his hand to silence the room. "Mr. Simmons, if you wish, you may continue."

"You bet I wish…" Edgar said under his breath, then out loud, "Yes, Sir, I wish to continue. Colleagues," he faced the audience, "I submit that heritage plays a role in each of our lives. We are who our parents and grandparents prepared us to be. My colleague should respect her heritage as well." He stepped back from his podium.

"My opponent has made an excellent point. My heritage involves grandparents and parents who valued education and shared their passion for learning with me. My mother encouraged me to pursue learning, to excel in school, and to embrace the education that will prepare me to fulfill my dream of opening the doors for others that my parents and grandparents opened for me."

The debate continued until each side completed their arguments. Professor Davidson rose and addressed the debaters. "Thank you for your participation," he said, then turned to the audience. "Thank you for your interest and your support of our project. Our judges will confer and will announce the winner of the debate within the next ten minutes."

The buzz of conversation grew until Professor Davidson tapped the microphone. The silence was immediate and profound while everyone waited for the judges' decision.

"The winner, according to the analysis of our judges, is Ms. Jackson's team."

Only one face registered disgust when the room erupted with cheers and applause.

Chapter 29

"Partners on this one?" Robin asked Tonya after Mr. Reed gave the directions for their final Contemporary Studies paper.

"Yep!" Tonya said.

"Let's split up," Katie suggested. "We're going to need to talk to each other and four conversations going on all at once won't work."

"Good idea," Leslie agreed. "Someone repeat exactly what Mr. Reed wants."

J.R. said, "He said we need to demonstrate how the issues and events of one decade in this century helped to shape today's American culture. We have scientific discoveries in the first decade, a world war in the second, the roaring '20s, the depression in the '30s, and another war in the '40s, do you see a pattern here?"

"Funny, Man," Mike chuckled. "The '50s are the Golden Age. I'm sure it's called that because all of us were born in the '50s, right?"

"So, what do you think about exploring the Roaring 20's and the emerging independence of women?" Robin asked Tonya.

"That option in the syllabus piqued my interest more than any of the others."

"Work's for me," Tonya said. "Let's get a spot by the stacks. We'll need to find references"

"We can focus on flappers, suffrage, and double standards for men and women. We can show the headway that women in the '20s made in establishing women's rights and paved the way for our fight for equality today."

Tonya said, "It's pathetic that it's 50 years later and we're still fighting the same battles."

"We'll need to highlight that point," Robin said. "We can show how hard it is to change culture. I guess we shouldn't point out that it's the men who are stubborn and entrenched. If they'd leave it to women to run things, the world would be organized, and we'd stand a chance of getting things done."

"I heard that!" J.R. said in a loud whisper from the next table. "And I refuse to admit that you might be right."

"I'll plow through the textbook to see what we can use," said Tonya, "and you check the stacks."

Tonya was turning pages and taking notes when Robin dropped a book on the table beside her. "Look what I found. This book says that the political effects of the women's rights movement were different from the Women's Suffrage. Suffrage was all about gaining the right to vote and ultimately achieving the 19th Amendment, and women's rights were about having the same rights as men like owning property."

"Super cool," Tonya said. "I think you may have found the framework for our paper!"

Settled in their seats, they listened to Mr. Wright describe the final project for their Humanities class. "On our last day of class, we'll have a multicultural breakfast. You will each prepare a dish that represents your heritage. Make enough to serve six people and label your dish so that we can group food from similar cultures together. From your chatter, I take it that you like the idea. Good, because that's not all. I would like you to come dressed in traditional attire. Each of you will have the opportunity to describe both your dish and your outfit. Each year I'm surprised and pleased with the wide variety of cultures our Crestmont students represent."

"Is there a grocery store nearby that carries exotic foods?" asked one student. "I mean stuff that we don't usually find on the shelves at Safeway. I'm going to make blintzes and I need matzoh meal."

"Finding what you need will be part of your planning. If the ingredients for your first choice aren't available, you'll have to have a Plan B."

Ms. Langston demonstrated giving a bed bath on one of the mannequins in the lab, then divided the class into small groups. She tolerated the silly comments and giggles as they practiced. After bed bath practice, Ms. Langston demonstrated the correct process for taking vital signs. "When someone says, *get the patients TPR,*" she explained, "they are referring to temperature, pulse, and respiration. BP, of course, is blood pressure. Pair up and practice on each other. It takes a bit of time to develop the touch and the hearing, but it will become second nature. "We'll be going to a nursing home next week where you will get to put your new skills into practice."

"Frannie if you pump that cuff up any higher, my arm will turn black and blue," Robin said.

"I know, I know… but if I don't get it high enough, I don't have time to hear the change." Frannie said. "Be quiet so I can hear, or I'll have to do it again. I hope I can do this on a real patient."

"What, I'm not real?" Robin said.

Frannie giggled, "No you're not."

"Thanks."

"I hope we get to do more than watch." Robin said as she dropped onto Nellie's back seat between Frannie and J.R. "This should be cool!"

"I've not been to a nursing home before," Frannie said.

"My grandmother was in one before she passed away," said J.R. "It was okay… they took good care of her there, but she just wasn't in good health. It was hard to visit."

"I'm sorry for your loss," Katie said.

"Thanks, it's okay it was a few years back."

"I've been helping Mom take care of Nana since her multiple sclerosis got so bad she couldn't walk at all," said Frannie. "She's so helpful that it's easy to take care of her. It'd be awful to take care of patients who just lie there and let you do all the work."

"I wouldn't worry about that, Frannie," Katie said. "They wouldn't ask us to do anything they don't think we're capable of doing. They pay attention to the patient's safety and ours. I'm sure we'll be fine."

"We won't be fine unless we get there," Leslie said. "Katie, get the map out of the glove compartment and help me figure out where we're going,"

Katie wrestled with the map until she found the address. "Take a right on Central Expressway and it's just the other side of downtown," she said, running her finger along the route. "It should only take us 10 to 15 minutes to get there. We're in good shape."

"I'm looking forward to next year when we'll have real clinicals," J.R. said. "These Intro trips just whet my appetite."

"That's probably the point," Katie said. "They're giving us a glimpse into our future in case there are some sophomores who decide it isn't what they had in mind. There's time for them to change majors without wasting credits."

"Ever the practical one," Robin said. Leslie pulled up in front of the nursing home. "Guys hop out and I'll find a place to park. No sense in all of us being late, I'll be there in a jiff."

The Crestmont nursing students clustered in groups in the lobby, nearly filling it to capacity. Frannie wrinkled her nose. "It smells awful in here," she announced. "And it's dingy, don't you think?" she said.

"Shhh," Katie grabbed her arm. "Not so loud, Frannie. It's not the newest building in town, but it's clean and tidy. I expect they're doing their best."

"What's with the frown?" Leslie asked Frannie as she joined the group.

"I'd just hate to think of Nana in a dump like this," Frannie said, just as Ms. Langston called for their attention.

"Let me introduce Mrs. Yolanda Hill and Ms. Carrie England, the registered nurses here at the Shady Oak Home. They will assign you to accompany the aides and help them take vitals and give bed baths."

Mrs. Hill, the elder of the two nurses, stepped forward. "I divided you alphabetically. That seemed easiest. Please come up when you hear your name and Carrie will introduce you to the aide with whom you'll be working today. You'll learn a great deal more by participating than watching, and the aides will appreciate all of the help you can give them."

Leslie and Frannie, both with surnames beginning with *B* were called first and left with their group. Katie, Robin, and J.R. found themselves together, and with one other student, they followed Elsie, their aide, to the second floor. Elsie popped into the first room on her left and emerged with two blood pressure monitors."

"I have all of the rooms on this side of the hall, all the even numbers," she said pointing down the right side of the corridor. "Each room has two patients. We'll start here in 202 and work our way to the other end. First, record the patient's TPR and BP, then each patient gets a bath. You know how to take vitals, right?"

Four heads bobbed up and down.

"I'll get two of you going in here," she pushed open the door to room 202, "and the other two in room 204."

Robin's heart sank. *"I'm in an old black and white silent movie. The furniture is gray metal, the upholstery is gray vinyl, the blankets are gray, and the patients match."*

"Good morning, Mr. Ames," Elsie chirped, "and Mr. Adams. These are nursing students from Crestmont University. They'll be helping me this morning. You two start here." She handed a sphygmomanometer to J.R. "Robin, their thermometers are on their bedside tables. You two come with me," she said to Katie and the fourth student. "I'll be right back, Gentlemen."

Robin and J.R. stood, immobile. "Well," croaked Mr. Ames with a wry smile. "Don't just stand there, make sure my heart is still beating, and it looks like Edgar might have croaked overnight."

Mr. Adams snorted, "Not likely. I wagered I'd outlast you and I aim to win that bet!"

Robin giggled and said, "Okay, you first, Mr. Ames." She prepared his thermometer while J.R. fitted the blood pressure cuff to Mr. Ames' thin upper arm. "Under your tongue," she said as she held the thermometer in front of his mouth.

"97.2," said Robin, rotating the thermometer to catch the light."

"112 over 84," J.R. announced, then looked around the room for somewhere to document the blood pressure and temperature.

"Lookin' won't do you no good," Mr. Ames cackled. "Elsie keeps a notepad in her pocket and scribbles everything down. They lock up our charts at the nurses' station. Can't imagine what's the big secret, but nobody ever said places like this gotta make sense. You might just go to jail for saying my blood pressure out loud, Sonny." He cackled again at Robin's and J.R.'s horrified expressions. "You oughta grab a paper towel over there and write those numbers down."

J.R. turned to Mr. Adams who pulled his covers up to his neck. "Mr. Adams," J.R. began.

"Don't you touch me!" Mr. Adams growled, bunching the covers under his chin. "No queer dude's putting his hands on me! No, siree. That ain't gonna happen!"

"But..." J.R. stammered, wide-eyed and rooted in place. "What?"

"Edgar," said Mr. Ames soothingly. "He's no such thing. Don't be picking on these kids. They'll never come back and they're just about the only visitors we ever get."

"You heard me, Faggot. And don't even think about my bath!"

"But, I'm..."

"You're what? You gonna tell me you ain't queer? Like I'm gonna believe THAT! Womens always been taking care of men, but guys don't touch other guys. The onliest reason a guy would be a nurse is if he ain't a real man."

"Mr. Adams," Robin protested. "That's not true!"

"You don't know nothin', Girl. You just stand back and learn a thing or two."

"That's ridiculous!" Robin drew herself to her full five foot five, planted her hands on her hips, and glared at Mr. Adams. "You've never laid eyes on him before. You have no right to make accusations like that. That's just wrong!"

"NURSE," croaked Mr. Adams, as Elsie burst in with Katie and the other student.

"What's wrong?" cried Elsie.

"Get this faggot outa here," then pointed at Robin, "and take that loud-mouth girl with you."

Elsie hustled the four students out of the room and pulled the door closed behind her. Before she could speak, Robin hissed, "He had no right, and whatever J.R. is or isn't is none of his business!"

"Well, I'm not a homosexual, that's for sure," said J.R., "but I agree it's none of his business even if I were."

"There's nothing you can do with folks like him," Elsie remarked. "They're set in their ways and they know they're right... and that's all there is to it. J.R., I am so sorry. I just never thought..."

"Not your fault, Elsie," J.R. assured her. "I agree there's no reasoning with folks like that. Scary thing is that accusations like that could land a person in jail."

Robin fumed. *Lesson learned. Be careful!*

Chapter 30

"I'll change quick," Robin said, "and we can walk to work together. We'll have time to talk and catch up on the way."

Tonya stood in the closet doorway and watched Robin take off her blouse and grab a clean shirt for work. She stepped close and stroked Robin's back.

"Mmmm, that feels so good," Robin purred, hunching her shoulders and turning in to Tonya's embrace. Tonya pulled her close and kissed her forehead. Robin tilted her head up and Tonya kissed her gently on the lips.

Robin gasped as the firebolt of pleasure shot from her lips to her toes and left her body quivering from the unexpected sensation. Her lips reached for Tonya's and they savored a long kiss.

"NOOOOO! STOP" Frannie yelled, shattering their euphoria. Frannie stood wide-eyed and gaping in the closet doorway. "STOP THAT! What are you DOING? Are you crazy? That's disgusting!" Frannie was panting with outrage.

Robin's heart thudded and time stopped. She clung to Tonya for another long moment, then turned slowly to face Frannie. She took a deep breath, gave Tonya's hand a squeeze, and said, "You go on. I'll deal with this."

"You sure?" Tonya asked, hesitating.

Robin nodded and Tonya slipped out, closing the suite door quietly behind her.

Robin, hands on her hips, stared back. "You finished screaming?"

Frannie collected herself slowly. "Robin, how could you? That's so wrong. Only sick people do that, and they go to jail, and…"

"Stop right there!" Robin said icily and pulled on her shirt. "You need to slam the door on your parents' warehouse of rights and wrongs and start thinking with your brain. You've learned so much since that first time you mouthed off in class. What happened to *you're entitled to your beliefs and others are entitled to theirs*? Where did you hide everything you've learned?"

Robin arched an eyebrow and glared at Frannie who remained rooted in place. "Am I getting through to you?" Robin raised her voice. "Are you listening?"

Frannie nodded. She whispered, "Robin, it's wrong. I *am* learning, but that doesn't change that some things are wrong. Sex is a man and woman thing. What you and Tonya were doing just isn't right. Besides, it's against the law and you'll get in trouble and it'll ruin your life. Why do you think you're always right and I'm always wrong?"

"Because this time you're wrong!" Robin retorted.

Frannie frowned and took a deep breath, preparing to defend herself when the essence of the dilemma dawned on Robin. "No. Wait a minute, Frannie. You're *not* wrong. What you believe is right for you and you're entitled to that. We're not debating what's right or wrong; we're talking about what we're going to *do* about the fact that we disagree."

Frannie cocked her head. "What do you mean?"

"I mean you're right. It's illegal and it could ruin my life. But it's my decision and I need for you to respect my right to make decisions that are different from the ones you would make. I'm not asking you to agree with me. I'm asking you to accept me for who I am."

"But Robin, it's illegal and you'll go to jail. How can I be okay with that?"

"That can't happen unless someone finds out. If you remember, last year you were in a position that could have ruined your life and what *you* were planning to do about it was illegal. I didn't think that was right, and I still don't, but I supported you and I've never mentioned it to anyone. I based my decisions on our friendship and what was best for you. I would have supported whatever decision you made for yourself."

"I appreciate that, but what's your point?"

"I want the same respect from you. I have to trust you to make decisions about what you say and do based on what's right for *me*, not on what you believe is right or wrong."

"What do you mean?"

"I mean that I have never uttered a word about last year… to anyone. I've kept your secret because I respect your right to manage your life, not because I thought what you did was right or wrong. I expect you to keep *my* secret, even though you don't agree with me. I need to know that you understand that it's *my* decision and you'll respect my privacy like I respect yours. I need to know that you'll never utter a word to *anyone,* no matter what."

"…I won't say anything."

"Can you promise me that?"

"I can promise to keep your secret, but I can't promise that I'll ever change my mind, and I won't pretend to understand."

"Thanks, Frannie. That's all I'm asking for."

"But I hate what you're doing."

"I didn't expect you to like my decision, but I need to trust that you will respect it. You're the one who pointed out it's illegal, and I know that. But I also know that it shouldn't be. People should have the right to make their own decisions about their private lives, and I'm going to do what I can about that. Our March against Violence is as much about women's rights as anything else. In the meantime, you're right about the trouble I could be in. Just a slip of the tongue to Missy could get me kicked out of school."

"How could you think I would tell Missy?" Frannie exclaimed.

"I didn't mean you'd tell her on purpose. My secret needs to be as important to you as yours is to me. I know you wouldn't hurt me on purpose, but I also know you often talk before you think. With this secret, there's no room for second chances."

"Can't you *ever* not criticize me? Give me a break!"

"Frannie, get real! I'm not criticizing you," Robin paused, "that is, not until I get so frustrated with you that I can't help it. I'm just telling the plain truth. I'm your roommate and your friend, and I'm trying to make a difference. Last year when I was warning you about Stephen, you thought I was just ragging on you, but I was trying to protect you."

"Well, you were right, but you *do* hurt my feelings. You hardly ever say anything nice. You're always so sarcastic, it's hard not to feel hurt."

"You're right, and I'm sorry. When I think nice things, I don't say them out loud."

"Like what?"

"Like I tell you that you spend way too much time and energy primping, but I don't tell you how pretty you look all the time. And I don't tell you how happy it makes me when I see you interact with children. You have a gift for connecting with them. I tell other people; I just don't tell you."

When Frannie smiled, Robin added, "You and I have never had a sister. I think sisters lookout for one another, even if they don't always act like they even like each other. We're kinda like sisters, you and I. It would be fantastic if you actually listened to me instead of just getting your feelings hurt, and I'll try just as hard not to sound like I'm ragging on you."

"Do you mean that?"

"I do. We must care about each other or we wouldn't have stuck together two years in a row."

"Well, then… I promise." Frannie giggled. "Pinky swear?"

"Pinky swear."

Chapter 31

"Intro to Nursing should be interesting today," Leslie said, "I never thought about joining the military as a nurse."

"Who would want to do that?" Frannie blurted. "You'd never get to see your husband and what woman would want to go to Vietnam anyway? And those drab uniforms are just awful; you can't accessorize anything."

"Frannie, that's not the point. The fantastic thing about a nursing career is that there are gobs of options and serving our country as a nurse is a great choice."

"Take your seats quickly," Ms. Langston said. An attractive twenties something woman in a Navy uniform stood next to her.

Frannie leaned over and whispered, "Well, as uniforms go, I like hers."

"Geez, Frannie, give it a rest," Robin muttered.

"Hello everyone," Ms. Langston began. "Let me introduce Lt. Linda Titleist. Linda is a 1967 Crestmont alumna. She graduated with honors, joined the Navy, and is now serving in Vietnam. She's from right here in Dallas, so when she comes home on leave, she makes time to share her experiences with our nursing students."

"Thank you so much for the invitation, Ms. Langston. I love interacting with Crestmont students and having the opportunity to introduce you to the military as a practice alternative. Today my talk is mental distress related to war, a problem that has been around since… well, since forever. Fright and anxiety on the battlefield and the trauma of seeing others die can create a variety of disorders. An assortment of terms has been used over the years. I'm sure you've heard of *shell shock*. Soldiers walking around dazed or confused were accused of malingering or cowardice and were ostracized or minimalized. Patients with battlefield psychoses may relive their experiences over and over in dreams and even when they are awake. These patients need our help and our patience to overcome this disorder and to take back control of their lives."

"Interesting," Leslie whispered. "I had no idea."

"Whether you endorse the Vietnam war or not, our servicemen and women are risking their lives for us and they deserve our respect and our help. Service personal returning stateside have been abused by the media and individuals who are not supportive of the war. When a soldier with mental trauma is confronted with abuse here at home, he feels like he's caught in a vice and there's no way out. Some become violent and abusive when, under normal circumstances, they would never act like that. Some unable to cope and without support can wind up in divorce, on the streets, or in jail making their lives even worse. Therapy involves teaching coping strategies to overcome the symptoms. Nurses not only treat this disorder in battlefield hospitals, but also back here at home."

Lt. Titleist paused and hands shot up around the room. She pointed to Robin.

"You mentioned that people with this condition are prone to violence particularly in the home environment. We are hosting a March against Violence on campus soon. Is there a way that we can work this disorder into that event? Maybe we could open some eyes."

"I think it's wonderful that you're calling attention to habits and practices that lead to violence. Battlefield trauma is a catalyst, like drugs and alcohol, that can lead to abusive behaviors. I hope you will emphasize treatment rather than punishment. Punishment may suit those who use violence to make a point, but these solders are different. They need our help."

Robin said, "My follow up question is, how do we recognize a pathologically abusive person from someone with this kind of disorder?"

"First, this type of psychosis is related to a traumatic experience, so it makes sense to suspect it when there's background to support the diagnosis."

"I'm afraid we've run out of time," said Ms. Langston. "Thank you for coming to speak to our class." A round of applause interrupted her. "Lt. Titleist will be returning to Vietnam to care for our servicemen and women. She focused today on a critical issue for our military personnel and emphasized that nurses are helping to make a difference for them. There are handouts by the door about military services."

"I wonder," Robin mused, *"if that asshole father of mine suffered from some disorder related to alcohol. He certainly drank all the time, but I never thought about his drinking as anything but rotten behavior. Even so, I doubt he would have done anything about it. He wasn't the kind to listen to anyone else. He's an angry man who should not be near women or children… but I wonder…"*

Leslie paced back and forth in the sitting area. When Robin couldn't stand it any longer, she stood and called into her bedroom, "Frannie, we're outa here. Leslie is wearing a hole in the carpet. C'mon already."

Leslie was out the door before Frannie responded, "I'll be there in a sec."

Katie glanced at the bedroom and raised an eyebrow. Robin shrugged and they followed Leslie. They were descending the front steps of Kirkwood Hall when Frannie caught up. "You could have waited a few more seconds," she pouted. "Two seconds wouldn't have hurt anything."

Robin said, "This way you take us seriously. You're getting better, but you have a ways to go." She moved up to walk beside Leslie. "This is the big day. We've been working on it for months, so relax and enjoy it. You've got it nailed!"

"I know, I know, but I need to double-check on everything. This turned out to be a much bigger event than we originally intended." Leslie said.

"It did, and that's great! It shows how much more support there is for the cause than we expected. You're fine. Take a deep breath. You've led the project well, and now it's up to the others to do the work they signed up for. Have fun with the day."

Leslie took a deep breath. "I suppose you're right. I just need to be doing something. The waiting is killing me."

"No joke." Robin laughed.

Robin watched Leslie's shoulders release when she saw that her team was already gathered and waiting at Simpson Hall. She climbed the steps and the group rallied around her. "Thank y'all for arriving early. You are awesome. Let's have fun with this!" She grinned and raised both hands in *okay* signs.

"*Nurseketeers*, all for one!" Robin called out, and Frannie, Katie, and Leslie raised their arms and replied, "and one for all!"

A guy in a black t-shirt sporting a gold coyote in a purple police uniform handed Leslie a bull-horn. "You'll need this to help get the groups lined up," he said. "When you're done with it, give it to any of the guys wearing a shirt like mine."

Robin watched as a sea of people gathered for the event. They wore t-shirts in all colors with *March against Violence* on the back. Event volunteers had versions of the Crestmont coyote reflecting their roles and others proclaimed their association with various campus organizations. The nursing students' coyotes wore a white uniform and a nursing cap. They'd decided against having the coyote holding a syringe when one SNA member pointed out that, for some, it could represent inappropriate drug use. They went with a coyote holding the hand of a child in a bed.

"I like your nurse's cap, J.R.," said Leslie.

"Give it a rest, Boss. "I looked for a black magic marker to make it disappear. Lucky for you…" he grinned.

As the participants gathered, Robin spotted a group of women walking purposefully toward them. They were dressed in white uniforms, from nursing caps to duty shoes. "Hey, guys," Robin said, pointing. "look at that! It's the entire nursing faculty."

The crowd followed her finger and began to cheer and clap.

Ms. Langston joined the Nurseketeers at the top of the Simpson Hall steps. "We wanted to show you how much we value the effort you have put into this March against Violence and how proud we are of you."

Leslie, near tears, was afraid to speak. Robin chimed in with "Thank you, Ms. Langston, and all of you for your support." Watching more faculty forming up behind their instructors, Robin added, "It looks like the other departments are following your lead."

"I can't believe this," said Leslie, finding her voice. It's beyond my wildest hope."

In addition to faculty, local businesses were represented. Robin waved to the Rob Rory Steakhauz employees clustered behind a huge placard painted with *March against Violence*. In each corner was a huge bull with RobRory Steakhauz emblazoned across his chest. Robin was all smiles when she saw Gram and the Davises dressed in T-shirts that matched the placard. Folks from other businesses were gathering behind the Steakhauz group.

Raising the bull horn to her mouth, Leslie said, "Thank you for participating and pledging to make a difference now and in the future against violence. Here are a few instructions before we begin. If you have questions, look for the students in the purple t-shirts with gold coyotes that say, *"I have the Answers."* The March organizers, the ones in t-shirts like mine, will be scattered throughout the crowd to keep everyone together. The March begins here and ends at the Blakemore Chapel. The university administrative staff will be on the chapel steps to greet us."

Robin noticed news reporters interviewing people, and photographers snapping photos. One photographer panned the crowd with a huge TV camera balanced on his shoulder. The Crestmont band was organizing in the oval. They would march in the center of the parade.

The security team leader reported. "The security team is distributed among the marchers and along the route."

"You are fantastic. Thanks for everything you've done." Leslie said.

"Take this walkie talkie so you can call me if you need me. We've positioned the SNA members at the end of the lineup as you requested. When the Nursing faculty showed up, we asked them to lead the parade."

Leslie beamed. "That's perfect, Leroy. We have nurses leading and ending the parade of marchers." She raised the bullhorn." Take your places. We're about to begin." With a nod to the band leader, the drums rolled, and the band burst into their first number. The nursing faculty strode down the path and the crowd flowed into step behind them.

The SNA group had just passed the tip of the oval when shouts of "Lesbos Go Home," "Whites Rule," and "Men Rock" erupted from among the bystanders. Greg and James led the group of hecklers into the parade of marchers, separating the nursing students from the others.

Leroy was on his walkie-talkie calling instantly for assistance from his team.

Robin maneuvered through the crowd to Greg and James and thrust her finger in Greg's face. "I should have known you'd be behind this. Get out of here! You couldn't do anything good if your life depended on it." The bystanders gaped at the confrontation.

"We're doing good," Greg shouted. "We're defending the rights of the white race, you nigger-lovin' creep. You got us kicked out of the Steakhauz."

Robin balled her fist and prepared for a roundhouse punch when Katie grabbed her arm. "We're marching *against* violence," Katie said. Robin whirled on her, then took a deep breath. She glared at Greg and James. "She's right, and here you are demonstrating how petty people use violence in place of intelligent expression."

Before she could continue, Leroy appeared with two uniformed police officers who grabbed Greg and James, handcuffed them, and hauled them off to a patrol car. The other hecklers scattered.

Leslie yelled to the team around her. "We are done with this nonsense. We have a March to complete. Let's catch up with the others."

The group fell in behind her, clapping and chanting, "Go, Leslie!" Leroy nodded and patted her on the back.

"Are you okay?" Katie asked Robin as she marched beside her.

"I'm not sure. I'm in the middle of a March against Violence and I got so mad I would have clocked that jerk if you hadn't stopped me."

"But you didn't. That's what counts."

The sea of marchers filled the entire space between the chapel and the university's main drag. Dean Abbott tapped the microphone at the top of the chapel steps and the crowd became quiet. "This marks a special day in the history of Crestmont University," he began. "Support for this event has been impressive, and I have the privilege of introducing Ms. Leslie Bleu, the sophomore nursing student who spearheaded the project. She was able to involve every student organization on campus as well as our entire community. Leslie..."

"Someone shouted "Les...lie, Les...lie" and the crowd picked up the chant. Leslie held the microphone and a flush spread from her neck to her forehead. "Thank you," she began, and the cheering slowly subsided. "Thank you, Dean Abbott and all of the administrative team and faculty, for your support. Violence should never occur... not in the community; not in the workplace; and not in the home. We marched today to underscore the importance of helping each person face life's challenges without resorting to violence. We marched against the physical abuse of women and children, but also against the emotional violence of racial discrimination, gender discrimination, and violence against any group of people just because they are different."

The crowd cheered again, and Leslie handed the microphone to Dean Abbott who held up a huge cardboard check for more than $1,000. He ceremoniously presented it to the President of the local chapter of the National Coalition Against Domestic Violence, founded only one year earlier.

"Thank you all," said Leslie, "for helping us make this happen. Snacks and beverages have been provided by the businesses in our community, and we have music and dancing. Enjoy the rest of the afternoon. Thank you, everyone."

The Nurseketeers crowded around Leslie. Mike gathered her into a bear hug and swung her around as though the 5'9" athlete was light as a feather. "You were wonderful!" he said. "Dance with me." Beaming she walked off with him.

"I'm hungry," Frannie announced.

"This way to the food," J.R. announced and led Missy and Frannie away.

"Where do you think you are going?" Katie challenged when Robin turned to leave.

Robin's expression was grim. "I just marched *against* violence and I nearly punched Greg's light out. I'm no different from my useless drunk of a dad and I'm not even drunk."

"Maybe you needed a moment to realize that we all need a little help along the way. Your anger was legitimate; those guys were out of line. You said yourself they substituted violence for intelligent expression. You just proved that violence is a decision, and you made the right one. Robin, this March was your idea and you let it be Leslie's opportunity to shine as a leader. That's what you should be celebrating."

Chapter 32

"This is an awesome day!" Frannie said, looking at the "A - Nice work!" written on the cover sheet of the Contemporary Studies paper that she and Katie had submitted.

"I'm major pumped we all aced the paper," Robin said, as Frannie did a circle dance.

"Mike and I don't need as much time to get ready as you ladies, so we'll change and meet you in the Kirkwood lobby. We can help carry the stuff for Mr. Wright's multicultural breakfast," J.R. said.

Robin fastened the gigantic ornamental safety pin to the green, black, yellow, and white plaid kilt that Gram had made her a few years back. It still fit her perfectly and the green knee socks matched the plaid. As she checked her outfit in the mirror, Frannie pirouetted out of the closet, the red skirt and white lace apron of her Octoberfest outfit flaring around her.

"You look adorable in that outfit, Frannie," Robin said.

At that moment, Tonya stepped out of the bathroom and Robin and Frannie gaped in awestruck silence.

"Wow," was all Frannie could manage as they stared at Tonya, regal in a full-length azure Kaftan. "How did you manage that head wrap? It's perfect with that dress and looks amazing with your dark skin." Frannie said.

An Indian Princess straight out of *Hiawatha*, who looked astonishingly like Katie, stepped into the room. Her smart leather dress was fringed and trimmed in authentic turquoise and red beads. She wore a beaded headband and her elegant sandals had thin strips of soft leather that wrapped her legs to her knees.

They trooped into the sitting room as Leslie emerged from her bedroom.

"*WHAT* are you wearing?" Frannie cried leaning back to take in Leslie's attire.

Leslie wore a full-length black gathered skirt with a three-inch waistband and a white blouse, covered by a full-length bib apron. She sported a straw hat and work boots. "You're looking at a Creole working woman from outside New Orleans. I'm making a statement for the working women of the world."

Frannie rolled her eyes and said, "Dear God, at least put on some lipstick. You look like you're on your way to milk the cows."

"Good one, Frannie," said Robin.

They laughed as they gathered their culinary cultural contributions. Two cowboys and a roaring twenties flapper in a slim green dress and a headband with a huge feather waited for them in the lobby.

"Tonya, you're gorgeous," said Missy, shaking her head. "That's all there is to it."

"Agreed," said J.R. "Y'all look amazing." He grinned at Leslie. "There's a message in there somewhere, right?"

"Right!" she replied and gave him a thumbs up.

"What's in here that smells so good," Mike asked as he took a large box from Leslie.

"We'll tantalize you with the smells and tease you with a description of our delicacies as we walk," Leslie said, "just no peeking in the box!"

"We have an array of cultures represented," Katie offered. "New Orleans gumbo, Irish potato cakes, southern cheese grits, bacon, sausage, biscuits with molasses, fried bologna, and an African sweet potato pie. Thanks to the bakery, we also have some German kolaches to go with this eclectic meal."

"We have enough food to feed an army," J.R. said, stacking several boxes to transport.

"Honey bear, I think that was the intent," Missy said. There are eight of us and we each made enough for six. Add that to what everybody else is bringing and we're gonna have a feast fit for several kings.

Chapter 33

"Leslie you are doing fine," Robin assured her nervous suitemate. "All you have to do is explain why you believe in the value of SNA and tell them what makes you a good candidate for Vice President. You can do this. Besides, you already have a leg up. They've seen you in action."

"I keep telling myself I'm fine, but the girl running against me is a junior. She has been here a whole year longer than I have."

"So what? Did she lead the March against Violence? Did she stand on the Chapel steps and thank hundreds of people for their contributions? The event was spectacular, and you led it from start to finish."

Frannie added, "Leslie, you did a great job. Everyone talked about it for the whole next week."

"Besides," said Katie, "running for an office and losing to a worthy opponent is hardly a failure. Two good candidates can't both win the election. If she wins because she's a junior, next year *you'll* have the advantage."

"Thanks, guys. I'm good," Leslie said. "Let's get seats before Sam starts the meeting."

"The first item on our agenda this evening," Sam said, "is a report on the March against Violence." Leslie joined Sam in the front of the room to give her report.

"With the contributions from local businesses and SNA t-shirt sales, we were able to cover all of the March expenses," Leslie reported, "*and* we donated more than $1,000 to the local chapter of the National Coalition Against Domestic Violence. They already have that big cardboard check; next week Dean Abbott, Ms. Langston, and I will deliver one they can actually cash." Leslie was rewarded with giggles throughout the room.

"My simple *thank you* cannot express my pride in the members of SNA or my appreciation for you, Ms. Langston, for organizing the nursing faculty to lead the March. Your efforts helped put nursing front and center on the agenda against violence." The nursing students responded with a standing ovation.

Ms. Langston nodded and patted her heart. "We are proud of you all, both for the outstanding job you did with the March and for the contribution we know that each of you will make to nursing when you graduate."

"I hope you have seen the news clip about the March," Leslie continued. "Thanks to Ms. Langston, there is a copy in the Montgomery Hall skills lab for anyone who would like to read it, or read it again," Leslie said, pointing to herself. Another round of giggles bolstered her confidence.

Robin winked and pumped her fist in support when Leslie sat, relief washing over her face.

"Our next agenda item, Sam continued, "is the election of officers for next year. Each candidate will have two minutes to address the group. There was a ballot placed on each chair. After the candidates speak, we'll vote. The Nominating Committee will collect and count the ballots, and I'll announce the 1972-73 slate of officers at the end of the meeting."

Robin whispered to Katie, "Leslie's hands are shaking, but she has this nailed!"

Leslie placed her notes on the lectern and delivered her speech without glancing at them once. "Involvement in SNA gives us the opportunity to participate in meaningful events like the March against Violence and prepares us to participate in professional issues like health policy, legislation, and the changing healthcare environment. SNA members are dedicated to making the world a better and healthier place for all."

The Nurseketeers gave Leslie a *thumbs up*, and J.R. hugged her shoulders when she collapsed into the chair beside him. Leslie fidgeted through the rest of the business agenda but snapped to attention when Sam asked the Nominating Committee for the election results.

Sam scanned the election results, then said, "I will call each newly-elected officer to the front, beginning with the Nominating Committee. We'll take a photo of the 1972-73 leadership group at the end of the meeting."

Robin hardly heard the names of the new officers until Sam said, "...and for Vice President, Leslie Blue has been elected." The Nurseketeers' cheers nearly drowned out Sam's announcement of Sally, their freshman dorm RA, as the new President.

"This calls for a celebration!" Robin announced. "Who's up for a DQ?"

Chapter 34

"We were so busy tonight I didn't even get a bathroom break," Robin said as she collapsed into a chair in Gram's pint-sized living room. "Don't know why half of Dallas chose this Friday to go out for dinner. You didn't have to wait up for me."

"It's not that late," Gram replied, "and I have some news. I received a letter from the Prosecutor's office about Harold's trial. They expect that it will make the docket in late July and they will need both of us to testify."

A flood of emotion kept Robin from responding as lust for revenge, revulsion for Harold, and trepidation at the thought of testifying in court consumed her. Gram watched Robin's face mirror the kaleidoscope of emotions.

"We'll be fine," Gram reassured her. "We have plenty of time to prepare."

Robin took a deep breath. "The good thing is that he'll get what he deserves." A tear trickled down each cheek. "It just won't bring her back."

The day before departure, all four girls were nearly packed. "Frannie, I'm going to miss you," said Robin.

"You're kidding, right?" Frannie said dully.

"Absolutely not," Robin replied, and Frannie brightened. "I want you to know how much it means to me that you honored my secret."

"It still makes me sick to think about it," Frannie said, wrinkling her nose.

"But you cared enough about me to protect me, and that's what true friends do for one another." Robin put her arms around Frannie, and Frannie burst into tears. "Hey, I just said thanks, not I hate you."

Frannie laughed through her tears. "I know you did, and I think you really meant it. They're happy tears. Thank you, too. All the good things I've learned were because you taught me, even though you could be nicer about it."

Robin laughed, too. "Summer will be over before you know it, and we'll have another year to get better at this friend business."

Katie stood in the doorway. "We're leaving in the morning, so Leslie and I thought we should have one last fling to celebrate our year. Let's go to the College Diner so we can include Tonya in the celebration.

"Cool beans!" Frannie chirped, and Robin gave her shoulders a squeeze.

"I'm in," said Robin. "Give us 15 minutes and I'll help my roomie finish packing her way-too-much stuff."

"Guys, I didn't know you'd be coming in tonight," Tonya said as the girls settled into a booth at the College Diner. "Fantastic timing, too, 'cuz I get off in ten minutes.'"

"We needed one last girl-fest before we scatter to for the four winds tomorrow." Katie said, "Cool that you'll be able to eat with us instead of stopping by while you're waiting tables."

"I'll bring your drinks to hold you for ten minutes, then we can eat."

They sipped and chatted until Tonya joined them. "I'm glad I hooked up with you guys this school year," she said as she pulled up a chair between Robin and Frannie. "I'm generally a loner and hanging with you guys was a treat. So, give me the short and sweet what-you're-going-to-do-this-summer. You first, Frannie."

"My folks and I will go to Atlantic City for a couple of weeks, but I'm going to see where I can volunteer while I'm home."

"What a cool idea, Roomie," said Robin. "You didn't tell me that."

"Well, last year when we got back to school," Frannie explained, "you all talked about how you worked during the summer. I felt like I wasted mine, so this summer will be different."

Robin snaked her arm around Frannie's shoulder and gave her squeeze. "And you studied with us most of the semester. There's hope for you yet!"

Frannie beamed.

"I'll work at the store and keep in shape," said Leslie. "Same ol', same ol', but I think there might be a few rough moments. Abita Springs is a small town and most folks won't know it hasn't been *Paul and Leslie* for some time."

"You'll be okay in that department, won't you?" Katie asked.

"I will," Leslie said. "Since I got the letter and we talked it over in the library. Paul did the right thing when he joined the Army, and his death is no one's fault. I don't feel responsible anymore. There's been so much activity this year with the SNA and the March against Violence... and Mike..."

"...and Mike," Robin said. "You guys make a great couple."

Leslie blushed.

"Speaking of couples" Robin continued, "John will be home for the summer, Katie. I'll bet you're anxious to catch up."

"He's already gotten most of the Nurseketeers news in letters, but he'll be glad to hear that we all made it through finals. Mainly, I want to hear about his first year. He listened to me rattle on most of last summer about our freshman year. I owe him," she laughed. "How about you, Tonya?"

"I thought about moving home for the summer, but I didn't want to lose my apartment. Also, it's easier to keep a job than get one, so it'll be me and the diner until you guys get back."

"I have good news," Gram said, as she helped Robin unpack from school. "Mr. Davis has found us a car. A friend of his ordered a new automobile and we can buy his current vehicle for a reasonable price. The timing is wonderful. We'll have the whole summer to enjoy it."

"Fantastic! I was going to lobby for a car so that we could explore on weekends, and to be honest, so Tonya and I could spend some time together. We can't do that here. It's way too risky."

"I know, Sweetheart. We did talk about inviting Tonya and her mother to take a driving trip with us. She seemed to like the idea."

"Neutral turf is great. We wouldn't be visiting in one another's homes. That could be awkward, don't you think?"

"I agree. Perhaps if Tonya's mother and I find some common ground, we could take trips to explore the countryside. It could help to make an awkward situation more comfortable. I stopped by the library today and got a book called *Texas from A to Z*. You'd be surprised how many historical sites and places of interest there are within driving distance. I didn't realize the number of small towns that have festivals. I'm excited about exploring our new world. It's nothing like Chicago."

"In lots of ways," Robin agreed.

Acknowledgments

Writing about the world of Robin and her suitemates, the *Nurseketeers*, is an adventure that allows us to engage with a myriad of wonderfully talented individuals without whose support we could not have completed our book. We are grateful to our beta reader team: J.D. Buchert, Amy Clark, Marcia Crosthwait, Chelsie Gable, Daryn Harrington, and Christine Roberts. They gave us perspective and helped us refine our vision and our storyline for the final manuscript of *Against the World*.

We are appreciative of the talented folks who help put the finishing touches on the book's cover (*Fresh Design*), interior design (*jetlaunch.net*), and printing (*Vervante*). A heartfelt thank you to our family and friends who allow us to stay focused on authoring the *Nurseketeers* series and to advance our mission of *sharing enjoyment, writing, and learning through meaningful stories about diverse nursing characters.*

Authors' Note

We hope that you enjoyed *AGAINST THE WORLD*. Ratings are instrumental to the success of a novel. We value your reviews and would appreciate your taking the time to leave us a review.

Visit our website at, https://www.bakergoodman.com/ and join our mailing list for notification of new releases and our blogs. *Friend us* on Facebook at Baker & Goodman Authors,

https://www.facebook.com/jt.bakergoodman

and follow our Author page at

https://www.facebook.com/bakergoodmanbooks

or email us at admin@bakergoodman.com

About the Authors

Joy Don Baker and Terri Goodman, nursing students in the '70s like their fictional characters in their *Nurseketeers Series,* and both writers in professional nursing literature. They met in the '80s and have remained friends for years. As co-authors, their mission is to share enjoyment, writing, and learning through meaningful stories about diverse nursing characters.

Both Baker and Goodman are well-established leaders in perioperative nursing. Dr. Baker teaches at the University of Texas at Arlington and served as the editor-in-chief of the *AORN Journal.* Dr. Goodman is an entrepreneur and an approved provider of continuing education as the principal at Terri Goodman & Associates.

Suitemates Robin, Frannie, Katie, and Leslie represent the rich diversity found among nurses. Follow the Nurseketeers as they face exciting challenges.

Baker and Goodman have also produced the award-winning book *A, B, & Cs of Author Partnering* the definitive how-to guide that leads readers through the process of creating a partnership, establishing a productive work environment, and producing a work of fiction, non-fiction, or journal article.

www.ingramcontent.com/pod-product-compliance
Lightning Source LLC
Chambersburg PA
CBHW071537110726
47908CB00007B/1920